forever

forever

maggie stiefvater

SCHOLASTIC PRESS

Library of Congress Cataloging-in-Publication
Data Available

ISBN 978-0-545-25908-8

10 9 8 7 6 5 4 3 2 1   11 12 13 14 15

Printed in the U.S.A.   23
First edition, July 2011

The text type was set in Adobe Garamond Pro.
Book design by Christopher Stengel

For those who chose
"yes"

Ach der geworfene, ach der gewagte Ball,
füllt er die Hände nicht anders mit Wiederkehr:
rein um sein Heimgewicht ist er mehr.

Oh, the ball that's thrown, the ball that dared,
Does it not fill your hands differently when it returns:
made weightier, merely by coming home.
— Rainer Maria Rilke

PROLOGUE

I can be so, so quiet.

Haste ruins the silence. Impatience squanders the hunt.

I take my time.

I am silent as I move through the darkness. Dust hangs in the air of the nighttime wood; the moonlight makes constellations of the particles where it creeps through the branches overhead.

The only sound is my breath, inhaled slowly through my bared teeth. The pads of my feet are noiseless in the damp underbrush. My nostrils flare. I listen to the beat of my heart over the sound of the muttering gurgle of a nearby creek.

A dry stick begins to pop under my foot.

I pause.

I wait.

I go slowly. I take a long time to lift my paw from the stick. I am thinking, *Quiet.* My breath is cold over my incisors. I hear a live, rustling sound nearby; it catches my attention and holds it. My stomach is tight and empty.

I push farther into the darkness. My ears prick; the panicked animal is close by. A deer? A night insect fills a long moment with clicking sounds before I move again. My heart beats rapidly in between the clicks. How large is the animal? If it's injured, it won't matter that I'm hunting alone.

Something brushes my shoulder. Soft. Tender.

I want to flinch.

I want to turn and snap it between my teeth.

But I am too quiet. I freeze for a long, long moment, and then I turn my head to see what is still brushing my ear with a feather touch.

It is a something that I can't name, floating in the air, drifting in the breeze. It touches my ear again and again and again. My mind burns and bends, struggling to name it.

Paper?

I don't understand why it is there, hanging like a leaf in the branch when it is not a leaf. It makes me uneasy. Beyond it, scattered on the ground, there are items imbued with an unfamiliar, hostile smell. The skin of some dangerous animal, shed and left behind. I shy away from them, lip curled, and there, suddenly, is my prey.

Only it is not a deer.

It is a girl, twisting in the dirt, hands gripping soil, whimpering. Where the moonlight touches her, she's stark white against the black ground. Fear ripples off her. My nostrils are full of it. Already uneasy, I feel the fur at the back of my neck prickle and rise. She is not a wolf, but she smells like one.

I am so quiet.

The girl doesn't see me coming.

When she opens her eyes, I am right in front of her, my nose nearly touching her. She was panting soft, heated breaths onto my face, but when she sees me, they stop.

We look at each other.

Every second that her eyes stay on mine, more fur raises along my neck and spine.

Her fingers curl in the dirt. When she moves, she smells less wolf and more human. Danger hisses in my ears.

I show her my teeth; I ease backward. All I can think of is retreat-ing, getting only trees around me, putting space between us. Suddenly I remember the paper hanging in the tree and the shed skin on the ground. I feel fenced in — this strange girl in front of me, that alien leaf behind me. My belly touches underbrush as I crouch, tail tucked between my legs.

My growl starts so slowly that I feel it on my tongue before I hear it.

I am trapped between her and the things that smell like her, mov-ing in the branches and lying on the ground. The girl's eyes are on mine still, challenging me, holding me. I am her prisoner and I cannot escape.

When she screams, I kill her.

CHAPTER ONE

· GRACE ·

So now I was a werewolf and a thief.

I'd found myself human at the edge of Boundary Wood. Which edge, I didn't know; the woods were vast, stretching for miles. Easily traveled as a wolf. Not so easy as a girl. It was a warm, pleasant day — a great day, by spring-in-Minnesota standards. If you weren't lost and naked, that is.

I ached. My bones felt as if they'd been rolled into Play-Doh snakes and then back into bones and then back into snakes again. My skin was itchy, especially over my ankles and elbows and knees. One of my ears rang. My head felt fuzzy and unfocused. I had a weird sense of déjà vu.

Compounding my discomfort was the realization that I was not only lost and naked in the woods, but naked in the woods near civilization. As flies buzzed idly around me, I stood up straight to look at my surroundings. I could see the backs of several small houses, just on the other side of the trees. At my feet was a torn black trash bag, its contents littering the ground. It looked suspiciously like it may have been my breakfast. I didn't want to think about that too hard.

I didn't really want to think about *anything* too hard. My thoughts were coming back to me in fits and starts, swimming into focus like half-forgotten dreams. And as my thoughts came back, I was remembering being in this moment — this dazed moment of being newly human — over and over again. In a dozen different settings. Slowly, it was coming back to me that this wasn't the first time I'd shifted this year. And I'd forgotten everything in between. Well, almost everything.

I squeezed my eyes shut. I could see *his* face, his yellow eyes, his dark hair. I remembered the way my hand fit into his. I remembered sitting next to him in a vehicle I didn't think existed anymore.

But I couldn't remember his name. How could I forget his *name*?

Distantly, I heard a car's tires echo through the neighborhood. The sound slowly faded as it drove by, a reminder of just how close the real world was.

I opened my eyes again. I couldn't think about him. I just wouldn't. It would come back to me. It would all come back to me. I had to focus on the here and now.

I had a few options. One was to retreat back into these warm, spring woods and hope that I'd change back into a wolf soon. The biggest problem with that idea was that I felt so utterly and completely human at the moment. Which left my second idea, throwing myself on the mercy of the people who lived in the small blue house in front of me. After all, it appeared I'd already helped myself to their trash and, from the look of it, the neighbors' trash as well. There were a lot of problems with this idea, however. Even if I felt completely human right now, who knew how long that would last? And I was naked and coming from the woods. I didn't know how I could explain that without ending up at the hospital or the police station.

Sam.

His name returned suddenly, and with it a thousand other things: poems whispered uncertainly in my ear, his guitar in his hands, the shape of the shadow beneath his collarbone, the way his fingers smoothed the pages of a book as he read. The color of the bookstore walls, how his voice sounded whispered across my pillow, a list of resolutions written for each of us. And the rest, too: Rachel,

Isabel, Olivia. Tom Culpeper throwing a dead wolf in front of me and Sam and Cole.

My parents. Oh, God. My parents. I remembered standing in their kitchen, feeling the wolf climbing out of me, fighting with them about Sam. I remembered stuffing my backpack full of clothing and running away to Beck's house. I remembered choking on my own blood. . . .

Grace Brisbane.

I'd forgotten all of it as a wolf. And I was going to forget it all again.

I knelt, because standing seemed suddenly difficult, and clutched my arms around my bare legs. A brown spider crawled across my toes before I had a chance to react. Birds kept singing overhead. Dappled sunlight, hot where it came through full strength, played across the forest floor. A warm spring breeze hummed through the new green leaves of the branches. The forest sighed again and again around me. While I was gone, nature moved on, normal as always, but here I was, a small, impossible reality, and I didn't know where I belonged or what I was supposed to do anymore.

Then, a warm breeze, smelling almost unbearably of cheese biscuits, lifted my hair and presented me with an option. Someone had clearly been feeling optimistic about this fair weather and had hung out a line of clothing to dry at the brick rambler next door. My eye was caught by the garments as the wind fluffed them. A line of neatly pinned-up possibilities. Whoever lived in the rambler was clearly a few sizes larger than me, but one of the dresses looked like it had a tie around the waist. Which meant it could work. Except, of course, it meant stealing someone's clothing.

I had done a lot of things that a lot of people might not consider strictly right, but stealing wasn't one of them. Not like this. Someone's nice dress that they probably had to wash by hand and hang up to dry.

And they had underwear and socks and pillowcases up on the line, too, which meant they were probably too poor to have a dryer. Was I really willing to take someone's Sunday dress so I would have a chance at getting back to Mercy Falls? Was that really the person I was now?

I'd give it back. When I was done.

I crept along the woodline, feeling exposed and pale, trying to get a better look at my prey. The smell of cheese biscuits — probably what had drawn me as a wolf in the first place — suggested to me that someone must be home. No one could abandon that smell. Now that I'd caught the scent, it was hard for me to think of anything else. I forced myself to focus on the problem at hand. Were the makers of the cheese biscuits watching? Or the neighbors? I could stay mostly out of sight, if I was clever.

My unlucky victim's backyard was a typical one for the houses near Boundary Wood, littered with the usual suspects: tomato cages, a hand-dug barbecue pit, television antennae with wires leading to nowhere. Push mower half covered with a tarp. A cracked plastic kiddie pool filled with funky-looking sand, and a family of lawn furniture with plasticky sunflower-printed covers. A lot of stuff, but nothing really useful as cover.

Then again, they'd been oblivious enough for a wolf to steal trash off their back step. Hopefully they were oblivious enough for a naked high school girl to nick a dress from their clothesline.

I took a deep breath, wished for a single, powerful moment that I could be doing something easy like taking a pop quiz in Calculus or ripping a Band-Aid off an unshaved leg, and then darted into the yard. Somewhere, a small dog began to bark furiously. I grabbed a handful of dress.

It was over before I knew it. Somehow I was back in the woods, stolen garment balled in my hands, my breath coming fast, my body hidden in a patch of what may or may not have been poison sumac.

Back at the house, someone shouted at the dog to *Shut up before I put you out with the trash!*

I let my heart settle down. Then, guiltily and triumphantly, I slid the dress over my head. It was a pretty blue flowered thing, too light for the season, really, and still a little damp. I had to cinch the back up quite a bit to make it fit me. I was almost presentable.

Fifteen minutes later, I had taken a pair of clogs off another neighbor's back steps (one of the clogs had dog crap stuck to one heel, which was probably why they'd been put outside to begin with) and I was strolling along the road casually, like I lived there. Using my wolf senses, giving in like Sam had showed me so long ago, I could create a far more detailed picture of the surrounding area in my head than I could with my eyes. Even with all this information, I had no real idea where I was, but I knew this: I was nowhere near Mercy Falls.

But I had a plan, sort of. Get out of this neighborhood before someone recognized their dress and clogs walking away. Find a business or some kind of landmark to get my bearings, hopefully before the clogs gave me a blister. Then: somehow get back to Sam.

It wasn't the greatest of plans, but it was all I had.

Chapter Two

· ISABEL ·

I measured time by counting Tuesdays.

Three Tuesdays until school was out for the summer.

Seven Tuesdays since Grace had disappeared from the hospital.

Fifty-five Tuesdays until I graduated and got the hell out of Mercy Falls, Minnesota.

Six Tuesdays since I'd last seen Cole St. Clair.

Tuesdays were the worst day of the week in the Culpeper household. Fight day. Well, every day *could* be a fight day in our house, but Tuesday was the surefire bet. It was coming up on a year since my brother, Jack, had died, and after a family screamathon that had spanned three floors, two hours, and one threat of divorce from my mother, my father had actually started going to group counseling with us again. Which meant every Wednesday was the same: my mother wearing perfume, my father actually hanging up the phone for once, and me sitting in my father's giant blue SUV, trying to pretend the back didn't still smell like dead wolf.

Wednesdays, everyone was on their best behavior. The few hours following counseling — dinner out in St. Paul, some mindless shopping or a family movie — were things of beauty and perfection. And then everyone started to drift away from that ideal, hour by hour, until, by Tuesday, there were explosions and fistfights on set.

I usually tried to be absent on Tuesdays.

On this particular one, I was a victim of my own indecision. After getting home from school, I couldn't quite bring myself to call Taylor or Madison to go out. Last week I'd gone down to Duluth with both of them and some boys they knew and spent two hundred dollars on shoes for my mother, one hundred dollars on a shirt for myself, and let the boys spend a third of that on ice cream we didn't eat. I hadn't really seen the point then, other than to shock Madison with my cavalier credit card wielding. And I didn't see the point now, with the shoes languishing at the end of Mom's bed, the shirt fitting weirdly now that I had it at home, and me unable to remember the boys' names other than the vague memory that one of them started with *J*.

So I could do my other pastime, getting into my own SUV and parking in an overgrown driveway somewhere to listen to music and zone out and pretend I was somewhere else. Usually I could kill enough time to get back just before my mother went to bed and the worst of the fighting was over. Ironically, there had been a million more ways to get out of the house back in California, back when I hadn't needed them.

What I really wanted was to call Grace and go walking downtown with her or sit on her couch while she did her homework. I didn't know if that would ever be possible again.

I spent so long debating my options that I missed my window of opportunity for escape. I was standing in the foyer, my phone in my hand, waiting for me to give it orders, when my father came trotting down the stairs at the same time that my mother started to breach the door of the living room. I was trapped between two opposing weather fronts. Nothing to do at this point but batten the hatches and hope the lawn gnome didn't blow away.

I braced myself.

My father patted me on my head. "Hey, pumpkin."

Pumpkin?

I blinked as he strode by me, efficient and powerful, a giant in his castle. It was like I'd time-traveled back a year.

I stared at him as he paused in the doorway by my mother. I waited for them to exchange barbs. Instead they exchanged a kiss.

"What have you done with my parents?" I asked.

"Ha!" my father said, in a voice that could possibly be described as *jovial.* "I'd appreciate if you put something on that covered your midriff before Marshall gets here, if you're not going to be upstairs doing homework."

Mom gave me a look that said *I told you so* even though she hadn't said anything about my shirt when I'd walked in the door from school.

"As in *Congressman* Marshall?" I said. My father had multiple college friends who'd ended up in high places, but he hadn't spent much time with them since Jack had died. I'd heard the stories about them, especially once alcohol was passed around the adults. "As in 'Mushroom Marshall'? As in the Marshall that boffed Mom before you did?"

"He's Mr. Landy to you," my father said, but he was already on his way out of the room and didn't sound very distressed. He added, "Don't be rude to your mother."

Mom turned and followed my father back into the living room. I heard them talking, and at one point, my mother actually laughed.

On a Tuesday. It was Tuesday, and she was laughing.

"Why is he coming here?" I asked suspiciously, following them from the living room into the kitchen. I eyed the counter. Half of the counter was covered with chips and vegetables, and the other half was clipboards, folders, and jotted-on legal pads.

"You haven't changed your shirt yet," Mom said.

"I'm going out," I replied. I hadn't decided that until just now. All of Dad's friends thought they were extremely funny and they were extremely not, so my decision had been made. "What is Marshall coming for?"

"Mr. Landy," my father corrected. "We're just talking about some legal things and catching up."

"A case?" I drifted toward the paper-covered side of the counter as something caught my eye. Sure enough, the word I thought I'd seen — *wolves* — was everywhere. I felt an uncomfortable prickle as I scanned it. Last year, before I knew Grace, this feeling would've been the sweet sting of revenge, seeing the wolves about to get payback for killing Jack. Now, amazingly, all I had was nerves. "This is about the wolves being protected in Minnesota."

"Maybe not for long," my father said. "Landy has a few ideas. Might be able to get the whole pack eliminated."

This was why he was so happy? Because he and Landy and Mom were going to get cozy and devise a plan to kill the wolves? I couldn't believe he thought that was going to make Jack's death any better.

Grace was in those woods, right now. He didn't know it, but he was talking about killing her.

"Fantastico," I said. "I'm out of here."

"Where are you going?" Mom asked.

"Madison's."

Mom stopped midway through ripping open a bag of chips. They had enough food to feed the entire U.S. Congress. "Are you *really* going to Madison's, or are you just saying you're going to Madison's because you know I'll be too busy to check?"

"Fine," I said. "I'm going to Kenny's and I don't know who I'm going to get to come with me. Happy?"

"Delighted," Mom said. I noticed, suddenly, that she was wearing the shoes that I'd bought her. It made me feel weird for some reason. Mom and Dad smiling and her wearing new shoes and me wondering if they were going to blow my friend away with a large caliber rifle.

I snatched my bag and went outside to my SUV. I sat in the stuffy interior, not turning the key or moving, just holding my phone in my hands and wondering what to do. I knew what I *should* do; I just didn't know if I wanted to do it. Six Tuesdays since I'd talked to him. Maybe Sam would pick up the phone. I could talk to Sam.

No, I *had* to talk to Sam. Because Congressman Marshall Landy and my dad might actually figure something out in their little potato-chip-fueled war council. I didn't have a choice.

I bit my lip and dialed the number for Beck's house.

"Da."

The voice on the other end of the phone was endlessly familiar, and the whisper of nerves in my stomach turned into howls.

Not Sam.

My own voice sounded unintentionally frosty. "Cole, it's me."

"Oh," he said, and hung up.

CHAPTER THREE

· GRACE ·

My growling stomach kept track of time for me, so it seemed like a lifetime before I came to a business. The first one I came to was Ben's Fish and Tackle, a gritty gray building set back in the trees, looking like it had grown out of the muddy ground that surrounded it. I had to pick my way over a pitted gravel parking lot flooded with snowmelt and rainwater to get to the door. A sign above the doorknob told me that if I was dropping off keys to my U-Haul truck, the drop box was around the side of the building. Another sign said they had beagle puppies for sale. Two males and one female.

I put my hand on the doorknob. Before turning it, I fixed my story in my mind. There was always a chance that they'd recognize me — with a little jolt, I realized I had no idea how long it had been since I'd first turned into a wolf or how newsworthy my disappearance might have been. I did know that in Mercy Falls, clogged toilets made headlines.

I stepped in, pushing the door behind me. I winced; the interior was incredibly hot and stank like old sweat. I navigated the shelves of fishing tackle, rat poison, and bubble wrapping until I got to the counter at the back. A small old man was bent over behind the counter, and it was clear even from here that he and his striped button-down were the source of the sweat smell.

"Are you here for the trucks?" The man straightened up and peered at me through square glasses. Racks of packing tape hung from the Peg-Board behind his head. I tried to breathe through my mouth.

"Hi," I said. "I'm not here for the trucks." I took a breath, looked slightly tragic, and proceeded to lie. "The thing is, me and my friend just had a giant fight and she made me get out of her car. I know, right? I'm sort of stranded. Is there any way I could use your phone?"

He frowned at me, and I allowed myself to wonder, briefly, if I was covered in mud and if my hair was a mess. I patted at it.

Then he said, "What, now?"

I repeated my story, making sure I kept it the same and continued to look tragic. I *felt* relatively tragic. It wasn't difficult. He still looked dubious, so I added, "Phone? To call someone to pick me up?"

"Well now," he said. "Long distance?"

Hope glimmered. I had no clue if it was a long distance call or not, so I replied, "Mercy Falls."

"Huh," he said, which didn't answer my question. "Well now."

I waited an agonizing minute. In the background, I heard someone barking sharply with laughter.

"My wife is on the phone," he said. "But when she's off, I suppose you can use it."

"Thank you," I said. "Where are we at, by the way? So I can tell my boyfriend where to pick me up?"

"Well now," he said again. I didn't think the phrase meant anything to him — he just said it while he was thinking. "Tell him we're two miles outside of Burntside."

Burntside. That was almost a thirty-minute drive from Mercy Falls, all twisty two-lane road. It was unsettling to think that I'd made my way all this distance without knowing, like a sleepwalker.

"Thanks," I said.

"I think you have some dog shit on your shoe," he added, kindly. "I can smell it."

I pretended to look at my shoe. "Oh, I think I do. I wondered about that."

"She'll be on for a while, now," he warned me. It took me a second to realize that he meant his wife and the phone.

I got his point. I said, "I'll look around," and he looked relieved, as if he had felt compelled to entertain me as long as I stood by the counter. As soon as I wandered to look at a wall of lures, I heard him go back to shuffling whatever he'd been shuffling behind the counter. And his wife kept talking and laughing her weird barking laugh, and the store kept on smelling like body odor.

I looked at fishing rods, a deer head wearing a pink baseball cap, and fake owls to scare birds away from your garden. There were containers of live mealworms in the corner. While I stared at them, my stomach churning with either squeamishness or the distant promise of the shift, the door opened again, admitting a man wearing a John Deere cap. He and the sweaty old man exchanged greetings. I fingered the edge of a bright orange hunting dog collar, most of my mind on my body, trying to decide if I was really going to shift again today.

Suddenly my attention focused on what the men were talking about. The man with the John Deere cap was saying, "I mean, something ought to be done. One of them took a bag of trash off my step today. The wife thought it was a dog, but I saw the print — it was too big."

Wolves. They were talking about the wolves.

Me.

I shrank, crouching as if I was looking at the bags of dog kibble on the lowest metal shelf.

The old man said, "Culpeper's trying to get something together, I heard."

John Deere guy made a noise that sort of growled out both his nostrils and mouth. "What, like last year? That didn't do jack shit.

Tickled their bellies is all it did. Is that really the price of fishing licenses this year?"

"It is," said the old man. "That's not what he's talking about now. He's trying to get them like they did in Idaho. With the helicopters and the — assassins. That's not the word. Sharpshooters. That's it. He's trying to get it legal."

My stomach turned over again. It felt like it always came back to Tom Culpeper. Shooting Sam. Then Victor. When was it going to be enough for him?

"Good luck getting that past the tree huggers," John Deere said. "Those wolves are protected or something like that. My cousin got into a heap of trouble for hitting one a few years ago. About wrecked his damn car, too. Culpeper's in for a climb."

The old man waited a long time to reply; he was making some sort of crinkling noise behind the counter. "Want some? No? Well now, but he's a big city lawyer himself. And his boy was the one that got himself killed by the wolves. He just might now, if anyone can. They killed that whole pack in Idaho. Or maybe Wyoming. Somewhere out there."

Whole pack.

"Not for taking trash," John Deere said.

"Sheep. I reckon it's a lot worse, wolves killing boys, instead of sheep. So he might get it through. Who knows?" He paused. "Hey, miss? Miss? Phone's up."

My stomach lurched again. I stood up, arms crossed over my chest, hoping and praying that John Deere didn't recognize the dress, but he only gave me a cursory glance before turning away. He didn't look like the kind of guy that normally noticed the finer points of what women were wearing anyway. I edged up next to him and the old man handed me the phone.

"I'll just be a minute," I said. The old man didn't even acknowledge I'd said anything, so I retreated to the corner of the store. The men continued talking, no longer about wolves.

With the phone in my hand, I realized I had three phone numbers I could call. Sam. Isabel. My parents.

I couldn't call my parents.

Wouldn't.

I punched in Sam's number. For a moment, before I hit SEND, I took a deep breath and closed my eyes and allowed myself to think about how desperately I wanted him to pick up the phone, more than I could let myself truly admit. My eyes pricked with tears, and I blinked fiercely.

The phone rang. Twice. Three times. Four. Six. Seven.

I had to come to grips with the idea that he might not pick up.

"Hello?"

At the voice, my knees felt wobbly. I had to crouch, all of a sudden, and put one of my hands on the metal shelf beside me to steady myself. My stolen dress pooled on the floor.

"Sam," I whispered.

There was silence. It lasted so long I was afraid he had hung up. I asked, "Are you there?"

He sort of laughed, a weird, shaky sound. "I — didn't believe it was really you. You're — I didn't believe it was really you."

I let myself think about it then: him pulling up in his car, his arms around my neck, me being safe, me being *me* once more, pretending I wasn't going to leave him again later. I wanted it so badly that it made my stomach ache. I asked, "Will you come get me?"

"Where are you?"

"Ben's Tackle. Burntside."

"Jesus." Then: "I'm on my way. I'll be there in twenty. I'm coming."

"I'll wait in the parking lot," I said. I wiped away a tear that had somehow managed to fall without me noticing.

"Grace —" He stopped.

"I know," I said. "I do, too."

· **SAM** ·

Without Grace, I lived in a hundred moments other than the one I currently occupied. Every second was filled with someone else's music or books I'd never read. Work. Making bread. Anything to fill my thoughts. I played at normalcy, at the idea that it was just one more day without her, and that tomorrow would bring her walking through my door, life going on as if it hadn't been interrupted.

Without Grace, I was a perpetual motion machine, run by my inability to sleep and my fear of letting my thoughts build up in my head. Every night was a photocopy of every day that had come before it, and every day was a photocopy of every night. Everything felt so wrong: the house full to the brim with Cole St. Clair and no one else; my memories edged with images of Grace covered in her own blood, shifting into a wolf; me, unchanging, my body out of the seasons' reach. I was waiting for a train that never pulled into the station. But I couldn't stop waiting, because who would I be then? I was looking at my world in a mirror.

Rilke said: *This is what Fate means: to be opposite, to be opposite to everything and nothing else but opposite and always opposite.*

Without Grace, all I had were the songs about her voice and the songs about the echo left behind when she'd stopped speaking.

And then she called.

When the phone rang, I was taking advantage of the warm day to wash the Volkswagen, scrubbing off the last of the salt and sand painted on from an eternity of winter snow. The front windows were rolled down so that I could hear music playing while I worked. It was a thumping guitar piece with harmonies and a soaring melody that I would forever associate with the hope of that moment, the moment that she called and said, *Will you come get me?*

The car and my arms were covered with suds, and I didn't bother to dry off. I just threw my phone on the passenger seat and turned the key in the ignition. As I backed out, I was in such a hurry that I revved the engine up high, high, high as I shifted gears from reverse to first, my foot slipping on the clutch. The ascending engine note matched the beat of my heart.

Overhead, the sky was huge and blue and filled with white clouds painted with thin ice crystals too far above the earth for me to feel, here on the warm ground. I was ten minutes down the road before I realized I had forgotten to roll up the windows; the air had dried the soap on my arms to white streaks. I met another car on the highway and passed it in a no passing zone.

In ten minutes, I would have Grace in my passenger seat. Everything would be all right. I could already feel her fingers laced in mine, her cheek pressed against my neck. It felt like years since I'd had my arms wrapped around her body, my hands pressed up against her rib cage. Ages since I'd kissed her. Lifetimes since I'd heard her laugh.

I ached with the weight of my hope. I fixated on the incredibly inconsequential fact that for two months, Cole and I had been living on dinners of jelly sandwiches and canned tuna and frozen burritos. Once Grace was back, we would do better. I thought we had a jar of spaghetti sauce and some dried pasta. It seemed incredibly important to have a proper dinner for her return.

Every minute closer to her. In the back of my head, nagging concerns pressed, and the biggest ones involved Grace's parents. They were certain that I'd had something to do with her disappearance, since she'd fought with them about me right before she shifted. In the two months that she'd been gone, the police had been out to search my car and question me. Grace's mother found excuses to walk by the bookstore when I was working, staring in the window while I pretended not to see. Articles about Grace's and Olivia's disappearances ran in the local paper, and they said everything about me but my name.

Deep down, I knew that this — Grace as a wolf, her parents as enemies, me in Mercy Falls in this newly minted body — was a Gordian knot, impossible to untangle and lay straight. But surely if I had Grace, it would work out.

I nearly drove by Ben's Fish and Tackle, a nondescript building mostly hidden by scrubby pines. The Volkswagen lurched as I pulled into the parking lot; the potholes in the gravel were deep and filled with muddy water that I heard splashing up on the undercarriage. Scanning the lot as I pulled in, I slowed. There were a few U-Hauls parked behind the building. And there, beside them, near the trees —

I pulled the car to the edge of the lot and climbed out, leaving it running. I stepped over a wooden railroad tie and stopped. At my feet, in the wet grass, lay a flowered dress. A few feet away from me, I saw an abandoned clog, and another yard beyond it, lying on its side, its mate. I took a deep breath, then knelt to pick up the dress. Balled in my hand, the fabric was scented softly with the memory of Grace. I straightened and swallowed.

From here, I could see the side of the Volkswagen, covered in filth from the parking lot. It was as if I had never washed it.

I climbed back behind the wheel, laying the dress in the backseat, and then I cupped my hands over my nose and mouth, breathing the same breaths over and over again, my elbows braced against the wheel. I sat there for several long moments, looking out over the dash at the left-behind set of shoes.

It had been so much easier when I was the wolf.

CHAPTER FOUR

· COLE ·

This was who I was, now that I was a werewolf: I was Cole St. Clair, and I used to be NARKOTIKA.

I had thought there'd be nothing left of me, once you took away the pounding bass of NARKOTIKA and the screams of a few hundred thousand fans and a calendar black with tour dates. But here it was, months later, and it turned out that there was fresh skin underneath the scab I'd picked off. Now, I was a fan of the simple pleasures in life: grilled cheese sandwiches without black flecks on the crust, jeans that didn't pinch the better parts of me, an inch of vodka, ten to twelve hours of sleep.

I wasn't sure how Isabel fit into this.

The thing was, I could go most of my week without thinking about grilled cheese and vodka. But I couldn't seem to say the same thing about Isabel. It wasn't like fantastic daydreams, either, the good sort of tease. It was more like jock itch. If you were really busy, you could almost forget about it, but then when you stopped moving, it was murder.

Almost two months and not a breath from her, despite a number of extremely entertaining voicemails on my part.

Voicemail #1: "Hi, Isabel Culpeper. I am lying in my bed, looking at the ceiling. I am mostly naked. I am thinking of . . . your mother. Call me."

And now she called?

No way.

I couldn't stay in the house with the phone looking at me like that, so I got my shoes and headed out into the afternoon. Since I'd taken Grace away from the hospital, I'd started digging further into discovering what made us wolves. Here in the bush, there was no way to look at us under the microscope and get real answers. But I'd planned out a few experiments that didn't require a lab — just luck, my body, and some balls. And one of said experiments would really run better if I could get my hands on one of the other wolves. So I'd been making forays into the forest. Actually, reccies. That was what Victor used to call our late-night convenience store runs to buy hasty meals constructed of plastic and dried cheese flavoring. I was performing reccies into Boundary Wood, in the name of science. I felt compelled to finish what I'd started.

Voicemail #2: The first minute and thirty seconds of "I've Gotta Get a Message to You" by the Bee Gees.

Today, the weather was warm and I could smell absolutely everything that had ever peed in the woods. I struck off on my usual path.

Cole, it's me.

God, I was going crazy. If it wasn't Isabel's voice, it was Victor's, and it was getting a little crowded inside my head. If I wasn't imagining removing Isabel's bra, I was willing the phone to ring, and if I wasn't doing that, I was remembering Isabel's father chucking Victor's dead body onto the driveway. In between them and Sam, I was living with three ghosts.

Voicemail #3: "I'm bored. I need to be entertained. Sam is moping. I may kill him with his own guitar. It would give me something to do and also make him say something. Two birds with one stone! I find all these old expressions unnecessarily violent. Like, ring around the rosy. That's about the plague, did you know? Of course you did. The plague is, like, your older cousin. Hey, does Sam talk to you? He says jack shit to me. God, I'm bored. Call me."

Snares. I was going to think about my experiments instead. Catching a wolf was turning out to be incredibly complicated. Using objects found in the basement of Beck's house, I'd rigged up a huge number of snares, traps, crates, and lures, and had caught an equally huge number of animals. Not a single member of *Canis lupus*. It was hard to say which was more aggravating — catching yet another use-less animal or figuring out a way to get it out of the trap or snare without losing a hand or an eye.

I was getting very fast.

Cole, it's me.

I couldn't believe that after all this time, she had called back, and her first words hadn't been some form of apology. Maybe that part was coming next, and I'd missed it by hanging up.

Voicemail #4: "Hotel California" by the Eagles, in its entirety, with every instance of the word California *replaced with* Minnesota.

I kicked a rotten log and watched it explode into a dozen black shards on the rain-soaked forest floor. So I'd refused to sleep with Isabel. My first decent act in several years. No good deed goes unpun-ished, my mother used to say. It was her motto. Probably she felt that way about changing my diapers now.

I hoped Isabel was still staring at her phone. I hoped she'd called back one hundred times since I'd gone outside. I hoped she felt infected like I did.

> Voicemail #5: "Hi, this is Cole St. Clair. Want to know two true things? One, you're never picking up this phone. Two, I'm never going to stop leaving long messages. It's like therapy. Gotta talk to someone. Hey, you know what I figured out today? Victor's dead. I figured it out yesterday, too. Every day I figure it out again. I don't know what I'm doing here. I feel like there's no one I can —"

I checked my traps. Everything was coated in mud from the rain that had kept me in the house for the past several days. The ground was slop under my feet and my traps were useless. Nothing in the one on the ridge. A raccoon in the one near the road. Nothing in the one in the ravine. And the trap near the shed, a new sort of snare, was completely demolished, the pegs ripped from the ground, trip wires everywhere, small trees snapped, and all the food eaten. It looked like I'd tried to trap Cthulhu.

What I needed was to think like a wolf, which was remarkably hard to do when I wasn't one.

I gathered up the ruined bits of snare and headed back to the shed to see if I could find what I needed to rebuild it. There was nothing wrong with life that some wire cutters couldn't fix.

Cole, it's me.

I wasn't going to call her back.

I smelled something dead. Not yet rotting, but soon.

I hadn't done anything wrong. Isabel could call me the twenty times that I'd called her.

Voicemail #6: "So, yeah, I'm sorry. That last message went a little pear-shaped. You like that expression? Sam said it the other day. Hey, try this theory on for size: I think he's a dead British housewife reincarnated into a Beatle's body. You know, I used to know this band that put on fake British accents for their shows. Boy, did they suck, aside from being assholes. I can't remember their name now. I'm either getting senile or I've done enough to my brain that stuff's falling out. Not so fair of me to make this one-sided, is it? I'm always talking about myself in these things. So, how are you, Isabel Rosemary Culpeper? Smile lately? Hot Toddies. That was the name of the band. The Hot Toddies."

I swore as a bit of wire from the snare in my hand cut my palm. It took me several moments to get my hands free of the mess of metal and wood. I dropped it onto the ground in front of me and stared at it. That piece of crap wasn't catching anything anytime soon. I could just walk away. Nobody had asked me to play Science Guy.

There was nothing saying that I couldn't just take off. I wouldn't be a wolf again until winter, and I could be hundreds of miles away by then. I could even go back home. Except that home was just the place where my black Mustang was parked. I belonged there just about as much as I belonged here with Beck's wolves.

I thought about Grace's genuine smile. About Sam's trust in my theory. About knowing that Grace had lived because of me. There was something vaguely glorious about having a purpose again.

I put my bloody palm to my mouth and sucked on the cut. Then I leaned over and picked all the pieces back up again.

Voicemail #20: "I wish you'd answer."

CHAPTER FIVE

· GRACE ·

I watched him.

I lay in the damp underbrush, my tail tucked close to me, sore and wary, but I couldn't seem to leave him behind. The light crept lower, gilding the bottom of the leaves around me, but still, he remained. His shouts and the ferocity of my fascination made me shiver. I clamped my chin onto my front paws, laid my ears back against my head. The breeze carried his scent to me. I knew it. Everything in me knew it.

I wanted to be found.

I needed to bolt.

His voice moved far away and then closer and then far again. At times the boy was so far I almost couldn't hear him. I half rose, thinking of following. Then the birds would grow quieter as he approached again and I would hurriedly crouch back into the leaves that hid me. Each pass was wider and wider, the space between his coming and going longer. And I only grew more anxious.

Could I follow him?

He came back again, after a long period of almost quiet. This time, the boy was so close that I could see him from where I lay, hidden and motionless. I thought, for a moment, that he saw me, but his expression stayed focused on some point beyond me. The shape of his eyes made my stomach turn uncertainly. Something inside me tugged and pulled, aching once again. He cupped his hands around his mouth, called into the woods.

If I stood, he would see me for certain. The force of wanting to be seen, of wanting to approach him, made me whine under my breath. I almost knew what he wanted. I almost knew —

"Grace?"

The word pierced me.

The boy still didn't see me. He'd just tossed his voice out into the emptiness, waiting for a reply.

I was too afraid. Instincts pinned me to the ground. *Grace.* The word echoed inside me, losing meaning with each repetition.

He turned, head bowed, and picked his way slowly away from me, toward the slanted light that marked the edge of the woods. Something like panic rose up inside me. *Grace.* I was losing the shape of the word. I was losing something. I was lost. I —

I stood up. If he turned, I was unmistakable now, a dark gray wolf against the black trees. I needed him to stay. If he stayed, maybe it would ease this terrible feeling inside me. The force of standing there, in plain sight, so close to him, made my legs quiver beneath me.

All he had to do was turn around.

But he didn't. He just kept walking, carrying the something that I'd lost with him, carrying the meaning of that word — *Grace* — never knowing how close he'd been.

And I remained, silently watching him leave me behind.

CHAPTER SIX

· SAM ·

I lived in a war zone.

When I pulled into the driveway, the music slapped its hands against the car windows. The air outside the house thumped with a booming bass line; the entire building was a speaker. The closest neighbors were acres away, so they were spared the symptoms of the disease that was Cole St. Clair. Cole's very being was so big that it couldn't be contained by four walls. It bled out the windows, crashed out of the stereo, shouted out suddenly in the middle of the night. When you took away the stage, you still had the rock star.

Since he'd come to live in Beck's house — no, *my* house — Cole had terraformed it into an alien landscape. It was as if he couldn't help destroying things; chaos was a side effect to his very presence. He spread every single CD case in the house over the living room floor, left the television turned to infomercials, burned something sticky into the bottom of a skillet and then abandoned it on the stove top. The floorboards in the downstairs hallway were lined with deep dimples and claw marks that led from Cole's room to the bathroom and back again, a lupine alphabet. He'd inexplicably take every glass out of the cupboard and organize them by size on the counter, leaving all the cabinet doors hanging open, or watch a dozen old '80s movies halfway through and leave the cassettes unrewound on the floor in front of the VCR he'd excavated from somewhere in the basement.

I made the mistake of taking it personally, the first time I came home to the mess. It took me weeks to realize that it wasn't about me. It was about him. For Cole, it was always about him.

I got out of the Volkswagen and headed toward the house. I wasn't planning on being here long enough to worry about Cole's music. I had a very specific list of items to retrieve before I went back out again. Flashlight. Benadryl. The wire crate from the garage. I'd stop by the store to get some ground beef to put the drugs in.

I was trying to decide if you still had free will as a wolf. If I was a terrible person for planning to drug my girlfriend and drag her back to my house to keep in the basement. It was just — there were so many ways to effortlessly die as a wolf, just one moment too long on a highway, a few days without a successful hunt, one paw too far into the backyard of a drunk redneck with a rifle.

I could feel that I was going to lose her.

I couldn't go another night with that in my head.

When I opened the back door, the bass line resolved itself into music. The singer, voice distorted by volume, shouted to me: *"Suffocate suffocate suffocate."* The timbre of the voice seemed familiar, and all at once I realized that this was NARKOTIKA, played loud enough for me to mistake the throbbing electronic backbeat for my heartbeat. My breastbone hummed with it.

I didn't bother to call out for him; he wouldn't be able to hear me. The lights he'd left on laid down a history of his comings and goings: through the kitchen, down the hall to his room, the downstairs bathroom, and into the living room where the sound system was. I momentarily considered tracking him down, but I didn't have time to hunt for him as well as Grace. I found a flashlight in the cabinet by the fridge and a banana from the island, and headed toward the hall. I promptly tripped over Cole's shoes, caked in mud, lying haphazardly in the doorway from the kitchen to the hall. I saw now that the kitchen floor was covered with dirt, the dull yellow lights illuminating where Cole's pacing had painted an ouroboros of filthy footprints in front of the cabinets.

I rubbed a hand through my hair. I thought of a swearword but didn't say it. What would Beck have done with Cole?

I was reminded, suddenly, of the dog that Ulrik had brought home from work once, a mostly grown Rottweiler inexplicably named Chauffeur. It weighed as much as I did, was a bit mangy around the hips, and sported a very friendly disposition. Ulrik was all smiles, talking about guard dogs and *Schutzhund* and how I would grow to love Chauffeur like a brother. Within an hour of its arrival, Chauffeur ate four pounds of ground beef, chewed the cover off a biography of Margaret Thatcher — I think it ate most of the first chapter as well — and left a steaming pile of crap on the couch. Beck said, "Get that damn langolier out of here."

Ulrik called Beck a *Wichser* and left with the dog. Beck told me not to say *Wichser* because it was what ignorant German men said when they knew they were wrong, and a few hours later, Ulrik returned, sans Chauffeur. I never did sit on that side of the couch again.

But I couldn't kick Cole out. He had nowhere to go but down from here. Anyway, it wasn't so much that Cole was intolerable. It was that Cole, undiluted, taken neat with nothing to cut through the loudness of him, was intolerable.

This house had been so different when it had been filled with people.

The living room went silent for two seconds as the song ended and then the speakers busted out another NARKOTIKA song. Cole's voice exploded through the hall, louder and brasher than real life:

Break me into pieces
small enough to fit
in the palm of your hand, baby

I never thought that you would save me
break a piece
for your friends
break a piece
just for luck
break a piece
sell it sell it
break me break me

My hearing wasn't as sensitive as it was when I was a wolf, but it was still better than most people's. The music was like an assault, something physical to push past.

The living room was empty — I'd turn the music off when I got back downstairs — and I jogged through it to get to the stairs. I knew there was an assortment of medicines in the downstairs bathroom's cabinet, but I couldn't get to them. The downstairs bathroom with its tub held too many memories for me to get through. Luckily, Beck, sensitive to my past, kept another store of medicines in the upstairs bathroom where there was no tub.

Even up here, I could feel the bass vibrating under my feet. I shut the door behind me and allowed myself the small comfort of rinsing the dried car-washing suds from my arms before I opened the mirror-fronted cabinet. The cabinet was full of the vaguely distasteful evidence of other people, as most shared bathroom cabinets were. Ointments and other people's toothpaste and pills for terms and conditions that no longer applied and hairbrushes with hair not my color in the bristles and mouthwash that had probably expired two years before. I should clean it out. I would get around to it.

I gingerly removed the Benadryl, and as I closed the cabinet, I caught a glimpse of myself in the mirror. My hair was longer than I'd ever let it get before, my yellow eyes lighter than ever against the dark circles beneath them. But it wasn't my hair or the color of my eyes that had caught my attention. There was something in my expression that I didn't recognize, something at once helpless and failing; whoever this Sam was, I didn't know him.

I snatched the flashlight and the banana off the corner of the sink. Every minute I spent here, Grace could be getting farther away.

I trotted down the stairs, two at a time, into the seething music. The living room was still empty so I crossed the floor to turn the stereo off. It was a strange place, the lamps by the tartan sofas casting shadows in every direction, no one here to listen to the fury exploding from the speakers. It was the lamps, more than the emptiness, that made me uncomfortable. They were slightly mismatched, with dark wood bases and cream shades; Beck had brought them back one day and Paul had declared that the house now officially looked like his grandmother's. Maybe because of that, the lamps never got used; we always used the brighter ceiling light instead, which made the faded reds in the couch less sad and kept the night outside. But now, the twin pools of lamplight reminded me of spotlights on a stage.

I stopped next to the couch.

The living room wasn't empty after all.

Out of the reach of the light, a wolf lay next to the couch, twitching and jerking, mouth parted, revealing its teeth. I recognized the color of the coat, the staring green eyes: Cole.

Shifting. I knew, logically, that he must be shifting — whether from wolf into human or human into wolf, I didn't know — but still, I felt uneasy. I watched for a minute, waiting to see if I would have to open the door to release him outside.

The pounding music fell into silence as the song ended; I still heard ghostly echoes of the beat whispering in my ears. I dropped my supplies softly onto the couch beside me, the hairs on the back of my neck prickling to wary attention. By the other couch, the wolf was still spasming, head jerking to the side again and again, senselessly violent and mechanical. His legs were ramrod straight away from him. Saliva dripped from his open jaws.

This wasn't shifting. This was a seizure.

I started with surprise as a slow piano chord rang out beside my ear, but it was only the next track on the CD.

I crept around the couch to kneel by Cole's body. A pair of pants lay on the carpet beside him, and a few inches away from them, a half-depressed syringe.

"Cole," I breathed, "what have you done to yourself?"

The wolf's head jerked back toward its shoulders, again and again.

Cole sang from the speakers, his voice slow and uncertain against a sparse backing of just piano, a different Cole than I'd ever heard:

If I am Hannibal
where are my Alps?

I had no one to call. I couldn't call 911. Beck was far out of reach. It would take too long to try to explain to Karyn, my boss at the bookstore, even if I could trust her to keep our secret. Grace might know what to do, but even she was in the woods, hidden from me. The feeling of impending loss sharpened inside me, like my lungs rubbed sandpaper with each inhalation.

Cole's body ripped through one spasm after another, head snapping back again and again. There was something deeply disturbing about the silence of it, the fact that the only sound accompanying all this abrupt motion was the hiss of his head rubbing the carpet while a voice he no longer possessed sang from the speakers.

I fumbled in my back pocket and pulled out my phone. There was only one person to call. I stabbed in the number.

"Romulus," Isabel said, after only two rings. I heard road noise. "I was thinking of calling you."

"Isabel," I said. I couldn't make my voice sound serious enough for some reason. It just sounded as if I were talking about the weather. "I think Cole's having a seizure. I don't know what to do."

She didn't even hesitate. "Roll him on his side so he doesn't drown in his own spit."

"He's a wolf."

In front of me, Cole was still seizing, at war with himself. Flecks of blood had appeared in his saliva. I thought he'd bitten his tongue.

"Of course he is," she said. She sounded pissed, which I was beginning to realize meant that she actually cared. "Where are you?"

"In the house."

"Well then, I'll see you in a second."

"You —?"

"I told you," Isabel said. "I was thinking of calling you."

It only took two minutes for her SUV to pull into the driveway. Twenty seconds later, I realized Cole wasn't breathing.

CHAPTER SEVEN

· SAM ·

Isabel was on the phone when she came into the living room. She threw her purse on the couch, barely looking at me and Cole. To the phone, she said, "Like I said, my dog is having a seizure. I don't have a car. What can I do for him here? No, this isn't for Chloe."

As she listened to their answer, she looked at me. For a moment, we both stared at each other. It had been two months and Isabel had changed — her hair, too, was longer, but like me, the difference was in her eyes. She was a stranger. I wondered if she thought the same thing about me.

On the phone, they'd asked her a question. She relayed it to me. "How long has it been?"

I looked away, to my watch. My hands felt cold. "Uh — six minutes since I found him. He's not breathing."

Isabel licked her bubblegum-colored lips. She looked past me to where Cole still jerked, his chest still, a reanimated corpse. When she saw the syringe beside him, her eyes shuttered. She held the phone away from her mouth. "They say to try an ice pack. In the small of his back."

I retrieved two bags of frozen french fries from the freezer. By the time I returned, Isabel was off her phone and crouching in front of Cole, a precarious pose in her stacked heels. There was something striking about her posture; something about the tilt to her head. She was like a beautiful and lonely piece of art, lovely but unreachable.

I knelt on the other side of Cole and pressed the bags behind his shoulder blades, feeling vaguely impotent. I was battling death and these were all the weapons I had.

"Now," Isabel said, "with thirty percent less sodium."

It took me a moment to realize that she was reading the side of the bag of french fries.

Cole's voice came out of the speakers near us, sexy and sarcastic: *"I am expendable."*

"What was he doing?" she asked. She didn't look at the syringe.

"I don't know," I said. "I wasn't here."

Isabel reached out to help steady one of the bags. "Dumb shit."

I became aware that the shaking had slowed.

"It's stopping," I said. Then, because I felt like being too optimistic would somehow tempt fate into punishing me: "Or he's dead."

"He's not dead," Isabel said. But she didn't sound certain.

The wolf was still, head lolled back at a grotesque angle. My fingers were bright red from the cold of the frozen fries. We were totally silent. By now, Grace would be far away from where she had called from. It seemed like a silly plan, now, no more logical than saving Cole's life with a bag of french fries.

The wolf's chest stayed motionless; I didn't know how long it had been since he'd taken a breath.

"Well," I said, quietly. "Damn."

Isabel fisted her hands in her lap.

Suddenly the wolf's body bucked again in another violent movement. His legs scissored and flailed.

"The ice," Isabel snapped. "Sam, wake up!"

But I didn't move. I was surprised by the ferocity of my relief as Cole's body buckled and twitched. This new pain I recognized — shifting. The wolf jerked and twitched and fur somehow sloughed and rolled back. Paws peeled into fingers, shoulders rippled and widened, the spine buckled. Everything shaking. The wolf's body stretched impossibly, muscles bulging against skin, bones audibly scraping one another.

And then it was Cole, gasping, his lips tinged blue, his fingers jerking and reaching for air. I could still see his skin stretching and remaking itself along his ribs with each shuddering breath. His green eyes were half-lidded, each blink almost too long to be a blink.

I heard Isabel suck in her breath and I realized that I should have warned her to look away. I put my hand on her arm. She flinched.

"Are you okay?" I asked.

"I'm fine," she replied, too fast to mean it. No one was fine after they saw that.

The next song on the CD started, and when the drums pattered an opening, one of NARKOTIKA's best-known songs, Cole laughed, silently, a laugh that saw no humor in anything, ever.

Isabel stood up, suddenly ferocious, like the laugh had been a slap.

"My work here's done. I'm going to go."

Cole's hand reached out and curled around her ankle. His voice was slurred. "IshbelCulprepr." He closed his eyes; opened them again. They were slits. "Youknow what-do." He paused. "Affer the beep. Beep."

I looked at Isabel. Victor's hands pounded posthumously on the drums in the background.

She told Cole, "Next time, kill yourself outside. Less cleanup for Sam."

"Isabel," I said sharply.

But Cole seemed unaffected.

"Was just," he said, and stopped. His lips were less blue now that he'd been breathing for a while. "Was just trying to find . . ." He stopped entirely and closed his eyes. A muscle was still twitching over his shoulder blade.

Isabel stepped over his body and snatched up her purse from the couch. She stared at the banana I'd left there beside it, eyebrows pulled down low over her eyes as if, out of everything that she'd seen today, the banana was the most inexplicable.

The idea of being alone in the house with Cole — with Cole, like this — was unbearable.

"Isabel," I said. I hesitated. "You don't have to go."

She looked back at Cole, and her mouth became a thin, hard thing. There was something wet caught in her long lashes. She said, "Sorry, Sam."

When she left, she shut the back door hard enough to make every glass Cole had left on the counter rattle.

Chapter Eight

· ISABEL ·

As long as I kept the speedometer needle above sixty-five, all I saw was the road.

The narrow roads around Mercy Falls all looked the same after dark. Big trees, then small trees, then cows, then big trees, then small trees, then cows. Rinse and repeat. I threw my SUV around corners with crumbling edges and hurtled down identical straightaways. I went around one turn fast enough that my empty coffee cup flew out of the cup holder. The cup pattered against the passenger side door and then rolled around in the footwell as I tore around another turn. It still didn't feel fast enough.

What I wanted was to drive faster than the question: *What if you'd stayed?*

I'd never had a speeding ticket. Having a hotshot lawyer father with anger-management issues was a fantastic deterrent; usually just imagining his face when he heard the news kept me safely under the limit. Plus, out here, there wasn't really any point to speeding. It was Mercy Falls, population: 8. If you drove too fast, you'd find yourself through Mercy Falls and out the other side.

But right now, a screaming match with a cop felt just about right for my current state of mind.

I didn't head toward home. I already knew that I could get home in twenty-two minutes from where I was. Not long enough.

The problem was that he was under my skin now. I'd gotten close to him again and I'd caught Cole. He came with a very specific set of symptoms. Irritability. Mood swings. Shortness of breath. Loss of appetite. Listless, glassy eyes. Fatigue. Next up, pustules and buboes, like the plague. Then, death.

I'd really thought I'd recovered. But it turned out I was just in remission.

It wasn't just Cole. I hadn't actually told Sam about my father and Marshall. I tried to convince myself that my father couldn't get the protection lifted from the wolves. Not even with the congressman. They were both big shots in their hometowns, but that was different from being a big shot in Minnesota. I didn't have to feel guilty about not warning Sam tonight.

I was so lost in my thoughts that I didn't realize my rearview mirror was full of flashing red and blue lights. The siren wailed. Not a long one, just a brief howl to let me know he was there.

Suddenly a screaming match with a cop didn't feel like such a brilliant idea.

I pulled over. Got my license out of my purse. Registration from the glove box. Rolled down the window.

When the cop came to my window, I saw that he wore a brown uniform and the big weird-looking hat that meant he was a state trooper, not a county cop. State cops never gave warnings.

I was so screwed.

He shone a flashlight at me. I winced and turned on the interior light of the car so he'd turn it off.

"Good evening, miss. License and registration, please." He looked a little pissed. "Did you know I was following you?"

"Well, obviously," I said. I gestured to the gearshift, put it into park.

The trooper smiled the unfunny smile my father did sometimes when he was on the phone. He took my license and the registration without looking at them. "I was behind you for a mile and a half before you stopped."

"I was distracted," I said.

"That's no way to drive," the cop said. "I'm here to give you a citation for going seventy-three in a fifty-five zone, all right? I'll be right back. Please don't move your vehicle."

He walked back to his car. I left the window open, even though bugs were starting to smack themselves against the strobe lights in my mirrors. Imagining my father's reaction to this ticket, I fell back into my seat and closed my eyes. I'd be grounded. My credit card taken away. Phone privileges gone. My parents had all sorts of torture devices they'd concocted back in California. I didn't have to worry about whether or not I should go see Sam or Cole again, because I would be locked in the house for the rest of my senior year.

"Miss?"

I opened my eyes and sat up. The trooper was by my window again, still holding my license and registration, a little ticket book beneath them.

His voice was different from before. "Your license says 'Isabel R. Culpeper.' Would that be any relation to Thomas Culpeper?"

"He's my father."

The trooper tapped his pen against his ticket book.

"Ah," he said. He handed me the license and the registration. "That's what I thought. You were going too fast, miss. I don't want to see you doing that again."

I stared at the license in my hands. I looked back at him. "What about —?"

The trooper touched the brim of his hat. "Have a safe night, Miss Culpeper."

CHAPTER NINE

· SAM ·

I was a general. I sat awake for most of the night poring over maps and strategies of how to confront Cole. Using Beck's chair as my fortress, I swiveled back and forth in it, scribbling fragments of potential dialogue on Beck's old calendar and using games of solitaire for divination. If I won this game, I would tell Cole the rules by which he had to live to stay in this house. If I lost, I would say nothing and wait to see what happened. As the night grew longer, I made more complicated rules for myself: If I won but it took me longer than two minutes, I would write Cole a note and tape it to his bedroom door. If I won and put down the king of hearts first, I would call him from work and read him a list of bylaws.

In between solitaire games, I tried out sentences in my head. Somewhere, there were words that would convey my concern to Cole without sounding patronizing. Words that sounded tactful but persuasive. That somewhere was not a place I could imagine finding.

Every so often, I crept out of Beck's office and down the dim gray hallway to the living room door, and I stood and watched Cole's seizure-spent body until I was certain I had seen him take a breath. Then frustration and anger propelled me back to Beck's office for more futile planning.

My eyes burned with exhaustion, but I couldn't sleep. If Cole woke up, I might speak to him. If I'd just won a game of solitaire. I couldn't risk him waking and me not speaking to him right away. I wasn't sure why I couldn't risk it — I just knew I couldn't sleep knowing he might wake up in the interim.

When the phone rang, I started hard enough to make Beck's chair spin. I let the chair complete its rotation, then cautiously picked up the receiver.

"Hello?"

"Sam," Isabel said. Her voice was brisk and detached. "Do you have a moment to chat?"

Chat. I had a special brand of hatred for the phone as a chatting medium. It didn't allow for spaces or silences or breaths. It was speaking or nothing, and that felt unnatural for me. I said, cautiously, "Yes."

"I didn't get a chance to tell you earlier," Isabel said. Her voice was still the sharp, enunciated words of a telephone bill collector. "My father is meeting with a congressman about getting the wolves taken off the protected list. Think helicopters and sharpshooters."

I didn't say anything. It wasn't what I thought she'd wanted to chat about. Beck's chair still had some momentum, so I let it turn another time. My tired eyes felt like they were being pickled in my skull. I wondered if Cole was awake yet. I wondered if he was still breathing. I remembered a small, stocking-hatted boy being pushed into a snowbank by wolves. I thought about how far away Grace must be by now.

"Sam. Did you hear me?"

"Helicopters," I said. "Sharpshooters. Yes."

Her voice was cool. "Grace, shot through the head from three hundred yards."

It stung, but in the way that distant, hypothetical horrors did, like disasters reported on the news. "Isabel," I said, "what do you want from me?"

"What I always want," she replied. "For you to do something."

And in that moment, I missed Grace, more than I had during any time in the past two months. I missed her so hard that it actually did make me catch my breath, like her absence was something real stuck in the back of my throat. Not because having her here would solve these problems, or because it would make Isabel let me be. But for the sharp, selfish reason that if Grace were here, she would have answered that question differently. She would know that when I asked, I didn't want an answer. She'd tell me to go sleep, and I would be able to. And then this long, terrible day would end, and when I woke up in the morning, everything would look more plausible. Morning lost its healing powers when it arrived and found you already wide-eyed and wary.

"Sam. God, am I talking to myself?" Over the line, I heard the chime cars made when a door was opened. And then a sharp intake of breath as the door shut.

I realized I was being an ingrate. "I'm sorry, Isabel. It's just been — it's been a really long day."

"Tell me about it." Her feet crunched across gravel. "Is he all right?"

I walked the phone down the hallway. I had to wait a moment to let my eyes adjust to the pools of lamplight — I was so tired that every light source had halos and ghostly trails — and waited for the requisite rise and fall of Cole's chest.

"Yes," I whispered. "He's sleeping."

"More than he deserves," Isabel said.

I realized that it was time to stop pretending to be oblivious. Probably well past time. "Isabel," I said, "what went on between you two?"

Isabel was silent.

"You aren't my business." I hesitated. "But Cole is."

"Oh, Sam, it's a little late to be pulling the authority card now."

I didn't think that she meant to be cruel, but it smarted. It was only by imagining what Grace had told me of Isabel — of her getting Grace through my disappearance, when Grace had thought I was dead — that kept me on the phone. "Just tell me. Is there something going on between you two?"

"No," Isabel snapped.

I heard the real meaning, and maybe she meant for me to. It was a *no* that meant *not at the moment.* I thought of her face when she saw the needle beside Cole and wondered just how big of a lie that *no* was. I said, "He's got a lot to work through. He's not good for anyone, Isabel."

She didn't answer right away. I pressed my fingers against my head, feeling the ghost of the meningitis headache. Looking at the cards on the computer screen, I could see that I had no more options. The timer said it had taken me seven minutes and twenty-one seconds to realize I'd lost.

"Neither," Isabel said, "were you."

Chapter Ten

· COLE ·

Back on the planet called New York, my father, Dr. George St. Clair, MD, PhD, Mensa, Inc., was a fan of the scientific process. He was a good mad scientist. He cared about the why. He cared about the how. Even when he didn't care about what it was doing to the subject, he cared about how you could state the formula to replicate the experiment.

Me, I cared about results.

I also cared, very deeply, about not being like my father in any way. In fact, most of my life decisions were based around the philosophy of not being Dr. George St. Clair.

So it was painful to have to agree with him on something so important to him, even if he'd never know about it. But when I opened my eyes, feeling like my insides had been pounded flat, the first thing I did was feel for the journal on the nightstand beside me. I had woken earlier, found myself alive on the living room floor — that was a surprise — and crawled to my bedroom to sleep or finish the process of dying. Now, my limbs felt like they'd been assembled by a factory with lousy quality control. Squinting in gray light that could've been any time of day or night, I opened the journal up with fingers that felt like inanimate objects. I had to turn past pages of Beck's handwriting to get to my own, and then I wrote the date and copied the format I'd used on the days before. My handwriting on the facing page was a bit sturdier than the letters I scratched down now.

EPINEPHRINE/PSEUDOEPHEDRINE MIX 4
METHOD: INTRAVENOUS INJECTION
RESULT: SUCCESSFUL
(SIDE EFFECTS: SEIZURE)

I closed the book and rested it on my chest. I'd pop the champagne over my discovery just as soon as I could stay awake. When progress stopped feeling so much like a disease.

I closed my eyes again.

CHAPTER ELEVEN

· GRACE ·

When I first became a wolf, I didn't know the first thing about how to survive.

When I'd first come to the pack, the things I didn't know wildly outnumbered the things that I did: how to hunt, how to find the other wolves when I got lost, where to sleep. I couldn't speak to the others. I didn't understand the riot of gestures and images that they used.

I knew this, though: If I gave into fear, I'd die.

I started by learning how to find the pack. It was by accident. Alone and hungry and feeling a hollow that food wouldn't fill regardless, I'd tipped my head back in despair and keened into the cold darkness. It was a wail more than a howl, pure and lonely. It echoed against the rocks near me.

And then, a few moments later, I heard a reply. A yipping howl that didn't last long. Then another. It took me a few moments to realize that it was waiting for me to respond. I howled again, and then, immediately, the other wolf replied. It had not finished howling when another wolf began, and another. If their howls echoed, I couldn't hear it; they were far away.

But far away was nothing. This body never got tired.

So I learned how to find the other wolves. It took me days to learn the mechanics of the pack. There was the large black wolf that was clearly in charge. His greatest weapon was his gaze: A sharp look would effectively send one of the other pack members to their belly. Anyone but the large gray wolf who was nearly as respected: He would merely flatten his ears back and lower his tail, only slightly deferential.

From them, I learned the language of dominance. Teeth over muzzle. Lips pulled back. Hair raised along spine.

And from the bottommost members of the pack, I learned about submission. The belly presented to the sky, the eyes directed downward, the lowering of one's whole body to look small.

Every day, the lowest wolf, a sickly thing with a running eye, was reminded of his place. He was snapped at, pinned to the ground, forced to eat last. I thought that being the lowest would be bad, but there was something worse: being ignored.

There was a white wolf who hovered on the edge of the pack. She was invisible. She wasn't invited into games, even by the gray-brown joker of the pack. He would even play with birds and he wouldn't play with her. She was a non-presence during hunts, untrusted, ignored. But the pack's treatment of her wasn't entirely unjustified: Like me, she didn't seem to know how to speak the language of the pack. Or perhaps I was being too kind. Really, it seemed like she didn't care to use what she knew.

She had secrets in her eyes.

The only time I saw her interact with another wolf was when she snarled at the gray wolf and he attacked her.

I thought he would kill her.

But she was strong; a scuffle through ferns ensued, and in the end the joker intervened, putting his body between the fighting wolves. He liked peace. But when the gray wolf shook himself and trotted away, the gray-brown joker turned back to the white wolf and showed his teeth, reminding her that though he'd stopped the fight, he didn't want her near.

After that, I decided not to be like her. Even the omega wolf was treated better. There was no place for an outsider in this world. So I crept up to the black alpha wolf. I tried to remember everything I'd seen; instinct whispered the parts that I couldn't quite remember. Ears flattened, head turned, shrunk down smaller. I licked his chin and begged for admittance to the pack. The joker was watching the exchange; I glanced at him and cracked a wolfish grin, just fast enough for him to see. I focused my thoughts and managed to send an image: me running with the pack, joining in the play, helping with the hunt.

The welcome was so boisterous and immediate that it was as if they'd been waiting for me to approach. I knew then that the white wolf was only rejected because she chose it.

My lessons began. As spring burst out around us, unfurling blossoms so sweet they smelled of rot, turning the ground soft and damp, I became the project of the pack. The gray wolf taught me how to creep up on prey, to run around and clamp down on a deer's nose as the others swept up its flanks. The black alpha taught me to follow scent trails at the edge of our territory. The joker taught me how to bury food and mark an empty stash. They seemed to take a peculiar joy in my ignorance. Long after I'd learned the cues for play, they would prompt me with exaggerated play bows, their elbows down to the ground, tails high and waving. When, hungry to the point of distraction, I managed to catch a mouse on my own, they pranced around me and celebrated as if I'd caught a moose. When they outstripped me on hunts, they'd return with a bit of the kill, like they would for a cub; for a long time, I stayed alive because of their kindness.

When I curled on the forest floor, crying softly, my body shaking and my insides ripped to shreds by the girl that lived inside me, the wolves stood watch, protecting me, though I wasn't sure what I needed to be protected from. We were the largest things in these woods, barring the deer, and even for them we had to run for hours.

And run we did. Our territory was vast; at first it seemed endless. But no matter how far we pursued our quarry, we circled and returned to the same stretch of woods, a long sloping stretch of ground broken by pale-barked trees. *Home. Do you like it?*

I would howl, at night, when we slept there. Hunger that could never be filled would well up inside me as my mind snatched at thoughts that didn't seem to fit inside my head. My howling would set off the others, and together we'd sing and warn others of our presence and cry for any members of the pack that weren't there.

I kept waiting for him.

I knew he wouldn't come, but I howled anyway, and when I did, the other wolves would pass images to me of what he'd looked like: lithe, gray, yellow-eyed. I would pass back images of my own, of a wolf by the edge of the woods, silent and cautious, watching me. The images, clear as the slender-leaved trees in front of me, made finding him seem urgent, but I didn't know how to begin to look.

And it was more than his eyes that haunted me. They were a door-way to other almost-memories, almost-images, almost-versions of myself that I couldn't catch, more elusive prey than the fastest deer. I thought I would starve for want of whatever that was.

I was learning to survive as a wolf, but I hadn't yet learned how to live as one.

Chapter Twelve

· GRACE ·

I shifted early one afternoon. "One" afternoon because I had absolutely no concept of time. I had no idea how long it had been since the last time I could fully remember being me, at Ben's Fish and Tackle. All I knew was that when I came to, I was in the little overgrown patio area near Isabel's house. My face was pressed against the damp dirt that covered the colorful mosaic I'd first seen several months ago. I'd been lying there long enough that the tiles had left a lined pattern in the side of my face. Down below me, ducks on the pond held terse conversations with each other. I stood up, testing my legs, and brushed most of the dirt and sticky wet leaf bits off me.

I said, "Grace." The ducks stopped quacking.

I was incredibly pleased by my ability to recall my own name. Being a wolf had drastically lowered my standards for miracles. Also, saying it out loud proved that I was sturdily human and could risk going up to the Culpeper house. The sun found me through the branches and warmed my back as I crept up through the trees. Checking to make sure that the driveway was empty — I was naked, after all — I made the run across the yard for the back door.

The last time Isabel had brought me here, the back door had been unlocked; I remembered commenting on it. Isabel had said, *I never remember to lock it.*

She'd forgotten again today.

I cautiously let myself in and found the phone in the spotless stainless-steel kitchen. The smell of food was so tantalizing that, for a moment, I just stood there, the phone in my hand, before I thought to dial.

Isabel picked up at once.

"Hi," I said. "It's me. I'm at your house. No one else is here."

My stomach growled. I eyed a bread box; a bagel wrapper poked out the bottom.

"Don't move," Isabel said. "I'm coming."

A half hour later, Isabel found me in her dad's hall of animals, eating a bagel, dressed in her old clothes. The room was actually fascinating, in a horrifying way. First of all, it was huge: two stories high, dim as a museum, and about as long as my parents' house was wide. It was also full of dozens of stuffed animals. I assumed Tom Culpeper had shot them all. Was it legal to shoot moose? Did they even have moose in Minnesota? It seemed like if anyone would have seen them, it would have been me. Perhaps he'd bought them instead. I imagined men in jumpsuits unloading animals with styrofoam taped to their antlers.

The door shut behind Isabel, loud and echoey like a church, and her heels tapped across the floor. The resonance of her footsteps in the hush only increased the church sensation.

"You look awfully happy," Isabel said, since I was still smiling at the moose. She stood beside me. "I came as fast as I could. I see you found my closet."

"Yes," I replied. "Thanks for that."

She picked at the sleeve of the T-shirt I wore, an old yellow T-shirt that read SANTA MARIA ACADEMY. "This shirt brings back horrible memories. I was Isabel C. back then, because my best friend was Isabel, too. Isabel D. Wow, was she ever a bitch."

"In case I shift, I didn't want to ruin anything nice." I glanced over at her; I was terribly glad to see her. Any other of my friends might have hugged me after I'd been gone for so long. But I didn't think Isabel hugged anyone, under any circumstances. My stomach twisted, warning me that I might not stay Grace for as long as I'd hoped. I asked, "Did your dad shoot all these?"

Isabel made a face. "Not all. Some of them he probably lectured to death."

We walked a few feet and I stopped in front of a glass-eyed wolf. I waited for the horror to hit, but it never came. Small round windows let in narrow shafts of light, casting circles of light at the stuffed wolf's paws. The wolf was shrunken and dusty and dull-haired and didn't look like it had ever been alive. Its eyes had been made in a factory somewhere and they didn't tell me anything about who the wolf might have been, animal or human.

"Canada," Isabel said. "I asked him. Not one of the Mercy Falls wolves. You don't have to keep staring at it."

I wasn't sure if I believed him.

"Do you miss California?" I asked. "And Isabel D.?"

"Yes," Isabel answered, then didn't elaborate. "Did you call Sam?"

"No answer." His phone had gone straight to voicemail; he'd probably let the battery run down again. And no one had answered at the house. I tried not to let my face show my disappointment. Isabel wouldn't understand, and I didn't feel like sharing my sorrow any more than Isabel did at the moment.

"For me, either," Isabel said. "I left a message at his work."

"Thanks," I said. But the truth was, I didn't feel very firmly Grace. Lately I had been staying human longer, awkwardly finding myself stranded in the middle of unfamiliar stretches of woods, but I still couldn't seem to stay human for longer than an hour. Sometimes I wasn't even human long enough to really register my change of bodies in my recently wolf brain. I had no idea of how much time had passed. All those days, silently marching by me . . .

I stroked the wolf's nose. It felt dusty and hard, like I was petting a shelf. I wished I was at Beck's house, sleeping in Sam's bed. Or even at my own house, getting ready to finish up my last month of school. But the threat of changing into a wolf dwarfed every other concern in my life.

"Grace," Isabel said. "My father is trying to get his congressman friend to help him get the wolves off the protected list. He wants to do an aerial hunt."

My stomach twisted again. I walked across the gorgeous hard-wood floor to the next animal, a fantastically huge hare forever frozen in midjump. It had a spiderweb between its back legs. Tom Culpeper — did he have to keep pursuing the wolves? Couldn't he stop? But I knew he couldn't. In his mind, it wasn't revenge, it was prevention. Righteous sword swinging. Keeping other people from suffering the same fate as his son. If I really, really tried, I could see it from his point of view and then I could stop thinking of him as a monster for two seconds, for Isabel's sake.

"You and Sam both!" Isabel snapped. "You don't even look both-ered. Don't you believe me?"

"I believe you," I replied. I looked at our reflections in the shiny wood. It was remarkably satisfying to see the dim, wavy shape of my human form. I felt a wave of nostalgia for my favorite jeans. I sighed. "I'm just a little tired of it all. It's a lot to deal with at the same time."

"But it has to be dealt with anyway. It doesn't matter if you like it or not. And Sam has the practical sense of a . . ." Isabel trailed off. Apparently she couldn't think of anything more fanciful than Sam.

"I know it has to be dealt with," I said wearily. My stomach lurched again. "What we need to do is move them, but I can't think about how to do that right now."

"Move them?"

I walked slowly to the next animal. Some kind of goose, running with its wings outstretched. Possibly it was supposed to be landing. The slanting afternoon light from above played with my sight and made the goose's black eye look like it was winking at me. "Obviously we have to get them away from your dad. He's not going to stop. There has to be someplace safer."

Isabel laughed, a short laugh that was more hiss than mirth. "I love that you came up with an idea in two seconds when Sam and Cole haven't come up with one in two months."

I looked at her. She was giving me a smirking sort of look, one eyebrow raised. It was probably meant to be admiring. "Well, it might not work. I mean, moving a pack of wild animals . . ."

"Yeah, but at least it's an idea. It's nice to see someone using their brain."

I made a face. We looked at the goose. It didn't wink again.

"Does it hurt?" Isabel asked.

I realized she was looking at my left hand, which had made its way to press on my side, all by itself. "Only a little," I lied. She didn't call me out on my untruthfulness.

We both jumped when Isabel's phone rang.

"That's for you," Isabel said, before she even dug it out. She looked at the screen and handed it to me.

My stomach jolted; I couldn't tell if it was from the wolf inside me or from sudden, inexplicable nerves.

Isabel smacked my arm; my skin crawled underneath her touch. "Say something."

"Hi," I said. More of a croak.

"Hi," Sam said, voice barely loud enough for me to hear. "How are you doing?"

I was very aware of Isabel standing beside me. I turned toward the goose. It winked at me again. My skin didn't feel like it was mine. "Better now."

I didn't know what I was supposed to say in two minutes after two months apart. I didn't want to talk. I wanted to curl up against him and fall asleep. More than anything, I wanted to be able to see him again, to see in his eyes that what we had had been real and that he wasn't a stranger. I didn't want a big gesture, an elaborate conversation — I just wanted to know that something was still the same when everything else had changed. I felt a surge of anger at the inadequate phone, at my uncertain body, at the wolves who'd made me and ruined me.

"I'm coming," he said. "Ten minutes."

Eight minutes too late. My bones ached. "I would really" — I paused to clench my teeth against the shivering. This was the worst part — when it was really starting to hurt but I knew that it was going to get more painful later — "like to get some cocoa when I'm back. I miss chocolate."

Sam made a soft noise. He could tell, and it hurt me, more than the shift, that he could. He said, "I know it's hard. Think of summer, Grace. Remember it will stop."

My eyes burned. I hunched my shoulders against the presence of Isabel.

"I want it to stop now," I whispered, and felt terrible for admitting it.

Sam said, "You —"

"Grace!" hissed Isabel, snatching the phone away from me. "You have to get out of here. My parents are home!"

She snapped the phone shut just as I heard voices from the other room.

"Isabel!" Tom Culpeper's voice rang out, distantly. My body was stretching and ripping inside. I wanted to fold in on myself.

Isabel propelled me toward a door; I stumbled into another room. She said, "Get in there. Be quiet! I'll take care of it."

"Isabel," I gasped, "I can't —"

The massive old lock at the other side of the hall cracked out like a shot, at the same moment that Isabel slammed the door shut in my face.

Chapter Thirteen

· ISABEL ·

For a single moment, I couldn't figure out if my father had seen Grace. His normally tidy hair was all disheveled and his eyes were full of shock or surprise or something else unguarded. He'd opened the door with such force that it banged into the wall behind it and bounced back again. The moose rattled; I waited for it to fall over. I'd never considered what an awesome sight it would be, to see all these animals start to tip like dominoes. My father was still shaking even after the moose had stopped.

I glowered at my father to cover my uneasiness. "Well, that was dramatic." I was leaning against the door to the piano room. I hoped that Grace wouldn't break anything in there.

"Thank God," my father said, as if I hadn't spoken. "Why the hell didn't you pick up your phone?"

I looked at him incredulously. I quite frequently let my parents' calls go through to voicemail. I called them *back*. Eventually. The fact that I'd let their calls beep through earlier today shouldn't have given them an ulcer.

Mom trailed into the room, her eyes bloodshot and her makeup a minor disaster. Considering that she normally made tears look like an accessory, I was impressed. I had thought this might be about the cop who'd stopped me, but I couldn't imagine Mom losing it over that.

I asked, suspiciously, "Why is Mom crying like that?"

My mother's voice was nearly a snarl. "Isabel, we gave you that cell phone for a reason!"

I was doubly impressed. Good for her. She normally let my father get all the good lines.

"Do you have it on your person?" my father asked.

"Jesus," I replied. "My person has it in her purse."

My father gave my mother a glance. "I expect you to pick it up from now on," he said. "Unless you are in class or missing a limb, I want that phone to be picked up and held to your ear when you see that it is us. Or you can say good-bye to it. A phone is a —"

"Privilege. Yeah, I know." I heard faint noises from inside the piano room behind me; to cover up the sound I began digging through my bag. When it had stopped, I pulled out my phone to prove that I had it. It showed twelve missed calls from my parents. And none from Cole, which, after over a month of having at least one missed call from him at all times, felt weird. I frowned. "So what's going on, anyway?"

My father said, "Travis called me and told me the police had just found a body in the woods. A girl, and they haven't identified her yet."

This was not good. I was glad that I knew that Grace was here, in the piano room making weird scratching noises. I realized Mom was still staring at me meaningfully; I was supposed to react.

I said, "And you just assumed that some random dead person was me?"

"It was near our property line, Isabel," Mom snapped.

Then my father said what I'd somehow known he was going to say. "She was killed by wolves."

I was filled with incredible anger, all of a sudden, at Sam and Cole and Grace, for doing nothing when I'd told them to do *something*.

There was more noise coming from the piano room. I spoke over the top of it. "Well, I've been at school or here all day. Hard to get killed at school." Then, because I realized I needed to ask or look guilty: "When will they know who she is?"

"I don't know," my father said. "They said she was in bad shape."

Mom said abruptly, "I'm going to go change out of these clothes." For a moment, I couldn't puzzle out the reason for her speedy exit. Then I realized she must've been thinking about my brother's death, imagining Jack torn apart by wolves. I was impervious; I knew how Jack had really died.

Just then, there was a thump from the piano room, clear enough that my father's eyes narrowed.

"I'm sorry I didn't pick up the phone," I said loudly. "I didn't mean to upset Mom. Hey. Something hit the bottom of my car on the way home. Would you look at it?"

I waited for him to refuse me, to charge into the other room and find Grace shifting into a wolf. But instead he sighed and nodded, already heading back toward the other door.

Of course there was nothing under my car for him to find. But he spent so long investigating that I had time to hurry back to the piano room to see if Grace had destroyed the Steinway. All I found was an open window and one of the screens pushed out into the yard. I leaned out and caught a glimpse of yellow — my Santa Maria Academy shirt, snagged on one of the bushes.

There had never been a worse time for Grace to be a wolf.

CHAPTER FOURTEEN

· SAM ·

So I had missed her again.

After the phone call, I lost hours to — nothing. Caught completely by the sound of Grace's voice, my thoughts chased each other, the same questions over and over. Wondering if I would have been able to see Grace if I'd gotten her message earlier, if I hadn't gone out to check the shed for signs of life, if I hadn't walked farther into the woods and shouted up through birch leaves to the sky, frustrated by Cole's seizure and Grace's absence and by just the weight of being me.

I drowned in the questions until the light failed. Hours gone, like I'd shifted, but I'd never left my own skin. It had been years since I'd lost time like this.

Once upon a time, that was my life. I used to look out the window for hours at a time, until my legs fell asleep beneath me. It was when I first came to Beck — I must've been eight or so, not long after my parents had left me with my scars. Ulrik sometimes picked me up under my armpits and pulled me back toward the kitchen and a life occupied by other people, but I was a silent, quivering participant. Hours, days, months gone, lost to another place that admitted neither Sam nor wolf. It was Beck who finally broke the spell.

He had offered me a tissue; it was a strange enough gift that it brought me to the present. Beck waved it at me again. "Sam. Your face."

I touched my cheeks; they weren't so much damp as sticky with the memory of continuous tears. "I wasn't crying," I told him.

"I know you weren't," Beck replied.

While I pressed the tissue to my face, Beck said, "Can I tell you something? There are a lot of empty boxes in your head, Sam."

I looked at him, quizzical. Again, it was a strange enough concept to hold my attention.

"There are a lot of empty boxes in there, and you can put things in them." Beck handed me another tissue for the other side of my face.

My trust of Beck at that point was not yet complete; I remember thinking that he was making a very bad joke that I wasn't getting. My voice sounded wary, even to me. "What kinds of things?"

"Sad things," Beck said. "Do you have a lot of sad things in your head?"

"No," I said.

Beck sucked in his lower lip and released it slowly. "Well, I do."

This was shocking. I didn't ask a question, but I tilted toward him.

"And these things would make me cry," Beck continued. "They used to make me cry all day long."

I remembered thinking this was probably a lie. I could not imagine Beck crying. He was a rock. Even then, his fingers braced against the floor, he looked poised, sure, immutable.

"You don't believe me? Ask Ulrik. He had to deal with it," Beck said. "And so you know what I did with those sad things? I put them in boxes. I put the sad things in the boxes in my head, and I closed them up and I put tape on them and I stacked them up in the corner and threw a blanket over them."

"*Brain* tape?" I suggested, with a little smirk. I was eight, after all.

Beck smiled, a weird private smile that, at the time, I didn't understand. Now I knew it was relief at eliciting a joke from me, no matter how pitiful the joke was. "Yes, brain tape. And a brain blanket over the top. Now I don't have to look at those sad things anymore. I could open those boxes sometime, I guess, if I wanted to, but mostly I just leave them sealed up."

"How did you use the brain tape?"

"You have to imagine it. Imagine putting those sad things in the boxes and imagine taping it up with the brain tape. And imagine pushing them into the side of your brain, where you won't trip over them when you're thinking normally, and then toss a blanket over the top. Do you have sad things, Sam?"

I could see the dusty corner of my brain where the boxes sat. They were all wardrobe boxes, because those were the most interesting sort of boxes — tall enough to make houses with — and there were rolls and rolls of brain tape stacked on top. There were razors lying beside them, waiting to cut the boxes and me back open.

"Mom," I whispered.

I wasn't looking at Beck, but out of the corner of my eye, I saw him swallow.

"What else?" he asked, barely loud enough for me to hear.

"The water," I said. I closed my eyes. I could see it, right there, and I had to force out the next word. "My . . ."

My fingers were on my scars.

Beck reached out a hand toward my shoulder, hesitant. When I didn't move away, he put an arm around my back and I leaned against his chest, feeling small and eight and broken.

"Me," I said.

Beck was silent for a long moment, hugging me. With my eyes closed, it seemed like his heartbeat through his wool sweater was the only thing in the world — and then he said, "Put everything in boxes but you, Sam. *You* we want to keep. Promise me you'll stay out here with us."

We sat like that for a long while, and when we stood up, all my sad things were in boxes, and Beck was my father.

Now, I went outside to the wide, ancient stump in the backyard, and I lay down on it so I could see the stars above me. Then I closed my eyes and slowly put my worries into boxes, one by one, sealing them up. Cole's self-destruction in one, Tom Culpeper in another. Even Isabel's voice got a box, because I just couldn't deal with it right now.

With each box, I felt a little lighter, a little more able to breathe.

The one thing I couldn't bring myself to put away was the sadness of missing Grace. That I kept. I deserved that. I'd earned it.

And then I just lay out there on the stump.

I had work in the morning, so I should have been sleeping, but I knew what would happen: Every time I closed my eyes, my legs would ache like I'd been running and my eyelids would twitch like they should be open and I'd remember that I needed to add names to the contacts in my cell phones and I'd think that really, one day, I should fold that load of laundry that I'd run a week ago.

Also, I'd think about how I really needed to talk to Cole.

The stump was wide enough in diameter that my legs only jutted over the side a foot or so; the tree — actually two of them grown together — must have been enormous when it had stood. It had black scars on it where Paul and Ulrik had used it as a base to set off fireworks. I used to count the age rings when I was younger. It had lived longer than any of us.

Overhead, the stars were wheeling and infinite, a complicated mobile made by giants. They pulled me amongst them, into space and memories. Lying on my back reminded me of being attacked by the wolves, long ago, when I'd been someone else. One moment I was alone, my morning and my life stretched out in front of me like frames in a film, each second only slightly different from the last. A miracle of seamless, unnoticed metamorphosis. And in the next moment, there were wolves.

I sighed. Overhead, satellites and planes moved effortlessly between the stars; a bank of clouds gestating lightning moved slowly in from the northwest. My mind flitted restlessly between the present — the ancient tree stump pressing sharply against my shoulder blades — and the past — my backpack crushed beneath me as the wolves pushed my body into a bank of snow left by the plow. My mother had armored me in a blue winter coat with white stripes on the arms and mittens too fluffy for finger movement.

In my memory, I couldn't hear myself. I only saw my mouth moving and the stick limbs of my seven-year-old self beating at the wolves' muzzles. I watched myself as if from outside my body, a blue and white coat trapped beneath a black wolf. Under its splayed paws, the garment looked insubstantial and empty, as if I had already vanished and left the trappings of my human life behind.

"Check this out, Ringo."

My eyes flew open. It took me a moment to register Cole next to me, sitting cross-legged on the stump. He was a dark black shape against a sky made gray in comparison, holding my guitar like its frame was spiked.

He played a D major chord, badly, with lots of buzzing, and sang in his low, gritty voice, *"I fell for her in summer"* — an awkward chord change and a melodramatic tip to his words — *"my lovely summer girl."*

My ears burned as I recognized my own lyrics.

"I found your CD." Cole stared at the guitar neck for a very long time before he put his fingers down on another chord. He'd placed every finger wrong on the fret, however, so the sound was more percussive than melodic. He let out an amiable grunt of dismay, then looked at me. "When I was going through your car."

I just shook my head.

"From blubber she is made, my lovely blubber girl," Cole added, with another buzzing D chord. He said, in a congenial voice, "I think I

might have ended up a lot like you, Ringo, if I'd been fed iced lattes from my mother's tits and had werewolves reading me Victorian poetry for bedtime stories." He caught my expression. "Oh, don't get your panties in a twist."

"They're untwisted," I replied. "Have you been drinking?"

"I believe," he said, "that I've drunk everything in the house. So, no."

"Why were you in my car?"

"Because you weren't," Cole said. He strummed the same chord. "Gets stuck in your head, did you notice? *I'd love to spend a summer with my lovely summer girl but I'm never man enough for my ugly summer squirrel. . . .*"

I watched a plane crawl across the sky, lights flashing. I still remembered writing that song, the summer before I met Grace for real. It was one of those that came out in a hurry, everything at once, me curled over my guitar on the end of my bed, trying to fit chords to the lyrics before the melody was gone. Singing it in the shower to lodge it firmly in my memory. Humming it while I folded laundry downstairs, because I didn't want Beck to hear me singing about a girl. All the while wanting the impossible, wanting what we all wanted: to outlast the summer.

Cole broke off his idle singing and said, "Of course, I like that one with the minor chord better, but I couldn't work it out." He made an attempt at a different chord. The guitar buzzed at him.

"The guitar," I said, "will only obey its master."

"Yeah," Cole agreed, "but Grace isn't here." He grinned at me slyly. He strummed the same D chord. "That's the only one I can play. Look at that. Ten years of piano lessons, Ringo, and you put a guitar in my hand and I'm a drooling baby."

Even though I'd heard him play the piano on the NARKOTIKA album, it was surprisingly difficult to imagine Cole taking piano lessons. To learn a musical instrument, you had to have a certain tolerance for tedium and failure. An ability to sit still helped, too.

I watched lightning jump from cloud to cloud; the air was getting the heavy feeling that comes before a storm. "You're putting your fingers too close to the fret. That's why you're buzzing. Move them farther behind the fret and press harder. Just your fingertips, too, not the pad."

I didn't think I'd described it very well, but Cole moved his fingers and played a chord perfectly, no buzzing or dead strings.

Looking dreamily up at the sky, Cole sang, *"Just a good-lookin' guy, sitting on a stump . . ."* He looked back to me. "You're supposed to sing the next line."

It was a game that Paul and I had used to play, too. I considered if I was too annoyed at Cole for making fun of my music to play along. After a slightly too long pause, I added, mostly the same note, half-hearted, *"Watching all the satellites."*

"Nice touch, emo-boy," Cole said. Thunder rumbled distantly. He played yet another D chord. He sang, *"I've got a one-way ticket to the county dump . . ."*

I sat up on my elbows. Cole strummed for me and I sang, *"'Cause I turn into a dog each night."*

Then I said, "Are you going to play that same chord for every single line?"

"Probably. It's my best one. I'm a one-hit wonder."

I reached for the guitar, and felt like a coward for doing it. To play this game with him felt like I was condoning the events of the night before; what he did to the house each week, what he did to himself every minute of every day. But as I took the guitar from him and strummed the strings lightly to see if it was in tune, it felt like a far more familiar language than any I would use to hold a serious conversation with Cole.

I played an F major.

"Now we're cooking with gas," Cole said. But he didn't sing another line. Instead, now that I was sitting with the guitar, he took my place, lying down on the stump and staring at the sky. Handsome and put together, he looked as if he had been posed there by an enterprising photographer, like last night's seizure hadn't even fazed him. "Play the minor chord one."

"Which —?"

"The good-bye one."

I looked at the black woods and played an A minor. For a moment, there was no sound except for some sort of insect crying out from the woods.

Then Cole said, "No, sing the actual song."

I thought of the little mocking change to his voice when he sang my summer girl lyrics and said, "No. I don't — no."

Cole sighed, as if he'd anticipated disappointment. Overhead, thunder rumbled, seemingly in advance of the storm cloud, which was cupping around the tops of the trees like a hand hiding a secret. Picking absently at the guitar because it made me feel calmer, I gazed upward. It was fascinating how the cloud, even between lightning flashes, seemed lit from within, collecting the reflected light of all the houses and cities that it passed over. It looked artificial in the black sky: purplish gray and sharply edged. It seemed impossible that something like it would exist in nature.

"Poor bastards," Cole said, his gaze still on the stars. "They must get pretty tired of watching us make the same damn mistakes all the time."

I suddenly felt incredibly lucky to be waiting. Because no matter how it gnawed at me, demanded my wakefulness, stole my thoughts, at the end of this endless waiting was Grace. What was Cole waiting for?

"Now?" Cole asked.

I stopped playing the guitar. "Now what?"

Cole shoved himself up and leaned back on his hands, still looking up. He sang, completely unself-conscious — but of course, why would he be? I was an audience two thousand bodies smaller than he was used to.

"One thousand ways to say good-bye, one thousand ways to cry . . ."

I strummed the A minor chord that started the song and Cole smiled a self-deprecating smile as he realized he'd started in the wrong key. I played the chord again, and this time I sang it, and I wasn't self-conscious, either, because Cole had already heard me through my car speakers and thus couldn't be disappointed:

> *One thousand ways to say good-bye*
> *One thousand ways to cry*
> *One thousand ways to hang your hat before you go*
> > *outside*
> *I say good-bye good-bye good-bye*
> *I shout it out so loud*
> *'Cause the next time that I find my voice*
> *I might not remember how*

As I sang *good-bye good-bye good-bye*, Cole began to sing the harmonies that I'd recorded on my demo. The guitar was a little out of tune — just the B string, it was always the B string — and we were a little out of tune, but there was something comfortable and companionable about it.

It was one frayed rope thrown across the chasm between us. Not enough to get across, but maybe just enough to tell that it wasn't as wide as I'd originally thought.

At the end, Cole made the hissed *haaaa haaaaa haaaaa* of fake audience noise. Then, abruptly, he stopped and looked at me, his head cocked. His eyes were narrowed, listening.

And then I heard them.

The wolves were howling. Their distant voices cadenced and melodic, discordant for a moment before falling back into harmonies. Tonight they sounded restless but beautiful — waiting, like the rest of us, for something we couldn't quite name.

Cole was looking at me still, so I said, "That's their version of the song."

"Needs some work," Cole replied. He looked at my guitar. "But not bad."

We sat in silence then, listening to the wolves howling between bursts of thunder. I tried unsuccessfully to pick out Grace's voice among them, but heard only the voices I'd grown up with. I tried to remind myself that I'd just heard her *real* voice on the phone earlier that afternoon. It didn't mean anything that her voice was absent now.

"We don't need the rain," Cole said.

I frowned at him.

"Back into the compound, I suppose." Cole slapped his arm and flicked an invisible insect off his skin with deft fingers. He stood up, tucked his thumbs into his back pockets, and faced the woods. "Back in New York, Victor —"

He stopped. Inside the house, I heard the phone ring. I made a mental note to ask him *What about New York?* but when I got inside, it was Isabel on the phone, and she told me that the wolves had killed a girl and that it wasn't Grace but I needed to turn on the damn television.

I turned it on and Cole and I stood in front of the couch. He crossed his arms while I thumbed through the channels.

The wolves were indeed on the news again. Once upon a time, a girl had been attacked by the wolves of Mercy Falls. The coverage then had been brief and speculative. The word then was *accident*.

Now it was ten years later and a different girl was dead and the coverage was never-ending.

The word now was *extermination*.

Chapter Fifteen

· GRACE ·

This was the nightmare.

Everything around me was solid black. Not the shape-filled black of my room at night, but the absolute depthless dark of a place with no light. Water splattered onto my bare skin, the driving sting of rain and then the heavier splash of water dripping from somewhere overhead.

All around me, I could hear the sound of the rain falling in a forest.

I was human.

I had no idea where I was.

Suddenly, light burst around me. Crouched and shaking, I had just enough time to see a forked snake of lightning strike beyond the black branches above me, my wet and dirty fingers outstretched before me, and the purple ghosts of tree trunks around me.

Then black.

I waited. I knew it was coming, but I still wasn't prepared when —

The crack of thunder sounded like it came from somewhere inside me. It was so loud that I clapped my hands over my ears and ducked my head to my chest before the logical part of me took over. It was thunder. Thunder couldn't hurt me.

But my heart was loud in my ears.

I stood there in the blackness — it was so dark that it *hurt* — and wrapped my arms around my body. Every instinct in me was telling me to find shelter, to make myself safe.

And then, again: lightning.

A flash of purple sky, a gnarled hand of branches, and eyes.

I didn't breathe.

It was dark again.

Black.

I closed my eyes, and I could still see the figure in negative: a large animal, a few yards away. Eyes on me, unblinking.

Now the hairs on my arms were slowly prickling, a slow, silent warning. Suddenly, all I could think about was that time when I was eleven. Sitting on the tire swing, reading. Glancing up and seeing eyes — and then being dragged from the swing.

Thunder, deafening.

I strained to hear the sound of an approach.

Lightning illuminated the world again. Two seconds of light, and there they were. Eyes, colorless as they reflected the lightning. A wolf. Three yards away.

It was Shelby.

The world went dark.

I started to run.

Chapter Sixteen

· SAM ·

I woke up.

I blinked, my eyes momentarily mystified by the brightness of my bedroom light in the middle of the night. Slowly, my thoughts assembled themselves, and I remembered leaving the light on, thinking I wouldn't be able to fall asleep.

But here I was, my eyes uncertain from sleep, my desk lamp casting lopsided shadows from one side of the room. My notebook had slid partially off my chest, all the words inside it off-kilter. Above me, the paper cranes spun on their strings in frantic, lumpy circles, animated by the air vent in the ceiling. They looked desperate to escape their individual worlds.

When it became obvious that I wasn't going back to sleep, I stretched my leg out and used my bare foot to turn on the CD player on the table at the end of my bed. Finger-picked guitar sounded through the speakers, each note in time with my heart. Lying sleepless in this bed reminded me of nights before Grace, when I'd lived in the house with Beck and the others. Back then, the population of paper cranes above me, scrawled with memories, had been in no danger of outgrowing their habitat as I slowly counted down toward my expiration date, the day when I'd lose myself to the woods. I'd stay awake long into the night, lost with wanting.

The longing then was abstract, though. I'd wanted something I knew I couldn't have: a life after September, a life after twenty, a life with more time spent *Sam* than *wolf*.

But now what I longed for wasn't an imagined future. It was a concrete memory of me slouched in the leather chair in the Brisbanes' study, a novel — *The Children of Men* — in my hand while Grace sat at the desk, biting the end of a pencil while doing homework. Saying nothing, because we didn't have to, just pleasantly intoxicated with the leather-scent of the chair around me and the vague smell of a roasted chicken hanging in the air and the sound of Grace sighing and turning her chair back and forth. Beside her, the radio hummed pop songs, top-40 hits that faded into the background until Grace tunelessly sang a refrain.

After a while, she lost interest in her homework and crawled into the chair with me. *Make room,* she said, though there was no way to make room. I protested when she pinched my thigh, trying to make herself fit into the seat beside me. *Sorry for hurting you,* she said right in my ear, but it wasn't really an apology, because you don't bite someone's earlobe to tell them you're sorry. I pinched her and she laughed as she pressed her face into my collarbone. One of her hands tunneled between the chair and my back to touch my shoulder blades. I pretended to read on and she pretended to rest against me, but she kept pinching my shoulder blade and I kept tickling her with my free hand, until she was laughing even as we kissed and kissed again.

There is no better taste than this: someone else's laughter in your mouth.

After a while, Grace fell asleep for real on my chest, and I tried, unsuccessfully, to follow her. Then I picked my book back up again and stroked her hair and read to the soundtrack of her breaths. The weight of her pinned my fleeting thoughts to the ground, and in that moment, I was more in the world than I'd ever been.

So now, looking at the paper cranes tugging urgently on their strings, I knew exactly what I wanted, because I'd *had* it.

I couldn't fall back asleep.

Chapter Seventeen

· GRACE ·

I couldn't outrun a wolf.

Neither of us could see very well in the dark, but Shelby had a wolf's sense of smell and a wolf's sense of hearing. I had bare feet tangled in thorns and blunt nails too short for attack and lungs that couldn't seem to get enough air. I felt powerless in this stormy wood. All I could think about was my memories of teeth in my collarbone, hot breath on my face, snow leaching my blood away from me.

Thunder cracked again, leaving behind the painfully fast crashing of my heart.

Panic wouldn't help.

Calm down, Grace.

I stumbled between lightning flashes, reaching out in front of me. Partially to spare myself from running into something, and partially in hopes of finding a tree with low enough branches to climb. That was the only advantage I had over Shelby — my fingers. But every tree here was either a skinny pine or a massive oak — no branches for twenty or fifty feet.

And behind me, somewhere: Shelby.

Shelby knew I'd seen her and so now she didn't take care to be quiet. Though she couldn't see any better than me in the darkness, I could hear her still tracking toward me in between lightning flashes, guided by her sense of smell and hearing.

I was more scared when I didn't hear her than when I did.

Lightning flickered. I thought I saw —

I froze, silent, waiting. I held my breath. My hair was plastered to my face and shoulders; a single wet strand was stuck to the corner of my mouth. It was easier to hold my breath than to resist the temptation to brush away that little bit of hair. Standing still, all I could think of were the small miseries: My feet hurt. The rain stung on my mud-smeared legs. I must have cut myself on unseen thorns. My stomach felt utterly empty.

I tried not to think about Shelby. I tried to concentrate on keeping my eyes locked on where I thought I'd seen my key to safety, so that when the lightning came again, I'd be able to map out a path.

Lightning flickered again, and this time I saw for certain what I thought I'd glimpsed earlier. Just barely, but it was there: the black outline of the shed where the pack kept supplies. It was several dozen yards to my right, above me, as if on a ridge. If I could make it there, I could slam that door in Shelby's face.

The forest went black and then thunder split the quiet. It was so loud that all other sound seemed to be sucked out of the world for a few seconds afterward.

In that noiseless dark, I bolted, hands in front of me, trying to stay true to the path to the shed. I heard Shelby behind me, close, snapping a branch as she jumped toward me. I *felt* more than heard her closeness. Her fur brushed my hand. I scrambled away and then

I

was

    falling

my hands grasped air

endless black

    falling

I didn't realize that I was crying out until all my breath was stolen and the sound was cut off. I hit something frigid and solid and my lungs emptied all at once. I only had a moment to realize that what I'd hit was water before I got a mouthful of it.

There was no up or down, just blackness. Just water coating my mouth and skin. It was so cold. So cold. Color exploded in front of my eyes, just a symptom in this blackness. My brain crying for air.

I clawed my way to the surface and gasped. My mouth was full of gritty, liquid mud. I felt it oozing down my cheeks from my hair.

Thunder grumbled above me, the sound seeming to come from far away; I felt like I was in the middle of the earth. Shivering almost too much to stand, I stretched my legs out and felt for the bottom. There — when I stood, the water came to the tip of my chin. It was freezing cold and filthy, but at least I could keep my head above water without tiring. My shoulders shook with involuntary tremors. I was so cold.

Then, standing in that frigid water, I felt it. A slow, slow path of nausea that started in my stomach and crawled up my throat. The cold. It was pulling at me, telling my body to shift.

But I couldn't shift. As a wolf, I'd have to swim to keep my head above water. And I couldn't swim forever.

Maybe I could climb out. I half swam, half stumbled through the icy water, reaching out. There must be a way out of this. My hands jammed into a craggy dirt wall that was perfectly vertical, stretching up higher than I could reach. My stomach twisted inside me.

No, I told myself. *No, you're not shifting, not now.*

I made my way around the wall, feeling for a possible escape. The sides stretched up and away from me, endless. I tried to get purchase in them, but my fingers wouldn't dig into the packed dirt, and the roots gave way under my weight, sending me back into the mud. My skin trembled, both from cold and the impending shift. I sucked in my frozen lower lip to try to steady it.

I could cry for help, but no one would hear me.

But what else could I do? The fact was this: If I turned into a wolf, I'd die. I could only swim for so long. All of a sudden, it seemed like a horrifying way to die, all alone, in a body that no one would ever recognize.

The cold pulled at me, flowed into my veins, unlocking the disease inside me. *No, no, no.* But I couldn't resist it anymore; I could feel the pulse in my fingers pounding as the skin bubbled into another shape.

The water sloshed around me as my body began to tear itself apart.

I screamed Sam's name into the darkness until I couldn't remember how to speak.

Chapter Eighteen

· SAM ·

"This is where the magic happens," Cole said. "Are you going to put on your leotard now?"

We were by the back entrance to the Crooked Shelf, the bookstore where I sometimes lived. I'd slept badly with the thunderstorm, and after last night's news, I hadn't wanted to come in to work, but there had been no way to get off my shift on such short notice. So in I went. I had to admit that the normalcy of it was assuaging my anxiety a little. Well, except for Cole. Every other day, I had left Cole behind when I went to work, and hadn't thought much of it. But this morning, I'd looked over while I was packing up and had seen him silently watching me getting ready to go, and I'd asked him if he wanted to come along. I didn't yet regret letting him come with me, but the morning was still young.

Cole squinted up at me from the base of the short stairs, arms braced on either stair rail, his hair a concerted mess. The uncomplicated morning light made him look disarming and at ease. Camouflage.

I echoed, "My leotard?"

"Yeah, your superhero shit," Cole said. "Sam Roth, werewolf by night, book retail specialist by day. Don't you need a cape for that?"

"Yes," I replied, unlocking the door. "Literacy rate in this country's appalling; you need a cape to even sell a cookbook. You're going to stay in the back if someone comes in, right?"

"No one's going to recognize me in a *bookstore*," Cole said. "Is the front of the store as crappy looking as the back?"

All of the stores on Main shared the same back alley, cluttered with spray-painted Dumpsters, weeds that looked like half-grown saplings, and plastic bags that had escaped death to tangle around the bases of staircases. Nobody came this way but owners and staff; I liked the disrepair because it was so far gone I didn't feel I had to try to clean it up.

"Nobody ever sees this part," I said. "It doesn't matter if it's pretty."

"So it's like track six on an album," Cole said. He smirked at some private joke. "So what's the plan, Stan?"

I pushed open the back door. "Plan? I have to work until noon. Isabel is supposed to come by sometime before then to tell me what she's found out since last night. Then, maybe, I'll put a bag on your head and we'll get lunch."

The back room was a mess of papers and boxes waiting to be put out for the trash. I had no taste for tidiness, and Karyn, the owner, had an arcane system of filing that made sense to no one but her. The first time Grace had seen the disorder, she'd been visibly horrified. Cole, on the other hand, just thoughtfully examined a box cutter and a stack of rubber-banded bookmarks while I turned the lights on.

"Put those back where you found them," I said.

As I did the business of opening up the store, Cole stalked around after me, his hands folded behind his back like a boy who'd been told not to break anything. He looked profoundly out of place here, a polished, aggressive predator moving amongst sunlit shelves that seemed folksy in comparison. I wondered if it was a conscious decision, his projected attitude, or if it was a by-product of the person within. And I wondered how someone like him, a furious sun, was going to survive in someplace like Mercy Falls.

With Cole's intent eyes on me, I felt self-conscious as I unlocked the front door, set up the register, turned on the music overhead. I doubted that he really appreciated the aesthetics of the store, but I felt a small, fierce bit of pride as he looked around. There was so much of me here.

Cole's attention was on the carpeted stairs near the back of the store. He asked, "What's upstairs?"

"Poetry and some special editions." Also, memories of me and Grace that were too piercing to relive at the moment.

Cole pulled a chick lit novel from an endcap, studied it vaguely, and put it back. He'd been here five minutes and he was already restless. I glanced at my watch, looking to see how long I had until Karyn arrived to relieve me. Four hours suddenly seemed like a very long time. I tried to remember the philanthropic impulse that had driven me to bring Cole.

Just then, as I turned toward the checkout counter, I caught an image out of the corner of my eye. It was one of those brief glances where you're amazed, afterward, at how much you've managed to see during the brief second of eye contact. One of those glances that should've been just a forgotten blur but was instead a snapshot. And the snapshot was this: Amy Brisbane, Grace's mother, walking past the big glass picture window of the bookstore toward her art studio. She held one arm across her chest, gripping the strap of her purse as if each jerky stride might pull it free from her shoulder. She wore a gauzy, pale scarf and that blank expression people put on when they want to become invisible. And I knew, right then, from that face, that she had heard about the dead girl in the woods, and she was wondering if it was Grace.

I should tell her it wasn't.

Oh, but there were a multitude of small crimes the Brisbanes had committed. I could easily bring back the memory of Lewis Brisbane's fist connecting with my face in a hospital room. Of being thrown out of their house in the middle of the night. Of going precious days without seeing Grace because they'd suddenly discovered parenting principles. I'd had so little, and they'd taken it from me.

But that face Amy Brisbane wore — I could still see it in my mind, even though her marionette strides had taken her past the storefront.

They had told Grace I was just a fling.

I bumped a fist into my palm again and again, torn. I was aware that Cole was watching me.

That blank face — I knew it was the same one I was wearing these days.

They'd made her last days as a human, as Grace, miserable. Because of me.

I hated this. I hated knowing what I wanted and knowing what was right and knowing that they weren't the same thing.

"Cole," I said, "watch the store."

Cole turned, an eyebrow raised.

God, I didn't want to do this. Part of me wanted Cole to refuse and thus make my decision for me. "No one will come in. I'll only be a second. I promise."

Cole shrugged. "Knock yourself out."

I hesitated one more second, wishing that I could just pretend it was someone else I'd seen walking on the sidewalk. After all, it had only been a face, half-hidden by a scarf, glimpsed for a second. But I knew what I'd seen.

"Don't burn anything down!" I pushed out the front door onto the sidewalk. I had to look away from the sudden brightness; the sun had only been able to peek in the front windows of the store, but outside, it came long and brilliant down the street. Squinting, I saw that Grace's mother had already made it most of the way down the block.

I hurried over the uneven sidewalk after her, pulled up short by two middle-aged ladies cackling over steaming coffee cups and then by a leathery old woman smoking in front of the thrift store and finally by a woman pushing a sidewalk-eating double stroller.

I had to run then, overly aware of Cole minding the store during my absence. Grace's mother hadn't even paused before crossing the street. I paused, breathless, on the corner, to let a pickup truck go by, before catching up with her in the shady alcove in front of her purple studio. Up close, she was a molting parrot; her hair was frizzily escaping from a band, one side of her blouse was tucked unevenly into her skirt, and the scarf I'd seen earlier had pulled free so that it was far longer on one side than the other.

"Mrs. Brisbane," I said, my voice catching as my lungs sucked in a breath. "Wait."

I wasn't sure what expression I was expecting her to wear when she saw that it was me. I'd braced myself for disgust or anger. But she just looked at me like I was — nothing. An annoyance, maybe.

"Sam?" she said after a pause, like she had to think to recall my name. "I'm busy." She was fumbling with the key in the lock, and not managing it. After a moment, she abandoned the key she'd been using and began digging in her purse for another. The bag was a massive, gaudy patchwork creation, full of clutter; if I needed any evidence that Grace was not her mother, that bag would have sufficed. Mrs. Brisbane didn't look at me as she dug through it. Her total dismissal — like I was not even worth fury or suspicion now — made me sorry that I'd come out of the store.

I took a step back. "I just thought you might not know. It's not Grace."

She jerked up to look at me so sharply that her scarf slid the rest of the way from her neck.

"I heard from Isabel," I said. "Culpeper. It's not Grace, the girl they found."

My little mercy felt less like a good idea as I realized that a suspicious mind could pull apart my story in a moment.

"Sam," Mrs. Brisbane said, in a very level voice, like she was addressing a young boy given to fibbing. Her hand hovered over her bag, fingers spread and motionless, like a mannequin. "Are you sure that's true?"

"Isabel will tell you the same thing," I said.

She closed her eyes. I felt a stab of satisfaction at the obvious pain she'd been feeling at Grace's absence, and then felt terrible for it. Grace's parents always managed that — making me feel like a worse version of myself. I ducked swiftly to pick up her scarf, awkward.

I handed the scarf to her. "I have to get back to the store."

"Wait," she said. "Come inside for a few moments. You have a few minutes, don't you?"

I hesitated.

She answered for me, "Oh, you're working. Of course you are. You — came out after me?"

I looked at my feet. "You looked like you didn't know."

"I didn't," she said. She paused; when I looked at her, her eyes were closed and she was rubbing the edge of the scarf on her chin. "The terrible thing, Sam, is that some other mother's daughter is dead out there and I can only be glad."

"Me, too," I said, very quietly. "If you're terrible, I am too, because I'm very, very glad."

Mrs. Brisbane looked at me then — really looked at me, lowering her hands and staring right at my face. "I guess you think I'm a bad mother."

I didn't say anything, because she was right. I softened it with a shrug. It was as close to lying as I could manage.

She watched a car go by. "Of course you know that we had a big fight with Grace before she — before she got sick. About you." She glanced up at me to see if this was true. When I didn't reply, she took it as a yes. "I had a lot of stupid boyfriends before I got married. I liked being with boys. I didn't like being alone. I guess I thought Grace was like me, but she's not really like me at all, is she? Because you two are serious, aren't you?"

I was still. "Very, Mrs. Brisbane."

"Are you sure you won't come in? It's hard to have a pity party out here where everyone can see me."

I thought, uneasily, about Cole in the store. I thought about the people I'd passed on the sidewalk. Two ladies with coffee. One smoking merchant. One lady with babies. The odds of Cole being able to get into trouble seemed fairly minimal.

"Just for a moment," I said.

Chapter Nineteen

· COLE ·

A bookstore was not the most entertaining place to be marooned. I wandered around for a few minutes, looking for books that might mention me, scuffing the carpet on the stairs backward so that it said my name in lighter colored tracks, and searching for something less offensively inoffensive to play on the radio overhead. The place smelled like Sam — or, I guess, he smelled like the store. Like ink and old building and something more leafy than coffee but less interesting than weed. It was all very . . . erudite. I felt surrounded by conversations I had no interest in participating in.

I finally found a book on how to survive worst-case scenarios and settled on the stool behind the counter, resting my feet next to the cash register while I paged through. *Being a werewolf* was not listed. Neither was *Recovering from addiction* or *Living with yourself.*

The door *ding*ed and I didn't lift my gaze, thinking it was just Sam returning.

"Oh, what are *you* doing here?"

I could identify her by the disdain in her voice and the rosiness of her perfume even before I looked up. God, she was hot. Her lips looked like they'd taste like Twizzlers. Her mascara was thick as paint and her hair was longer than before — I could have wrapped its icy blondeness twice around my finger, not that I was imagining such things. As she let the door close slowly behind her, her edible lips parted.

"Welcome to the Crooked Shelf," I said, raising an eyebrow. "Can I help you find something? Our self-help section is extensive."

"Oh, you should know," Isabel said. She was holding two paper cups and she forcefully put them down on the counter, away from my feet. She regarded my face with something like contempt. Or maybe fear. Did Isabel Culpeper possess this emotion? "What the hell was Sam thinking? You know anyone can walk by on the street and see your face through those windows, right?"

"Nice view for them," I said.

"Must be nice to be so carefree."

"Must be nice to be so worried about other people's problems." Something slow and unfamiliar was moving through my veins. I was both surprised and impressed when I realized it was anger. I couldn't remember the last time I'd been angry — I was sure it had been something between me and my father — and I couldn't remember what I was supposed to do about it.

"I'm not playing mind games with you," she said.

I looked at the coffee cups she'd brought in. One for her, one for Sam. Such generosity seemed unlike the Isabel I knew. "Would you play mind games with Sam?" I asked.

Isabel stared at me for a long moment, and then she shook her head. "God, could you be any more insecure?"

The answer to that question was always yes, but I didn't appreciate her bringing up my less public vices. I leaned forward to examine the two drinks, while Isabel gazed at me with slow death simmering in her eyes. Removing the lids, I looked at the contents. One of them was something that smelled suspiciously healthy. Green tea, maybe, or possibly horse pus. The other one was coffee. I took a drink of the coffee. It was bitter and complicated, just enough cream and sugar to make it drinkable.

"That," she said, "was mine."

I smiled broadly at her. I didn't feel like smiling, but I hid that by smiling bigger. "And now it's mine. Which means we're almost even."

"God, Cole, what? Even for what?"

I looked at her and waited for it to come to her. Fifty points if she got it in thirty seconds. Twenty points if she got it in a minute. Ten points if she got it in . . . Isabel just crossed her arms and looked out the window as if she were waiting for paparazzi to descend on us. Amazingly, she was so angry that I could *smell* it. My wolf senses were on fire with it; my skin prickled. Buried instincts were telling me to react. Fight. Flight. Neither seemed applicable. When she didn't say anything, I shook my head and made a little phone gesture by my ear.

"Oh," Isabel said, and she shook her head. "Are you serious? *Still?* The calls? Come on, Cole. I wasn't going to do that with you. You're toxic."

"Toxic?" I echoed. Actually, I'd be lying if I said I wasn't flattered. There was a strength to that word that was tempting. *Toxic.* "Yes, toxicity. It's one of my finer features. Is this because I didn't sleep with you? Funny, normally girls yell at me because I *did* screw them."

She gave her hard little laugh: *Ha. Ha. Ha.* Her heels clicked as she strode around the counter to stand right next to me. Her breath was hot on my face; her anger was louder than her voice. "This look on my face is because I was standing *this close* to you two nights ago, watching you twitch and drool because of whatever you'd stuck in your veins. I pulled you out of that hole once. I'm on the edge looking in anyway, Cole. I can't be around someone else who is. You're dragging me down with you. I'm trying to get out."

And again, this is how Isabel always worked her magic on me. That little bit of honesty from her — and it wasn't that much — took the wind out of my sails. The anger I'd felt before was strangely hard to sustain. I took my legs off the counter, slowly, one at a time, and then I turned on the stool so I was facing her. Instead of backing up to give me more room, she stayed right there, standing between my legs. A challenge. Or maybe a surrender.

"That," I said, "is a lie. You only found me in the rabbit hole because you were already down there."

She was so close to me that I could smell her lipstick. I was painfully aware that her hips were only an inch away from my thighs.

"I'm not going to watch you kill yourself," Isabel said. A long minute passed where we heard nothing but the roar of a delivery truck as it drove down the street outside. She was looking at my mouth, and suddenly she looked away. "God, I can't stay here. Just tell Sam I'll call him."

I reached out and put my hands on her hips as she tried to turn. "Isabel," I said. One of my thumbs was on bare skin, right above the waist of her jeans. "I wasn't trying to kill myself."

"Just chasing a high?" She attempted to turn again; I held on. I wasn't holding tight enough to keep her, but she wasn't pulling hard enough to get away, so we stayed as we were.

"I wasn't trying to get high. I was trying to become a wolf."

"Whatever. Semantics." Isabel wouldn't look at me now.

Letting go of her, I stood up so that we were face-to-face. I'd learned a long time ago that one of the finest weapons in my arsenal was my ability to invade personal space. She turned to look at me and it was her eyes and my eyes and I felt a surging sensation of *right*ness, of saying the right thing at the right time to the right person, that too-rare sensation of having the right thing to say and believing it, too:

"I'm only going to say this once, so you better believe me the first time. I'm looking for a cure."

CHAPTER TWENTY

· SAM ·

She — *Amy*, I tried to think of her as *Amy* instead of as *Grace's mother* — wrangled the door open and led me through a shady ante-room in a more muted purple than the front, and then into a startlingly bright main room full of canvases. The light was pouring in through the back wall of windows, which looked out onto a shabby lot with old tractors parked in it. If you ignored the view, the space itself was pro-fessional and classy — light gray walls, like a museum, with picture wires hanging from white molding along the ceiling. Paintings hung on the walls and leaned against the corners; some of them looked like they were still wet.

"Water?" she asked.

I stood in the middle of the room and tried not to touch anything. It took me a moment to put the word *water* in context: to drink, not to drown in.

"I'm fine," I told her.

Before, when I'd seen Amy's work, it had been strange and whimsical — animals in urban areas, lovers painted in odd colors. But all the canvases I saw now had been drained of life. Even if they were paintings of places — alleys and barns — they felt like barren planets. There were no animals, no lovers. No focal point. The only canvas that had any subject was the one currently on her easel. It was a huge canvas, nearly as tall as I was, and it was all white except for a very small figure sitting in the lower left corner. The girl's back was to the viewer, shoulders hunched up, dark blond hair down her back. Even facing away, it was unmistakably Grace.

"Go ahead, psychoanalyze me," Amy said as I looked at the paintings.

"I'm trying to quit," I said. And making that little joke felt like a cheat, like last night, when I'd played the singing-the-next-line game with Cole when I should've been grilling him. I was consorting with the enemy.

"Say what you're thinking, then," she said. "You make me nervous, Sam. Did I ever say that? I guess I should have. Here, I'll say it. You never said anything when you were with Grace, and I didn't know how to deal with that. Everyone says something to me. I can make anyone talk. The longer you went without saying anything, the more I wondered what the problem was."

I looked at her. I knew I was only proving her point, but I didn't know what to say.

"Oh, now you're just messing with me," she went on. "What are you thinking?"

I was thinking lots of things, but most of them needed to stay thoughts, not words. All of them were angry, accusatory. I turned toward the Grace on the canvas, her back toward me, an effective barrier. "I was thinking that *that* is not a Grace that I ever knew."

She walked across the studio to stand next to me. I moved away from her. I was subtle, but she noticed it. "I see. Well, this is the only Grace I know."

I said, slowly, "She looks lonely. Cold." I wondered where she was.

"Independent. Stubborn." Amy let out a sudden sigh and whirled away from me, making me start. "I didn't think I was being a horrible mother. My parents never gave me any privacy. They read every book I read. Went to every social event I went to. Strict curfew. I lived under a microscope until I got to college and then I never went home again.

I still don't talk to them. They still look at me under that giant glass." She made a binoculars motion at me. "I thought we were great, me and Lewis. As soon as Grace started wanting to do stuff on her own, we let her. I won't lie — I was really happy to have my social life back, too. But she was doing great. Everyone said that their kids were acting out or doing badly in school. If Grace had started doing badly, we would've changed."

It didn't sound like a confession. It sounded like an artist's statement. Conflict distilled into sound bites for the press. I didn't look at Amy. I just looked at that Grace on the canvas. "You left her all alone."

There was a pause. She hadn't expected me to say anything, maybe. Or maybe she just hadn't expected me to disagree.

"That's not true," she said.

"I believe what she told me. I saw her cry over you guys. That was real. Grace isn't dramatic."

"She never asked for more," Amy said.

Now I looked at Amy — fixed her with my yellow eyes. I knew it made her uncomfortable; it made everyone uncomfortable. "Really?"

Amy held my gaze for a few seconds and then looked away. I thought she was probably wishing she had left me on the sidewalk.

But when she looked back, her cheeks were wet and her nose was getting unbecomingly red. "Okay, Sam. No bullshit, right? I know there were times I was selfish. There were times I saw what I wanted to see. But it goes both ways, Sam — Grace wasn't the warmest daughter in the world, either." She turned away to wipe her nose on her blouse.

"Do you love her?" I asked.

She rested her cheek against her shoulder. "More than she loves me."

I didn't answer. I didn't know how much Grace loved her parents. I wished I was with her instead of here, in this studio, not knowing what to say.

Amy walked to the adjacent bathroom. I heard her blow her nose loudly before she returned from the bathroom. She stopped several feet away from me, dabbing her nose with a tissue. She had the weird look on her face that people get when they're about to be more serious than they are used to.

"Do *you* love her?" she asked.

I felt my ears burn, though I wasn't embarrassed by how I felt. "I'm here," I said.

She chewed her lip and nodded at the floor. Then, not looking at me, she asked, "Where is she?"

I didn't move.

After a long moment, she lifted her eyes to me. "Lewis thinks you killed her."

It didn't feel like anything. Not yet. Right now, they were just words.

"Because of your past," she said. "He said that you were too quiet and strange, and that your parents had messed you up. That there was no way you couldn't be ruined after that, and that you'd killed Grace when you found out he wouldn't let her see you again."

My hands wanted to make themselves into fists by my sides, but I thought that would look bad, so I forced them to hang, loose. They felt like deadweights at my sides, swollen and not belonging to my body. All the while, Amy was watching me, gauging my reaction.

I knew she wanted words, but I didn't have any that I wanted to say. I just shook my head.

She smiled a sad little smile. "I don't think you did. But then — where is she, Sam?"

Uneasiness budded slowly inside me. I didn't know if it was from the conversation, or the paint fumes, or Cole back at the store by himself, but it was there, nonetheless.

"I don't know," I said, truthfully.

Grace's mom touched my arm. "If you find her before we do," she said, "tell her I love her."

I thought of Grace and that empty dress balled in my hand. Grace, far, far away and unreachable in the woods.

"No matter what?" I asked, though I didn't think she could possibly say it in a way that would convince me. I separated my hands; I realized I had been rubbing a thumb over one of my scarred wrists.

Amy's voice was firm. "No matter what."

And I didn't believe her.

CHAPTER TWENTY-ONE

· ISABEL ·

The problem with Cole St. Clair is that you could believe everything he said, and, also, you couldn't believe anything he said. Because he was just so grandiose that it was easy to believe he could accomplish the impossible. But he was also such an incredible dirtbag that you couldn't really trust a single thing he said, either.

The problem was that I *wanted* to believe him.

Cole hooked his fingers in his back pockets, as if proving that he wasn't going to touch me unless I made the first move. With all the books behind him, he looked like one of those posters you see in libraries, the ones with celebrities advocating literacy. COLE ST. CLAIR SAYS NEVER STOP READING! He looked like he was enjoying himself up there on the moral high ground.

And he looked damn good.

I was reminded suddenly of a case that my dad had worked on. I didn't really remember the details properly — it was probably several different cases run together, actually — just some loser who'd been convicted of something in the past and was now being accused of something else. And my mom had said something like *Give him the benefit of the doubt.* I'd never forgotten my father's reply, because it was the first and only clever thing I thought he'd ever said: *People don't change who they are. They only change what they do with it.*

So if my father was right, it meant that behind those earnest green eyes staring into mine, it was the same old Cole, perfectly capable of being that person he was before, lying on the floor drunk out of his mind and working up the nerve to kill himself. I didn't know if I could take that.

I said finally, "And your cure for werewolfism was . . . epilepsy?"

Cole made a disinterested noise. "Oh, that was just a side effect. I'll fix it."

"You could have died."

He smiled, the wide, gorgeous smile that he knew very well was wide and gorgeous. "But I didn't."

"I don't think that counts," I said, "as not being suicidal."

Cole's tone was dismissive. "Taking risks is not being suicidal. Otherwise, skydivers need serious help."

"Skydivers have parachutes or whatever the hell it is skydivers have!"

Cole shrugged. "And I had you and Sam."

"We didn't even know that you —" I broke off, because my phone was ringing. I stepped away from Cole to look at it. My dad. If there had ever been a time to let it go through to voicemail, this was it, but after my parents' tirade yesterday, I had to pick it up.

I was aware of Cole's eyes on me as I flipped the phone open. "Yeah, what?"

"Isabel?" My father's voice was both surprised and . . . buoyant.

"Unless you have another daughter," I replied. "Which would explain a lot."

My father acted like I hadn't spoken. He still sounded suspiciously good-tempered. "I dialed your number by accident. I meant to call your mother."

"Well, no, you got me. What were you calling her for? You sound high," I said. Cole's eyebrows jerked up.

"Language," my father replied automatically. "Marshall just called me. The girl was the last straw. He's got word that our wolf pack is coming off the protected list and they're setting up an aerial hunt. The state's going to do it — no rednecks with rifles this time. We're talking helicopters. They're going to do it properly, like Idaho."

I said, "It's definitely happening?"

"Just a question of when they can schedule it," my father said. "Collect the resources and manpower and all that."

Somehow, that last sentence drove it home for me — "resources and manpower" was such a bullshit Marshall phrase that I could imagine my father repeating the words after hearing them on the phone only minutes before.

This was it.

Cole's face had changed from the lazily handsome expression he'd worn before. Now, something in my voice or face must have tipped him off, because he was looking at me in a sharp, intense way that made me feel exposed. I turned my face away.

I asked my father, "Do you have any idea of when? I mean, at all?"

He was talking to someone else. They were laughing and he was laughing back. "What? Oh, Isabel, I can't talk. A month, maybe, they said. We're working on moving it up, though — it's a question of the helo pilot and getting the area pinned down, I think. I'll see you when I get home. Hey — why aren't you in school?"

I said, "I'm in the bathroom."

"Oh, well, you didn't have to pick up in school," my father said. I heard a man say his name in the background. "I have to go. Bye, pumpkin."

I snapped the phone shut and stared at the books in front of me. There was a biography of Teddy Roosevelt face-out.

"Pumpkin," Cole said.

"Don't start."

I turned and we just looked at each other. I wasn't sure how much he'd heard. It didn't take much to get the gist. There was still something about Cole's face that was making me feel weird. Like before, life had always been a little joke that he found a little funny but mostly lame. But right now, in the face of this new information, this Cole was — *uncertain*. Just for two seconds, it was like I saw all the way down to the inside of him, and then the door *ding*ed open and that Cole was gone.

Sam stood in the doorway of the store, the door slowly swinging shut behind him.

"Bad news, Ringo," Cole said. "We're going to die."

Sam looked at me, a question in his eyes.

"My dad did it," I said. "The hunt's going through. They're waiting on the helo pilot."

Sam stood there by the front door for a long, long moment, his jaw working slightly. There was something odd and resolute about his expression. Behind him, the back of the open sign said CLOSED.

The silence stretched out so long that I was about to say something, and then Sam said, with strange formality, "I'm getting Grace out of those woods. The others, too, but she's my priority."

Cole looked up at that. "I think I can help you there."

CHAPTER TWENTY-TWO

· SAM ·

The woods were slimy and still from days of rain. Cole led the way, the certainty in his steps proving how often he'd taken the paths. Isabel had reluctantly left for school, and when Karyn had arrived to replace me, Cole and I had headed back to Beck's house as quickly as we could. While we were in the car, Cole had told me his brilliant idea for catching Grace: traps.

I couldn't quite believe that all this time that I'd thought Cole was spending his days trashing the house, he'd also been trying to trap animals. Wolves. I supposed everything about Cole was so unpredictable that I couldn't be legitimately surprised.

"How many of these things do you have?" I asked, as we picked through the woods. I could have been thinking about Isabel's news, the impending hunt, but I focused on making my way through the trees. The world was so damp that it took quite a bit of concentration. Water from last night's storm dripped on me as I used branches for handholds, and my feet slid sideways beneath me.

"Five," Cole said, stopping to knock his shoe on a tree trunk; chunks of mud fell out the treads. "Ish."

"'Ish'?"

Cole kept walking. "I'm making one for Tom Culpeper next," he said, without turning around.

I couldn't say I disagreed.

"And what is it you're planning on doing, if you catch one?"

Cole made an exaggerated noise of disgust as he stepped over a pile of old deer droppings. "Find out what makes us shift. And find out if you're really cured."

I was surprised that he hadn't asked me for a blood sample yet.

"Maybe," Cole said thoughtfully, "I'll enlist you for a bit of benign experimentation next."

Apparently I was getting to know him better than I thought. "Maybe not," I said.

As we walked, I suddenly caught a whiff of something that reminded me of Shelby. I stopped, turned in a slow circle, stepped carefully over a whiplike, bright green branch of thorns at my feet.

"What are you doing, Ringo?" Cole asked, stopping to wait.

"I thought I smelled . . ." I broke off. I didn't know how to explain.

"The white wolf? The pissy one?"

I looked at him, and his expression was canny.

"Yes. Shelby," I said. I couldn't find whatever scent it was that I'd caught before. "She's bad news. Have you seen her recently?"

Cole nodded, terse. I felt a knot of disappointment settle, cold and undigested, in my stomach. I hadn't seen Shelby in months now, and I had hoped, optimistically, that she'd abandoned the woods. It wasn't unheard of for wolves to leave their packs. Most packs had a scapegoat, picked on and driven away from food, pushed outside of the pack hierarchy, and they'd often travel hundreds of miles to start another pack, somewhere far away from their tormentors.

Once upon a time, Salem, an older wolf I'd never known as a human, had been the omega of the Boundary Wood pack. But I had seen enough of Shelby when I was clawing my way through the meningitis to know that she had fallen low in Paul's eyes and thus low in the pack. It was as if he knew, somehow, what she had done to me and Grace.

"Bad news how?" Cole asked.

I didn't want to tell him. To talk about Shelby was to take the memories of her out of the boxes I'd carefully put them away in, and I didn't think I wanted to do that. I said warily, "Shelby prefers being a wolf. She . . . had a bad childhood, somewhere, and she isn't quite right." As soon as I said the words, I hated them, because it was the same thing that Grace's mom had just said about me.

Cole grunted. "Just the way Beck likes them." He turned away and began to walk, vaguely following the trail Shelby had left behind, and after a moment, I did, too, though I was lost in my thoughts.

I remembered Beck bringing Shelby home. Telling us all to give her time, give her space, give her something that she needed but we couldn't offer. Months had gone by, then, a warm day, like this. Beck had said, *Could you go see what Shelby's gotten up to?* He didn't really think she was up to something, or he would've gone himself.

I'd found her outside, crouched by the driveway. She started when she heard me approach, but when she saw it was me, she turned back around, unconcerned. I was like air to her: neither good nor bad. Just there. So she didn't react when I walked directly up to where she crouched, her white-blond hair hiding her face.

She had a pencil in her hand, and she was using it to scry in bits of innards, stretching loops of intestines straight with the tip of the pencil. They looked like worms. There was some metallic green and oily-looking organ nestled among them. At the other end of the guts, a few inches away, a starling jerked and bicycled its legs, upright on its chest and then its side, held fast to Shelby's pencil by the grip of its own intestines.

"This is what we do to them, when we eat them," Shelby had said. I remember just standing there, trying to hear any trace of emotion in her voice. She pointed to the bird's mangled chest cavity with another pencil she held in her other hand. I remembered that it was one of my pencils, from my room. Batman. Freshly sharpened. The idea of her in my room felt more real and horrifying than the tortured animal kicking up dust on the edge of the concrete drive.

"Did you do that?" I asked. I knew she had.

As if I hadn't spoken, Shelby said, "This is where its brain is. An ostrich's eye is bigger than its brain."

She pointed to the starling's eye. I could see the tip of the pencil resting directly on the shining black surface and something inside me clenched, bracing itself. The starling lay perfectly still. Its pulse was visible in its exposed innards.

"No —" I said.

Shelby stuck my Batman pencil through the starling's eye. She smiled at it, a faraway smile that had nothing to do with joy. Her gaze shifted in my direction though she didn't turn her head.

I stood there, my heart racing as if I was the one who'd been attacked. My breath came in uneven, sick jerks. Looking at Shelby and the starling, black and white and red, it was hard to remember what happiness felt like.

I had never told Beck.

Shame made me a prisoner. I hadn't stopped her. It had been my pencil. And in penance, I never forgot that image. I carried it with me, and it was a thousand times heavier than the weight of that little bird's body.

And what rough beast, its hour come round at last,
Slouches toward Bethlehem to be born?

I wished Shelby was dead. I wished that this scent, the one that both Cole and I were following, was just a phantom of her, a relic instead of a promise. Once upon a time, it would have been good enough for her to just leave the woods in search of another pack, but I was not that Sam anymore. Now, I hoped she was someplace she could never return from.

But the scent of her, lingering in the damp underbrush, was too strong. She was alive. She'd been here. Recently.

I stopped then, listening.

"Cole," I said.

He stopped immediately, something in my voice warning him. For a moment, there was nothing. Just the grumbling, alive smell of the woods waking up as they warmed. Birds shouting from tree to tree. Far away, outside the woods, a dog barking, sounding like a yodel. And then — a distant, faint, anxious sound. If we hadn't stopped, the noise of our feet would've obliterated it. But now, clearly, I heard the whistling, whimpering sound of a wolf in distress.

"One of your traps?" I asked Cole softly.

He shook his head.

The sound came again. Something like misgiving tugged in my stomach. I didn't think it was Shelby.

I held my finger to my lips and he jerked his chin to show he understood. If there was an injured animal, I didn't want to drive it away before we could help.

We were suddenly wolves ourselves, in human skins — soundless and watchful. As when I had hunted, my strides were long and low, my feet barely clearing the forest floor. My stealth wasn't something I had to consciously recollect. I just pulled away my humanness, and there it was, just underneath, waiting for me to recall it back to the surface.

Beneath my feet, the ground was slick and slimy with the wet clay and sand. As I descended into a shallow ravine, arms outstretched for balance, my shoes slid, leaving behind misshapen prints. I stopped.

Listened. I heard Cole hiss as he struggled to keep his balance behind me. The sound of the wolf's whimper came again. The distress in it plucked something deep inside me. I crept closer.

My heart was loud in my ears.

The closer I got, the more wrong it felt. I could hear the whistling of the wolf, but I also heard the sound of water, which didn't make sense. No river ran through the bottom of this ravine, and we were nowhere near the lake. Still: splashing.

A bird sang over us, loud, and a breeze lifted the leaves around me, showing their pale undersides. Cole was looking at me but not quite at me, listening. His hair was longer than when we'd first met, his color better. He looked, strangely, like he belonged here, aware and tense in these woods. The breeze was sending petals around us, though there was no flowering tree in sight. It was an ordinary, beautiful spring day in these woods, but my breath was coming unevenly and all I could think was *I will remember this moment for the rest of my life.*

Suddenly, I had a clear, perfect sensation of drowning. Of water, cold and slimy, closing over the hair on the top of my head, of water burning my nostrils, of my lungs held tight in its grip.

It was a fragmented memory, entirely out of place. How wolves communicated.

And then I knew where the wolf was. I abandoned my stealth and scrambled the last few yards.

"Sam!" snapped Cole.

I barely stopped in time. Beneath my right foot, the ground sloughed away, falling with a splash. I pulled back to a safer distance and peered down.

Below me, the clay was shockingly yellow, a scratch of unreal color below the dark leaves. It was a sinkhole, freshly made, judging from the newly exposed tree roots, witches' fingers that poked crook-edly out of the slick sides. The edge of the pit was jagged where it had

collapsed; the rain must've been too much for the roof of an under-
ground cavern. The resulting hole was eight or ten or fifteen feet deep,
it was hard to tell. The bottom was filled with something like yellow-
orange water or mud, thick enough to cling to the sides, thin enough
to drown in.

Floating in the water was a wolf, its fur clogged and tufted with
mud. It wasn't whimpering now, just drifting in the water. Not even
kicking its legs. Its coat was too filthy for me to identify.

"Are you alive?" I whispered.

At my voice, the wolf kicked convulsively and lifted its head to
look at me.

Grace.

I was a radio tuned to all stations at the same time, so many
thoughts inside me that none of them counted.

Now I could see the evidence of her struggles: claw marks in the
soft clay at the water line, chunks of dirt pried from the side of the pit,
a track worn smooth by a body sliding back down into the water. She
had been here a while, and when she looked at me, I could see that she
was tired of fighting. I saw, too, that her eyes were knowing, pensive,
full of understanding. If not for the cold water around her, holding her
body in wolf form, she'd probably be human.

That made it so much worse.

Beside me, Cole sucked in a breath before saying anything.
"Something for it to climb on? Something to at least —"

He didn't finish, because I was already scouting around the mouth
of the sinkhole, looking for something that would be of help. But with
Grace in wolf form, what could I do? The water was at least six feet
below me, and even if I managed to find something long enough to
lower into the pit — maybe there was something in the shed — it
would have to be something she could walk on, since she couldn't
climb. Could I even convince her to walk on something? If she had her

hands, her fingers, this still wouldn't be easy, but at least it wouldn't be impossible.

"This is all useless," Cole said, nudging a branch with his foot. The only wood near the pit was a couple of crumbling, rotten pine trees downed by storms and age, nothing useful. "Is there anything back at the house?"

"A ladder," I said. But it would take me at least thirty minutes to get there and back. I didn't think she had thirty more minutes. It was cold up here in the shade of the trees, and I thought that it must be colder down in the water. How cold did it have to be for hypothermia? I crouched back at the edge of the pit, feeling helpless. That same dread I'd felt when I saw Cole seizing was slowly poisoning me.

Grace had made her way to the side of the pit nearest me, and I watched her attempt a foothold, her legs trembling with fatigue. She didn't even manage to leverage herself an inch out of the water before her paws smeared back down the wall. Her head was only just above water, her trembling ears tipped at half-mast. Everything about her was exhausted, cold, beaten.

"It won't last until we get the ladder," Cole said. "It hasn't got that much stamina left."

I felt sick with the plausibility of her death. I said miserably, "Cole, it's Grace."

He looked at me then, instead of at her, his expression complicated.

Below us, the wolf flicked her eyes up toward me, holding my gaze for a moment, her brown eyes on my yellow ones.

"Grace," I said. "Don't give up."

It seemed to steel her: She began to swim again, this time toward another part of the wall. It was painful to recognize Grace in this grim determination. Again she tried to climb, one shoulder forced into the muck, the other paw scrabbling above the water at the steep wall. Her hind paws were braced on something below the surface of the water. Straining upward, muscles twitching, she pressed against the clay wall, shutting one eye to keep the mud out. Shivering, she looked at me with her one open eye. It was so easy to look past the mud, past the wolf, past everything else, and into that eye, right into Grace.

And then the wall gave way. In a cascade of mud and grit, she splashed into the water. Her head vanished beneath the sludge.

There was an infinite moment where the brown water was perfectly still.

In those seconds that it took for her to fight her way back to the surface, I made up my mind.

I stripped off my jacket, stood at the edge of the sinkhole, and, before I could think of the countless horrific consequences, I went in.

I heard Cole say my name, too late.

I half slid, half fell into the water. My foot touched something slick, and before I had a chance to determine whether it was the bottom of the pit or merely a submerged root, I was swallowed.

The grit of the water stung my eyes for a second before I closed them. In the moment of that blackness, time disappeared, became an arbitrary concept, and then I found my footing and lifted my head above the surface.

"Sam Roth, you bastard," Cole said. There was admiration in his voice, which probably meant I'd made a poor decision.

The water came just to my collarbone. It was slimy as mucus and bitterly, bitterly cold. I felt like I had no skin, standing in this pit. It was just my bones and this frigid water passing around them.

Grace pressed against the opposite wall, her head against the mud, her expression torn between wariness and something her lupine face couldn't convey. Now that I knew the depth of the sinkhole, I realized that she must be on her back legs, leaning against the wall to save her strength.

"Grace," I said, and, at the sound of my voice, her eyes hardened into fear. I tried not to take it personally; wolf instincts took precedence, no matter what humanity I thought I'd seen in them earlier. Still, I had to rethink my plan of trying to lift her toward the edge of the hole. It was hard to concentrate; I was so cold that my goose bumps hurt. Every old instinct I had was telling me to get out of the cold before I shifted.

It was so cold.

Above me, Cole was crouched at the edge of the pit. I could feel his restlessness, hear the unasked question, but I didn't know how to answer him.

I moved toward her, just to see how she reacted. She jerked back, defensively, and lost her footing. She vanished into the water, and this time, she was gone for the space of several breaths. When she emerged, she tried unsuccessfully to find her previous resting place, but the wall wouldn't hold her. She paddled feebly, nostrils huffing above the water. We didn't have much time.

"Should I come down there?" Cole asked.

I shook my head. I was so cold that my words were more breath than voice. "Too — cold. You'll — shift."

Near me, the wolf whistled, very quietly, anxious.

Grace, I thought, closing my eyes. *Please remember who I am.* I opened my eyes.

She was gone. There was just a slow, thick ripple moving toward me from where she'd sank.

I lunged forward, my shoes sinking into the soft floor of the pit, and scooped my arms through the water. Agonizing seconds went by where all I felt was silt on arms, roots on my fingertips. The pool that had seemed small from above now felt vast and depthless.

All I could think was: *She's going to die before I can find her. She's going to die inches from my fingertips, sucking water into her nose and breathing mud. I will live this moment again and again every day of my life.*

Then, finally, my fingers touched something more substantial. I felt the solidness of her wet fur. I wrapped my arms underneath to lift her up and get her head above water.

I needn't have worried about her snapping. In my arms, she was a limp thing, lightweight with the water buoying her up, pathetic and broken. She was a golem of twigs and mud, cold as a corpse already from her hours in the water. Brown water bubbled from her nostrils.

My arms wouldn't stop shaking. I leaned my forehead against her muddy cheek; she didn't flinch. I felt her ribs pressing against my skin. She breathed another sticky, dirty-water breath.

"Grace," I whispered. "This isn't how it ends."

Each of her exhalations was wet and raspy. My mind was a jostle of ideas and plans — if I could get her farther out of the water, if I could keep her warmer, if I could keep her above water until she got some strength back, if Cole could get the ladder — but I couldn't focus on any one of them. Keeping her face above the liquid mud, I moved around slowly, feeling with my feet for whatever she'd stood on earlier.

I looked up to the edge of the hole. Cole was gone.

I didn't know what to feel.

Moving slowly, I found a slick, fat root that supported my weight, and I braced myself against the wall, Grace's wolf body in my arms. I hugged her to me until I felt her strange fast heartbeat against my chest. She was shivering now, whether from fear or exhaustion, I didn't know. I didn't know, either, how I was going to get us out of here.

I knew this, though: I wasn't letting go.

Chapter Twenty-Three

· COLE ·

Running as a wolf was effortless. Every muscle was built for it. Every part of a wolf body worked together for seamless, constant motion, and the wolf mind just wouldn't hold on to the concept of tiring at some point in the future. So there was only running like you would never stop, and then: stopping.

As a human, I felt clumsy and slow. My feet were useless in this mud, collecting so much crap on the bottom that I had to knock it off to continue. By the time I reached my destination, the shed, I was out of breath and my knees ached from running uphill. No time to stop, though. I already had half an idea of what to retrieve from the shed, unless a better idea presented itself. I pushed open the door and peered inside. Stuff that had seemed infinitely practical when I'd seen it before now seemed useless and fanciful. Bins of clothing. Boxes of food. Bottled water. A television. Blankets.

I tore the lids off the bins marked SUPPLIES, looking for what I really wanted: some kind of cable, bungee cord, rope, ball python. Anything I could fasten around the mouth of a bin to turn it into a sort of dumbwaiter for wolves. But there was nothing. This was like kindergarten for werewolves. Snack time and nap supplies.

I swore into the empty room.

Maybe I should have risked the extra time to go back to the house for the ladder.

I thought about Sam, shivering down in that hole with Grace in his arms.

I had a sudden flash of memory: Victor's cold body at the bottom of a hole, dirt flung over him. It was only a trick of my thoughts, and an untrue one at that — Victor had been wrapped up when we buried him — but it was enough. I wasn't burying another wolf with Sam. Especially not Grace.

The thing I was beginning to figure out about Sam and Grace, the thing about Sam not being able to function without her, was that that sort of love only worked when you were sure both people would always be around for each other. If one half of the equation left, or died, or was slightly less perfect in their love, it became the most tragic, pathetic story invented, laughable in its absurdity. Without Grace, Sam was a joke without a punch line.

Think, Cole. What is the logical answer?

My father's voice.

I closed my eyes, imagined the sides of the pit, Grace, Sam, myself at the top. Simple. Sometimes the simplest solution was the best.

Opening my eyes, I grabbed two of the bins and upended them, dumping their contents onto the floor of the shed, abandoning everything in them but a towel. I nested the bins inside each other, along with the towel, and tucked the lids under my arm. It seemed like the best weapons in my life had always been the most innocuous: empty plastic bins, a blank CD, an unmarked syringe, my smile in a dark room.

I slammed the shed door behind me.

· **GRACE** ·

I was dead, floating in water deeper than me and wider than me.

I was

bubbling breath

clay in my mouth
black-star vision
a moment
then a moment
then I was
Grace.
I was floating, dead in water colder than me and stronger
than me.
Stay awake.
The warmth of his body tugged at my skin
ripped
Please, if you can understand me
I was inside out
everything was yellow, gold, smeared over my skin
Stay awake
I
was
awake
I
was

· COLE ·

The pit was eerily silent when I got to it, and I half expected, for some
reason, to find both Sam and Grace dead. Once upon a time, I
would've stolen that feeling and written a song, but that time was
long gone.

And they weren't dead. Sam looked up at me when I crept to the
edge of the hole. His hair was plastered to his head in the sort of
unstudied disarray that hands normally lifted to fix without thinking,
but of course Sam had no hands free. His shoulders shook with the

cold and he ducked his chin to his chest as he shuddered. If I hadn't known what he held in his arms, I would have never guessed that small, dark form was a live animal.

"Heads up," I said.

Sam looked up just as I dropped the two bins down. He winced as water exploded upward, splattering my skin with cold drops. I felt the wolf inside me jerk at the sensation, dissipating almost instantly. It was a weird reminder that eventually, I'd turn back into a wolf, and not because I'd stuck myself with a needle or otherwise experimented on myself. Eventually I'd shift because I couldn't help it.

"C-cole?" Sam asked. He sounded bewildered.

"Stand on the bins. One might be enough. How heavy is she?"

"N-not."

"Then you can hand her up to me." I waited while he moved stiffly through the water to the closest bin. It was bobbing on the surface; he was going to have to push it under the surface and turn it upside down in order for it to be a step. He tried to lean to grab the edge of it while still holding Grace; her head flopped away from his chest, limp and unresponsive. It was clear that he couldn't manipulate the bin without putting Grace down, and to put Grace down was to drown her.

Sam stood there, just staring at the floating bin, his arms tremoring under Grace. He was absolutely motionless. His head was tilted slightly to the side, regarding the water or something just past it. Both of his shoulders were slanted steeply to point at the ground. Victor had trained me to recognize what that meant. Giving up was the same in every language.

There are times that you sat back and let others play their solo and there are times you got up and took control of the music. And the truth is, I've never looked as good sitting still.

I said, "Watch — !" and not really giving Sam a chance to react, I slid down into the hole. There was a brief moment of utter vertigo, where my body wasn't sure how much farther I was falling and when I needed to brace myself, and then I caught my arm on the side just before pitching under the surface of the liquid mud. "Hot *damn*," I breathed, because the water was cold, cold, cold.

Behind a layer of grit, Sam's face was uncertain, but he saw what I meant to do. "B-better hurry."

"You think?" I said. Sam was right, though — the cold water was jerking and twisting and poking fingers at me, prodding for the wolf inside me. I tipped the first bin and water poured into it, the weight tugging it down beneath the surface. Working by feel, trying to hold my twisting stomach still inside me, I turned the bin and pushed it into the sludge at the bottom. I reached for the other, let it fill with water, stacked it sideways on top. Grabbed the floating lid and pressed it on top.

"H-hold it steady," Sam said. "L-let me get her and . . ."

He didn't finish, but he didn't have to. He shifted her in his arms and stepped onto the first bin. I reached out with my free hand to steady him. His arm was the exact temperature of the mud. Grace looked like a dead dog in his arms as he climbed onto the next. The bins teetered precariously; I was the only thing keeping them from tumbling under his weight.

"Fast," I hissed. God, the water was cold; I couldn't get used to it. I was going to turn into a wolf, and *no* I was not going to, not right now — I gripped the edge of the bins. Sam was on the bin with Grace and his shoulder was at the edge of the pit. He closed his eyes for a bare second. He whispered *sorry*, and then tossed the wolf's body up and out of the pit, onto dry ground. It was only a few feet, but I saw that it pained him. He turned to me. He was still shaking with the cold.

I was so close to wolf that I could taste it in my mouth.

"You come out first," Sam said, his teeth gritted to keep his voice steadier. "I don't want you to change."

It wasn't really me who mattered, wasn't me who absolutely had to climb out of this hole, but Sam didn't leave room for argument. He clambered off the bins and splashed heavily into the water beside me. There was a knot the size of my head in my guts, clenching and unclenching. I felt like my fingers were inside my diaphragm, tiptoeing their way up my throat.

"Climb," Sam said.

My scalp crept and crawled. Sam reached out and grabbed my jaw, hard enough that his fingertips were painful against my jawbone. He stared into my eyes, and I could feel the wolf in me responding to that challenge, this unspoken instinct that lent force to his command. I didn't know this Sam.

"Climb," he ordered. "Get out!"

And said like that, I had to. I crawled up the bins, my body twitching, my fingers finding the edge of the sinkhole. Every second that I was out of the water I felt more human and less wolf, though I could smell the stink of myself, of the near-shift. It washed over me every time I turned my head. Pausing a bit to gather my senses, I slithered out of the sinkhole on my stomach. It was not the sexiest move I'd ever performed, but I was impressed nonetheless. A few feet away, Grace lay on her side, motionless but breathing.

Below me, Sam climbed unsteadily onto the first bin and waited a long moment to find his balance.

"I . . . I'm only going to have a second before this thing falls," Sam said. "Can you —"

"Got it," I replied.

He was wrong; he had less than a second. He had only barely made it onto the second bin, crouching, when they began to tip below him. He reached up and, almost in the same moment, I grabbed his arm. The bins fell back into the water below, the splash more muffled than I would've expected, as Sam swung his other arm up for me to grab. I braced myself against the soggy edge of the sinkhole and backed up. It was a good thing that Sam was a gangly guy with limbs made of twigs, because otherwise we would've both ended up back in the pit.

Then it was over. I was leaning back on my arms, out of breath. Not a single part of me untouched by the slimy mud of the sinkhole. Sam sat beside Grace, clenching and unclenching his fists, looking at the small balls of clay that formed when he did. The wolf lay quietly next to him, breaths fast and jerky.

Sam said, "You didn't have to come down there."

"Yes, I did," I said.

I looked up and found him already looking back at me. In the dark of the woods, his eyes looked very pale. So strikingly wolf's eyes. I remembered him grabbing my jaw and telling me to climb, appealing to my wolf instincts if nothing else. The last time someone had stared me in the face like that, ordered me to listen and to focus through the change, it had been the first time I'd shifted. The voice had been Geoffrey Beck's.

Sam reached out and touched Grace's side; I saw his fingers move as they traced the ribs hidden beneath the fur. "There's a poem that goes like this," he said. *Wie lange braucht man jeden Tag, bis man sich kennt.*"

He kept touching the wolf's ribs, his eyebrows furrowed, until the wolf lifted its head slightly, uneasy. Sam put his hands in his lap. "It means '*how long it takes us, each day, to know each other*.' I haven't really been fair to you."

Sam was saying it didn't matter, but it kind of did, too. "Save your kraut poetry for Grace," I said, after a pause. "You're getting your weird all over me."

"I'm serious," Sam said.

I said, not looking at him, "I'm serious, too. Even cured, you're really incredibly abnormal."

Sam wasn't laughing. "Take the apology, Cole, and I won't say anything about it again."

"Fine," I said, standing up and tossing him the towel. "Apology accepted. In your defense, I didn't really deserve 'fair.'"

Sam carefully tucked the towel around the wolf's body. She jerked away at his touch, but she was too tired to really react. "It's not the way I was brought up," he said finally. "People shouldn't have to earn kindness. They should have to earn cruelty."

I thought, suddenly, of how this conversation would have gone down differently with Isabel here. She would've disagreed. But that was because, with Isabel, cruelty and kindness were sometimes the same thing.

"Anyway," Sam said. But he didn't say anything else. He scooped up Grace's body, all wrapped tightly in the towel so that she couldn't move even if she found the strength. He started toward the house.

Instead of following him, I walked back to the edge of the sinkhole and looked in. The bins still floated in the thin mud below, so covered in the dirty paste that it was impossible to see their original color. There was no motion on the surface of the water, nothing to betray its depth.

I spit into the hole. The mud was so thick it didn't even ripple outward where my spit landed. It would've been hell to die in. It occurred to me that every single way I'd tried to die had been an easy way. It hadn't seemed like it at the time, when I lay on the floor and said *enoughenoughenoughenoughjustgetmeout* to no one. I had never really considered that it was a privilege to die as Cole and not as something else.

CHAPTER TWENTY-FOUR

· ISABEL ·

There was this thing that my parents used to do to me and Jack, before Jack died. They'd pick a time when we were most likely to be doing something that we wanted to be doing, sometimes homework but more often plans with friends — opening night of a movie you were dying to see was always a likely time — and then they would kidnap us.

They would take us to Il Pomodoro. That is "The Tomato" for those of you who, like me, do not speak cornball. Il Pomodoro was an hour and a half away from Mercy Falls in the middle of nowhere, which was saying a lot, because Mercy Falls was also the middle of nowhere. Why travel from one non-destination to another? Because while most people knew my father as a hard-assed trial lawyer who eviscerated his opponents with the ease of a velociraptor on speed, I knew the truth, which was that my father turned into a melting kitten in the hands of Italian men who served him garlic breadsticks while a tenor warbled sweetly in the background.

So, having just powered through a school day, dying to be done so that I could drive over to Beck's house to see what Sam and Cole were up to, with a million other things on my mind, I should have realized that it was a prime parental kidnapping environment. But it had been over a year. I was unprepared and my defenses were down.

I had no sooner stepped out of the school than my phone rang. Of course it was my father, so I had to pick it up or risk his righteous wrath. Flipping the phone open, I waved Mackenzie on; she wiggled her fingers over her shoulder without looking back at me.

"Yeah, what," I said, hitting the button on my keys to see how far away I could be and still unlock the car.

"Come right back home when you're done," my father said. I heard the hiss of running water behind him and the snap of a makeup case. "We're going to Il Pomodoro tonight and we're leaving as soon as you get here."

"Are you *serious*?" I asked. "I have homework and I have to be up early tomorrow. You can go without me; it'll be romantic."

My father laughed with ruthless mirth: *Ha. Ha. Ha.* "We're going with a group, Isabel. A little celebration party, as it were. Everyone wants to visit with you. It's been a long time." My mother's voice murmured in the background. "Your mother says that if you go, she'll pay for the oil change on your vehicle."

I jerked open the door on my SUV and scowled at the puddle I was standing in. Everything was soggy this week. Warm air rushed out of the car, a sign that it was spring — it had actually gotten warm enough to heat the inside of the car while it was shut up. "She already promised me that for taking her dry cleaning the other day."

My father relayed this information to my mother. There was a pause. "She is saying that she will take you to Duluth for something called high/lowlights. Wait, is this about your hair? I'm not really a fan of —"

"I really don't want to go," I interrupted him. "I had plans." Then a thought occurred to me. "What are you celebrating again? Is this about the wolf hunt?"

"Well, yes, but we won't be talking about that *all* night," my father said. "It will be fun. We'll —"

"Good. Fine. I'll go. Tell mom I need a haircut more than color. Not with that doofus guy she likes, either. He makes me look like a

soccer mom. I think he learned how to do hair from nineties sitcoms."
I climbed into my car and started it, trying not to think about the
evening ahead of me. The things I did for Grace and Sam that I would
never do for anybody else.

"This makes me happy, Isabel," my father said. I frowned at the
steering wheel. But I kind of believed him.

Every time we came to Il Pomodoro, I wondered how it had managed
to suck in my parents. We were Californians, for crying out loud, who
should know a quality culinary experience when we saw one. And yet
here we were at a red-and-white-checked table listening to some poor
college graduate sing opera at the end of our table while we perused
the menu and snacked on four different kinds of bread, none of which
looked Italian and all of which looked Minnesotan. The room was
dark and the ceiling was low and made of acoustic tile. It was an
Italian American tomb with a side of pesto.

I had done my best to stick to my father during the seating
process, because there were about fifteen people, and the whole point
of coming to this thing was to be close enough to hear what he said.
Still, I ended up with a woman named Dolly sitting between us. Her
son, who looked like he'd done his hair by standing backward in
a wind tunnel, sat on the other side of me. I picked at the ends of
my breadstick and tried not to let my elbows touch either of my
neighbors.

There was a flash as something flew across the table, landing
directly inside the neckline of my shirt, nestling on my breasts. Across
from me, a fellow wind-tunnel survivor — a brother, maybe — was
smirking and shooting glances at my neighbor. Dolly was oblivious,
talking across my father to my mother on the other side of him.

I leaned across the table toward the crumb-thrower. "Do that
again," I said, loud enough to be heard over the opera singer, Dolly,

my mother, and the smell of the breadsticks, "and I will sell your first-born child to the devil."

When I sat back, the boy next to me said, "He's annoying, sorry." But I could tell that what he really meant was *What a great conversation starter, thanks, bro!* Of course, Grace would have said, *Maybe he was just being nice*, because Grace thought nice things about people. Jack would have agreed with me, though.

Actually, it was really hard not to think about how the last time I'd been here, Jack had been sitting across the table from me, the rows and rows of wine bottles behind him, just like the kid across the table from me now. Jack had been a jerk that night, even though I tried not to remember that part. It felt like I wasn't missing him properly if I let myself remember how much I'd despised him sometimes. Instead I tried to remember what he looked like when he was grinning and dirty in the driveway, though these days it felt more like I was remembering a memory of a memory of his smile instead of remembering the smile itself. When I thought too hard about that, it made me feel weightless and untethered.

The opera singer ceased singing, to polite applause, and moved to the small stage on the side of the restaurant, where she conferred with another person in an equally demoralizing costume. My father took the opportunity to knock his spoon against his glass.

"A toast, for those of us who are drinking tonight," he said. Not really standing, just half rising. "To Marshall, for believing this could be done. And to Jack, who can't be here with us tonight" — he paused, then said — "but would be bugging us for a glass of his own if he were."

I thought it was a crappy toast, even if it was true, but I let Dolly and the neighbor boy knock their glasses against my water glass. I sneered at the boy across the table and withdrew my glass before he could lift his to mine. I'd get the crumb out of my shirt later.

Marshall sat at the end of the table, and his voice boomed in a way that my father's didn't. He had a carrying, congressional sort of voice, the kind that sounded good saying things like *Less of a tax burden on the middle class* and *Thank you for your donation* and *Honey, could you bring me my sweater with the duck on it?* He said, conversational and resonant, "Did you know that you folks have the most dangerous wolves in North America?" He smiled, broad and pleased to share this information with us. His tie was loosened like he was here among friends, not working. "Until the Mercy Falls pack became active, there had been only two confirmed fatal wolf attacks in North America. Total. On humans, of course. Out west, they had quite a few livestock taken down, that's for sure, that's why they put that two hundred twenty wolf quota out there in Idaho."

"That's how many wolves the hunters could take?" asked Dolly.

"You betcha," Marshall said, a Minnesota accent presenting itself so unexpectedly that I was surprised.

"That seems like a lot of wolves," Dolly replied. "Do we have that many wolves here?"

My father broke in smoothly; in comparison to Marshall, he sounded more elegant, more cultured. Of course we were sitting in Il Pomodoro, so how cultured could he be, but still. "Oh, no, they estimate the Mercy Falls pack to be only twenty or thirty animals. At most."

I wondered how Sam would take this conversation. I wondered what he and Cole had decided to do, if anything. I remembered that strange, resolute look on Sam's face in the store, and it made me feel hollow and incomplete.

"Well, what makes our pack so dangerous, then?" Dolly wondered, her chin resting in a circle of her fingers. She was performing a trick that I'd done often enough to recognize. The interested ignorance routine was excellent for commanding attention.

"Familiarity with humans," my father answered. He made a gesture at one of the waiters: *We're ready.* "The big thing that keeps wolves
away is fear, and once they have no fear, they're just large, territorial
predators. There have, in the past, in Europe, India, been wolf packs
that were notorious man-killers." There was no trace of emotion in his
voice: When he said *man-killer*, he was not thinking *Jack-killer*. My
father had a purpose now, a mission, and as long as he was focused on
that, he would be fine. This was the old Dad, powerful and frustrat-
ing, but ultimately someone to be proud of and awed by. I hadn't seen
this version of my father since before Jack died.

I realized bitterly that if it hadn't been Sam and Grace and Cole at
stake, I would've been happy at this moment, even sitting in Il
Pomodoro. My mother and father, smiling and chatting like old times.
Just a small price to pay for all this. I could have my parents back —
but I had to lose all of my real, true friends.

"Oh, no, they have significant populations in Canada," my father
was explaining to the man across from him.

"It's not a numbers game," Marshall added, because no one was
going to say it if he didn't. No one had any real response to that. We
all jumped in surprise as the singer began again. I saw Marshall's
mouth clearly form *My God*, but you couldn't hear him over the rush-
ing soprano.

At the same time that I felt my phone vibrate against my leg,
something tickled at my shirt collar. I looked up to see the muppet
across the table grinning stupidly at me, having launched another
crumb into my shirt. The music was too loud to say something to him
this time, which was good, because everything I could think of
involved four-letter words. Moreover, every time I looked to his side
of the table, I thought again about Jack sitting here with us and
how now we were all sitting around talking about the animals that
had killed him and not about how he would never be sitting in this

restaurant again. I jerked when something touched me again, this time my hair. It was the boy next to me, his fingers next to my temple.

"— got some in your hair," the guy shouted over the singing. I held up my hand like *Stop, just stop*.

My father was leaning over the table toward Marshall, engaged in a benevolent shouting match, trying to be heard over something that sounded a lot like Bizet. I heard him shout, "From the air, you can see everything." I retrieved my phone and flipped it open. Seeing Sam's number made me feel a strange knot of nerves in my stomach. He'd sent me a text, full of typos.

we founf her. was badf but cole pulle through likea hero.

thjought youd want to know. s

It was hard to picture the words *Cole* and *hero* in the same sentence. *Hero* seemed to indicate some kind of gallantry. I tried to text back under the table, out of the view of helpful boy next to me and Dolly on the other side, saying just that I was at dinner listening to details and I'd talk later. Or come by. When I texted *come by*, I once again felt that twitch in my stomach, and a breathless rush of guilt, for no particular reason that I could name.

The singing stopped then, and there was clapping around me — Dolly had her hands up by her face and was clapping right by my ear — but my father and Marshall kept on talking, leaning on the table toward each other, as if there had never been any music.

My father's voice was clear: "— drive them out from the woods, like we did before, but with more manpower, state blessing, Wildlife Services and all that, and once they're north of Boundary Wood in the open, the helicopters and sharpshooters take over."

"Ninety percent success rate in Idaho, you said?" Marshall

asked. He had a fork poised over an appetizer like he was taking notes with it.

"Then the rest don't matter," my father said. "Without the pack, they can't survive alone. Takes more than two wolves to take down enough game."

My phone vibrated again in my hands, and I flipped it open. Sam, again.

i thoughtshe was going to die isabel. i am so relievef it hurts.

I heard the boy across the table laughing and knew that he'd thrown something else at me that I hadn't felt. I didn't want to glance up at him because I'd just see his face against the wall where Jack's had been. Suddenly I knew that I was going to be sick. Not in the future, not in a "distinct possibility" way, but in a "right this moment I had to leave before I embarrassed myself" way.

I pushed back my chair, jostling it into Dolly, who was in the middle of asking a stupid question. I wound my way through tables and singers and appetizers made out of sea creatures that didn't come from anywhere near Minnesota.

I got to the bathroom — one room, no stalls, all kitted out like a home bathroom instead of a restaurant bathroom — and shut myself inside. I leaned back against the wall, my hand over my mouth. But I wasn't sick. I started to cry.

I shouldn't have let myself, because I was going to have to go back out there, and I'd have a swollen, red nose and pink eyes and everyone would know — but I couldn't stop. It was like they were choking me, my tears. I had to gasp to breathe around them. My head was full of Jack sitting at the table, being a jerk, the sound of my father's voice talking about the sharpshooters in helicopters, the idea that Grace had nearly died without me even knowing it, stupid boys throwing stuff into my shirt, which was probably cut too low for a family dinner anyway, Cole looking down at me on the bed, and the thing that had set me off, Sam's honest, broken text about Grace.

Jack was gone, my father always got what he wanted, I wanted and hated Cole St. Clair, and no one, no one would ever feel that way about me, the way that Sam felt about Grace when he sent that text.

I was sitting on the floor of the bathroom now, my back up against the cupboard beneath the sink. I remembered just how scathing I had been when I'd found Cole ruined on the floor of Beck's house — not the last time, but when he'd told me he needed to get out of his body or kill himself. I'd thought he was so weak, so selfish, so self-indulgent. But I got it now. Right in that moment, if someone had said, *Isabel, I can make it go away, take this pill* . . . I might have taken it.

There was a knock on the door.

"It's occupied," I said, angry that my voice sounded thick and unlike me.

"Isabel?" My mother's voice.

I had been crying so hard that my breath was hitching. I tried to speak evenly. "I'll be out in a second."

The knob turned. In my haste, I hadn't locked the door.

My mother stepped into the room and shut the door behind her. I looked down, humiliated. Her feet were the only thing I could see, inches from my own. She was wearing the shoes I'd bought her. That made me want to cry again, and when I tried to swallow my sob, it made an awful strangled sound.

My mother sat down on the bathroom floor next to me, her back to the sink as well. She smelled like roses, like me. She put her elbows up on her knees and rubbed a hand over her composed Dr. Culpeper face.

"I'll tell them you threw up," my mother said.

I put my head in my hands.

"I've had three glasses of wine. So I can't drive." She took out the keys and held them low enough that I could see them through the crack between my fingers. "But you can."

"What about Dad?"

"Dad can get a ride with Marshall. They're a good couple."

I looked up then. "They'll see me."

She shook her head. "We'll go out the door on this side. We don't have to go past the table. I'll call him." She used a tissue from her purse to dab my chin. "I hate this goddamn restaurant."

"Okay," I said.

"Okay?"

"Okay."

She stood up and I took her hand so she could pull me up. "You shouldn't sit on the floor, though — it's filthy and you could pick up rotavirus or MRSA or something. Why do you have a piece of bread in your shirt?"

I picked the crumbs delicately out of my shirt. Standing next to each other in the mirror, my mother and I looked eerily similar, only my face was a tearful, disheveled ruin and hers was not. The exact opposite of the twelve months leading up to this point.

"Okay," I said. "Let's go before they start singing again."

Chapter Twenty-Five

· GRACE ·

I didn't remember being woken up. I just remembered *being*. I sat up, blinking against the harsh light, cupping my face in my hands and smoothing my skin. I ached — not like from a shift, but like I had been caught under a landslide. Beneath me, the floor was a cold and unforgiving tile. There was no window and a row of blinding light-bulbs above the sink made everything permanent daylight.

It took me a moment to pull myself together enough to look around and then another moment to process what I was seeing. A bathroom. A framed postcard of some mountains next to the sink. A glass-walled shower, no tub. A closed door. Recognition dawned all at once — this was the upstairs bathroom at Beck's house. *Oh.* What that meant hit me all at once: I'd made it back to Mercy Falls. I'd made it back to Sam.

Too stunned to be properly appreciative, I climbed to my feet. Beneath my toes, the tile of the floor was spread with mud and dirt. The color of it — a sick yellow — made me cough, choking on water that wasn't there.

Movement caught my eye, and I froze, my hand over my mouth. But it was just me: In the mirror, a naked version of Grace with a lot of ribs and wide eyes looked out, her mouth covered by fingers. I lowered my hand to touch my lowest rib and, as if on cue, my stomach growled.

"You look a little feral," I whispered to myself, just to watch my mouth move. I still sounded like me. That was good.

On the corner of the sink sat a pile of clothing, folded with the extreme tidiness of someone who generally either folded a lot of clothing or none at all. I recognized it from my backpack, the one I'd brought when I came to Beck's house however many months ago. I pulled on my favorite long-sleeved white T and a blue T-shirt over the top of it; they were like old friends. Then jeans and socks. No bra or shoes — they were both back at the hospital, or wherever things left behind at hospitals by bleeding girls went.

What it came down to was this: I was a girl who turned into a wolf, and I had almost died, and the thing that was going to bother me the most all day was that I was going to have to go around without a bra.

Underneath the clothing was a note. I felt a weird little tickle in my stomach when I saw Sam's familiar handwriting, all run together and barely legible.

GRACE — THIS IS POSSIBLY THE WORST THING I'VE EVER DONE, SHUT MY GIRLFRIEND IN MY BATHROOM. BUT WE DIDN'T KNOW WHAT ELSE TO DO WITH YOU UNTIL YOU SHIFTED. I PUT YOUR CLOTHING IN HERE. DOOR'S NOT LOCKED SO YOU CAN JUST OPEN IT SOON AS YOU HAVE FINGERS. I CAN'T WAIT TO SEE YOU. — S

Happiness. That's what the feeling was. I held the note in my hands and tried to remember the events he'd written about. I tried to remember being shut in here, being retrieved from the woods. It was like trying to remember an actor's name after being shown his vaguely familiar face. My thoughts danced maddeningly out of my reach. Nothing, nothing, and then — I was choking on the memory of darkness and mud. Shelby. I remembered Shelby. I had to swallow, hard, and I looked up at myself in the mirror again. My face was afraid, my hand pressed to my throat.

I didn't like what my face looked like afraid; it looked like some other girl I didn't recognize. I stood there and composed it carefully until the Grace in the mirror was the one I knew, and then I tried the doorknob. As Sam had said, it was unlocked, and I stepped into the hall.

I was surprised to find that it was night. I could hear the hum of appliances downstairs, the whisper of air through heating vents, the sounds an occupied house made when it thought no one was listening. I remembered that Sam's room was to my left, but its open doorway was dark. To my right, another door at the end of the hall stood open, and light spilled out into the hallway. I chose that option, padding past photographs of Beck and others smiling and, weirdly enough, a collection of socks nailed to the wall in an artistic pattern.

I peered into the bright doorway and found Beck's room. After half a second, I realized that I had no true reason to believe it to be Beck's room. It was all rich greens and blues, dark wood and simple patterns. A reading lamp on the bedside table illuminated a stack of biographies and a pair of reading glasses. There was nothing particularly identifying about it. It was just a very comfortable and simple room, in the same way that Beck seemed comfortable and simple.

But it wasn't Beck who lay on the mattress; it was Cole, sprawled crosswise, his feet dangling off the edge, toes pointing at the floor. A little leather book lay on its face beside him. On his other side was a mess of loose papers and photographs.

Cole looked asleep among the mess. I started to back out, but when my foot hit a creaky section of floor, he made a noise into the blue comforter.

"Are you awake?" I asked.

"Da."

He turned his face as I came around to the end of the bed. I felt like I was in a hotel room then, this nice, tidy, unfamiliar room with its sparse color-coordination, glowing desk lamp, and its sense of abandonment.

Cole looked up at me. His face was always a shock: so good look-ing. I had to make a conscious effort to put that aside in order to be able to talk to him like a real person. He couldn't help what his face looked like. I was going to ask him where Sam was, but on second thought, that seemed pretty rude, to just use Cole as a signpost.

"Is this Beck's room?" I asked.

Cole stretched his arm out across the comforter toward me and made a thumbs-up.

"Why are you sleeping here?"

"I wasn't sleeping," Cole said. He rolled onto his back. "Sam never sleeps. I'm trying to learn his secrets."

I rested my butt on the end of the bed, not quite sitting, not quite standing. The idea of Sam not sleeping made me a little sad. "Are his secrets in these papers?"

Cole laughed. His laugh was a short, percussive thing that seemed like it belonged on an album. I thought it was a lonely sort of sound. "No, these are Beck's secrets." He groped out until his fingers reached the leather journal. "Beck's journal." He rested his other hand on some of the loose papers. I saw now that he was lying on even more of them. "Mortgage and wills and trust paperwork and dental records and pre-scriptions for drugs that Beck tried to cure the pack with."

I was surprised, a little, to hear that such things existed, but I shouldn't have been. Those weren't things that Sam generally would have sought out — facts were not the most interesting thing to him — and quite possibly it had been information he'd grown up know-ing and already found not useful. "Do you think Beck would be very pleased that you were going through his stuff?" I softened the question with a smile.

Cole said, "He's not here." But then he seemed to think better of his short answer, because he said, voice earnest, "Beck said he wanted me to take over for him. Then he left. This is the only way I know how to learn anything. It beats the hell out of reinventing the wheel."

"I thought Beck wanted Sam to take over for him?" Then I answered my own question. "Oh — I guess he thought that Sam wasn't changing back. That's why he recruited you."

Well, that was why he recruited *someone*. Why he had chosen Cole in specific was less certain. At some point he must have seen this guy in front of me and thought that he would make a good pack leader. At some point he must've seen something of himself in Cole. I thought I could see it, maybe. Sam had Beck's gestures, but Cole had . . . the strength of Beck's personality? The confidence? There was something like the force of Beck's character in Cole; where Sam was kind, Cole was driven.

Again Cole laughed that same cynical laugh. And again, I heard the bravado in it, but, it was like Isabel, where I had learned that you took away the cynical bit and heard the truth: the weariness and the loneliness. I still missed a lot of the nuances that Sam picked up on, but it wasn't hard to hear when you were listening for it.

"*Recruiting* is such a noble-sounding verb," Cole said, sitting up, pulling his legs toward him to sit cross-legged. "It makes me think about men in uniforms and great causes and signing up to protect the American way. Beck didn't want me to die. That's why he chose me. He thought I was going to kill myself, and he thought he would save me."

I wasn't going to let him get away with that.

"People kill themselves every day," I said. "It's, like, thirty thousand Americans a year or something like that. Do you really think that's why he chose you? I don't. It's just not logical. Out of everyone in the world, obviously he picked you for a very specific reason, especially considering that you're famous and otherwise a risk. I mean, logic. *Logic.*"

Cole smiled at me then, this sudden, broad thing that was pleasing in its *real*ness. "I like you," he said. "You can stay."

"Where's Sam?"

"Downstairs."

"Thanks," I said. "Hey — has Olivia shown up here yet?"

His expression didn't change, signaling his ignorance as much as anything he could say. My heart sank, just a little. "Who?" he asked.

"One of the other wolves," I said. "One of my friends who was bitten last year. My age."

It pained me to think of her out in the woods going through the same thing I was.

Something strange flitted across Cole's face then, too fast for me to interpret it. I just wasn't that good at reading faces. He looked away from me, gathering up some of the papers, stacking them against his foot and then putting them down in such a way that they immediately became disorderly again. "Haven't seen her."

"Okay," I said. "I'd better go find Sam." I moved toward the door, feeling a strange little bubble of nerves in my rib cage. Sam was here, I was here, I was very firmly in my skin. I *would* be with him again. I was suddenly and irrationally afraid that I would see him and things would be different, somehow. That what I felt wouldn't match up with what I saw, or that he would've changed how he felt about me. What if we had to start all over again, from scratch? I was filled at the same time with the knowledge that my fears were completely unfounded and with the realization that they just weren't going to move until I saw Sam again.

"Grace," Cole said as I started to leave.

I stopped in the doorway.

He shrugged. "Never mind."

By the time I got out into the hall, Cole was already laid back on the bed, papers spread under him and over him and around him, surrounded by everything that Beck had left behind. He could have so easily looked lost, surrounded by all those memories and words, but instead, he looked buoyed, buffered by the pain that had come before him.

Chapter Twenty-Six

· ISABEL ·

There was something about driving with my parents that always made me a worse driver. No matter how much time I'd spent with my hands gripped on a steering wheel, put a parental unit in the passenger seat and instantly I started braking too hard and turning too soon and hitting the wipers when I reached for the radio knob. And though I'd never been one to talk to people who couldn't hear me (Sam Roth was turning out to be the notable exception to that), with a parent in the car, suddenly I found myself snarling at other drivers' poor vanity plate choices or grousing about their slowness or commenting on their signal light coming on a full two miles before they planned to turn off.

Which was why, when my headlights illuminated the truck-thing half-pulled off the road, its nose pointing into the ditch, I said, "Oh, stellar parking job there."

My mother, who'd become drowsy and benevolent from the wine and the hour, came to sudden attention. "Isabel, pull in behind them. They might need help."

I just wanted to get home so that I could call Sam or Cole and find out what was going on with Grace. We were two miles from the house; this felt a little unfair on the part of the universe. In the far-off edge of my headlights, the stopped vehicle looked a little disreputable. "Mom, you're the one who said to never stop in case I get raped or picked up by a Democrat."

Mom shook her head and pulled a compact out of her purse. "I never said that. That sounds like your father." She flipped down the visor to look at herself in the small, lighted mirror. "I would've said Libertarian."

I slowed to a crawl. The truck — it was turning out to be a truck with one of those tall caps over the bed, the kind that you probably have to show ID proving you're over fifty to buy — looked like it probably belonged to a drunk who'd stopped to puke.

"What would we do, anyway? We can't . . . change a tire." I struggled to think of what would make someone pull over, other than puking.

"There's a cop," Mom said. Sure enough, I saw that a cop car was parked by the side of the road as well; its lights had been blocked by the hulking truck. She added casually, "They might need medical assistance."

Mom lived in hope of someone needing medical assistance. She was always very eager for someone to get hurt on the playground when I was little. She eyed line cooks at fast-food restaurants, waiting for a kitchen disaster to strike. In California, she used to stop at accidents all the time. As a superhero, her line was: *"DOES ANYONE NEED A DOCTOR? I AM A DOCTOR!"* My father told me once that I needed to go easy on her; she'd had a hard time getting her degree because of family issues, and she just liked the novelty of being able to tell people she was a doctor. Okay, fine, self-actualize yourself, but really, I thought she'd gotten over it.

Sighing, I pulled in behind the truck. I did a better job than him of getting my vehicle off the road, but that wasn't saying much. My mother deftly leaped from the SUV, and I followed her more slowly. There were three stickers on the back of the truck: GO ARMY, HANG UP AND DRIVE, and, inexplicably, I'D RATHER BE IN MINNESOTA.

On the other side of the truck, a cop was talking to a red-haired man who was wearing a white T-shirt and suspenders because he had a belly and no ass. More interestingly, I could see a handgun sitting on the driver's seat through the open door of the truck.

"Dr. Culpeper," said the officer warmly.

My mother adopted her caramel voice — the one that oozed richly about you so slowly you didn't realize you were possibly being suffocated. "Officer Heifort. I just stopped to see if you needed me."

"Well, that's decent of you, for sure," Heifort said. He had his fingers linked in his gun belt. "This your daughter? She's pretty as you, Doc." My mother demurred. Heifort insisted. The red-haired man shifted his weight from foot to foot. They spoke briefly about the mosquitoes this time of year. The red-haired man said that they weren't near as bad as they were going to be. He called them "skeeters."

"What's the gun for?" I asked.

They all looked at me.

I shrugged. "Just wondering."

Heifort said, "Well. Seems Mr. Lundgren here decided to take the wolf hunt into his own hands and do a bit of spotlighting."

The red-haired Mr. Lundgren protested, "Well, now, Officer, you know that's not what went down. I just *happened* upon it and shot from my truck. That's not quite the same."

"I suppose not," Heifort said. "But there is a dead animal here and no one's supposed to be shooting much of anything after sundown. Much less with a .38 revolver. I know you know better, Mr. Lundgren."

"Wait," I said. "You *killed* a wolf?" I shoved my hands in the pockets of my jacket. Even though it wasn't that cold, I shivered.

Heifort gestured over toward the front of the truck, shaking his head.

"My husband told me no one was allowed to hunt them until the aerial hunt," my mother said, her caramel voice a bit harder. "To keep from scaring them into hiding."

"That's the truth," Heifort said.

I moved away from them to the ditch where Heifort had gestured, aware that the red-haired man was watching me dolefully. Now I could see a ridge of fur from an animal lying on its side in the grass.

Dear God and possibly Saint Anthony, I know I ask for a lot of stupid things, but this one is important: Please don't let that be Grace.

Even though I knew that she was supposed to be safe with Sam and Cole, I sucked in a breath and stepped closer. The ticked fur ruffled in the breeze. There was a small bloody hole in its thigh, another in its shoulder, and finally, one just behind the skull. The top of its head was a little gross where the bullet had come out the other side. If I wanted to see if the eyes were familiar, I would have to kneel, but I didn't bother checking.

"This is a coyote," I said accusingly.

"Yes, ma'am," Heifort replied, genial. "Big one, right?"

I let out my breath. Even a city girl like myself could tell the difference between a wolf and a coyote. I was back to assuming Mr. Lundgren had had one too many or just really wanted to try out his new handgun.

"You haven't had too much trouble like this, have you?" Mom was asking Heifort. She was asking it in that way she did when she wanted to know something for my father rather than for herself. "People taking matters into their own hands? You're keeping it under wraps?"

"We're doing the best we can," Heifort said. "Most people are being real good about it. They don't want to spoil things for those helos. But I wouldn't be surprised if we had a mishap or two before the real deal. Boys will be boys." This was with a gesture toward Mr. Lundgren, as if he were deaf. "Like I said, doing the best we can."

My mother looked less than satisfied. Her tone was a bit chilly when she said, "That's what I tell my patients, too." She frowned at me. "Isabel, don't touch that."

As if I was anywhere near it. I climbed back up through the grass to join her.

"You haven't been drinking tonight, have you, Doc?" Heifort asked, as Mom turned to go. He and Mom both wore matching looks. Candy-coated hostility.

My mother flashed him a large smile. "Oh, yes." She paused to let him consider this. "But Isabel's driving. Come on, Isabel."

When we got back into the car, no sooner had the door slammed than my mother said, "*Hicks.* I hate that man. This may have cured me of my philanthropic nature for good."

I didn't believe it for a second. Next time she thought she might be able to help, she'd be jumping out of the car again before it stopped rolling. Whether or not they wanted her.

I guess I was turning out a lot like my mother.

"Dad and I have been talking about moving back to California," Mom said. "When this is all over."

I narrowly avoided wrecking the car. "And you were going to tell me . . . when?"

"When it became more definite. I have a few leads on jobs out there; it's just a question of their hours and how much we can sell the house for."

"Again," I said, a little breathless, "you were going to tell me *when?*"

My mother sounded perplexed. "Well, Isabel, you're about to go off to college, and all but two on your list are there. It will make it easier for you to visit. I thought you hated it here."

"I did. I do. I just — I can't believe you didn't tell me it was an option, before —" I wasn't sure how to end the sentence, so I just stopped.

"Before what?"

I threw one of my hands up in the air. I would have thrown both, but I had to keep one on the wheel. "Nothing. California. Great.

Yahoo." I thought about it — stuffing my giant coats in boxes, having a social life, living someplace where not everyone knew the sordid history of my dead brother. Trading Grace and Sam and Cole for a life of cell phone plans, seventy-three-degree days, and textbooks. Yes, college in California had always been the plan, in the future. Apparently, however, the future was getting here faster than I'd expected.

"I can't believe that man mistook a coyote for a wolf," my mother mused as I pulled into our driveway. I remembered when we'd first moved here. I'd thought the house looked like something out of a horror movie. Now, I saw that I'd left my light on in my third-floor bedroom and it looked like something out of a children's book, a big sprawling Tudor with one yellow window on the top floor. "They look nothing alike."

"Well," I said, "some people see what they want to see."

Chapter Twenty-Seven

· GRACE ·

I found Sam leaning on the front porch railing, a long, dark form barely visible in the night. It was funny how Sam, with just the curve of his shoulders and the way he ducked his chin, could convey so much emotion. Even for someone like me, someone who thought a smile was a smile was a smile, it was easy to see the frustration and sadness in the line of his back, the bend of his left knee, the way one of his slender feet was rolled on its side.

I felt suddenly shy, as uncertain and excited as I had been the first time I met him.

Without turning on the front light, I joined him at the railing, not sure of what to say. I felt like I wanted to jump up and down and grab him around the neck and punch his chest and grin like a crazy person or cry. I wasn't sure what the protocol for this was.

Sam turned to me, and in the dim light from the window, I saw that there was stubble on his chin. While I was gone, he had gotten older. I reached up and scrubbed his stubble with my hand, and he smiled ruefully.

"Does that hurt?" I asked. I rubbed his stubble against the grain. I'd missed touching him.

"Why would it?"

"Because it's going the wrong way?" I suggested. I was overwhelmingly happy to be standing here, my hand on his unshaven cheek. Everything was terrible, but everything was fine, too. I wanted to be smiling, and I thought my eyes probably already were, because he was sort of smiling, too, a puzzled one, like he wasn't certain if that was what he meant to do.

"Also," I said, "hi."

Sam did smile then, and said softly, "Hey, angel." He put his lanky arms around my neck in a fierce hug, and I wrapped mine around his chest to squeeze him as hard as I could. I loved to kiss Sam, but no kiss could ever be as wonderful as this. Just his breath against my hair and my ear smashed up against his T-shirt. It felt like together, we were a sturdier creature, Grace-and-Sam.

Still locking me in his arms, Sam asked, "Did you eat something yet?"

"A bread sandwich. I also found some clogs. Not to eat."

Sam laughed softly. I was so glad to hear it, so hungry to hear him. He said, "We aren't very good at shopping."

Into his shirt — he smelled like fabric softener — I mumbled, "I don't like grocery shopping. It's the same thing over and over every week. I'd like to make enough money, one day, that someone else would do it for me. Do you have to be rich for that? I don't want a fancy house. Just someone else to do the shopping."

Sam considered. He hadn't loosened his hold on me yet. "I think you always have to do your own shopping."

"I'll bet the Queen doesn't shop for herself."

He blew a breath out over the top of my hair. "But she always eats the same thing every day. Eel jellies and haddock sandwiches and scones with Marmite."

"I don't think you even know what Marmite is," I said.

"It's something you put on bread and it's disgusting. That's what Beck told me." Sam pulled his arms free and leaned on the railing instead. He eyed me. "Are you cold?"

It took me a moment to realize the implication: *Will you shift?*

But I felt good, real, firmly me. I shook my head and joined him at the railing. For a moment we just stood there in the darkness and looked out into the night. When I glanced over at Sam, I saw that his hands were knotted together. The fingers of his right hand squeezed his left thumb so tightly that it was white and bloodless.

I leaned my head against his shoulder, just his T-shirt between my cheek and his skin. At my touch, Sam sighed — not an unhappy sigh — and said, "I think those are the northern lights."

I shifted my gaze without lifting my head. "Where?"

"Over there. Above the trees. See? Where it's sort of pink."

I squinted. There were a million stars. "Or it could be the lights from the gas station. You know, that QuikMart outside of town."

"That's a depressing and practical thought," Sam said. "I'd rather it was something magical."

"The aurora borealis isn't any more magical than the QuikMart," I pointed out. I had done a paper on it once, so I was more aware of its science than I might have otherwise been. Though I had to admit that I did find the idea of solar wind and atoms playing together to create a light show for us a little magical anyway.

"That's also a depressing and practical thought."

I lifted my head and shifted to look at him instead. "They're still beautiful."

"Unless it really is the QuikMart," Sam said. He looked at me then, in a pensive way that made me feel a little fidgety. He said, reluctantly, as if suddenly remembering his manners, "Are you tired? I'll go back in with you, if that's what you want."

"I'm not tired," I said. "I want to just be with you for a while. Before everything gets difficult and confusing."

He frowned off into the night. Then, all in a rush, he said, "Let's go see if those really are the northern lights."

"You have an airplane?"

"I have a Volkswagen," he replied valiantly. "We would have to get someplace darker. Farther away from the QuikMart. Into the wilds of Minnesota. You want to?"

And now he had the shy little grin on his face that I loved. It felt like ages since I had seen it.

I asked, "Do you have your keys?"

He patted his pocket.

I gestured upstairs. "What about Cole?"

"He's sleeping, like everyone else at this time of night," Sam said. I didn't tell him that Cole wasn't sleeping. He saw my hesitation and mistook the meaning of it. "You're the practical one. Is it a bad idea? I don't know. Maybe it's a bad idea."

"I want to go," I said. I reached down and took his hand firmly. "We won't be gone long."

Getting into the Volkswagen in the dark driveway, the car rumbling to life, it felt like we were conspiring to something greater than just chasing lights in the sky. We could be going anywhere. Chasing the promise of magic. Sam turned up the heat all the way while I moved my seat back — someone had moved it all the way forward. Reaching over the center console, Sam briefly squeezed my hand before grabbing the gearshift and backing out of the driveway.

"Ready?"

I grinned at him. For the first time since the hospital, since before the hospital, I felt like the old Grace, the one who could do anything she put her mind to. "I was born ready."

We raced down the street. Sam reached over to brush the top of my ear with his finger; the action made him send the car slightly crooked. Looking hurriedly back to the road, he laughed at himself, just a little, as he straightened the wheel.

"Watch out the window," he said. "Since I can't seem to remember how to drive. Tell me where to go. Where it's brightest. I'm trusting you."

I pressed my face against the window and squinted at the hint of lights in the sky. At first, it was hard to tell which direction the lights were coming from, so I just directed Sam down the darkest roads first, farthest away from house lights and town. And now, as the minutes passed, it became easier to find a path north. Every turn took us farther away from Beck's house, farther away from Mercy Falls, farther away from Boundary Wood. And then, suddenly, we were miles away from our real lives, driving down a straight-arrow road under a wide, wide sky punched through with hundreds of millions of stars, and the world was vast around us. On a night like tonight, it wasn't hard to believe that, not so long ago, people could see by starlight alone.

"In 1859," I said, "there was a solar storm that made the northern lights so strong, people could read by them."

Sam didn't doubt my facts. "Why do you know this?"

"Because it's interesting," I said.

His smile was back. The little amused one that meant that he was charmed by my overdeveloped left brain. "Tell me something else interesting."

"The auroras were so strong that telegraph people shut off their batteries and ran their telegraphs by the power of the auroras instead," I said.

"They did not," Sam said, but it was clear that he believed me. "Tell me something else interesting."

I reached over to touch his hand where it rested on the gearshift. When I ran my thumb over the inside of his wrist, I felt goose bumps raise underneath my fingers. My fingertips found his scar, the skin unnaturally smooth, the edges still puckered and lumpy.

"I can't feel anything on my scar," he said. "It's got no sensation in it."

I briefly closed my hand around his wrist, thumb pressed tightly into his skin. I could feel the flutter of his pulse.

"We could keep going," I said.

Sam was silent, and at first I thought he didn't understand what I meant. But then I saw him working his hands on the steering wheel. By the light of the dashboard, I saw that he still had mud underneath the nails of his right hand. Unlike me, he hadn't left his dirty skin behind.

I asked him, "What are you thinking?"

His voice sounded sticky when he replied, like he had to dislodge the words to get them out. "That this time last year, I wouldn't have wanted to." Sam swallowed. "I was thinking that now, if we could, I would. Can you imagine it?"

I could. I could imagine a life someplace far away, starting over from scratch, just us. But as soon as I pictured it — Sam's socks draped over a window radiator, my books spread across a tiny kitchen table, dirty coffee mugs upside down in the sink — I thought of what I would leave behind: Rachel and Isabel and Olivia and, finally, my parents. I had left them so conclusively, through the dubious miracle of my shift, that my old anger at them felt dull and remote. They had no power over my future now. Nothing did, except for the weather.

Then, suddenly, out Sam's window, I saw the aurora, clear and bright, obviously not a reflection of any store's lights. "Sam, Sam! Look! Turn, turn, turn, go that way!"

Twisting slowly in the sky above to our left was a sinuous, shaggy ribbon of pink. It pulsed and brightened like a living thing. Sam pulled a left at a narrow, barely paved road that led through an unending black field. The car dipped through potholes and weaved, loose gravel rattling behind us. My teeth snapped as we went over a bump. Sam made an *ahhhhhhhh* sound so that his voice modulated crazily with the jolting vibration of the Volkswagen.

"Stop here!" I ordered.

The field rolled out for acres in every direction. Sam pulled up the parking brake and together we peered out the windshield.

Hanging in the sky directly above us was the aurora borealis. Like a brilliant pink road, it snaked through the air and disappeared behind the trees, a darker purple aura clinging to one side of it. The lights shimmered and stretched, growing and receding, striving and shrinking. One moment the light was a singular thing, a path to heaven, the next moment it was a collection of many, an army made of light, marching ever northward.

"Do you want to get out?" Sam asked. My hand was already on the door handle. Outside, the air was cold enough to have teeth to it, but I was fine, for now. I joined Sam at the front of the car, where he leaned on the hood. When I leaned back on my hands next to him, the hood was hot from the engine, a buffer against the cool night.

Together we gazed up. The flat black field around us made the sky as big as an ocean. With the wolf inside me and Sam beside me, both of us strange creatures, I felt we were somehow an intrinsic part of this world, this night, this boundless mystery. My heart thumped faster, for a reason I couldn't pinpoint. I was suddenly very aware that Sam was just inches away from me, watching with me, his breaths visible in front of his face.

"This close, it is so hard to believe," I said, and my voice caught for some reason on *believe*, "that it isn't magic."

Sam kissed me.

His kiss landed sort of on the side of my mouth because my face was still turned up, but it was a real kiss, not a careful one. I turned toward him so that we could kiss again, properly. My lips were hot with the unfamiliar feeling of his stubble and when he touched my arm, I was hyperaware of the rough calluses on his fingertips against my skin. Everything inside me felt raw-edged and hungry. I couldn't understand how something we'd done so many times could feel so strange and new and terrifying.

When we kissed, it didn't matter that I had been a wolf hours ago, or that I would be a wolf again. It didn't matter that a thousand snares were laid for us as soon as we left this moment. All that mattered was this: our noses touching, the softness of his mouth, the ache inside me.

Sam pulled away to press his face into my neck. He remained there, hugging me fiercely. His arms were tight enough around me to constrict my breathing, and my hip bone was pressed against the hood hard enough to hurt, but I would never, ever tell him to let me go.

Sam said something, but his voice was inaudible against my skin.

"What?" I asked.

He released me and looked to where my hand rested on the hood. He pressed the ball of his thumb on the top of my index finger and studied the shape of our fingers together as if it was something fascinating. "I missed looking at your face," he said softly. But he didn't look at my face when he said it.

Above us, the lights shimmered and changed. They had no beginning or end, but it looked like they were leaving us anyway. I thought again about the mud beneath his fingernails, the abrasion on his temple. What else had happened while I'd been in the woods?

"I missed *having* my face," I said. In my head, it had seemed like it would be funny, but when I said it, neither of us laughed. Sam took his hand back and lifted his eyes to the aurora borealis. Sam was still looking off into the sky like he was thinking of nothing, and suddenly I realized, I was being cruel, not saying anything lovey to him after he had said it to me, not saying anything that he needed after being gone for so long. But the moment to say something right back was gone, and I didn't know how to say something that wouldn't sound corny. I thought about saying *I love you* to him, but even thinking about saying it out loud made me feel strange. I didn't know why it should; I did love him, so much it hurt.

But I didn't know how to say that. So I held out my hand, and Sam took it.

· SAM ·

Outside of the car, the lights were even more dazzling, as if the cold air around us moved and shimmered with violet and pink. I stretched my free hand above me as if I could brush the aurora. It was cold, but a *good* cold, the sort that made you feel alive. Over our heads, the sky was so clear that we could see every star that could see us. Now that I had kissed Grace, I couldn't stop thinking about touching her. My mind was full of the places I had yet to touch: the soft skin inside the bend of her elbow, the curve right above her hip bone, the line of her collarbone. I wanted to kiss her again, so badly, I wanted *more* of her, but instead, we held hands, our heads tipped back, and together we slowly turned, looking up into the infinity. It was like falling, or like flying.

I was torn between wanting to rush out of this moment, toward that *more*, and wanting to stay in it, living in a state of constant anticipation and constant safety. As soon as we stepped back into the house, the hunt of the wolves would become a real thing again, and I wasn't ready.

Grace, out of the blue, asked, "Sam, are you going to marry me?"

I jerked, looking over at her, but she was still gazing up into the stars as if she'd merely asked about the weather. Her eyes, however, had a sort of hard, squinty look about them that belied the nonchalant sound of her voice.

I didn't know what she expected me to say. I felt like laughing out loud. Because I realized all in a rush that of course she was right — yes, the woods would claim her for the cold months, but she wasn't dying; I hadn't lost her for good. And I had her right here, now. In comparison, everything else seemed small, manageable, secondary.

Suddenly the world seemed like a promising, friendly place. Suddenly I saw the future, and it was a place I wanted to be.

I realized that Grace was still waiting for an answer. I pulled her closer, until we were nose to nose under the northern lights. "Are you asking?" I said.

"Just clarifying," Grace replied. But she was smiling, a tiny, genuine smile, because she had already read my thoughts. By her temple, little flyaway blond hairs drifted in the breeze; they looked like they must tickle, but she didn't twitch. "I mean, instead of living in sin."

And then I did laugh, even though the future was a dangerous place, because I loved her, and she loved me, and the world was beautiful and awash with pink light around us.

She kissed me, very lightly. "Say okay." She was starting to shiver.

"Okay," I said. "It's a deal."

It felt like a physical thing, held in my hands.

"Do you really mean it?" she asked. "Don't say it if you don't really mean it."

My voice didn't sound as earnest as I felt. "I really mean it."

"Okay," Grace said, and just like that, she seemed content and solid, certain of my affections. She gave a little sigh and rearranged our hands so that our fingers were intertwined. "Now you can take me home."

CHAPTER TWENTY-EIGHT

· SAM ·

Back at home, Grace fell into my bed and asleep at about the same moment, and I envied her easy friendship with slumber. She lay motionless in the eerie, deathlike sleep of the exhausted. I couldn't join her; everything inside me was awake. My mind was on continuous playback, giving me the events of the day again and again, until they seemed like one long creation, impossible to pull apart into separate minutes.

So I left her upstairs and made my soft way downstairs. In the kitchen, I dug through my pocket to drop my car keys on the counter. It seemed wrong that the kitchen looked the same. Everything should've looked different after tonight. A television humming upstairs was the only indication that Cole was in residence; I was glad for the solitude. I was filled with so much happiness and sadness that I couldn't think of speaking. I could still feel the shape of Grace's face pressed into my neck and see her face when she gazed up at the stars, waiting for my answer. I wasn't ready, yet, to dilute that by speaking out loud.

Instead, I sloughed off my jacket and went to the living room — Cole had left this television on, too, though it was muted, so I switched it off and found my guitar where I'd left it leaning against the armchair. The body of it was a bit grubby from being outside; there was a new nick in the finish where either Cole or I had been too careless with it.

Sorry, I thought, because I still didn't want to speak out loud. I picked the strings softly; the change in temperature from outside to inside had put it a little bit out of tune, but not as much as I would have thought. It was still playable, though I took the moment to make it perfect. I put the strap over my head, familiar and easy as a favorite shirt, and I remembered Grace's smile.

Then I began to play. Variations on a G major chord, the most wonderful chord known to mankind, infinitely happy. I could live inside a G major chord, with Grace, if she was willing. Everything uncomplicated and good about me could be summed up by that chord. It was the second chord Paul had ever taught me, sitting here on that ancient plaid couch. First chord: E minor. "Because," Beck had said, passing through the room, quoting one of his favorite movies, a memory that stung a little now, "into every life, a little rain must fall."

"Because," corrected Paul, "into every song, we must have a minor bridge."

Dire E minor was straightforward for a newbie like myself. It was so much harder to play the halcyon G major. But Paul made the cheerfulness seem effortless.

It was that Paul I remembered right now, not the Paul who had pinned me to the snow as a child. Just like it was the Grace that slept upstairs that I remembered now, not the wolf with her eyes that we had found in the sinkhole.

I had spent so much of life being afraid or living in the memory of being afraid.

No more.

I stepped my fingers all around the chord as I walked down the hallway, toward the bathroom. The light was already on, so I didn't have to stop playing as I stood there, looking at the bathtub at the other side of the room.

Darkness pressed on either side of my vision, memories pushing at me. I kept playing my guitar, plucking a song about the present to shove back the past. I stood there, eyes fixed on the empty tub.

Water tipped and steadied

washed with blood

The weight of the guitar's shoulder strap grounded me. The pressure of the strings against my fingers held me in the here and now. Upstairs, Grace slept.

I took a step into the bathroom; my reflection in the mirror startled me as it moved. I held still to study myself. Was that my face, now?

water snaking up the fabric of my shirt

this is not sam

three two

I walked my fingers up to a C major. Filled my head with everything I could do with that chord: *She came to me in summer, my lovely summer girl*. I held on to the words Grace had said earlier. *Are you going to marry me?*

Grace had done so much of the work, saving me. Now it was time to save myself.

My fingers never stilled as I walked toward the tub, my guitar singing if I wouldn't, and I stood by the bathtub, looking in. For a moment, it was just an ordinary, mundane object, just a dry basin waiting to be filled.

Then my ears began to ring.

I saw my mother's face.

I couldn't do this.

My fingers found G major and they played one thousand variations of it without me, songs they could play while my thoughts ran to other things. Songs that were a piece of something bigger than me, some unending reservoir of happiness that anyone could tap.

I hesitated, my chords echoing off the tile back at me. The walls were close around me; the doorway seemed far behind me.

I stepped into the bathtub, my shoes squeaking softly on the dry surface. My heart hammered against my T-shirt. Bees hummed inside my head. One thousand minutes other than this one lived in here: minutes with razors, minutes where everything that was me gurgled down the drain, minutes with hands pinning me in the water. But there was also Grace holding my head above the surface, Grace's voice calling me back to myself, Grace taking me by the hand.

And more important than all of those was *this* minute. The minute when I, Sam Roth, had come here under my own power, my music held in my hands, strong, finally, strong.

Rilke said:

> *For among these winters there is one so endlessly winter*
> *that only by wintering through it will your heart survive.*

That was how Cole found me, an hour later. Sitting cross-legged in the empty bathtub, my guitar in my lap, my fingers teasing out a G major chord, singing a song I'd never sung before.

Chapter Twenty-Nine

· SAM ·

wake me up
wake me up, you said

but I was sleeping, too
I was dreaming

but now I'm waking up
still waking up

I can see the sun

CHAPTER THIRTY

· GRACE ·

I was wide awake.

Everything in the room was still and black, and I was sure I had just been dreaming of exactly this moment, only with someone standing by the bed.

"Sam?" I whispered, thinking that it had been only minutes I'd been sleeping, that he'd woken me up when he came to bed.

From behind me, I heard Sam make a low-pitched sleep sound. I could feel, now, that it was not blankets pushed up against me but instead a Sam-blanket. Under normal circumstances, this small gift of his presence would have thrilled me and then lured me back to sleep, but I was so certain that someone had been standing by the bed that it was disconcerting to realize that he was firmly entrenched next to me instead. The hairs on the back of my neck prickled, wary. As my eyes slowly adjusted to the darkness, Sam's paper cranes became visible, swaying and tipping, moved by an invisible wind.

I heard a sound.

It wasn't quite a crash. It was an interrupted crash, like something falling and being caught. I held my breath, listening — it was coming from somewhere downstairs — and was rewarded with another muffled thump. The living room? Something knocking something over in the backyard?

"Sam, wake up," I said urgently. Looking over, I had a disorienting jolt when I saw the reflections of Sam's eyes in the darkness beside me; he was already awake and was silent. Listening, like me.

"Did you hear that?" I whispered.

He nodded. I didn't so much see it as hear his head rubbing on the pillowcase behind him.

"Garage?" I suggested. He nodded again.

Another muffled scrape seemed to confirm my assessment. Sam and I tumbled out of bed in slow motion; both of us were still clothed in what we'd worn to chase the aurora borealis. Sam led the way down the stairs and then the hall, so it was me who first saw Cole emerging from the hallway to the downstairs bedrooms. His hair was crazily spiked. I had never thought, before, that he had spent any time on it at all — surely careless rock stars didn't have to work at looking like careless rock stars — but now it was clear that spiky was its natural state and he took care to keep it from being that way. He wore only sweatpants. He looked more annoyed than alarmed.

In a low voice several degrees closer to sleep than wakefulness, Cole said, "What the hell?"

The three of us stood there, a bare-footed posse, and listened for another few minutes. There was nothing. Sam rubbed a hand through his hair, leaving it comically fanned. Cole held up a finger to his lips and pointed through the kitchen toward the garage door entrance. Sure enough, if I held my breath, I could still hear scuffling coming from that direction.

Cole armed himself with the broom from beside the fridge. I opted for a knife from the wooden block on the counter. Sam gave us both bemused looks and went empty-handed.

We stood outside the door, waiting for another noise. A moment later, another crash sounded out, this one louder than before, *ding*ing off metal. Cole looked at me and raised his eyebrows, and at the same time, he opened the door and I reached in to hit the garage light.

And there was:

nothing.

We looked at each other, mystified.

Into the garage, I said, "Is there anybody in here?"

Cole, sounding betrayed, said to Sam, "I can't believe there was another car here all along and you didn't tell me."

The garage was, like most garages, filled to capacity with weird and smelly things that you didn't want to keep in the house. Most of the space was filled by a crappy red BMW station wagon, dusty with the lack of use, but there were also the requisite lawn mower, a workbench covered with small metal soldiers, and a Wyoming license plate above the door that said BECK 89.

My eyes were drawn back to the station wagon.

I said, "Shh. Look!"

There was a weed whacker leaning askew against the hood of the car. I stepped into the garage ahead of the boys to lean it back up, and then noticed the slightly ajar hood. I pressed an experimental hand on it. "Was this like this before?"

"Yes. For the last decade," Sam said, joining me. The BMW was not a thing of beauty, and the garage still smelled like whatever fluid it had been leaking last. He pointed to a crate of tools knocked over by the rear fender of the BMW. "That wasn't like that, though."

"Also," Cole said, "listen."

I heard what Cole had heard: a sort of scuffling underneath the car.

I started down but Sam caught my arm and knelt down himself to look.

"For crying out loud," he said. "It's a raccoon."

"Poor thing," I said.

"It could be a rabid baby-killer," Cole told me primly.

"Shut up," Sam said pleasantly, still peering under the vehicle. "I'm wondering how to get it out."

Cole stepped past me, holding the broom like a staff. "I'm more interested in how it got in."

He walked around the back of the car to the side door of the garage, which was slightly open. He tapped on the open door. "Sherlock found a clue."

· SAM ·

I said, "Sherlock should figure out how to get this guy out."

"Or girl," Cole said, and Grace regarded him approvingly. Holding the knife from the kitchen, she looked stark and sexy and like someone I didn't associate with her body. Her repartee with Cole maybe should've made me jealous, but instead it made me glad — evidence, more than anything else, that I was starting to think of Cole as a friend. Everyone harbored the secret fantasy that everyone who was friends with them would also be friends with each other.

I padded to the front of the garage, grit pressing uncomfortably into the bottom of my bare feet, and tugged the garage door open. It rolled up into the ceiling with a terrific crash and the dark driveway with my Volkswagen spread out before me. It was an eerie and lonesome landscape. The cool night air, scented with new leaves and buds, bit at my arms and toes, and some potent combination of the cool breeze and the wide, wide night quickened my blood and called to me. I was momentarily lost with the force of my wanting.

With some effort, I turned back to Cole and Grace. Cole was already poking experimentally around the bottom of the car with the broomstick, but Grace was looking out into the night with an expression that I felt mirrored mine. Something like contemplation and yearning. She caught me looking at her and her face didn't change. I felt like — I felt like she *knew* how I felt. For the first time in a very long time, I remembered waiting in the woods for her to shift, waiting for us both to be wolves at the same time.

"Come on, you bastard," Cole said to the animal under the car. "I was having an excellent dream."

"Should I be on the other side with something else?" Grace asked, her eyes on me just a second longer before she turned back.

"A knife is a bit excessive," I suggested, stepping away from the garage door. "There's a push broom over there."

. She looked at the knife before setting it down on a birdbath — another failed grounds beautification attempt by Beck.

"I hate raccoons," observed Cole. "This is why your idea of moving the wolves is somewhat problematic, Grace."

Grace, armed with a push broom, inserted the bristly end under the car with grim efficiency. "I hardly find this to be an apt comparison."

I could see the masked nose of the raccoon poking out from under the BMW. In a sudden rush, it bolted away from Cole's broomstick and ran directly by the open garage door to hide behind a watering can on the other side of the car.

"Why, you dumb bastard," Cole said wonderingly.

Grace walked over and pushed on the watering can, gently. There was a moment's hesitation, and the raccoon bolted directly back under the car. Again, completely bypassing the open door. Grace, an ardent disciple of logic, threw up her free hand. "The door is *right* there. It's the entire wall."

Cole, looking a bit more enthusiastic than the job called for, rummaged around beneath the car with the broomstick again. Duly terrified by this onslaught, the raccoon bolted back to the watering can. The smell of its fear was strong as the rank scent of its coat, and vaguely contagious.

"This," Cole said, the broomstick braced on the ground beside him, looking like Moses in sweatpants, "is the reason raccoons don't take over the planet."

"This," I said, "is the reason we keep getting shot at."

Grace looked down at the raccoon where it was huddled in the corner. Her expression was pitying. "No complicated logic."

"No spatial sense," I said. "Wolves have plenty of complicated logic. Just no human logic. No spatial sense. No sense of time. No sense of boundaries. Boundary Wood is too small for us."

"So we move the wolves someplace better," Grace said. "Someplace with a better human-to-acre ratio. Someplace with fewer Tom Culpepers."

"There are always Tom Culpepers," I said at the same time that Cole said it, and Grace smiled ruefully at both of us.

"It would have to be pretty remote," I said. "And it couldn't be private property, unless it was ours, and I don't think we're that rich. And it couldn't have existing wolves already, or there's a good chance they'd kill a lot of us in the beginning. And there would have to be prey there, or we'd just die of starvation anyway. Plus, I'm not sure how you'd catch twenty-odd wolves. Cole's been trying and he's not had much luck even getting one."

Grace had her stubborn face on, which meant she was losing her sense of humor as well. "Better idea?"

I shrugged.

Cole scratched his bare chest with the end of the broomstick and said, "Well, you know, they've been moved before."

He had both Grace's and my undivided attention.

Cole said, tone lazy, infinitely used to slowly doling out things other people wanted to hear, "Beck's journal starts when he's a wolf. But the journal doesn't start in Minnesota."

"Okay," Grace said, "I'll bite. Where?"

Cole pointed the broomstick at the license plate above the door, BECK 89. "Then the real wolf population started to come back and, like Ringo here said, started killing the part-time wolves, and he decided their only option was to move."

I felt an odd sense of betrayal. It wasn't that Beck had ever lied to me about where he'd come from — I was sure I'd never asked him directly if he'd always been here in Minnesota. And it wasn't like that license plate wasn't in plain sight. It was just — Wyoming. Cole, benevolent interloper that he was, knew things about Beck that I didn't. Part of me said it was because Cole had the balls to read Beck's journal. But another part of me said that I shouldn't have had to.

"So does it say how he did it?" I asked.

Cole gave me an odd look. "A little."

"A little how?"

"Only said that Hannah helped them a lot."

"I've never heard of Hannah," I said. I was aware that I sounded wary.

"You wouldn't have," Cole said. Again he had that funny expression. "Beck said that she hadn't been a wolf very long, but she couldn't seem to stay human as long as the others. She stopped shifting that year after they moved. He said she seemed more capable of holding human thoughts when she was a wolf than the others. Not much. But remembered faces and returned to places she'd been as a human, but as a wolf."

Now I knew why he was looking at me. Grace was looking at me, too. I looked away. "Let's get this raccoon out of here."

We stood there in silence for a few moments, a little trippy with sleep loss, until I realized that I heard movement from closer to me. I hesitated for a moment, my head cocked, listening to identify the source.

"Oh, hey," I noted. Crouched behind a plastic garbage can, right beside me, was a second, larger raccoon, looking up at me with leery eyes. Far better at hiding than the first one, obviously, as I had been completely unaware of its presence. Grace craned her neck, trying to see over the car what I was looking at.

I didn't have anything in my hands but my hands, so that's what I used. I reached down and took the handle of the garbage can. And very slowly, I pushed it toward the wall, forcing the raccoon out the other side.

Instantly, the raccoon tore along the wall and straight out the door into the night. No pause. Just straight out the garage door.

"Two of them?" Grace asked. "Th —" She stopped as the first raccoon, inspired by the success of the escaping raccoon, bolted out after it, no detours to watering cans along the way.

"Pf," she said. "As long as there's not a third. *Now* it figures out the concept of the door."

I headed to the garage door to close it, but as I did, I caught a glimpse of Cole. He was staring out after the raccoons, his eyebrows pulled together in a face that, for once, wasn't arranged to best affect the viewer.

Grace started to speak and then followed my gaze to Cole. She fell quiet.

For a full minute, we were silent. In the distance, the wolves had begun to howl, and the hair on my neck was crawling.

"There's our answer," Cole said. "That's what Hannah did. That's how we get the wolves out of the woods." He turned to look at me. "One of us has to lead them out."

CHAPTER THIRTY-ONE

· GRACE ·

It felt like camp when I woke up in the morning.

When I was thirteen, my grandmother had paid for me to go to summer camp for two weeks. Camp Blue Sky for Girls. I'd loved it — two weeks with every moment planned out, every day accounted for, ready-made purpose printed out on colored 8.5" x 11" fliers poked in our cubby holes each morning. It was the opposite of life with my parents, who laughed at the idea of schedules. It was fantastic and the first time I realized that there might be other right ways to happiness than the one prescribed by my parents. But the thing about camp was that it *wasn't* home. My toothbrush was grubby from being poked into the small pocket of my backpack by a mother who forgot to buy plastic baggies before I left. The bunk bed crushed my shoulder uncomfortably when I tried to sleep. Dinner was good but salty and just a little too far away from lunch, and unlike at home, I couldn't just go to the kitchen and get some pretzels. It was fun and different and just that tiny bit wrong that made it disconcerting.

So here I was at Beck's house, in Sam's bedroom. It wasn't properly home — *home* still conjured up the memory of pillows that smelled like my shampoo, and my beat-up old copies of John Buchan novels that I'd gotten from a library sale so they were doubly dear, and the running-water-shaving-sound of my father getting ready for work, and the radio speaking to itself in low, earnest tones in the study, and the endlessly comfortable logic of my own routine. Did that home even exist for me anymore?

Sitting up in Sam's bed, I was sleep-stupid and surprised to find him lying beside me, rolled up to the wall with his fingers splayed against it. I couldn't remember a morning I'd ever woken up before him, and feeling a bit neurotic, I watched him until I saw his chest rise and fall under his ratty T-shirt.

I climbed out of the bed, expecting him to wake up at any moment, half hoping he would, half hoping he wouldn't, but he remained in his crooked little sleeping pose, looking like he'd been tossed onto the bed.

I had that toxic combination of not enough sleep and too much wakefulness pumping through me, so it took me longer than I would've thought to make it out to the hallway and then another moment to remember where the bathroom was, and when I got there, I had no hairbrush and no toothbrush and the only thing I could find to wear was one of Sam's T-shirts with a logo on it from a band I didn't recognize. So I used his toothbrush, telling myself with every stroke across my teeth that this was no grosser than kissing him, and almost believing it. I found his hairbrush next to a disreputable-looking razor and used one but not the other.

I looked in the mirror. It felt like I was living life on the wrong side of it. Time passing didn't mean anything here. I said, "I want to tell Rachel I'm alive."

It didn't sound unreasonable, until I started thinking about how it could go wrong.

I checked back in the bedroom — Sam was still sleeping — and headed downstairs. Part of me wanted him to be awake, but the other part of me liked this quiet feeling of being both alone and not lonely. It reminded me of all the times I'd sat reading or doing homework with Sam in the same room. Together but silent, two moons in companionable orbit.

Downstairs, I found Cole sprawled on the couch, sleeping with one arm stretched above his head. Remembering that there was a coffeepot in the basement, I tiptoed down the hall and crept down the stairs.

The basement was a cozy but somewhat disorienting place — draftless and windowless, all the light coming from lamps, making it impossible to tell the time. It was strange to be back in the basement, and I felt a weird, misplaced sense of sadness. The last time I'd been down here had been after the car crash, talking with Beck after Sam had shifted into a wolf. I'd thought he was gone forever. Now it was Beck who was lost.

I started the coffeepot and sat in the chair I'd sat in when I spoke to Beck. Behind his empty chair stretched the bookshelves with the hundreds of books he'd never read again. Every wall was covered with them; the coffeepot was nestled on the few inches of shelf not occupied by books. I wondered how many there were. Were there ten in a foot of shelf space? Maybe one thousand books. Maybe more than that. Even from here, I could see that they were tidily organized, nonfiction by subject, battered novels by author.

I wanted a library like this by the time I was Beck's age. Not *this* library. A cave of words that I'd made myself. I didn't know if that would be possible now.

Sighing, I stood and browsed the shelves until I found that Beck had a few education books, and then I sat on the floor with them, carefully setting my coffee mug beside me. I wasn't sure how long I'd been reading when I heard the stairs creak softly. Glancing up, I saw a set of bare feet descending: Cole, looking musty and sleep-tussled, a line in the side of his face where the couch pillow had pressed into it.

"Hi, Brisbane," he said.

"Hi," I said. "St. Clair."

Cole unplugged the coffeepot and brought the entire thing over to the floor where I was. He topped my coffee up and poured a cup for himself, silent and solemn during the entire process. Then he turned his head to read the titles of the books I'd pulled out.

"Distance learning, eh? Heady stuff first thing in the morning."

I ducked my head. "This is all Beck had."

Cole read further. "Acing the CLEP test. Legitimate online degrees. How to be an educated werewolf without leaving the comfort of your own basement. Bothers you, doesn't it? School, I mean."

I glanced up at him. I hadn't thought I sounded upset. I hadn't thought I *was* that upset. "No. Okay, yeah. It does. I wanted to go to college. I wanted to finish high school. I *like* studying." I realized after I'd said it that Cole had chosen NARKOTIKA over college. I wasn't sure how to explain the thrill I used to get when I considered college. I wasn't sure how to describe the anticipation when I looked at course catalogs — all those possibilities — or just the sheer pleasure of opening up a new notebook and a new textbook next to it. The appeal of being someplace with a bunch of other people who also liked studying. Of having a tiny apartment that I could rule like a queen, my way, all the time. Feeling a little silly, I added, "I guess that sounds corny, doesn't it."

But Cole looked thoughtfully into his coffee cup and said, "Mmm, studying. I'm a fan, myself." He pulled one of the books to him and opened it to a random page. The chapter heading read *Studying the World From Your Armchair* and there was a graphic of a stick figure doing just that. "Do you remember everything that happened in the hospital?"

He was asking in that *ask me more* way, so I did. He detailed the events of the night, from when I'd started throwing up blood, to Sam and him taking me to the hospital, to Cole puzzling out science to save me. And then he told me about my father punching Sam.

I thought I must've misunderstood him. "He didn't really hit him, though, right? I mean, you just mean that he . . ."

"No, he whaled him," Cole remarked.

I took a sip of my coffee. I wasn't sure what was weirder, to consider my dad punching Sam, or to realize how much I had missed while lying in a hospital bed or shifting. Suddenly the time I spent as a wolf felt even more like lost time, hours I'd never get back. Like my effective lifespan had been abruptly halved.

I stopped thinking about that, and started thinking about my father hitting Sam instead.

"I think," I said, "that makes me angry. Sam didn't hit him back, did he?"

Cole laughed and poured himself some more coffee.

"And so I was never really cured," I said.

"No. You just didn't shift, which isn't the same thing. The St. Clairs — I hope you don't mind, I'm naming the werewolf toxins after myself, for purposes of the Nobel Peace Prize or Pulitzer or whatever — were all built up inside you."

"So Sam's not cured, either," I said. I put my coffee cup down and shoved the books away from me. For it all to have been a waste — everything we'd done — it was just too much. The idea of a big library and a red coffeepot of my own seemed completely unreachable.

"Well," Cole replied, "I don't know about that. After all, he made himse — Oh, look, here's miracle boy now. Good morning, Ringo."

Sam had descended nearly silently and now he stood at the base of the stairs. His feet were bright red from a shower. Seeing him made me feel slightly less pessimistic, though his presence wouldn't solve anything that wasn't already solved.

"We were just talking about the cure," Cole said.

Sam padded across the floor to me. "The band?" He sat down cross-legged next to me. I offered him coffee and, reliably, he shook his head.

"No, yours. And the one I've been working on. I've been spending a lot of time thinking about how you make yourself shift."

Sam made a face. "I don't make myself shift."

"Not often, Ringo," Cole admitted, "but you do."

I felt a little prickle of hope. If anybody could figure out how the Boundary Wood wolves worked, I thought it would be Cole. He'd saved me, hadn't he?

"Like when you saved me from the wolves," I said. "And what about in the clinic when we injected you?" That night seemed so long ago, in Isabel's mom's clinic, willing the wolf that was Sam to become human. Again, the memory of sadness pressed on me. "Have you figured anything out about it?"

Sam looked petulant as Cole started to talk about adrenaline and Cole St. Clairs in the system and how he was trying to use Sam's unusual shifts as the basis of a cure.

"But if it was adrenaline, wouldn't someone saying 'boo' make you shift?" I asked.

Cole shrugged. "I tried using an EpiPen — that's pure adrenaline — and it worked, just barely." Sam frowned at me, and I wondered if he was thinking what I was thinking — that "barely" working sounded dangerous.

Cole said, "It's just not making my brain react the right way; it's not triggering the shift the same way that cold or the St. Clair buildup does. It's hard to replicate when you have no idea what it's actually doing. It's like drawing a picture of an elephant from the sound it makes in the next cage over."

"Well, I'm impressed you even figured out it was an elephant,"

Sam said. "Apparently, Beck and the rest didn't even have the species right." He stood up and held his hand out for me. "Let's go make breakfast."

But Cole wasn't done. "Oh, Beck just didn't want to see it," he said dismissively. "He didn't really want to lose that time as a wolf. You know what, if my father were involved in all this, he'd whip out some CAT scans, some MRIs, about fourteen hundred electrodes, throw in a couple vials of poisonous meds and a car battery or two, and three or four dead werewolves later, he'd have his cure. Hot damn, he's good at what he does."

Sam lowered his hand. "I wish you wouldn't talk about Beck like that."

"Like what?"

"Like he's —" Sam stopped. He frowned at me, as if the way to end the sentence was hidden in my expression. I knew what he had been about to say. *Like you.* Cole's mouth wore the slightest of hard smiles.

"How about this?" Cole said. He gestured at the chair Beck had sat in before, making me think that he, too, had had a conversation with Beck in this basement. That was an odd thing to consider, for some reason: Cole having a history with Beck that we were unaware of. "How about you tell me who Beck was for you, and I'll tell you who he was for me? And then, Grace, you can tell us whose version sounds like the real one."

"I don't think —" I started.

"I knew him for twelve years," Sam interrupted. "You knew him for twelve seconds. My version wins."

"Does it?" Cole asked. "Did he tell you about what he was like as a lawyer? Did he tell you about living in Wyoming? Did he tell you about his wife? Did he tell you about where he found Ulrik? Did he tell you what he was doing to himself when Paul got to him?"

Sam said, "He told me how he became a wolf."

"Me, too," I said, feeling like I should back Sam up. "He told me he was bitten in Canada and met up with Paul in Minnesota."

"Not that he was in Canada with a death wish, and that Paul bit him there to keep Beck from killing himself?" Cole asked.

"He told you that because that was what you needed to hear," Sam said.

"And he told you the story about hiking and about Paul being already here in Minnesota because it was what *you* needed to hear," Cole said. "Tell me how Wyoming fits into this, because he didn't tell either of us about that. He didn't come from Canada to Mercy Falls when he discovered there were already wolves here, any more than he was bitten while he was out hiking. He simplified the story so he wouldn't look bad to you. He simplified it for me because he didn't think it was relevant for convincing me. Don't tell me you haven't doubted him, Sam, because it's not possible. The man arranged for you to be infected and then adopted you. You had to have thought about it."

My heart hurt for Sam, but he didn't look down or away. His face was completely blank. "I've thought about it."

"And what is it that you're thinking?" Cole asked.

Sam said, "I don't know."

"You must be thinking something."

"I don't know."

Cole stood up and took the step to stand right next to Sam, and the sheer force of the way he did was intimidating, somehow. "Don't you want to ask him about it?"

Sam, to his credit, didn't look intimidated. "That's not really an option."

Cole said, "What if it was? What if you could have him for fifteen minutes? I can find him. I can find him and I have something that should force him to shift. Not for long. But long enough to talk. I have to say I have some questions for him, too."

Sam frowned. "Do what you want with your own body, but I'm not going to mess with someone who can't give me his consent."

Cole's expression was deeply aggrieved. "It's adrenaline, not prom sex."

Sam's voice was stiff. "I am not going to risk killing Beck just to ask him why he didn't tell me he lived in Wyoming."

It was the obvious answer, the one that Cole had to know that Sam would give. But Cole had that small, hard smile on his face again, barely there. "If we caught Beck and I made him human," he said, "I might be able to start him back over, like Grace. Would you risk his life for that?"

Sam didn't answer.

"Tell me yes," Cole said. "Tell me to find him, and I will."

And this, I thought, was why Sam and Cole could not get along. Because when it came down to it, Cole made bad decisions for good reasons, and Sam couldn't justify that. Now, Cole dangled this tempting thing in front of Sam, this thing he wanted more than anything, along with the thing that he wanted the least. I wasn't sure which answer I wanted him to give.

I saw Sam swallow. Turning to me, he said softly, "What do I say?"

I didn't know what to tell him that he didn't already know. I crossed my arms. I could think of a thousand reasons for and against, but all of them started and ended with the wanting I saw on Sam's face now. "You have to be able to live with yourself," I told him.

Cole said, "He'll die out there anyway, Sam."

Sam turned away from both of us, his hands linked behind his head. He stared at the rows and rows of Beck's books.

Not looking at either of us, he said, "Fine. Yes. Find him."

I met Cole's eyes and I held them.

Upstairs, the teakettle began to scream, and Sam wordlessly bounded up the stairs to silence it — a glad excuse, I thought, to leave the room. My stomach had an uncertain lump in it at the thought of trying to prompt Beck to shift. I'd forgotten too easily how much we risked every time we tried to learn more about ourselves.

"Cole," I said, "Beck means everything to him. This isn't a game. Don't do anything you aren't sure of, okay?"

"I'm always sure of what I do," he said. "Sometimes I was just never sure there was supposed to be a happy ending."

Chapter Thirty-Two

· GRACE ·

That first day back as me was odd. I couldn't settle without my clothing and my routine, knowing that the wolf that was me was still lurching around unpredictably inside my limbs. In a way, I was glad for the uncertainty of being a new wolf, because I knew that it would eventually settle into the same temperature-based shift that Sam had had when I met him. And I loved the cold. I didn't want to fear it.

In an attempt to settle myself into some kind of normalcy, I suggested that we make a proper dinner, which turned out to be more difficult than I'd expected. Sam and Cole had stocked the house with a strange combination of foods, most of which could be described as "microwavable" and few that could be described as "ingredients." But I found the things for making pancakes and eggs — which was always an appropriate meal, I thought — and Sam moved in wordlessly to assist while Cole lay on the floor in the living room, staring at the ceiling.

I glanced over my shoulder. "What's he doing? Could I have the spatula?"

Sam passed the spatula to me. "His brain hurts him, I think." He slid behind me to reach the plates, and for a moment, his body was pressed against mine, his hand on my waist to steady me. I felt a fierce rush of longing.

"Hey," I said, and he turned, plates in hand. "Put those down and come back here."

Sam started toward me but then, as he did, movement caught my eye.

"*Hst* — what's that?" I asked, my voice dropping to a whisper. "Stop!"

He froze and followed my gaze as I found what had caught my eye — an animal moving across the dark backyard. The grass was illuminated by the light coming from the two kitchen windows. For a moment, I lost sight of it, and then, there, by the covered barbecue grill.

For a moment, my heart felt light as a feather, because it was a white wolf. Olivia was a white wolf, and I hadn't seen her in so long.

But then Sam breathed, "Shelby," and I saw as she moved that he was right. There was none of the lithe grace that Olivia had had as a wolf, and when the white wolf lifted her head, it was a darting, suspicious move. She looked at the house, her eyes definitely not Olivia's, and then she squatted and peed by the grill.

"Oh, nice," I said.

Sam frowned.

We watched silently as Shelby made her way from the grill to another point in the middle of the yard, where she marked territory again. She was alone.

"I think she's getting worse," Sam said. Outside the window, Shelby stood for a long moment, staring at the house. I felt, uncannily, that she was looking at us in the kitchen, though we had to be just motionless silhouettes to her, if we were anything. Even from here, though, I could see her hackles rising.

"She" — we both started as Cole's voice came from behind us — "is psychotic."

"What do you mean?" I asked.

"I've seen her about when I do the traps. She's brave and she's mean as hell."

"Well, I knew that," I said. With a little shudder, I remembered without fondness the evening that she had thrown herself through a plate glass window to attack me. And then, her eyes in the lightning storm. "She's tried to kill me more times than I care to remember."

"She's scared," Sam interrupted softly. He was still watching Shelby, whose eyes were right on him, no one else. It was terribly eerie. "She's scared, and lonely, and angry, and jealous. With you, Grace, and Cole, and Olivia, the pack's changing really fast and she doesn't have much further to fall. She's losing everything."

The last pancake I'd started was burning. I snatched the pan from the stove top. "I don't like her around here."

"I don't . . . I don't think you have to worry," Sam said. Shelby was still motionless, staring at his silhouette. "I think she blames me."

Suddenly, Shelby started, at the same time that we heard Cole's voice across the backyard: "Clear off, you psychotic bitch!"

She slid off into the darkness as the back door slammed.

"Thanks, Cole," I said. "That was incredibly subtle."

"That," replied Cole, "is one of my finest traits."

Sam was still frowning out the window. "I wonder if she —"

The phone rang from the kitchen island, interrupting him, and Cole retrieved it. He made a face and then handed the handset to me without answering it.

The caller ID was Isabel's number. I said, "Hello?"

"Grace." I waited for some comment on my humanness, something offhand and sarcastic. But she only said that: *Grace.*

"Isabel," I said back, just to say something. I glanced at Sam, who appeared puzzled, reflecting my expression.

"Is Sam still there with you?"

"Yeah. Do you . . . want to talk to him?"

"No. I just wanted to make sure that you —" Isabel stopped. There was a lot of noise behind her. "Grace, did Sam tell you they'd found a dead girl in the woods? Killed by wolves?"

I looked at Sam, but he couldn't hear what Isabel had said.

"No," I said, uneasy.

"Grace. They know who she was."

Everything inside me was very quiet.

Isabel said, "It was Olivia."

Olivia.

Olivia.

Olivia.

I saw everything around me with perfect precision. There was a photograph on the fridge of a man standing beside a kayak and giving a peace sign. There was also a dingy magnet in the shape of a tooth with a dental office's name and number on it. Next to the fridge was a counter that had a few small nicks all the way down to some colorless surface. On it was an old glass Coca-Cola bottle that had a pencil and one of those pens that looked like a flower stuck in it. The kitchen tap dripped every eleven seconds, the drop of water running clockwise around the lip of the faucet before working up enough nerve to fall into the sink below. I'd never noticed how everything in this kitchen was a warm color. Browns and reds and oranges, all worked through the counters and cabinets and tiles and faded photographs stuck into the doors of the cabinets.

"What did you say?" Sam demanded. "What did you say to her?"

I couldn't figure out why he would ask me that when I hadn't said anything. I frowned at him and saw that he was holding the phone, which I didn't remember giving to him.

I thought, *I am a terrible friend because I don't hurt at all. I'm just here looking at the kitchen and thinking that if it were mine, I'd find a rug for it so my feet wouldn't be so cold on the bare floor. I must not have loved Olivia, then, because I don't even feel like crying. I am thinking about rugs and not about how she's dead.*

"Grace," Sam said. In the background, I saw Cole move off, holding the phone, talking into it. "What do you need from me?"

I thought it was a very strange question to ask. I just looked at him. "I'm okay," I said.

Sam said, "You're not."

"I am," I said. "I'm not crying. I don't even feel like crying."

He smoothed my hair back from my ears, pulling it behind my head like he was making a ponytail, holding it in his fist. Into my ear, he said, "But you will."

I leaned my head on his shoulder; it seemed incredibly heavy just then, impossible to hold up. "I want to call people and find out if they're okay. I want to call Rachel," I said. "I want to call John. I want to call Olivia." Too late, I realized what I'd said, and I opened my mouth as if I could somehow take it back and insert something more logical.

"Oh, Grace," Sam said, touching my chin, but his pity was a distant thing.

On the phone, I heard Cole say, in a completely different voice than I'd ever heard him use before, "Well, there's not much we can do about it now, is there?"

CHAPTER THIRTY-THREE

· SAM ·

That night, Grace was the wakeful one. I felt like an empty cup, bobbing and tipping to admit rivulets of slumber; it was only a matter of time before it filled up enough to pull me under entirely.

My room was dark except for the Christmas lights strung around the ceiling, tiny constellations in a claustrophobic sky. I kept meaning to pull out the cord beside the bed and put us in darkness, but fatigue whispered in my ear and distracted me. I couldn't understand how I could be so tired after I'd finally slept the night before. It was like my body had reacquired its taste for sleep now that I had Grace back, and it couldn't get enough.

Grace sat next to me, her back leaned up against the wall, legs tangled in bedsheets, and ran the flat of her hand up and down my chest, which wasn't helping me feel any more awake.

"Hey," I murmured, reaching up toward her with my hand, my fingertips just barely able to brush her shoulder. "Come down here with me and sleep."

She stretched out her fingers and rested them on my mouth; her face was wistful and not like her, a mask of Grace worn by another girl in this half-light. "I can't stop thinking." It was a familiar enough sentiment that I pushed up onto my elbows; her fingers slipped off my lips, back to my chest.

"You should be lying down," I said. "That will help."

Grace's expression was doleful and unsure; she was a little girl. I sat up the rest of the way and pulled her toward me. Together we lay back against my headboard, her head lying on my chest where her hand had been before. She smelled like my shampoo.

"I can't stop thinking about her," Grace whispered, braver now that we weren't looking at each other. "And then I start thinking about how I'm supposed to be at home right now, and, Sam, I don't want to go back."

I wasn't sure what to say to that. I didn't want her to go back, either, but I knew she wasn't supposed to be here. If she were human, cured, I would've told her that we had to go back and talk to her parents. We would've made it work; we would've made them understand that we were serious, and then I would have lived without her in my bed until she moved in on the proper terms. I would've hated it, but I'd have lived with it. I'd told her I wanted to do it right with her, and I still did.

But now there was no right. Now Grace was a girl who was also a wolf, and as long as she said that she didn't want to go back, and as long as I remained unsure of how her parents would react, this was where I wanted her. One day soon there would be hell to pay for these stolen moments together, but I didn't think we were wrong to have them. I ran my fingers through her hair until I hit a tiny knot and had to pull them out to start again. "I won't make you."

"We have to figure it out eventually," Grace said. "I wish I was eighteen. I wish I'd moved out a long time ago. I wish we were already married. I wish I didn't have to think of a lie."

At least I wasn't the only one who thought that they wouldn't do well with the truth. "Nothing," I said, with utmost certainty, "will get solved tonight." After I said it, I recognized, with some irony, Grace's own reasoning, the statement that she had used many times before to try to lure me to sleep.

"It all just keeps going round and round and round," Grace said. "Tell me a story."

I stopped touching her hair because the repetitive comfort of it was making me fall asleep again. "A story?"

She said, "Like you told me about Beck teaching you to hunt."

I tried to think of an anecdote, something that didn't need too much explaining. Something that would make her laugh. Every Beck story seemed tainted now, colored by doubt. Everything about him that I hadn't seen with my own eyes now felt apocryphal.

I cast about for another memory, and said, "That BMW wagon wasn't the first car Ulrik had. When I first came here, he had a little Ford Escort. It was brown. And very ugly."

Grace sighed, as if this were a comforting start to a bedtime story. She fisted a handful of my T-shirt; the action woke me up instantly and guiltily made me think of at least four things that were not bed-time stories or selfless ways to comfort a grieving girl.

I swallowed and focused on my memory instead. "There was a lot wrong with it. When you went over bumps, it would scrape on the ground. The exhaust, I think. Once, Ulrik hit a possum in town and he dragged it all the way back home."

Grace laughed a small, soundless laugh, the sort you laugh when you know you're expected to.

I pressed on. "It always smelled like something going wrong, too. Like brakes sticking or rubber burning or maybe just like he hadn't got all the possum off." I paused, remembering all the trips I'd made in that car, sitting in the passenger seat, waiting in the car while Ulrik ran into the grocery store for some beer or standing beside the road as Beck swore at the silent engine and asked me why he hadn't just taken his own damn car. That was back in the days when Ulrik had been human a lot, when his bedroom had been right next to mine, and I used to get woken up by the sound of noisy lovemaking, though I was pretty sure Ulrik was alone. I didn't tell Grace that part.

"It was the car that I used to drive to the bookstore," I said. "Ulrik bought that BMW wagon from a guy who was selling roses by the side of the road in St. Paul, so I got the Escort. Two months after I'd gotten my license, I got a flat tire in it." I'd been sixteen in the most naive sense of the word: simultaneously euphoric and terrified to be driving home from work by myself for the first time, and when the tire made an incredible noise that sounded like a gun going off by my head, I thought I might die.

"Did you know how to change tires?" Grace asked. She asked the question like she did.

"Not a chance. I had to pull it over in the slush by the side of the road and use the cell phone I'd just been given for my birthday to call Beck for help. First time I was using the phone, and it was to say I couldn't change a flat tire. Totally unmanning."

Grace laughed again, softly. "Unmanning," she repeated.

"Unmanning," I assured her, glad to hear that little laugh. I thought back to the memory. Beck had been a long time getting there, dropped off by Ulrik on his way to work. Ignoring my bleak expression, Ulrik waved cheerily at me from the window of the BMW: "Later, boy-o!" His wagon vanished into the oncoming gloom, the taillights neon red in the snow gray world.

"So Beck arrived," I said, aware then that I had included an anecdote with Beck after all, though I hadn't meant to. Maybe all of my anecdotes had Beck in them. "He said, 'So you've killed the car, then?'

"He had been all bundled in coats and gloves and scarves, but despite them, he'd already been shivering. He'd whistled when he saw the comically deflated tire. 'That's a beauty. You run over a moose?'"

"Had you?" Grace asked.

"No," I said. "Beck made fun of me and showed me where the spare tire was and —"

I dropped off. I'd meant to tell the story of when Ulrik had finally sold the Escort, how he'd cooked four pounds of bacon and put it in the trunk when people came to look at it because he'd read that real estate agents baked cookies to sell houses to women. Instead I'd somehow gotten sidetracked in my drowsiness and the story I'd started now ended with Beck's smile vanishing in the time it took for headlights to come over the hill and disappear on the other side — with a pile of scarves and sweaters and gloves on the ground behind the Escort and me with a useless tire iron in my hand and the memory of Beck saying half my name as he shifted.

"And what?"

I tried to think if there was a way that I could spin the story, to make it more cheerful, but as I did, I remembered an aspect of it that I hadn't thought about for years. "Beck shifted. I was still there with the damn tire iron and still was just as dumb as before."

It had just been me, picking up his coat and countless shirts from the ground, knocking the bulk of the gritty snow from them, throwing the lot of them in the back of the Escort. Allowing myself one good door slam. Then linking my arms behind my head and turning away from the road and the car. Because the loss of Beck had not yet begun to sting. The fact that I was stranded by the road, on the other hand, had sunk in immediately.

Grace made a quiet, sad noise, sorry for that Sam long ago, though it took that Sam a long time to realize what he'd really lost in those few minutes.

"I was there for a while, staring at all the useless junk in the back — like, Ulrik had a hockey mask in the trunk, and it kept on looking at me like *You're an idiot, Sam Roth.* And then I heard this car pull up behind me — I totally forgot about this part until just now, Grace — and who do you think stopped to see if I needed help?"

Grace rubbed her nose on my shirt. "I don't know. Who?"

"Tom Culpeper," I said.

"No!" Grace pulled back so that she could look at me. "Really?" Now she looked more like herself in the dim light, her hair mussed from lying on my chest and her eyes more alive, and my hand that rested on her waist wanted desperately to slide inside her shirt to map a course up the dip of her spine, to touch her shoulder blades and make her think only of me.

But it wasn't a bridge I would start across by myself. I didn't know where we stood. I was good at waiting.

"Yes," I said, instead of kissing her. "Yes, it was Tom Culpeper."

Grace lay back down on my chest. "That's crazy."

"You're Geoffrey Beck's kid," Tom Culpeper had observed. Even in the dim light, I had seen that his SUV was crusted with ice and sand and salt — snirt, Ulrik always called it, a combination of snow and dirt — and that the headlights cast a crooked path of light across me and the Escort. He had added, after some thought, "Sam, right? Looks like you need a hand."

I remembered thinking at the time how relieving it was to hear my name said in such an ordinary voice, to wipe out the memory of how Beck had said it as he'd shifted.

"He helped me out," I said. "He seemed different then, I guess. That must've been soon after they moved here."

"Did he have Isabel with him?" Grace asked.

"I don't remember Isabel." I considered. "I try really hard not to think of him as evil, Grace. Because of Isabel. I don't know what I would have thought of him, if not for the wolves."

"If not for the wolves," Grace said, "neither of us would've given him any thought at all."

"This story was supposed to have bacon in it," I admitted. "It was supposed to make you laugh."

She sighed heavily, like the weight of the world had crushed the breath out of her, and I knew how she felt.

"That's okay. Turn off the lights," she replied, reaching down to tug the comforter over both of us where we lay. She smelled faintly like wolf, and I didn't think she'd make it all the way through the night without shifting. "I'm ready for today to be over."

Feeling far less sleepy than before, I dropped my arm off the side of the bed to pull the plug out of the wall. The room went dark and, after a moment, Grace whispered that she loved me, sounding a little sad. I wrapped my arms tightly around her shoulders, sorry that loving me was such a complicated thing.

Her breaths were already slowing as I whispered it back to her. But I didn't sleep. I stayed awake, thinking of Tom Culpeper and Beck, how the truth of them seemed so buried inside. I kept seeing Culpeper walking across the snow toward me, his nose already red from the cold, perfectly willing to help a boy he didn't know change a tire in the freezing evening. And between repeated flashes of that image, I kept seeing the wolves plunging out of the morning to shove my small body to the ground, to change my life forever.

Beck had done that. Beck had decided to take me. Long before my parents decided they didn't want me, he had planned to take me. They had just made it easy for him.

I didn't know how I could live with that knowledge, without it eating me up, without it poisoning every happy memory I had of growing up. Without it ruining everything Beck and I had.

I didn't understand how someone could be both God and the devil. How the same person could destroy you and save you. When everything I was, good and bad, was knotted with threads of his making, how was I supposed to know whether to love or hate him?

In the middle of the night, Grace woke up, her eyes wide, her body shuddering. She said my name, just like Beck had said it all those years ago by the side of the road, and then, like Beck, she left me with nothing but an empty suit of clothing and one thousand unanswered questions.

CHAPTER THIRTY-FOUR

· ISABEL ·

Sam's cell phone called me at seven A.M. the next morning. Normally I would've been getting ready for school at seven A.M., but it was a weekend, which meant that instead I was lying on my bed, pulling on my running shoes. I ran because I was vain and it gave me great legs.

I flipped open the phone. "Hello?" I wasn't sure what I expected.

"I knew it," Cole said. "I knew you'd pick up the phone if you thought it was Sam."

"Oh my God. Are you for real?"

"I am for very real. Can I come inside?"

I jumped off my bed and went to the window, peering around. I could just see the edge of a rather ugly station wagon at the end of the driveway.

"Is that you in that perv-mobile?"

"It smells," Cole said. "I would invite you to come out here and talk to me in the privacy of the car, but it's pretty powerful stuff, whatever is making it smell."

"What do you want, Cole?"

"Your credit card. I need to order a fishing net, some hardware, and a couple of tranquilizers that I swear are totally over-the-counter. Also, I need them overnighted."

"Tell me you're just trying to be funny."

"I told Sam I could catch Beck. I'm going to build a pit trap using the pit Grace helpfully found by falling into it and bait it with Beck's favorite food, which he helpfully recorded in his journal while telling an anecdote about a kitchen fire."

"You are trying to be funny. Because otherwise, this sounds like an insane person on the telephone."

"Scent is the strongest tie to memory."

I sighed and lay back down on my bed, phone still at my ear. "What does this have to do with keeping you all from being killed by my father?"

There was a pause. "Beck moved the wolves once before. I want to ask him about it."

"And a fishing net, some hardware, and drugs will help you to do that?"

"If not, it's all the makings of a very good time."

I stared at the ceiling. Long ago, Jack had thrown Silly Putty at the place where the ceiling tipped to meet the roof-slanted wall, and it still stuck there.

I sighed. "Fine, Cole, fine. I'll meet you at the side door, by the little stairs you went up before. Park that thing someplace my parents won't see when they wake up. And don't be loud."

"I'm never loud," Cole said, and the phone went silent in my hand at the same time my bedroom door opened.

Still lying on my back, I looked upside down to the door and was unsurprised to see Cole letting himself in. He shut the door carefully behind him. He was wearing cargo pants and a plain black T-shirt. He looked famous, but I was beginning to realize that was a function of the way he stood, not of what he wore. In my room, which was all floating, light fabrics and pillows that shone and mirrors that smiled back at you, Cole looked out of place, but I was beginning to figure out that that, too, was a function of how he was, not where he was.

"So today you're Cross-Country Barbie," he said. I remembered I was in my running shoes and shorts. He walked to my dresser and sprayed a puff of my perfume into the air. A Cole in the dresser mirror waved his hand through the mist.

"Today I'm Humor-Free Barbie," I replied. Cole picked up my rosary from the dresser, his thumb over one of the beads. The way he held it made it look like a familiar gesture, though it was hard to imagine Cole St. Clair entering a church without catching fire. "I thought that side door was locked."

"Not so much."

I closed my eyes. Looking at him was making me feel . . . tired. I felt the same weight inside me that I'd felt at Il Pomodoro. I thought, possibly, that what I really needed was to go where nobody knew me and start over again, with none of my previous decisions, conversations, or expectations coming with me.

The bed sighed as Cole climbed onto it and lay on his back beside me. He smelled clean, like shaving cream and the beach, and I realized he must have taken special care before he came over here today. That made me feel weird, too.

I closed my eyes again. "How is Grace doing? About Olivia?"

"I wouldn't know. She shifted last night so we locked her in the bathroom."

"I wasn't friends with Olivia," I said. It seemed important for him to know. "I didn't know her, really."

"Me neither." Cole paused. He said, in a different voice, "I like Grace."

He said it like it were a very serious thing, and for a moment, I thought he meant it as *"I like Grace"* which I couldn't even properly comprehend. But then he clarified. "I like how she is with Sam. I don't think I ever believed in love, not really. Just thought it was something James Bond made up, a long time ago, to get laid."

We lay there, not speaking, for a few more minutes. Outside, birds were waking up. The house was silent; the morning was not cold enough to trip the heater. It was hard to not think about Cole lying right there beside me, even if he was quiet, especially since he smelled good and I could remember exactly what it felt like to kiss him. I could remember, too, exactly the last time I'd seen Sam kiss Grace, and I remembered, more than anything, the way Sam's hand looked, pressing against her as they kissed. I didn't think that was what it looked like when Cole and I had kissed. Thinking about it was making it get all loud and crowded inside me again, the wanting Cole and the doubting that it was the right thing to want him. I felt guilty, dirty, euphoric, as if I had already given in.

"Cole, I'm tired," I said. As soon as I said it, I had no idea why I had.

He didn't reply. He just lay there, quieter than I thought he could be.

Irritated by his silence, I battled whether or not I should ask him if he'd heard me.

Finally, in a quiet so deep that I heard his lips part before he spoke, he said, "Sometimes, I think about calling home."

I was used to Cole being self-centered, but this, I felt, was a new low in our relationship, him hijacking my confession with one of his own.

He said, "I think that I'll just call home and tell my mom that I'm not dead. I think I'll call my dad and ask him if he'd like to have a little chat about what meningitis does to you on a cellular level. Or I think I'll call Jeremy — he was my bassist — and I'll tell him that I'm not dead, but I don't want to be looked for anymore. To tell my parents that I'm not dead but I'm never coming home." He was quiet for such a long time then that I thought he was done. He was quiet long enough that I could see the morning light in my airy, pastel room get a little brighter as the mist began to burn off.

Then he said, "But it just makes me tired even thinking about it. It reminds me of that feeling I had before I left. Like my lungs were made of lead. Like I can't even think about starting to care about anything. Like I either wish that they were all dead, or I was, because I can't stand the pull of all that history between us. That's before I even pick up the phone. I'm so tired I never want to wake up again. But I've figured out now that it was never them that made me feel that way. It was just me, all along."

I didn't reply. I was thinking again about that revelation in the bathroom in Il Pomodoro. That wanting to just be done, for once, to feel done, to not want anything. Thinking of how precisely Cole had described the fatigue inside me.

"I'm part of what you hate about yourself," Cole said. It wasn't a question.

Of course he was part of what I hated about myself. Everything was part of what I hated about myself. It wasn't really personal.

He sat up. "I'll go."

I could still feel the heat of the mattress from where he'd been. "Cole," I said, "do you think I'm lovable?"

"As in 'cuddly and'?"

"As in 'able to be loved,'" I said.

Cole's gaze was unwavering. Just for a moment, I had the strange idea that I could see exactly what he had looked like when he was younger, and exactly what he'd look like when he was older. It was piercing, a secret glimpse of his future. "Maybe," he said. "But you won't let anybody try."

I closed my eyes and swallowed.

"I can't tell the difference between not fighting," I said, "and giving up."

Despite my eyelids being tightly shut, a single, hot tear ran out of my left eye. I was so angry that it had escaped. I was so angry.

Beneath me, the bed tipped as Cole edged closer. I felt him lean over me. His breath, warm and measured, hit my cheek. Two breaths.

Three. Four. I didn't know what I wanted. Then I heard him stop breathing, and a second later, I felt his lips on my mouth.

It wasn't the sort of kiss I'd had with him before, hungry, wanting, desperate. It wasn't the sort of kiss I'd had with anyone before. This kiss was so soft that it was like a memory of a kiss, so careful on my lips that it was like someone running his fingers along them. My mouth parted and stilled; it was so quiet, a whisper, not a shout. Cole's hand touched my neck, thumb pressed into the skin next to my jaw. It wasn't a touch that said *I need more.* It was a touch that said *I want this.*

It was all completely soundless. I didn't think either of us was breathing.

Cole sat back up, slowly, and I opened my eyes. His expression, as ever, was blank, the face he wore when something mattered.

He said, "That's how I would kiss you, if I loved you."

He stood up, looking unfamous, and retrieved the car keys from where they'd slid out onto the bed. He didn't look at me when he left, shutting the door behind him.

The house was so noiseless that I heard his step down the stairs, the first five or so slow and hesitating, and then all the rest in a rush.

I put my thumb on my neck where Cole's had been and closed my eyes. It didn't feel like fighting or like giving up. I hadn't realized there was a third option, and even if I had, I wouldn't have guessed it had anything to do with Cole.

I exhaled, my breath long and noisy over lips that had just been kissed. Then I sat up and pulled out my credit card.

Chapter Thirty-Five

· SAM ·

I didn't particularly feel like going into work the next morning, since the world was coming to an end, but I couldn't think of a compelling and plausible explanation to give Karyn, so I left home and drove into Mercy Falls. I couldn't bear the sounds of Grace the wolf, either, clawing disasters into the walls of the downstairs bathroom, so it was a mercy, in a way, to leave, though I felt guilty for feeling that way. Just because I wasn't there to be reminded of her panic didn't mean that she wasn't feeling it while I was gone.

It was a beautiful day, no sign of rain for the first time in a week. The sky was the dreamy, high blue of summer, months early, and the leaves of the trees looked one thousand colors of green, from electric, plastic shades to a hair lighter than black. Instead of parking behind the store as I usually did, I parked on Main Street, far enough away from the center of downtown that I wouldn't have to feed a parking meter. In Mercy Falls, that was only a handful of blocks. I left my jacket on the passenger seat of the Volkswagen, put my hands in my pockets, and started to walk.

Mercy Falls wasn't rich, but it was quaint, in its way, so by virtue of its quaintness, it had a pretty thriving downtown. Charm, plus proximity to the beautiful Boundary Waters, brought tourists, and tourists brought money. Mercy Falls offered several blocks of boutique-sort shops to part them from their cash. The shops were largely of the sort that kept husbands waiting in the car or sent them poking around in the hardware store on Grieves Street, but still I glanced in windows as I walked. I kept to the edge of the sidewalk so that the cautious morning sun could reach me. It felt good on my skin, a small consolation prize in this terrible and wonderful week.

I made it a few yards past a shop that sold clothing and knick-knacks, and I stopped and doubled back to stand in front of the window. A headless mannequin in the window wore a white summer dress. It was just a simple thing: thin straps up over the shoulders, a loose tie round the middle. The fabric was something that I thought was called eyelet. I imagined Grace in it, the narrow straps over her shoulders, a triangle of bare skin below her throat, the hem falling just above her knee. I could imagine her hips beneath the thin material, my hands bunching the fabric at her waist when I pulled her to me. It was a carefree dress, a dress that was about summer and ankle-high grass and blond hair streaked paler by the confident sun.

I stood there for a long moment, looking at it, wanting what it stood for. It seemed like such a foolish thing to be thinking of right now when so much else was at stake. Three times I shifted my weight, about to step off, to go back on my way. And every time that image of Grace — wind lifting the edge of the dress, pressing the fabric flat to her belly and breasts — kept me fixed in front of the window.

I bought it. I had four twenties in my wallet — Karyn had paid me in cash last week — and I left with one of them and a little bag with the dress nestled in the bottom. I backtracked to put it in my car and then went on to the Crooked Shelf, eyes on the sidewalk running ahead of me, feeling the warmth and uncertainty of having bought a gift that cost more than a day of working. What if she didn't like it? Maybe I should have been saving for a ring. Even if she had really meant it and did want to marry me, which seemed like an impossible thing, a ring seemed far off. I had no idea what a ring cost, and maybe I needed to start saving. What if I told her I'd got her a present and that was what she expected and I disappointed her? I felt simultaneously like the oldest nineteen-year-old on the planet and the youngest — what was I doing thinking about rings, and why hadn't I thought of it sooner? And perhaps in all her practical nature Grace would be annoyed that I'd bought her a gift instead of doing something about the hunt.

So it was these things I wrestled as I walked into the bookstore. With my mind so far from my body, the store felt like a lonely, timeless place as I opened it up. It was Saturday, so an hour after I opened the store, Karyn came in the back door, sequestering herself away in the tiny back room to do ordering and reconciling. Karyn and I had an easy relationship; it was nice to know she was in the shop even when we didn't speak.

There were no customers and I was restless, so I walked back to the workroom. The sun was coming in the front windows full and strong, reaching long hands all the way back here. It warmed my body, comfortingly hot, as I leaned on the doorway.

"Hi," I said.

Karyn was already sitting surrounded by drifts of invoices and book catalogs. She looked up at me with a pleasant smile. To me, everything about Karyn was always pleasant — she was one of those women who always seemed comfortable with themselves and the world, whether they were in polar fleece or pearls. If she thought any differently about me since Grace disappeared, she didn't show it. I wished I could tell her how much I had needed that from her, that unchanging pleasantness. "You look happy," she said.

"Do I?"

"Happier," she said. "Have we been busy?"

I shrugged. "It's been quiet. I swept. And removed some tiny handprints from the front windows."

"Children — who needs them?" Karyn asked. It was a rhetorical question. She mused, "If it would get warm, we'd get people. Or if that

Tate Flaugherty sequel would come out already, we'd have them in scads. Maybe we should do up the front window for it. What do you think, an Alaskan theme for *Mayhem in Juneau?*"

I made a face. "It seems to me Minnesota just got done with its Alaskan theme."

"Aha. Good point."

I thought about my guitar, the northern lights over my head, the songs I needed to write about the past few days.

"We should do music biographies," I said. "That'd make a nice window."

Karyn gestured to me with her pencil. "Point to the man." She lowered the pencil and tapped it on the letter in front of her, a gesture that suddenly reminded me of Grace. "Sam, I know that Beck is . . . ill, and this might not be a priority for you, but have you thought about what you're doing for college?"

I blinked at the question and crossed my arms. She looked at my crossed arms as though they were part of my answer. I said, "I — hadn't given it a lot of thought yet." I didn't want her to think I was unmotivated, though, so I said, "I'm waiting to see where Grace goes to school."

I realized, half a moment later, that this statement was wrong, for about three different reasons, primary amongst them being that Grace was officially missing.

Karyn didn't look pitying or puzzled, however. She just gave me a long, pensive look, her lips set in a small line and one of her thumbs sort of resting on the bottom of her chin. I felt, then, like she *knew*, somehow, about us, and that this was merely a pretense that Beck and I played with her.

Don't ask.

She said, "I was just wondering because, if you're not going to school right away, I was going to ask if you wanted to work full-time here."

It was not what I'd expected her to say, so I didn't answer.

Karyn said, "I know what you're thinking, that it's not a lot of money. I'll up your hourly by two dollars."

"You can't afford that."

"You sell a lot of books for us. It would make me feel better to know that you're always the one behind the counter. Every day you're sitting on that stool is a day I don't have to worry about what's going on in here."

"I —" Really, I was grateful for the offer. Not because I needed the money, but because I needed the trust. My face felt warm, a smile pending.

Karyn pressed on, "I mean, I feel a little guilty, trying to keep you out of college for another year, but if you're waiting anyway . . ."

I heard the front-door bell ring as it opened. One of us was going to have to go up there, and I was glad for it. Not because the conversation was awkward or terrible, but the opposite. I needed a moment to process this, to hold all this at an arm's length so I could be sure of my face and my words when I spoke again. I felt like I looked too ungrateful, too slow. I asked, "Can I think about it?"

"I would've been amazed if you didn't," Karyn said. "You're a little predictable, Sam."

I grinned at her and turned to head back to the front, which is how I happened to be smiling when the police officer first saw me.

My smile melted away. Actually, it remained for just a moment too long, my lips pulled up to show an emotion that had vanished seconds before. The police officer could have been there for anything. He could've been there to talk to Karyn. He could've been there with just a quick question.

But I knew he wasn't.

I saw now that he was Officer William Koenig. Koenig was young, understated, familiar. I wanted to think that our previous exchanges would weight things in my favor, but his face told me everything I needed to know. His expression was the purposefully blank one of someone who was being made to regret his past kindnesses.

"You're a hard man to find, Sam," Koenig said as I slowly approached him. My hands felt sort of useless hanging at my sides.

"Am I?" I asked. I felt prickling, defensive, although his tone was light. Being found was not something I cared for. Being looked for wasn't something I liked, either.

"I told them this was the place to find you," Koenig said.

I nodded. "That's a pretty fair guess." I felt like I should ask him *What can I do for you?* but I didn't really want to know. Mostly I wanted to be left alone to process everything that had happened to me in the past seventy-two hours.

"We actually need to ask you a few questions," Koenig said. Behind him, the door *ding*ed as a woman came in. She had a giant purple bag that I couldn't stop staring at.

"Where are your self-help books?" she asked me. She seemed utterly oblivious to the fact that there was a police officer in front of me. Maybe people spoke with police officers on a casual basis all the time. It was hard to imagine.

If Koenig hadn't been there, I would have told her that every book ever written was a self-help book and could she be more specific? And she would've left with four books instead of one, because that was what I did. But with Koenig there, I just said, "Over there. Behind you."

"Back at the department," Koenig said. "For your privacy."

For my privacy.

This was bad.

"Sam?" Koenig said.

I realized I was still watching that purple leather bag move slowly through the store. The woman's cell phone had rung and now she was yammering on it. "Okay," I said. "I mean, I have to, don't I?"

Koenig said, "You don't have to do anything. But things are a lot less ugly without a warrant."

I nodded my head. Words. I needed to say something. What did I need to say? I thought of Karyn, sitting there in the back, thinking all was fine up front because I was here. "I need to tell my boss that I'm leaving. Is that all right?"

"Of course."

I felt him drifting after me as I headed to the back of the store. "Karyn," I said, leaning on the doorframe. I could not make my voice casual, but I tried. It occurred to me that I didn't normally address her by her name, and it felt wrong in my mouth. "I'm sorry. I have to go for a little bit. Um, Officer Koenig — they would like me to go in for questions."

For one second, her expression stayed the same, and then everything about it hardened. "They *what*? Are they here now?"

She pushed out of her chair and I backed up so that she could stand in the doorway and confirm that Koenig was standing in the aisle, staring up at one of the paper cranes that I'd hung from the balcony above.

"What's going on now?" she asked. It was her brisk, efficient voice that she used when she was speaking to a difficult customer; it stood for no crap and kept emotion out of it. Business Karyn, we both called it. It turned her into a completely different person.

"Ma'am," Koenig said apologetically — this was a natural response to Business Karyn — "one of our investigators has questions for Sam. He asked if I would bring him back for a chat in some privacy."

"A chat," Karyn echoed. "The sort of chat that would be better with a lawyer present?"

"That's entirely up to Sam. But he's not being charged with anything right now."

Right. Now.

Karyn and I both heard it. *Right now* was another way of saying *yet.* She looked at me. "Sam, do you want me to call Geoffrey?"

I knew my face gave me away, because she answered her own question. "He's not available, is he?"

"I'll be okay," I said.

"This strikes me as harassment," Karyn said to Koenig. "He's an easy target because he's not the same as everyone else. If Geoffrey Beck were in town, would we be having this conversation?"

"With all due respect, ma'am," Koenig said, "if Geoffrey Beck were in town, he would probably be the one we were questioning."

Karyn sealed her lips shut, looking unhappy. Koenig stepped back out of the center aisle to gesture toward the front door. Now I could see a police car double-parked in front of the store, waiting for us.

I was intensely grateful to Karyn for standing up for me. For acting like I was her business. She said, "Sam, call me. If you need anything. If you feel uncomfortable. Do you want me to come with?"

"I'll be okay," I said again.

"He'll be all right," Koenig said. "We are not trying to back anyone into a corner here."

"I'm sorry I have to leave," I told Karyn. Usually she only came in for a few hours on Saturday morning and then left the shop in the hands of whoever was working. Now I'd ruined her entire day.

"Oh, Sam. You didn't do anything wrong," Karyn said. She came over and hugged my shoulders, hard. She smelled like hyacinths. To Koenig, she said — Business Karyn vanishing as accusation slipped into her tone — "I hope this is worth it for you guys."

Koenig led me down the aisle toward the front door. I was infinitely aware that the woman with the big purple bag was watching me go, cell phone still up to her ear. Her phone speaker was turned up loud enough that we could both hear the woman on the other side of the line say, *"Are they arresting him?"*

"Sam," Koenig said. "Just tell the truth."

He didn't even know what he was asking for.

Chapter Thirty-Six

· COLE ·

After I left the Culpeper house, I just drove. I had Ulrik's old BMW wagon, some of the money I'd brought, no one to tell me not to go.

On the radio, I was listening to a song by a band that had opened for us once. They had been such a train wreck live that I'd felt positively virtuous, a difficult feat to accomplish at that point. I should've thanked them for making us look good. The lead singer's name had been Mark or Mike or Mack or Abel or something like that. Afterward, he'd come up to me, ferociously drunk, and told me I was his biggest influence. I could see the resemblance.

Now, a million years later, I listened to the DJ describe the single as the band's one hit. I kept driving. I still had Sam's phone in my pocket, and it wasn't ringing, but for once, I didn't care. I felt like I'd left a message for Isabel that didn't require a callback. It was enough to have said it.

My windows were rolled down and my arm was out, the wind buffeting it, my palm moist from grabbing mist. The Minnesota landscape stretched out on either side of the two-lane road. It was all scrubby pines and flat houses and rocks stacked randomly and lakes suddenly glinting behind trees. I thought the residents of Mercy Falls must have decided to build ugly houses to make up for all the natural beauty. Keep the place from exploding, or something, from an excess of picturesque.

I kept thinking about what I'd told Isabel, about thinking of calling my family. I'd been mostly truthful. The idea of calling my parents felt impossible and unpalatable. In the Venn diagram that was me and them, the shape where our circles overlapped was empty.

But I still thought about calling Jeremy. Jeremy the resident bassist-yogi. I wondered what he was doing without me and Victor. I liked to think that he'd used his money to go backpacking across India or something. The thing about Jeremy, the thing that made me almost willing to call him and no one else, was that he and Victor had always known me better than anyone. That was what all NARKOTIKA really was: a way of knowing Cole St. Clair. Victor and Jeremy had spent years of their lives helping describe the particular pain of being me to hundreds of thousands of listeners.

They did it so often that they could do it without me. I remembered one interview where they did it so well that I never bothered to answer another interview question again. We were being interviewed in our hotel room. It was first thing in the morning because we had a flight to catch later. Victor was hungover and pissy. Jeremy was eating breakfast bars at the tiny, glass-topped desk in the room. The room had a narrow balcony with a view to nothing, and I had opened the door and was lying out there on the concrete. I had been doing sit-ups with my feet hooked on the bottom rung of the railing, but now I was just staring at jet trails in the sky. The interviewer sat cross-legged on one of the unmade beds. He was young and spiked and pressed and named Jan.

"So who does most of the songwriting?" Jan had asked. "Or is it a group thing?"

"Oh, it's a group thing," Jeremy said, in his slow, easy way. He'd picked up a Southern accent at the same time he'd acquired Buddhism. "Cole writes the lyrics, and then I bring him coffee, and then Cole writes the music, and Victor brings him pretzels."

"So you do most of the writing, then, Cole?" Jan raised his voice so that I could hear him better out on the balcony. "Where do you get your inspiration?"

From my vantage point on the balcony, staring straight up, I had two viewing options: the brick sides of the buildings across the street, or one square of colorless sky above me. All cities looked the same when you were on your back.

Jeremy snapped a piece of his breakfast bar off; we could all hear the crumbs rustle across the table. From the other bed, still sounding like he was PMSing, Victor said, "He won't answer that."

Jan sounded genuinely puzzled, as if I was the first to refuse him. "Why?"

"He just won't. He hates that question," Victor said. His feet were bare; he clicked the bones in his toes. "It is kind of a stupid question, man. Life, right? That's where we get our inspiration."

Jan scribbled something down. He was left-handed and writing looked awkward for him, as if he were a Ken doll with parts assembled slightly wrong. I hoped he was writing down *Never ask that question again.* "Okay. Um. Your EP *One/Or the Other* just debuted in Billboard's top ten. What are your thoughts on that incredible success?"

"I'm buying my mother a BMW," Victor said. "No, I'm just buying Bavaria. That is where BMWs are from, right?"

"Success is an arbitrary concept," Jeremy said.

"The next one will be better," I said. I hadn't said it out loud before, but now I had, so it was true.

More writing. Jan read the next question from his paper. "Uh, that means that you guys knocked out the Human Parts Ministry album from the top ten, where it had been for over forty weeks. Sorry, forty-one. I swear there won't be typos in the final interview. So, Joey of Human Parts Ministry said he thought 'Looking Up or Down' was such a long-lived hit because so many people identified with the lyrics. Do you think listeners out there identify with the lyrics of *One/Or the Other*?"

One/Or the Other was about the Cole that I heard in the monitors on stage versus the Cole that paced the hotel halls at night. This was what *One/Or the Other* was: It was the knowledge that I was surrounded by adults with lives that I could never imagine living. It was the humming noise inside me that told me to do *something* and found nothing to do that meant anything, the bit of me that was like a fly smashing itself again and again on a windowpane. It was the futility of aging. It was a piano piece gotten right the first time. It was the time I picked Angie up for a date and she was wearing a cardigan that made her look like her mother. It was roads that ended in cul-de-sacs and careers that ended with desks and songs screamed in a gymnasium at night. It was the realization that this was life, and I didn't belong here.

"No," I said. "I think it's about the music."

Jeremy finished his breakfast bar. Victor cracked his knuckles. I watched people the size of germs fly overhead in a plane the size of an ant.

"I read you were a choir boy, Cole," Jan said, consulting his notes. "Are you still a practicing Catholic? Are you, Victor? Jeremy, I know you're not."

"I believe in God," Victor offered. He didn't sound convincing.

"You, Cole?" Jan prompted.

I watched empty sky, waiting for another plane. It was that or look at the blank sides of the buildings. One/Or the Other.

"Here's what I know about Cole," Jeremy said. Punctuated by the silence, it sounded like he was in a pulpit. "Cole's religion is debunking the impossible. He doesn't believe in *impossible*. He doesn't believe in *no*. Cole's religion is waiting for someone to tell him it can't be done so he can do it. Anything. Doesn't matter what that something is, so long as it can't be done. Here's an origin story for you. In the beginning of time there was an ocean and a void, and God made the ocean into the world and he made the void into Cole."

Victor laughed.

"I thought you said you were a Buddhist," Jan said.

"Part-time," Jeremy replied.

Debunking the impossible.

Now, the pines stretched up so high on either side of the road that it felt like I was tunneling to the middle of the world. Mercy Falls was an unnumbered stretch of miles behind me.

I was sixteen again, and the road unwound in front of me, endless possibilities. I felt wiped clean, empty, forgiven. I could drive forever, anywhere. I could be anyone. But I felt the pull of Boundary Wood around me and, for once, the business of being Cole St. Clair no longer felt like such a curse. I had a purpose, a goal, and it was the impossible: finding a cure.

I was so close.

The road flew by beneath the car; my hand was cold from being in the wind. For the first time in a long time, I felt powerful. The woods had taken that void that was me, the thing I thought that could never be full, never be satisfied, and they'd made me lose everything — things I never knew I wanted to keep.

And in the end, I was Cole St. Clair, cut from a new skin. The world lay at my feet and the day stretched out for miles.

I slid Sam's cell phone out of my pocket and dialed Jeremy's number.

"Jeremy," I said.

"Cole St. Clair," he replied, slow and easy, like he wasn't surprised. There was a pause on the other side of the line. And because he knew me, he didn't have to wait for me to say it. "You're not coming home, are you?"

Chapter Thirty-Seven

· SAM ·

They questioned me in a kitchen.

The Mercy Falls Police Department was small and apparently ill-prepared for questioning. Koenig led me past a room full of dispatchers — they stopped mid-conversation to watch me — and two offices full of desks and uniforms bowed around computers, and finally into a tiny room with a sink, refrigerator, and two vending machines. It was lunchtime and the room smelled overwhelmingly like microwaved Mexican dinners and vomit. It was excruciatingly hot.

Koenig directed me into a light wooden chair at a folding table and cleared off a few napkins, a plate with a half-eaten lemon bar, and a can of soda. Dumping them in the trash, he stood just outside the door, his back to me. All I could see of him was the back of his head, the straight edge of his stubble-short hair on the back of his neck eerily perfect. He had a dark burn scar at the edge of his hair; the scar trickled to a point that disappeared into the collar of his shirt. It occurred to me that there was a story behind the scar — maybe not as dramatic as the story of my wrists, but a story nonetheless — and the fact that everyone had a story behind some mark on their inside or outside suddenly exhausted me, the gravity of all those untold pasts.

Koenig was speaking in a low voice to someone in the hall. I only caught snatches of his words. "Samuel Roth . . . no . . . warrant . . . body? . . . what he finds."

My stomach felt instantly sick, crushed by the heat. It was churning and turning over and I suddenly had the horrible feeling that, despite the heat, *because* of the heat, I was going to shift here in this little room and there would be no way out.

I lay my head on my arms; the table smelled like old food but was cool against my skin. My stomach pinched and squeezed and, for the first time in months, I felt unsafe in my own skin.

Please don't shift. Please don't shift.

I repeated this in my head with every breath.

"Samuel Roth?"

I lifted my head. A pouch-eyed officer was standing in the doorway. He smelled like tobacco. It felt like everything in this room was designed as a specific assault on my wolf senses.

"I'm Officer Heifort. Do you mind if Officer Koenig is in the room while we talk?"

I didn't trust myself to talk, so I just shook my head, my arms still pressed against the table. The contents of my chest felt weightless and loose inside me.

Heifort pulled out the chair opposite — he had to pull it out quite a bit to make room for his paunch. He had a notepad and a folder that he laid on the table in front of him. Behind him, Koenig appeared in the doorway, arms crossed over his chest. Koenig looked infinitely more like a cop to me, very official and built, but still, the familiarity of his presence had a calming effect. The paunchy detective looked far too delighted by the concept of questioning me.

"What we're gonna do," he said, "is we're gonna ask you a few questions and you just answer them the best you can, all right?" His voice had a joviality that didn't make it to his eyes.

I nodded.

"Where's your daddy at these days, Sam? We haven't seen Geoffrey Beck around for a long while," Heifort asked.

I said, "He's been sick." It was easier to say a lie that I'd used before.

"That's too bad," Heifort said. "Sick how?"

"Cancer," I said. I looked at the table and mumbled, "He's getting treatment in Minneapolis."

Heifort wrote this down. I wished he hadn't.

"What's the address of the center, do you know?" he asked.

I shrugged. I tried to invest the shrug with sadness.

Koenig said, "I'll help track it down later."

Heifort wrote that down, too.

I said, "What am I being questioned about?" I suspected that this was not really about Beck, but about Grace, and some essential part of me resisted the idea of being taken into custody for the disappearance of someone I had been holding in my arms the night before.

"Well, since you asked," Heifort said, and slid the folder out from under the notepad. He removed a photo and put it in front of me.

It was a close-up of a foot. A girl's foot, slender and long. Both foot and what I could see of the bare leg rested among leaves. There was blood between the toes.

There was a long pause between my breath and the next one.

Heifort placed another photograph on top of that one.

I winced and looked away, both relieved and horrified.

"Does that mean anything to you?"

It was an over-flashed photograph of a naked girl, pale as snow, thin as a whisper, sprawled in the leaves. Her face and neck were a disaster zone. And I knew her. The last time I'd seen that girl she'd had a tan and a smile and a pulse.

Oh, Olivia. I'm so sorry.

"Why are you showing me that?" I asked. I couldn't look at the photo. Olivia hadn't deserved to be killed by wolves. No one deserved to die like that.

"We were hoping you might tell us," Heifort said. As he spoke, he laid out more photos in front of me, each a different vantage point of the dead girl. I wanted him to stop. Needed him to stop. "Seeing as she was found a few yards from Geoffrey Beck's property line. Naked. After being missing for quite a long time."

A bare shoulder smeared with blood. Skin written with dirt. Palm to the sky. I closed my eyes, but I couldn't stop seeing the images from the photos. I could feel them burrowing into me, living inside me, becoming something to populate my nightmares.

"I didn't kill anyone," I said. It sounded false when I said it. Like it was in a language I didn't speak, and I said it with inflection so wrong that the words didn't even make sense together.

"Oh, this was the work of wolves," Heifort said. "They killed her. But I don't think they put her on that property naked."

I opened my eyes, but I didn't look at the photographs. There was a bulletin board on the wall, and there was a piece of paper tacked there that said PLEASE CLEAN THE MICROWAVE IF YOUR LUNCH EXPLODES IN THERE. THNX, MANAGEMENT.

"I swear I had nothing to do with it. I didn't know where she was. This wasn't *me*." I had this heavy, heavy feeling inside me that I knew who it was, though. I added, "Why would I possibly do that?"

"Honestly, son, I have no idea," Heifort said. I wasn't sure why he said *son*, as the rest of his tone was entirely at odds with it. "Some sick son of a bitch did this, and it's hard for me to get in that mindset. What I do know is this: Two young girls who knew you have disappeared in the last year. You were the last person to see one of them. Your foster father hasn't been heard from in months and you're the only one who seems to know where he is. Now there's a body near your residence, naked and half-near starved, and it seems like the sort of thing only a really troubled SOB would do. And I have right now in front of me a guy who was abused by his parents and they tell me that screws you up pretty well. Would you care to comment on that?"

His voice was slow and genial the entire time he spoke. Koenig was studying a print of a ship that had never been anywhere near Minnesota.

When Heifort had first started speaking, a tiny fleck of anger had scratched and twisted inside me, and every moment he kept on, that fleck grew and grew. After everything I'd lived through, I was not going to be reduced to a one-sentence definition. I lifted my gaze to Heifort's and held it. I saw his eyes tighten a bit and knew that, as always, the yellow of mine was disconcerting. I felt suddenly, utterly calm, and somewhere in my voice, I heard echoes of Beck. "Is there a question in there, Officer? I thought you wanted me to account for my time or describe my attachment to my father or tell you I would do anything for Grace. But it sounds an awful lot like really what you want me to do is defend my mental health. I can't tell what it is you think I've done. Are you accusing me of kidnapping girls? Or killing my father? Or do you just think I'm screwed up?"

"Hey now," Heifort said. "I didn't accuse you of anything, Mr. Roth. You just slow that teen rage right down now, because no one is accusing you of anything."

I didn't feel bad for lying to him earlier, if he was going to lie to me now. Like hell he wasn't accusing me.

"What do you want me to say?" I shoved all the photos of the girl — Olivia — at him. "*That's* horrible. But I didn't have anything to do with it."

Heifort left the photos where they were. He turned in his chair to give Koenig a meaningful glance, but Koenig's expression didn't change. Then he turned back around to me, his chair groaning and clicking. He rubbed one pouched eye. "I want to know where Geoffrey

Beck and Grace Brisbane are, Samuel. I've been round the block enough times to know that coincidences don't just happen. And you know what the common factor is between all these things? You."

I didn't say anything. I wasn't the common factor.

"So are you going to cooperate and tell me something about all this, or are you going to make me do it the hard way?" Heifort asked.

"I don't have anything to tell you," I said.

Heifort looked at me for a long time, as if he were waiting for my expression to betray something. "I think your daddy didn't do you any favors training you in lawyer talk," he said finally. "Is that all you got to say?"

I had lots more to say, but not to him. If it had been Koenig asking, I would have told him that I didn't want Grace to be missing. That I wanted Beck back. That he wasn't my *foster* father, he was my father. That I didn't know what was going on with Olivia, but that I was just trying to keep my head above water. I wanted them to leave me alone. That was all. Just leave me alone to work through this on my own.

I said, "Yes."

Heifort was just frowning at me. I couldn't tell if he believed me or not. After a space, he said, "I guess we're done for now. William, take care of him, would you?"

Koenig nodded shortly as Heifort pushed away from the table. Breathing felt slightly easier after Heifort had gone down the hall.

"I'll take you back to your car," Koenig told me. He made an efficient gesture that meant for me to stand. I did — surprised, for some reason, that the floor felt solid beneath my feet. My legs felt vaguely jellied.

I started down the hall after Koenig, but he stopped when his cell phone rang. He retrieved it from his duty belt and examined it.

"Hold on," Koenig said. "I have to take this call. Hello, William Koenig. Okay, sir. Wait. What happened now?"

I put my hands in my pockets. I felt light-headed: strung out from the questioning, from not eating, from the images of Olivia. I could hear Heifort's voice booming through the open door of the dispatch room to my left. The dispatchers laughed at something he said. It was weird to think that he could just switch it off like that — righteous anger at that girl's death instantly changing to office jokes in the next room over.

Koenig, on the phone, was trying to convince someone that if his estranged wife had taken his car that it was not theft as it was co-marital property.

I heard, "Hey, Tom."

There were probably dozens of Toms in Mercy Falls. But I knew instantly which one it was. I recognized the odor of his aftershave and the prickling of my skin.

The dispatch room had a window to the hall on the opposite side from us, and I saw Tom Culpeper. He was jingling his keys in the pocket of his coat — one of those barn coats described as *rugged* and *classic* and *four hundred dollars* that were usually worn by people who spend more time in Land Rovers than barns. His face had the gray, sagging look of someone who hasn't slept, but his voice sounded smooth and in control. Lawyer voice.

I tried to decide what was worse: risk talking to Culpeper, or brave the puke smell in the kitchen. I contemplated retreat.

Heifort said, "Tom! Hey, devil. Hold on, let me get you in." He breezed out of the dispatch room, down the dogleg hall that led around to the room where Culpeper was, and opened the door. He clapped a hand on Culpeper's shoulder. Of course they knew each other. "You here for work or are you just stirring up trouble?"

"Just coming to see about that coroner's report," Culpeper said. "What did Geoffrey Beck's kid have to say about it?"

Heifort stepped back just enough that Culpeper could see past him to where I stood.

"Speak of the devil," Culpeper said.

It would've been polite to say hi. I didn't say anything.

"How's your old man?" Culpeper asked. When he asked, it was deeply ironic, not only because it was clear that he didn't care, but also because Culpeper was so far from the sort of person that would say "old man" that it was obvious he was being sarcastic. He added, "I'm surprised he's not down here with you."

My voice was stiff. "He would be if he could."

"I've been talking with Lewis Brisbane," Culpeper said. "Speaking of legal advice. The Brisbanes know I'm there for them if they need it."

I couldn't quite bring myself to fully ponder the implications of Tom Culpeper acting as lawyer and confidant for Grace's parents. In any case, the possibility of any cordial future with them seemed incredibly distant. The possibility of *any* future that I had hoped for seemed incredibly distant.

"You really are completely gorked, aren't you?" Tom Culpeper said with wonder, and I realized I had been silent for too long, unaware of what my expression had been doing while I was lost in my dismay. He shook his head, not so much cruel as struck by the strangeness of us misfits. "Word for the wise: Try the insanity plea. God bless America. Beck always has liked them cracked."

Heifort, to his credit, tried not to smile.

Koenig snapped his phone shut. His eyes were narrowed. "Gentlemen," he said, "I am taking Mr. Roth back to his vehicle now, unless you need him for anything else."

Heifort shook his head, slow and portentous.

Culpeper turned toward me, his hands in his pockets. There was no anger in his voice. Of course, there wouldn't be — he had all the cards in this game. "When you next see your father," he told me, "you can tell him that his wolves will all be gone in fourteen days. Should've been done a long time ago. I don't know what you all thought you were playing with, but it's done."

And I saw Tom Culpeper looking after me, not vindictive. Just a raw wound reopened too frequently to ever heal. How could I judge him? He didn't know the truth. He couldn't know. He thought they were nothing but animals, and us careless neighbors with misplaced priorities.

But I also saw this: It would not stop until we were dead.

Koenig took my arm and looked over his shoulder at Culpeper. "I think you are confusing the son with the father, Mr. Culpeper."

"Maybe," Culpeper said. "You know what they say about apples and trees, though."

The thing about that saying was that it was pretty true.

Koenig said, "It's time to go."

Chapter Thirty-Eight

· GRACE ·

Sam was late coming home.

I wouldn't be worried.

Without him, I was restless and useless in Beck's house; at least when I was a wolf, I didn't feel my lack of purpose and goal so strongly. I'd never realized just how much of my day, before, was filled with homework and cooking and planning crazy things with Rachel and yet more homework and Olivia and library visits and repairing the loose board on the deck because Dad would never get around to it. Reading was a reward for work, and without work, I couldn't seem to settle down with a book, though Beck's basement was full of them.

All I'd thought about before was graduating with good enough grades that I didn't have to worry about where I went to college. And then, after I'd met Sam, keeping him human was added to that list.

Now, neither of those things really applied.

I had so much free time that free time was meaningless. I felt like I did on school breaks. Mom had said once that I didn't know how to have downtime and that I should be sedated when I didn't have school. I had thought that was a little harsh of her, but now, it made sense.

I washed the six articles of clothing I had at Beck's house, cleaned the backlog of dishes in the sink, and finally, I called Isabel because I couldn't call anybody else and if I didn't talk to someone, I'd start crying about Olivia and that wouldn't do anybody any good.

"Tell me why it's a bad idea to tell Rachel I'm alive," I said as soon as Isabel picked up her phone.

"Because she will go crazy and then break down and make a scene and eventually her parents will find out and she won't lie and then everyone will know," Isabel said. "Any other questions? No."

"Rachel can be sensible."

"She just found out that one of her friends had her throat torn out by wolves. She won't be sensible."

I didn't say anything. The only thing that kept me sane was keeping Olivia's death abstract. If I started thinking about how it had happened, how it couldn't have been quick, how she didn't deserve to die — if I started thinking about what it had felt like to lie in the snow and have my skin jerked off my bones by wolves, imagining that Sam hadn't been there to stop them — I couldn't believe that Isabel had said it. I wanted to hang up right then. The only thing that kept me on the phone was the knowledge that if I hung up, I'd be all alone with that image of her death rolling around in my head again and again.

Isabel said, "At least that's how I was with Jack. *Sensible* is not a word I would've used for myself."

I swallowed.

"Grace, don't take it so personally. It's fact. The sooner that you get a grip on the facts, the better you'll be. Now stop thinking about it. Why do you want to tell Rachel?"

I blinked until my eyes were clear. I was glad Cole wasn't here. He thought that I was some sort of iron maiden and I didn't like to convince him otherwise. Only Sam was allowed to see what a mess I really was, because Sam knowing felt like *me* knowing. I told Isabel, "Because she's my friend and I don't want her thinking I'm dead. And because I'd kind of like to talk to her! She's not as silly as you think."

"So sentimental," Isabel said. Not in a mean way. "You asked me to tell you why it was a bad idea, and I did. I'm not going to change my answer."

I sighed. It was uneven and conveyed more unhappiness than I meant for it to.

"Fine," Isabel snapped, as if I'd yelled at her. "Talk to her. Don't blame me if she can't handle the truth." She laughed then, at some joke that only she got, before going on. "I wouldn't tell her the wolf part, only the alive part. I mean, assuming you listen to me."

"I always listen to you. Except when I don't."

"There's the old Grace. That's better. I was starting to think you'd become completely lame."

I smiled then, to myself, because it was the closest I'd get to emotional truth from Isabel. Then another thing occurred to me.

"Could you do something else for me?" I asked Isabel.

"It never ends."

"Well, I don't know how else to find out. I don't even know if you can find this out without making people suspicious. But if anyone could, you could."

"Keep the compliments coming, Grace. Every bit helps."

"Your hair is also really nice," I said, and she laughed her hard laugh. "I want to know if I could still graduate, if I did summer school."

"Wouldn't that require you to be *human*? Not that some of the mouth-breathers there this year seem to be."

"I'm getting there," I said. "I think I could make it work. Once I get unmissing."

"You know what you need?" Isabel asked. "A good lawyer."

I'd already thought about it. I wasn't sure what Minnesota State Law said about runaways, which was what I was sure to be classified as. It seemed incredibly unfair that I might end up with a mark on my record because of this, but I'd deal with it. "I know this girl whose father is one."

Now Isabel really laughed. "I'll find out," she said. "Only you would be concerned about finishing high school while you're turning into another species in your spare time. It's slightly refreshing to see that some things never change. Geek. Nerd. Teacher's pet. Oh — pet — that has become funny now that you grow fur."

"I'm glad I could amuse you," I said, pretending to be hurt.

Isabel laughed again. "Me, too."

CHAPTER THIRTY-NINE

· SAM ·

This time, Koenig gestured for me to ride in the front seat of the police car. The car had gotten hot under the unmitigated attention of the sun, and Koenig combated the heat by cranking the air-conditioning on full blast. It was so cold that little drops of moisture kept hitting my face. The wolf that must still be inside me didn't stir. Everything smelled like pine cleaner.

Koenig turned off the radio. It was playing '70s rock.

I was thinking about Culpeper shooting my family from a helicopter.

The only sound in the car was the occasional crackle of the radio clipped on Koenig's shoulder. My stomach growled, audibly, and Koenig leaned across me to let the glove box fall open into my knees. There was a package of crackers in there, and two candy bars.

I took the crackers.

"Thanks," I said. They hadn't been offered in such a way that gratitude felt uncomfortable.

Koenig didn't look at me. "I know that Heifort was wrong," he said. "I know what the common factor is, and it's not you."

I realized that he had not turned toward the bookstore. We were headed away from Mercy Falls, not toward it.

"Then what is it?" I asked. There was something like anticipation hanging in the air. He could have said *Beck* or *Boundary Wood* or anything, really. But I didn't think he was going to.

"The wolves," Koenig said.

I held my breath. The dispatcher's voice, fuzzy, crackled over the radio. "Unit Seventeen?"

Koenig pressed a button on the radio and leaned his head toward his shoulder. "I'm en route with a passenger. Will call when I'm clear."

"Ten-four," she replied.

He waited a moment, and then he said, still not looking at me, "Now tell me the truth, Sam, because there is no more time for dancing around it. Tell me now, the truth, not what you told Heifort. Where is Geoffrey Beck?"

The tires were loud on the road. We were nowhere near Mercy Falls. Trees flew by us, and I remembered the day I drove to get Grace from the tackle shop. It seemed like a million years ago.

There was no way I could trust him. There was no way that he was prepared for the truth, and even if he was, this was our number one rule: We didn't tell anyone about ourselves. Especially not an officer of the law who had just been standing in the room while I was accused of kidnapping and murder.

"I don't know," I muttered. Barely audible over the road noise.

Koenig set his mouth and shook his head. "I was there at the first wolf hunt, Sam. It wasn't legal, and I regret it. The whole town was choking on Jack Culpeper's death. I was there when they drove them through the woods to get them up against the lake. I saw a wolf that night and I have never, ever forgotten it. They are going to drive those wolves from the woods and shoot every single one of them from the air, Sam, and I saw the paperwork to prove it. Now I am going to ask you again, and you are going to tell me the truth because you and the wolves are out of options except for me. Tell me straight, Sam. *Where is Geoffrey Beck?*"

I closed my eyes.

Behind my eyelids, I saw Olivia's dead body. And I saw Tom Culpeper's face.

"He's in Boundary Wood."

Koenig let out a long, long hiss of breath between his teeth.

"Grace Brisbane, too," he said. "Right?"

I didn't open my eyes.

"And you," Koenig said. "You were there. Tell me that I am crazy. Tell me I am wrong. Tell me that when I saw a wolf that night with Geoffrey Beck's eyes, I was wrong."

Now I opened my eyes. I had to see what his face looked like when he said this. He was staring straight through the windshield, eyebrows drawn together. The uncertainty made him younger; made the uniform less daunting.

"You're not wrong," I said.

"There is no cancer."

I shook my head. Koenig didn't turn his head, but he nodded a tiny nod, as if to himself.

"There are no leads on Grace Brisbane not because she disappeared, but because she is —" Koenig stopped himself. He couldn't say it.

I realized that I was letting a lot ride on this moment. On whether or not he finished this sentence. Whether he grabbed the truth like Isabel had, or whether he pushed it away or warped it to fit some religion or changed it to match a less strange worldview, like my parents had.

I kept looking at him.

"A wolf." Koenig kept his eyes on the road, but his hands twisted around the steering wheel. "We cannot find her or Beck because they're wolves."

"Yes."

Koenig shook his head. "My father used to tell me wolf stories. He told me he had a friend in college who was a werewolf, and we used to laugh at him. We could never tell if he was telling a story or telling the truth."

"It's true." My heart was thudding with our secret hanging out there between us. Suddenly, in light of his suspicions, I was replaying every conversation I'd had with Koenig. I was trying to see if it changed how I saw him, and it didn't.

"Then why — I cannot believe I am asking this, but why are they staying wolves if the pack is about to be eliminated?"

"It's involuntary. Temperature based. Wolf in winter, human in summer. Less time every year, and eventually we stay a wolf forever. We don't keep our human thoughts when we shift." I frowned. This explanation was getting less true every day that we spent with Cole. It was a strangely disorienting feeling, to have something you'd relied on for so long start to change, like finding out that gravity no longer worked on Mondays. "That's grossly oversimplified. But it's the basic rules of it." I felt weird saying *grossly oversimplified*, too; a phrase like that was only because Koenig spoke so formally.

"So Grace —"

"Is missing because she's still unstable in this weather. What is she supposed to tell her parents?"

Koenig considered. "Are you born a werewolf?"

"No, good old horror movie technique. Biting."

"And Olivia?"

"Bitten last year."

Koenig snorted softly. "Just incredible. I knew it. I kept finding things that led me back to that, and I could not believe it. And when Grace Brisbane disappeared out of the hospital and left just that bloody hospital gown behind . . . they said she was dying, that there was no way that she could have left under her own power."

"She needed to shift," I said softly.

"Everyone in the department blamed you. They have been looking for a way to crucify you. Tom Culpeper more than anyone. He has Heifort and everyone else lapping out of a bowl." Now he sounded a little bitter, and it made me look at him in an entirely different way. I could see him out of uniform, at home, getting a beer out of the fridge, petting his dog, watching TV. A real person, something separate from the uniformed identity I'd assigned him. "They would very much like to hang you with this."

"Well, that's great," I said. "Because all I can do is tell them I didn't do anything. Until Grace gets stable enough to reappear. And Olivia . . ."

Koenig paused. "Why did they kill her?"

My head was full of Shelby, her eyes on me through the kitchen window, the desperation and anger I thought I'd seen there. "I don't think there was a 'they.' There's one wolf that has been behind all of the problems. She attacked Grace before. She attacked Jack Culpeper, too. The others wouldn't kill a girl. Not near summer. There are other ways to get food." I had to try, very deliberately, to push away the memory of Olivia's destroyed body.

We rode in silence for a minute or two.

"So, this is the situation," Koenig said, and I was kind of charmed, now, to see that he sounded like a cop no matter what he said. "They have clearance to eliminate the pack. Fourteen days is not very long. You are telling me that some of them probably will be unable to shift before then, and some of them cannot shift at all. So we're talking mass murder."

Finally. It was relieving and terrifying to hear Culpeper's plan defined as such.

"And there are not many options here. You could reveal the wolves for what they are, but —"

"I don't think that's a good idea," I said hurriedly.

"— I was going to say that I do not think that is feasible. Telling Mercy Falls that they have a pack of wolves carrying an incurable infectious disease right after we discover that they have killed a girl . . ."

"Won't end well," I finished.

"And the other option is to try to motivate more animal rights groups to save the pack as wolves. It didn't work in Idaho, and I think the time frame will be impossible, but . . ."

I said, "We thought of moving them."

Koenig stilled. "Go on."

I stumbled over the words. Koenig was so precise and logical that I felt, again, as if I needed to match it. "Someplace farther away from people. But then . . . it could just put us in a worse situation, unless we know what the people are like. And I don't know what the pack will be like in a new place, without boundaries. I don't know if I should try to sell Beck's house to buy land, or what. There's not enough money to buy a complete territory. Wolves range hugely, over miles and miles. So there's always a chance of trouble."

Koenig drummed his fingers on the wheel, eyes narrowed. A long moment of silence went by. I was glad of it. I needed it. The ramifications of my confession to Koenig felt unpredictable.

"I am just talking as I'm thinking," Koenig said finally, "but I have property, a few hours farther up in the Boundary Waters. It was my father's, but I just inherited it."

I started, "I . . . don't . . ."

"It's a peninsula," Koenig interrupted me. "Pretty big one. Used to be an old resort, but that's all shut down because of old family politics. The end of it is fenced off. Not the best of fence, just box wire between trees in some places, but it could be reinforced."

He glanced over at me at the same time that I looked at him, and I knew we were both thinking: This might be it.

"I don't think a peninsula, even a big one, would be big enough to support the pack. We'd have to feed them," I said.

"So you feed them," Koenig said.

"And are there campers?" I asked.

"It faces mining land," Koenig replied. "Mining company hasn't been active since sixty-seven, but they hold on to the land. There's a reason why the resort didn't make it."

I chewed my lip. It was hard to believe in hope. "We'd still have to get them there, somehow."

"Quietly," Koenig advised. "Tom Culpeper won't consider relocation an alternative to their deaths."

"And quickly," I said. I was thinking about how long Cole had been unsuccessfully trying to trap wolves, however, and how long it would take to catch twenty-odd wolves and how we would transport them hours north.

Koenig was silent. Finally, he said, "Maybe it's not a good idea. But you can consider it an option."

An option. Option meant a plausible course of action, and I wasn't sure it was even that. But what else did we have?

CHAPTER FORTY

· GRACE ·

The interminable day finally ended when Sam came home with a pizza and an uncertain smile. Over the pizza, Sam told me everything that Koenig had said. We sat cross-legged on the floor of his room, his desk lamp and Christmas lights turned on, the pizza box between us. The desk lamp was next to the one sloping wall by the roof, and the way the wall diverted the light made the room seem warm and cave-like. The CD player by Sam's bed was turned on, low, some smoky voice singing to a piano.

Sam described everything that had happened, making a little sweeping motion with his fingers across the floor with each one, as if unconsciously moving the last thing out of the way before he told me the next. Everything was a sort of a wreck, and I felt completely adrift, but I couldn't help but think how much I liked to look at him in this low yellow light. He was not as soft as when I'd first met him, not as young, but the angles of his face, his quick gestures, the way he sucked in his lower lip to think before going on — I was in love with all of it.

Sam asked me what I thought.

"Of?"

"All of it. What do we do?"

He was stunningly trusting of my ability to logic it all through. It was such a lot to take in — Koenig guessing the secret of the wolves, the idea of moving being plausible, the thought of trusting all our fates to someone we barely knew. How did we know that he would keep our secret?

"I need another piece of pizza to answer that," I said. "Didn't Cole want any?"

Sam said, "He told me he was fasting. I don't think I want to know why. He didn't seem unhappy."

I pulled the crust off a piece of pizza; Sam took what was left. I sighed. The idea of leaving Boundary Wood was a disheartening one. "I'm thinking it wouldn't have to be permanent. The wolves being on the peninsula, I mean. We could come up with a better idea later, after the hunt business had all died down."

"We have to get them out of the woods first." He closed the pizza box and traced the logo with a finger.

"Did Koenig say he'd help you get out of trouble? I mean, about me being missing? Obviously he knows you didn't kidnap and kill me," I said. "Does he have some way to get them off your back?"

"I don't know. He didn't say anything."

I tried to keep the frustration out of my voice; I wasn't really frustrated with *him*. "Don't you think that's kind of important?"

"I guess? The wolves have only got two weeks. I can worry about clearing my name afterward. I don't think the cops can find anything to pin on me," Sam said. But he wasn't looking at me.

"I thought the cops didn't suspect you anymore," I said. "I thought Koenig knew."

"*Koenig* knows. No one else. He can't just tell them I'm innocent."

"Sam!"

He shrugged, not meeting my gaze. "There's nothing I can do about it right now."

The thought of him being questioned in the police department was acutely painful. The idea that my parents might think him capable of hurting me was even worse. And the possibility that he could be tried for murder was unthinkable.

An idea presented itself.

"I have to tell my parents," I said. I thought about my conversation with Isabel earlier that day. "Or Rachel. Or someone. I have to let someone know that I'm alive. No dead Grace, no murder mystery."

"And your parents will be understanding," Sam said.

"I don't know what they'll be, Sam! But I'm not going to just let you — let you go to jail." I wadded my napkin and threw it at the pizza box angrily. We'd so narrowly avoided being pulled apart — it seemed appalling to think that after everything else, an entirely man-made, unscientific event might be what finally separated us. And there was Sam, looking guilty, as if he believed that he'd been responsible for my supposed death. "No matter how bad my parents are, that's worse."

Sam looked at me. "Do you trust them?"

"Sam, they're not going to try to kill me," I snapped.

I stopped and put my hands over my nose and mouth, my breath coming out in a rush.

Sam's face didn't change. The napkin he had been very carefully ripping apart stilled in his hands.

I covered my whole face now. I couldn't stand to look at him. "I'm sorry, Sam," I said. "I'm sorry." The thought of his face, unchanging, gaze steady and lupine — I felt tears trying to tease themselves out of my eyes.

I heard the floor creak as he stood up. I pulled my hands away from my face. "Please don't go," I whispered. "I'm sorry."

"I got you a present," Sam said. "I forgot it in the car. I'm going to go get it." He touched the top of my head as he went quietly out, shutting the door.

So I was still feeling like the most terrible person in the world when he gave me the dress. He was sitting on his knees in front of me like a penitent, watching my face carefully as I pulled it out. For some reason I thought, at first, that it would be skimpy underwear, and I felt relieved and disappointed, somehow, when it was a pretty summer dress instead. I couldn't seem to sort out my emotions lately.

I flattened the top out with my hand, smoothing the fabric, looking at the fine straps. It was a dress for a hot, carefree summer, which felt like a long time from now. I looked up at Sam and saw that he was biting the inside of his lip, watching my reaction.

"You're the nicest boy ever," I told him, feeling undeserving and terrible. "You didn't have to get me anything. I like thinking about you thinking about me when I'm not around." I reached out and put my hand on his cheek. He turned his face and kissed my palm; his lips inside my hand made something inside me squeeze. My voice was a little lower when I said, "Should I go try it on now?"

In the bathroom, it took me several long minutes how to work out putting it on, though there was nothing complicated about it. I was unused to wearing dresses, and I felt like I had nothing on. I stood on the edge of the tub to look in the mirror, trying to imagine what had made Sam look at this dress and say *Get that for Grace.* Was it because he thought I would like it? Because he thought it was sexy? Because he wanted to get me something and this happened to be the first thing? I wasn't sure why it made a difference whether he had asked a salesgirl what his girlfriend would like versus found it hanging on a hanger and imagined my body in it.

In the mirror, I thought I looked like a college girl, confident, pretty. Sure of what would show off her body to its best advantage. I smoothed the front of the dress; the skirt tickled and teased my legs. I could just see the curve of my breasts. Suddenly it seemed very urgent to go back to the room so that Sam could see me. It seemed very urgent to make him look at me and touch me.

But when I made it back to the room and slid in the doorway, I was abruptly self-conscious. Sam was sitting on the floor, leaning against his bed with his eyes closed, listening to the music, far away from this room, but he opened his eyes when I shut the door behind me. I made a face, twisted my hands behind my back.

"What do you think?" I asked.

He scrambled to his feet.

"Oh," he said.

I said, "The only thing is that I couldn't do the tie in the back myself."

Sam took a breath and stepped to me. I could feel my heart pounding, though I couldn't understand why it was. He picked up the ties where they attached to the side of the dress and put his arms behind me. But instead of tying them, he dropped the ties and pressed his hands up against my back, his hands hot through the thin cotton of the dress. It felt like there was nothing between his fingertips and my skin. His face rested on my neck. I could hear him breathing; each breath sounded measured, restrained.

I whispered, "You like it, then?"

Then, all of a sudden, we were kissing. It felt like such a long time since we'd kissed like this, like it was deadly serious — for a second, all I thought was, *I just ate pizza*, until I realized that Sam had, too. Sam slid his hands around to rest on my hips, wrinkling the fabric, erasing my doubt, his fingers tight with wanting. Just that, just the heat of his palms through the dress, holding my hips, was enough to make my insides twist fiercely. I was wound so tightly it hurt. A little sigh escaped from me.

"I can stop," he said, "if you're not ready."

"Don't," I said. "Don't stop."

So, kneeling on the bed, we kept kissing, and he kept touching, careful, like he had never touched me before. It was like he couldn't remember what shape I'd had before, and he was rediscovering it. He felt where my shoulder blades pressed against the fabric of the dress. Skimmed his palm along my shoulders. His fingers traced along the swell of my breast at the edge of the dress.

I closed my eyes. There were other things in the world that demanded our attention, but right now, all I could think of were my thighs and Sam's hands running up them under my skirt, pushing the fabric up like summer clouds around me. When I opened my eyes, my hands pressed on top of Sam's hands, there were a hundred shadows beneath us. Every one of them was Sam or me, but it was impossible to tell which was which.

Chapter Forty-One

· COLE ·

This new concoction felt like poison.

Sometime after midnight, I stepped outside. It was black as death on the other side of the back door, but I listened to make certain I was alone. My stomach was tight with hunger, a sensation at once painful and productive. Concrete proof that I was working. The fasting had made me jittery and watchful, a cruel sort of high. I lay my notebook with the details of my experiments on the step so that Sam would know where I'd gone if I didn't come back. The woods hissed at me. They didn't sleep even if everyone else did.

I rested the needle against the inside of my wrist and closed my eyes.

My heart was already kicking like a rabbit.

In the syringe, the liquid was colorless as spit and thin as a lie. In my veins, it was razors and sand, fire and mercury. A knife notched every vertebrae in my spine. I had exactly twenty-three seconds to wonder if I'd killed myself this time and eleven more to realize that I was hoping I hadn't. Three more after that to wish that I'd stayed in my bed. That left two to think *holy shit*.

I burst out of my human body, splitting my skin so fast that I felt it slough off my bones. My heart was exploding. Overhead, the stars wheeled and focused. I grabbed for the stair, the wall, the ground, anything that wasn't moving. My notebook skidded off the back step, my body plummeting to join it, and then I was running.

I'd found it. The mixture I was going to use to jerk Beck from his wolf body.

Even as a wolf, I was still healing, joints knitting back together, skin stitching shut along my spine, cells reinventing themselves with every massive stride I took. I was an incredible machine. This wolf body I wore was keeping me alive even as it dragged at and stole my human thoughts.

You're Cole St. Clair.

One of us had to be able to maintain our thoughts if we were going to move the wolves. Had to at least be able to remember enough to gather the wolves together, get them to one place. There had to be some way to convince a wolf brain to keep a simple goal.

Cole St. Clair

I tried to hold on to it. I wanted to hold on to it. What good was it, to make myself shift, to conquer the wolf for just a few moments, when I didn't get to keep the triumph of it?

Cole

There was nothing these woods had to say that I couldn't hear. The wind was screaming past my ears as I ran. My paws were sure over fallen branches and through brambles, toenails clicking when I scrambled across exposed rocks. The ground dropped out beneath me, dipping into a culvert, and I sailed over it. Halfway through the air, I realized I wasn't alone. Half a dozen bodies leaped with me, light shapes in the dark night. Their scents identified them, more specific than names. My pack. Surrounded by these other wolves, I was secure, certain, invincible. Teeth snapped by my ear, playful, and images flashed between us: The culvert growing to a ravine. The soft ground where a dusty rabbit warren waited to be dug up. The sky, black and endless above us.

Sam Roth's face.

I hesitated.

The images surged back and forth, harder to catch as most of the wolves left me behind. My thoughts were stretching larger to hold the concept of a name and a face. *Sam Roth.* I dropped to a walk, the image and the words held in my head until they had no association with each other. When one of the wolves doubled back to jostle against me, I snapped at it until it realized I was not up for a wrestle. The other wolf licked at my chin, confirming the dominance I already assumed. After a moment, I snapped at it again, just for some quiet. I padded back the way I had come, nose to the ground, ears pricked. I scouted for something I couldn't quite understand.

Sam Roth.

I moved slowly through the dark woods, cautious. If nothing else, I hunted for an explanation for that image tossed to me: a human face.

My spine stung as my hackles rose, fast and inexplicable.

Then her body hit me.

The white she-wolf buried her teeth in my ruff as I staggered for my balance under her weight. She'd taken me by surprise and her grip wasn't great, so with a snarl, I shook her off. We circled each other. Her ears were pricked, listening to my movement; the darkness masked me. Her white coat, on the other hand, stood out like a wound. Everything about her posture was aggressive. She didn't smell afraid, but she wasn't large. She would back down, and if she didn't, the fight wouldn't last long.

I underestimated her.

When she hit me the second time, her paws wrapped around my shoulders like an embrace, and her teeth found a hold beneath my jawbone. Her grip ground closer and surer to my windpipe. I let her push me onto my back so that I could kick her belly with my back legs. It only broke her hold for a moment. She was fast, efficient, fearless. She had my ear next, and I felt the heat exploding out of me before I felt the wetness of the blood. When I twisted away from her, it felt like my skin was shredding between her teeth. We charged up against each other, chest to chest. Seizing her throat, I crumpled skin and fur in my teeth, hanging on with all I was worth. She was out of my grip like she was water.

Now she had a hold on the side of my face, and her teeth scraped bone. She got a better grip, and this was the one that mattered.

My eye.

I scrambled backward, desperate, trying to dislodge her before she ruined my face, destroyed my eye. I had no pride. I whimpered and flattened my ears back, trying to submit, but she wasn't interested. There was a snarl rippling out of her that vibrated through my skull. My eye would explode with the sound if she didn't puncture it first.

Her teeth slid closer. My muscles were trembling. Bracing themselves already for the pain.

Suddenly she cried out and released me. I backed up, shaking my head, blood matting the side of my face, my ear still screaming pain. In front of me, the white wolf cowered submissively before a large gray wolf. A black wolf stood just behind him, ears pricked with aggression. The pack had returned.

The gray wolf turned toward me, and behind him, I saw the white wolf's ears instantly lift from their position of surrender. Without his gaze on her, everything about her bristled with rebellion. Everything said *I give up, for now, while you're watching.* Her eyes were unflinching on me. It was a threat, I understood now. I was meant to take my place below her in the pack, or someday fight her again. Maybe the pack wouldn't be around then to stop her.

I wasn't ready to back down.

I stared back.

The gray wolf took a few steps to me, passing me images of my torn face as he did. He nosed my ear cautiously. He was wary; I was smelling less and less of wolf and more and more of the thing I was when I wasn't a wolf. My strange body was working hard to heal my face and to pull me back into a human. It wasn't cold enough to keep me in this skin.

The white wolf stared at me.

I could feel that I didn't have long. My brain was stretching again.

Beside me, the gray wolf growled, and I jerked until I realized that it was directed at the she-wolf. He stepped away from me, still growling, and now, the black wolf was growling, too. The white wolf stepped back. One step, then another. They were leaving me.

A shudder twitched through my body, ending just under my eye, stinging. I was shifting. The gray wolf — Beck — snapped at the white wolf, pushing her farther away from me.

They were saving me.

The white wolf met my gaze one last time. *This time.*

CHAPTER FORTY-TWO

· ISABEL ·

I spent the weekend waiting for Grace to call and invite me over to Beck's house, and when I finally realized that she was probably waiting for me to invite myself as usual, it was Monday. And by then, Cole's box of dangerous toys had arrived and I figured I could deliver it and see Grace at the same time. Then it wasn't like I was going over specially to see Cole. I knew what was good for me. Even if I didn't like it.

When Cole answered the front door of Beck's house, he was shirtless and faintly sweaty. He looked like he'd been excavating with his bare hands and he had a bit of bruising around his left eye. He wore a smile across his entire face, wide and benevolent. It was a very grand-looking expression, even though he had bedhead and was wearing only sweatpants. There was something undeniably theatrical about Cole, even when his stage was the mundane.

"Good morning," he said. He peered at the warm day. "It's so Minnesota out here. I hadn't realized."

It was a gorgeous day, one of the perfect spring days that Minnesota seemed to have no problem inserting in between weeks of frigid weather or into the middle of a summer heat wave. The lawn smelled like the boxwoods that were planted unevenly in front of the house.

"It's not morning anymore," I said. "Your stuff is in the car. You didn't say what kind of sedatives, so I got the worst I could find."

Cole rubbed his filthy palm across his chest and stretched his neck up as if he could see what I'd brought from the front step. "How well you know me. Come in, I was just making a fresh pot of uppers. I had a helluva night."

Music was blaring from the living room behind him; it was hard to believe that Grace was in the same house as it. "I don't know if I'm coming in," I said.

Cole laughed, a very cavalier laugh that completely dismissed my statement as fanciful, and walked barefoot to my SUV. "Front seat or backseat?"

"Very back." It wasn't a huge box and I could've carried it, but I preferred to see Cole's arms wrapped around it instead.

"Come into my workshop, little girl," Cole said.

I followed him into the house. It felt cooler than the outside, and smelled like something burnt. The howlingly loud music had a back-beat that vibrated in the soles of my shoes; I had to nearly shout to be heard over it. "Where are Sam and Grace?"

"Ringo left in his car a few hours ago. He must've taken Grace with him. I don't know where they went."

"You didn't ask?"

"We're not married," Cole said, and added, in a humble tone, "yet."

He kicked the door shut behind him, his arms full of the box, and said, "Kitchen."

With the music providing a chaotic soundtrack, I led the way into the kitchen, where the burnt smell was most potent. It looked like a disaster zone. The counter was all glasses, markers, syringes, books, a bag of sugar ripped open and rolled down to show its contents. Every one of the cabinets was covered with photographs of the wolves of Mercy Falls in their human bodies. I tried not to touch anything.

"What's burning?"

"My brain," Cole replied. He used the last available counter space to shove the box next to the microwave. "Sorry about the mess. We're having amitriptyline for dinner."

"Does Sam know you've turned his kitchen into a drug lab?"

"It's Sam Roth approved, yeah. Do you want coffee before we go set up this trap?"

Sugar gritted under the heels of my boots. I said, "I never said I was going to help you set it up."

Cole examined the inside of a mug before setting it down on the island in front of me and filling it with coffee. "I read between the lines. Sugar? Milk?"

"Are you high? Why are you never wearing a shirt?"

"I sleep naked," Cole said. He put both milk and sugar in my coffee. "As the day goes on, I put on more and more clothing. You should've come over an hour ago."

I glared at him.

He said, "Also, I am not high. It offends me that you had to ask." He didn't look offended.

I took a sip of the coffee. It wasn't horrible. "What are you really working on here?"

"Something to not kill Beck," he said. He managed to seem both dismissive and possessive of the chemicals in the room. "Do you know what would be really excellent? If you helped me get into your high school's lab this evening."

"As in break in?"

"As in I need a microscope. I can only make so many scientific discoveries with a research lab built out of Legos and Play-Doh. I need real equipment."

I regarded him. This Cole, electric and confident, was hard to resist. I scowled. "I'm not helping you break into my school."

Cole held out his hand. "Fine. I would like my coffee back, then."

I hadn't realized how much I'd had to raise my voice to be heard over the music until there was a pause between tracks and I could lower it. "It's mine now," I said, echoing what he'd said to me back at the bookstore. "I might help you get into my mom's clinic, though."

"You're a mensch," he said.

"I have no idea what that means," I replied.

"Me neither. Sam said it the other day. I liked the sound of it."

That was pretty much all you needed to know about Cole, right there. He saw something he didn't quite understand, liked it, and just took it to be his.

I dug in my tiny purse. "I brought you something else, too."

I handed him a little die-cast Mustang, black and shiny.

Cole accepted it and set it in the open palm of his hand. He stood still; I hadn't realized that he hadn't been before that moment. After a pause, he said, "Bet this one gets better mileage than my real one."

He drove it along the edge of the counter, making a soft, ascending sound for the engine note as he did. At the end of the island, he had it take off into the sky. He said, "I'm not letting you drive it, though."

"I wouldn't look good in a black car," I said.

Cole suddenly snaked his arm out and grabbed my waist. My eyes widened. He said, "You'd look good in anything. Perfect ten, Isabel Culpeper."

He started to dance. And all at once, because Cole was dancing, I was dancing. And this Cole was even more persuasive than the last one. This was everything about Cole's smile made into a real thing, a physical object made out of his hands looped around me and his long body pushed up against mine. I loved to dance, but I'd always been aware that I was dancing, aware of what my body was doing. Now, with the music thumping and Cole dancing with me, everything became invisible but the music. *I* was invisible. My hips were the booming bass. My hands on Cole were the wails of the synthesizer. My body was nothing but the hard, pulsing beat of the track.

My thoughts were flashes in between the downbeats.

beat:

my hand pressed on Cole's stomach

beat:

our hips crushed together

beat:

Cole's laugh

beat:

we were one person

Even knowing that Cole was good at this because it was what he *did* didn't make it any less of an amazing thing. Plus, he wasn't trying to be amazing without me — every move of his body was to make us move together. There was no ego, just the music and our bodies.

When the track ended, Cole stepped back, out of breath, half a smile on his face. I couldn't see how he could stop. I wanted to dance until I couldn't stand up. I wanted to crush our bodies against each other until there was no pulling them apart.

"You're an addiction," I told him.

"You should know."

Chapter Forty-Three

· SAM ·

Because Grace was feeling more solidly herself, we spent the day out. She ducked down inside the car as I ran into the Dollar Parade to buy her some socks and T-shirts and ventured into the grocery store to buy the things on a list she'd written for me. There was pleasure in the mundane, in the pretense of routine. It was only marred by the knowledge that Grace was trapped in that car, officially missing, and I was tied to Boundary Wood, tangled in the pack still, and we were both prisoners in Beck's house, waiting for our sentences to be commuted.

We took the groceries home and I folded Grace's list into a paper crane and tied it to my bedroom ceiling with the others. It strained toward the window in the current from the air vent, but when I bumped it with my shoulder, its string was only long enough to tangle it with the crane next to it.

"I want to go see Rachel," Grace said.

"Okay," I replied. I already had my keys in my hand.

We got to Grace's old high school well before school let out, so we sat together in silence and waited until the bell rang. As soon as it did, Grace ducked into the backseat, out of sight.

There was something odd and terrible about sitting outside her old school, watching the seniors begin to trickle out in groups, waiting for the buses. They moved in knots of twos and threes. Everything was bright colors: Day-Glo messenger bags hanging on shoulders, brilliant shirts with team mottos, fresh green tree leaves by the parking lot. Their conversations were silent with my windows rolled up, and without the benefit of sound, I thought that they could communicate entirely with their body language. There were so many hands punched in the air, shoulders bumping, heads thrown back in laughter. They didn't need the words, if they were willing to be silent long enough to learn to speak without them.

I looked at the clock on the car. We'd only been here a few minutes, but it seemed longer. It was a beautiful day, closer to summer than spring, one of those days where the cloudless blue sky seemed high and far out of reach. The high schoolers kept coming out of the school, none of them familiar yet. It was ages ago that I'd waited for Grace to come out of class, back when I'd had to hide from the weather.

I felt so much older than all of them. They were seniors, so some of them might have been my age, which seemed unfathomable. I couldn't imagine walking among them, backpack slung over my shoulder, waiting for a bus or walking to my car. I felt like I'd never been that young. Was there an alternate universe where a Sam Roth had never met the wolves, never lost his parents, never left Duluth? What would that Sam look like, going to school, waking up on Christmas, kissing his mother's cheek on graduation day? Would that Sam without scars have a guitar, a girlfriend, a good life?

I felt like a voyeur. I wanted to go.

But there she was. Dressed in a straight brown dress with striped purple stockings underneath it, Rachel was walking alone to the far side of the parking lot, a sort of grim march. I rolled down my window. There was no way to do this that didn't feel like a page out of a murder mystery. *The boy called to her from his car. She approached; she knew he was suspected by the police, but he'd always seemed kind. . . .*

"Rachel!" I called.

Rachel's eyes were wide and it took a long time for her to arrange her face into something more pleasant. She stopped about ten feet from my driver's side window, her feet clapped together and her hands holding both of her backpack straps.

"Hi," she said. She looked wary, or sad.

"Can I talk to you a minute?"

Rachel glanced back toward the school, then to me. "Sure," she said. She didn't come any closer. That distance stung. It also meant that everything I said to her would be shouted across ten feet of parking lot.

"Do you mind if we're, um, a little closer?" I asked.

Rachel shrugged, but didn't come any closer.

I left the car running and got out, shutting the door behind me. Rachel didn't move as I approached her, but her eyebrows moved slightly closer to her eyes.

"How are you doing?" I asked gently.

Rachel looked at me, her lower lip firmly caught in her teeth. She was so incredibly sad looking that it was hard to think that Grace's decision to come here was wrong.

"I'm so sorry about Olivia," I said.

"Me, too," Rachel said. She said it in this brave way. "John is doing bad."

It took me a moment to remember that John was Olivia's brother. "Rachel, I'm here about Grace."

"What about Grace?" Her voice was guarded. I wished that she trusted me, but I guessed she had no reason to.

I grimaced and looked at the students filing onto the buses. It looked like an advertisement for a school: perfect blue sky, brilliant green leaves, eye-buggingly yellow school buses. Rachel only added to the image; those stripes looked like you had to order them out of a catalog. Rachel was Grace's friend. Grace believed that she could keep a secret. Not just a secret, but *our* secret. Even trusting Grace's judgment, it was surprisingly difficult to relinquish the truth. "I need to know you can keep a secret first, Rachel."

Rachel said, "They're saying some pretty bad things about you, Sam."

I sighed. "I know. I've heard them. I hope you know that I wouldn't hurt Grace, but . . . you don't have to trust me for this, Rachel. I just want to know that, if it was something important, something really important, you could keep a secret. Be honest."

I could see that she *wanted* to let down her guard.

"I can keep a secret," she said.

I bit my lip and closed my eyes for just a second.

"I don't think you killed her," she said, very matter-of-fact, like she was saying that she didn't think it would rain tonight, because there were no clouds. "If that helps."

I opened my eyes. It did help. "Okay. Here's the thing, and it's going to sound crazy, but . . . Grace is alive, she's still here in Mercy Falls, and she's okay."

Rachel leaned toward me. "Are you keeping her tied up in your basement?"

The bad thing about that was that I sort of *was*. "Funny, Rachel. I'm not keeping her tied up against her will. She's hiding and she doesn't want to have to come out yet. It's sort of a hard situation to —"

"Oh my God, you got her pregnant," Rachel said. She threw her hands up in the air. "I knew it. I *knew* it."

"Rachel," I said. "Rach. *Rachel.*"

She was still talking. "— like everything we used to talk about and still, no, did she use her brain? No. She —"

"Rachel," I said. "She's not pregnant."

She eyed me. I thought both of us were growing a bit fatigued with the conversation. "*Okay.* So then, what?"

"Well, it's going to be a bit difficult to believe. I don't really know how to tell you. Maybe it would be better from Grace."

"Sam," Rachel said, "we all had to take sex ed."

"Rachel, no. She told me I should say 'Peter of the Plentiful Pecs' to you. I have no idea what that means, but she said you'd know it was her then."

I could see the words working through her as she processed the meaning and considered whether I could have gotten them through nefarious means. She asked, wary, "Why isn't she telling me this herself, then?"

"Because you wouldn't come over to the car!" I said. "She can't get out of the car, and I can. She's supposed to be missing, remember? If you'd actually come over to the car when I called to you, she was going to wave at you from the backseat."

When she still hesitated, I rubbed my hands over my face. "Look, Rachel, just go over there and look yourself. I'll stand here. No chance that I'm going to brain you with a beer bottle and put you in my trunk. Will that make you feel any better?"

"If you stand farther away, maybe," Rachel said. "I'm sorry, Sam, but I watch TV. I know how these things go."

I pressed my fingers into the bridge of my nose. "Look. Call my cell phone. It's in the car. She's in the car. She'll pick it up and you can talk to her yourself. You don't have to get anywhere near it."

Rachel pulled her cell phone out of the side pocket of her backpack. "Tell me your number."

I recited it and she punched it, her fingers pecking the buttons. "It's ringing," she said.

I pointed at the Volkswagen. Through the closed door, my cell phone was vaguely audible.

"No one is picking up," Rachel said accusingly. Just as she said it, the driver's side window rolled down and Grace looked over from the passenger seat.

"For crying out loud," she said in a loud whisper, "you're going to make everybody suspicious just standing around there. Are you guys going to get in, or what?"

Rachel's eyes were perfectly round.

I held my hands up on either side of my head. "Now do you believe me?"

"Are you going to tell me why she's undercover?" Rachel replied.

I gestured toward Grace. "I think that will sound better coming from her."

CHAPTER FORTY-FOUR

· GRACE ·

I had thought that the sheer fact of *me* would be enough for Rachel. The fact that I was living and breathing seemed like a pretty powerful recommendation for Sam's innocence, but when it came down to it, Rachel was still uncertain. It took several minutes to coax her into the car, even after she had seen me in it.

"Just because you have Grace doesn't mean that I'm sure about this," Rachel said, peering at the open back door with a dubious expression. "For all I know, you've been giving her psychedelic mushrooms in your basement and you'd like to do the same thing to me."

Sam glanced back at the school, his light eyes narrowed against the warm sun. He was probably thinking the same thing as me: Namely, that most everyone in Mercy Falls mistrusted him, and if someone noticed him standing at the back of a parking lot with an uncertain-looking girl, things could get unpleasant. He said, "I'm not exactly sure how to counteract that allegation."

"Rachel, I am not drugged," I said. "Just get in the car."

Rachel frowned at me and then looked back to Sam. "Not until you tell me why you want to stay hidden."

"It's sort of a long story."

Rachel crossed her arms. "Summarize."

"It really, really ought to be explained."

Rachel didn't move. *"Summarize."*

I sighed. "Rachel, I keep turning into a wolf. Don't freak out."

She waited for me to say something else, for it to make sense. But there wasn't any way to make it easy for her, not when I had to *summarize*.

"Why would I freak out?" Rachel asked. "Just because you're a crazy person saying crazy things? Of course you turn into a wolf. And I also turn into a zebra. Check out the stripes, they're a leftover."

"Rachel," Sam said gently, "I promise it makes a lot more sense when it's explained. If you give Grace a chance to — someplace *private* — it will still be weird, but not impossible."

Rachel looked at him, aghast, and then back at me. "Sorry, Grace. But I just don't think it sounds like the greatest idea to let him drive me back to his lair." She held out her hand to Sam, who looked at it as if it might be a weapon. Wiggling her fingers, she added, "Let me drive."

"Drive . . . to my house?" Sam asked.

Rachel nodded.

Sam looked a little flustered, but to his credit, his voice didn't change. "How is that any different than if I drive us there?"

"I don't know! It will make me feel better." Her hand was still out for the key. "In the movies, no one drives themselves to their own deaths."

Sam looked at me. His face said, *Grace, help!*

"Rachel," I said firmly. "Do you even know how to drive a stick shift?"

"No," Rachel said. "But I'm a fast learner."

I gave her a look. "Rachel."

"Grace, you have to admit this is pretty weird. Say it. You disappearing from the hospital and Olivia is — and Sam suddenly shows up with you and, well, the freaky hallucinogenic mushrooms are looking more and more realistic, especially when you start talking about wolves. Because next step is for Isabel Culpeper to show up saying that everybody's going to be abducted by aliens and I have to tell you, I can't take that in my fragile emotional state. I think that —"

I sighed. "Rachel."

"Fine," she said. She threw her bag in the backseat and climbed in after.

As we headed toward Beck's house, Sam in the driver's seat, me beside him, Rachel in the backseat, I felt suddenly and inexplicably homesick, somehow frantic with the thought of my lost life. I couldn't think what I was so desperately missing — surely not my parents, who hadn't been around enough to be missed — until I realized that the emotion was being triggered by the wildly sweet strawberry scent of Rachel's shampoo. And *that* I missed. Afternoons and evenings with Rachel, holed up in her room or taking over my parents' kitchen or following Olivia on one of her photography treks. I wasn't homesick, not really, because that required a home. I was personsick. Lifesick.

I turned to the backseat and stretched out my hand to Rachel, my fingers not quite long enough to reach her. She didn't say anything, just took my hand and clutched it tightly. We rode like that for the rest of the trip, me half-twisted and her leaning forward a little, our hands resting on the back of my seat. Sam didn't say anything, either, except for *Oh, sorry* when he shifted gears too soon and the car shuddered a bit.

Later, when we got back to the house, I told her everything, the whole story, from the moment the wolves dragged me from the swing to the day I'd almost died in my own blood. And everything in between. Sam looked more nervous than I'd ever seen him, but I wasn't worried. From the moment that I held Rachel's hand in the car, I'd known that in this strange new life, Rachel was one of the things I was going to get to keep.

CHAPTER FORTY-FIVE

· ISABEL ·

I was against felonies when a misdemeanor would do. Using the school's lab would have constituted breaking and entering. Using one of the spare keys for my mother's office was merely unlawful entry. It was just common sense. I'd parked my SUV in the grocery store parking lot across the road so that anyone driving by the clinic would see nothing out of the ordinary. I would have made an excellent criminal. Maybe I still would. I was young yet and it was possible med school wouldn't work out.

"Do *not* break anything," I told Cole as I gestured for him to go in before me. Possibly a futile plea, where Cole St. Clair was involved.

Cole stalked down the hallway, eyeing the posters on the walls. The low-income clinic was a part-time project for my mother, who also put in time with the local hospital. When my mother had first opened the clinic, the walls had been decorated with art that she didn't have room for in the house or had gotten tired of. She wanted the clinic to seem homelike, she had said when we first came to Mercy Falls. After Jack had died, she'd given away a lot of art from home, and once she got over that, she'd taken the pieces from the clinic walls to replace them. Now the clinic was generally decorated with a decor I liked to call *late pharmaceutical period*.

"All the way at the end, to the right," I said. "Not that. That's the bathroom."

The afternoon light was fading as I locked the door behind me, but it didn't matter. When I turned on the buzzing fluorescent lights overhead, it became clinic time, where all times are the same. I'd always told Mom that if she really wanted the clinic to feel "home-like," real lightbulbs would go a long way toward making it feel like a house instead of a Wal-Mart.

Cole had already disappeared into my mother's tiny lab room, and I slowly trailed after. I'd cut class to take the package to Cole, but I hadn't slept in — I'd been up and running. Then I'd helped Cole set up his incredibly industrial-looking pit trap, taking care not to fall into the sinkhole he said they'd pulled Grace out of. And now back here, waiting until the clinic was closed in order to come back in, telling my parents I was going to a student council meeting. I was ready to take a break. We hadn't had much food to speak of and I was feeling vaguely martyred for the whole werewolf cause. I paused in the reception area to open the tiny fridge under the counter. I grabbed two juices and carried them back with me. Juice was better than nothing.

In the lab room, Cole was already settled backward on a chair and leaning over the counter where the microscope was. He held one of his hands up in the air, pointing toward the ceiling. It only took me a moment to realize that he'd pricked his finger and was holding his hand up to slow the bleeding.

"Do you want, like, a Band-Aid, or are you fine doing the Statue of Liberty thing?" I asked. I put the juice next to him and then, on second thought, screwed off the lid and held the bottle to his mouth so he could get a drink. He waved his bloody finger in a sort of thank-you.

"I couldn't find the Band-Aids," Cole said. "Which is to mean, I didn't look. Is this methanol? Oh, look, it is."

I found him a Band-Aid and rolled another chair next to him. It didn't take much rolling. The lab room was really the storage room, drawers and shelves stuffed with prescription drug samples and trials, boxes of cotton balls and swabs and tongue depressors, bottles of rubbing alcohol and hydrogen peroxide. A urinalysis machine, microscope, blood tube rotaror. There wasn't much room for two chairs and two bodies in them.

Cole had smeared some of his blood on a glass slide and was peering at it through the microscope.

"What are you looking for?" I asked him.

He didn't answer; his eyebrows were pulled down close to his eyes in an expression of such deep thought that I suspected he hadn't even heard me. I sort of liked seeing him like that, not performing, just . . . being Cole, as hard as he could. He didn't resist as I took his hand and swabbed off the blood.

"For crying out loud," I said, "what did you use to open yourself up, a butter knife?" I applied a Band-Aid and released his hand. He immediately used it to adjust the microscope.

The silence seemed to last forever, but it was probably only a minute. Cole sat back from the microscope, not looking at me. He laughed, a short, breathy laugh of disbelief, his hands tented in front of him, fingertips pressed together. He rested his fingers on his lips.

"Christ," he said, and then he laughed again, that abbreviated laugh.

I was annoyed. "What?"

"Just — look." Cole pushed his chair back and physically pulled mine over to take its place. "What do you see?"

I wasn't going to be able to see jack shit, since I didn't know what I was looking for, that's what. But I humored him. I put my eye against the microscope and peered in. And Cole was right — I could immediately see what he saw. There were dozens of red blood cells beneath the scope, colorless and normal. There were also two red dots.

I pulled back. "What is that?"

"It's the werewolf," Cole said. He was jerking his spinning chair back and forth on its axis. "I knew it. I *knew* it."

"Knew *what*?"

"Either I have malaria or that is what the wolf looks like. Hanging out there in my cells. I *knew* it was behaving like malaria. I knew it. Christ!"

He stood up, because sitting down wouldn't cut it anymore.

"Great, boy genius. What does that mean for the wolves? Can you cure it like malaria?"

Cole was looking at a chart on the wall. It depicted the growth stages of a fetus in vibrant colors that hadn't been seen since the sixties. He waved a hand at me. "Malaria can't be cured."

"Don't be stupid," I said. "They cure people of malaria."

"No," Cole said, and he traced the shape of one of the fetuses with his finger. "They just stop it from killing them."

"So you're saying there's no cure," I said. "But there's a way to stop them from . . . you've already stopped Grace from dying. I don't understand what the revelation is here."

"Sam. Sam's the revelation. This is just confirmation. I need to do more work. I need paper," Cole said, turning toward me. "I need . . ." He broke off, his temporary high slowly unwinding. It felt anticlimactic, coming out here for a scientific reveal that was only half-baked, one I couldn't understand. And being in the clinic after dark was reminding me of when Grace and I had brought Jack here. It was bringing back all that failure and loss and pretty much making me want to curl up on my bed back at home.

"Food," I suggested. "Sleep. That's what I need. To get the hell out of here."

Cole frowned at me, as if I'd suggested "ducks" and "yoga."

I stood up and faced him. "Unlike those of you with raging wolf infections inside them, I have school in the morning, especially since I skipped today to be here."

"Why are you pissed?"

"I'm not pissed," I said. "I'm tired. I just want to go home, I guess." The idea of going home didn't sound that great, either, though.

"You're pissed," he said. "I'm almost there, Isabel. I've almost got something. I think I — I'm really close. I need to talk to Sam. If I can get him to talk to me."

And then he was just a tired, good-looking guy, not a rock star with tens of thousands of fans who wondered where he was or a genius with a brain so big that it rebelled against being used and tried to invent ways to hurt itself instead.

Looking at him looking like that, I felt like I needed something from him, or somebody, and that probably meant that he also needed something from me, or somebody, but the revelation was like looking at spots on a slide. Knowing that it meant something to somebody wasn't the same as it meaning something to you.

And then I heard a familiar sound — the crack of the lock on the door at the end of the hall as the dead bolt unlocked. Someone else was here.

"Shit, shit, shit!" I hissed. I had two seconds to devise a plan. "Get your stuff and get under the counter!" Cole grabbed his slide and juice and Band-Aid wrapper and I checked to make sure he was pushed underneath the counter before I hit the light to the lab room and slid underneath with him.

The door at the end of the hall opened with a slow series of pops, then clunked heavily shut again. I heard my mother's irritated sigh, loud and dramatic enough to be heard all the way in the lab room. I hoped her irritation was because she thought someone had left the hall light on.

There was nothing of Cole but the glint of his eyes in the darkness, the light from the hall reflecting on them. There was not a lot of space under the counter, so we were knee to knee, foot crushed on top of foot, impossible to tell whose breath was whose. We were both absolutely silent, listening to my mother's progress. I heard her heels click into one of the first rooms — probably the reception area. She was there for a several moments, shuffling around. Cole readjusted one of his feet so that my boot wasn't pressing into his ankle bone. I heard something in his shoulder pop as he moved. He braced one of his arms on the wall behind me. I somehow had a hand between his legs, so I withdrew it.

We waited.

My mother said, very clearly, "Dammit." She crossed the hall into one of the exam rooms. I heard more paper shuffling. It was black as sleep in the cubby beneath the counter, too dark for my eyes to get used to, and it felt like we had more legs between the two of us than we really ought to. My mother dropped papers; I could hear the whoosh and ticking of them spreading over the floor and tapping into the exam table. She didn't swear this time, though.

Cole kissed me. I should have told him to stop, to keep still, but I wanted it. I didn't move from where I was curled up against the wall, just let him kiss me and kiss me again. It was the sort of kiss that would take a long time to recover from. You could take each of our kisses, from the very first moment we'd met, and put them on slides under a microscope, and I was pretty sure what you'd find. Even an expert would see nothing on the first one, and then on the next one, the start of something — mostly outnumbered, easily destroyed — and then more and more until finally this one, something that even the untrained eye could spot. Evidence that we'd probably never be cured of each other, but we might be able to keep it from killing us.

I heard the sound of my mother's footsteps a second before the light to the lab room went on. Then a heavy sigh.

"Isabel, why?"

Cole leaned away and so we were like two possums behind a Dumpster when she stood back to look at us. I saw her doing a quick vitals check: We had all our clothing on, nothing was rumpled, we weren't injecting ourselves with anything. She looked at Cole; Cole smiled lazily back at her.

"You — you're from . . ." my mother started. She squinted at him. I waited for her to say NARKOTIKA, though I'd never imagined her a fan. But she said, "The boy from the stairs. From the house. The naked one. Isabel, when I said I didn't want you to do this in the house, I didn't mean to take it to the clinic. Why are you under this counter? Oh, I don't want to know. I just don't."

I didn't really have anything to say.

My mother rubbed one of her eyebrows with a hand that was holding a closely printed form. "God, where is your car?"

"Across the road," I said.

"Of course it is." She shook her head. "I am not telling your father I saw you here, Isabel. Just, please, do not . . ." She didn't define what I was supposed to avoid doing. Instead, she threw my half-drunk bottle of juice in the trash can by the door, and turned the light out again. Her shoes receded down the hallway and then there was the popping of the outside door opening and closing. The clunk of the dead bolt.

In the darkness, Cole was invisible, but I could still feel him beside me. Sometimes you didn't have to see something to know it was there.

I felt a tickle on my skin; it took me a moment to realize that Cole was driving his die-cast Mustang up my arm. He was laughing to himself, hushed and infectious, as if there was still any reason to be quiet. He turned the car around at my shoulder and headed back down toward my hand, the wheels skidding on my skin a bit when he laughed.

I thought it was the truest thing I'd ever heard from Cole St. Clair.

CHAPTER FORTY-SIX

· SAM ·

I didn't realize how accustomed I'd become to a lack of routine until we had one. Somehow, with Grace back in the house and Cole's scientific exploration more focused, our lives took on a sheen of normalcy. I became diurnal again. The kitchen once more became a place for eating; on the counter, prescription drug bottles and scribbled notes were slowly exchanged for cereal boxes and coffee mugs with rings in the bottom. Grace shifted only once in three days, and even then just for a few hours, returning shakily to bed after shutting herself in the bathroom for the duration. The days felt shorter, somehow, when night and sleeping came on a schedule. I went to work and sold books to whispering customers and came home with the feeling of a condemned man given a few days' reprieve. Cole spent his days trying to trap wolves and fell asleep in a different bedroom each night. In the mornings, I caught Grace putting out pans of stale granola for the pair of raccoons, and in the evenings, I caught her wistfully looking at college websites and chatting with Rachel. We were all hunting for something elusive and impossible.

The wolf hunt was on the news most nights.

But I was — not quite happy. Pending happy. I knew this was not really my life; it was a borrowed life. One that I was temporarily wearing until I could sort out my own. The date of the wolf hunt felt far away and implausible, but it was impossible to forget. Just because I couldn't think of what to do didn't mean that something didn't need to be done.

On Wednesday, I called Koenig and asked him if he could give me directions to the peninsula so I could properly investigate its potential. That's what I said — "properly investigate." Koenig always seemed to have that effect on me.

"I think," Koenig said, with an emphasis on *think* that indicated he really meant *know*, "that it would be better if I took you out there. Wouldn't want you getting the wrong peninsula. I can do Saturday."

I didn't realize that he had made a joke until we'd hung up, and then I felt bad for not laughing.

On Thursday, the newspaper called. What did I have to say about the Grace Brisbane missing persons case?

Nothing, that was what I had to say. Actually, what I had said to my guitar the night before was

> *you can't lose a girl you misplaced years before*
> *stop looking*
> *stop looking*

But the song wasn't ready for public consumption, so I just hung up the phone without saying anything else.

On Friday, Grace told me that she was coming with Koenig and me to the peninsula. "I want Koenig to see me," she said. She was sitting on my bed matching socks while I tried out different ways of folding towels. "If he knows I'm alive, there can't be a missing persons case."

Uncertainty made an indigestible lump in my stomach. The possibilities sown by that action seemed to grow rapid and fierce. "He'll say you have to go back to your parents."

"Then we'll go see them," Grace said. She threw a sock with a hole in it to the end of the bed. "Peninsula first, then them."

"Grace?" I said, but I wasn't sure what I was asking her.

"They're never home," she said recklessly. "If they're home, me talking to them was meant to be. Sam, don't give me that look. I'm tired of this . . . *not knowing.* I can't relax, waiting for the ax to fall. I'm not going to have people suspecting you of — of — whatever it is they think you did. Kidnapped me. Killed me. Whatever. I can't fix very much these days, but I can fix that. I can't take the idea of them thinking of you that way."

"But your parents . . ."

Grace made a massive ball of socks without mates between her hands. I wondered if I'd unknowingly been wandering about all this time in socks that didn't quite match. "They only have a couple of months until I'm eighteen, Sam, and then they can't say anything about what I do. They can choose the hard way and lose me forever as soon as my birthday rolls around, or they can be reasonable and we can one day be on speaking terms with them again. Maybe. Is it true that Dad punched you? Cole says he punched you."

She read the response in my face.

"Yeah," she said, and she sighed, the first evidence that this topic held any pain for her. "And that is why I'm not going to have a problem having this conversation with them."

"I hate confrontation," I muttered. It was possibly the most unnecessary thing I had ever said.

"I don't understand," Grace said, stretching out her legs, "how a guy who never seems to wear any socks has so many ones that don't match."

We both looked at my bare feet. She reached out her hand as if she could possibly reach my toes from where she sat. I grabbed her hand and kissed her palm instead. Her hand smelled like butter and flour and home.

"Okay," I said. "We'll do it your way. Koenig, then your parents."

"It's better to have a plan," she said.

I didn't know if that was true. But it felt true.

Chapter Forty-Seven

· ISABEL ·

I hadn't forgotten about Grace's request for me to find out about summer school, but it took me quite awhile to figure out how to go about tracking down the answer. It wasn't as if I could pretend it was for me, and the more precise my questions got, the more I'd draw suspicion. In the end, I figured out a solution by accident. Emptying out my backpack, I found an old note from Ms. McKay, my favorite teacher from last year. Which wasn't saying much, but still. This particular note dated from my "problematic period" — my mother's words — and in it, Ms. McKay let me know that she would be happy to help me if I would let her. It reminded me that Ms. McKay was good at answering questions without asking any of her own.

Unfortunately, everyone else also knew this about Ms. McKay, so there was always a line to see her after last period. She didn't have an office, just the English classroom, so to an outsider, it looked like five students were waiting desperately to get in there and learn some Chaucer.

The door opened and closed as Hayley Olsen left the classroom and the girl in front of me went in. I moved forward one step and leaned against the wall. I hoped Grace knew how much I did for her. I could have been at home doing nothing by now. Daydreaming. The quality of my daydreams had improved exponentially as of late.

Footsteps slapped up behind me, followed by a sound that was unmistakably a backpack hitting the ground. I glanced back.

Rachel.

Rachel was like a caricature of a teen. There was something incredibly self-aware with the way she presented herself: the stripes, the quirky smocks, the braids and the twisted knobs she put her hair into. Everything about her said *quirky, fun, silly, naive*. But, this: There was innocence and there was projected innocence. I had nothing against either, but I liked to know what I was dealing with. Rachel knew darn well how she wanted people to see her, and that was what she gave them. She wasn't an idiot.

Rachel saw me looking but pretended not to. My suspicion had already settled, however.

"Fancy seeing you here," I said.

Rachel flashed me a grimace that lasted about as long as a movie frame; too fast for the human eye to properly perceive. "Fancy."

I leaned toward her, my voice lowered. "You wouldn't be here to talk about *Grace*, would you?"

Her eyes widened. "I'm already seeing a counselor, but that's none of your business."

She was good.

"Right. I'm sure you are. So you aren't going in to confess anything to Ms. McKay about her or the wolves," I said. "Because that would be so incredibly dumb, I can't begin to tell you."

Rachel's face cleared suddenly. "You know."

I just gave her a look.

"So it really is true." Rachel rubbed her upper arm and studied the floor.

"I've seen it."

Rachel sighed. "Who else knows?"

"Nobody. It's staying that way, right?"

The door opened and closed. The student in front of me went in; I was next. Rachel made an annoyed noise. "Look, I didn't do my

English reading! That's why I'm here. Not for anything about Grace. Wait. That means that you *are* here for her."

I wasn't sure how she'd managed to come to that conclusion, but it didn't change the fact that she was right. For half a second, I considered telling Rachel that Grace had asked me to find out about summer school for her, mostly because I wanted to rub in that Grace had trusted me first and I was shallow that way, but it wouldn't really be useful.

"Just finding out about some graduating credits," I said.

We stood in the awkward silence of people who had a friend in common and not much else. Students passed down the other side of the hall, laughing and making weird noises because they were guys and that was mostly what high school boys did. The school continued to smell like burritos. I continued to devise my method of questioning Ms. McKay.

Rachel, leaning against the wall and looking at the lockers on the other side of the hall, said, "Makes the world seem bigger, doesn't it?"

The naïveté of the question irritated me, somehow. "It's just another way to die."

Rachel looked at the side of my head. "You really do default to bitch, don't you? That'll only work as long as you're young and hot. After that, you'll only be able to teach AP History."

I looked at her and narrowed my eyes. I said, "I could say the same for *quirky*."

Rachel smiled a wide, wide smile, her most innocent one yet. "So what you're saying is you think I'm hot."

Okay, Rachel was all right. I wouldn't give her the satisfaction of a smile back, but I felt my eyes giving me away. The door opened. We regarded each other. As far as allies went, I guessed Grace could do worse.

As I went in to see Ms. McKay, I thought that Rachel actually was right. The world seemed bigger every day.

CHAPTER FORTY-EIGHT

· COLE ·

Another day, another night. We — Sam and I — were in the QuikMart a few miles away from the house, the sky black as hell above us. Mercy Falls proper was still another mile away; this convenience store was mostly for the oh-shit-I-forgot-to-get-milk moments. Which was exactly why we were at the QuikMart. Well, it's why Sam was there. Partially because we had no milk and partially because I was beginning to learn that Sam didn't sleep without someone there to tell him to, and I wasn't about to tell him. Normally this would fall to Grace, but Isabel had just called with the exact model of the helicopter that would be carrying the sharpshooters and we were all a little on edge. Grace and Sam had engaged in a wordless argument that somehow managed to involve only their eyes and then she had won, because she started making scones, and Sam had sulked on the couch with his guitar. If she and Sam ever had kids, they'd be gluten-intolerant out of self-defense.

Scones required milk.

So Sam was here for milk because the grocery store closed at nine. I, on the other hand, was at the QuikMart because if I spent another second in Beck's house, I was going to break something. I was figuring out more about the wolf science every day, but the hunt was almost here. In a few days, my experiments would be about as useful as medical research on the dodo bird.

Which brought us to QuikMart at eleven P.M. Inside the store, I pointed to a rack of condoms and Sam gave me a look completely devoid of humor. He'd worn too few or too many to see the amusement in it.

I broke off to navigate the aisles of the store, full of nervous energy. This crappy little service station felt like the real world. The real world, months after I'd murdered NARKOTIKA by disappearing with Victor. The real world where I smiled at security cameras and somewhere, they might smile back at me. Country music wailed low through speakers hung next to the sign for the bathrooms (FOR *PAYING* CUSTOMERS ONLY). The plate glass windows were painted with the green-black night that only lived outside of service stations. No one was awake but us, and I'd never been more awake. I browsed candy bars that sounded better than they tasted, checked tabloids for mention of me out of habit, looked at the racks of overpriced cold medications that no longer had the ability to impair either my ability to sleep or drive, and realized there was nothing here in this store that I wanted.

In my pocket, I felt the weight of the little black Mustang Isabel had given me. I couldn't stop thinking about it. I slid the car out and drove it over racks to where Sam stood in front of the milk case, his hands in the pockets of his jacket. Though he faced the milk, his face wore an undirected frown, his thoughts consumed by a problem somewhere else.

"Two percent is a nice compromise between skim and whole, if you're having problems deciding," I said. I kind of wanted Sam to ask me about the Mustang, to ask what the hell I was doing with it. I was thinking about Isabel, about shifting into a wolf for the first time, about the black sky pressing against the windows outside.

Sam said, "We're running out of time, Cole."

The electronic bell of the QuikMart door opening kept him from saying more, or me from answering him. I didn't turn to look, but some sort of instinct made the skin crawl at the back of my neck.

Sam had not turned his head, either, but I saw that his expression had changed. Sharpened. *That* was what I was subconsciously reacting to.

In my head, memories flashed. Wolves in the woods, ears pricked and swiveling, suddenly at attention. Air sharp in our nostrils, scent of deer on the breeze, time to hunt. The wordless agreement that it was time to act.

By the counter, I heard the murmur of voices as the newcomer and the clerk exchanged greetings. Sam put his hand on the handle of the cooler but didn't open it. He said, "Maybe we don't actually need milk."

· SAM ·

It was John Marx, Olivia's older brother.

Speaking with John had never been easy for me — we barely knew each other, and every encounter we'd ever had had been on tense terms. And now his sister was dead and Grace was missing. I wished we hadn't come. There was nothing to do but to carry on as usual. John wasn't quite in line; he was staring at the gum. I slouched up to the counter beside him. I could smell alcohol, which was depressing, because John had seemed so young before.

"Hi," I said, barely audible, just so I got credit for saying it.

John did the man-nod, a curt jerk of the head. "How are you doing." It was not a question.

"Three twenty-one," the clerk told me. He was a slight man with permanently lowered eyes. I counted out bills. I didn't look at John. I prayed that he didn't recognize Cole. I eyed the security camera, watching all of us.

"Did you know that this is Sam Roth?" John asked. There was silence until the clerk realized that John was talking to him.

The clerk darted a glance up at my damning yellow eyes and then back down to the bills I'd placed on the counter, before replying politely, "No, I didn't."

He knew who I was. Everyone knew. I felt a surge of friendliness toward the clerk.

"Thanks," I told him as I took my change, grateful for more than the coins. Cole pushed off the counter next to me. Time to go.

"Aren't you going to say anything?" John asked me. I heard misery in his voice.

My heart jerked inside me as I turned toward him. "I'm sorry about Olivia."

"Tell me why she died," John said. He took a step toward me, unsteady. A breath laced with some kind of alcohol — hard, neat, and recent, by the odor — gusted toward me. "Tell me why she was there."

I held a hand out, palm toward the ground. A sort of *That close is good. No closer.* "John, I don't kn —"

John swatted my hand away, and at that gesture, I saw Cole move restlessly. "Don't lie to me. I know it's you. I *know* it is."

This was a little easier. I couldn't lie, but this didn't require one. "It wasn't me. I didn't have anything to do with her being there."

The clerk said, "Good conversation to take outside!"

Cole opened the door. Night air rushed in.

John seized a mighty handful of my T-shirt at the shoulder. "Where's Grace? Why out of everyone in the world, why my sister, why Grace? Why them, you sick —"

And I saw in his face or heard in his voice or felt in that grip on my shirt what he was going to do next, so when he swung at me, I lifted an arm and deflected his blow. I couldn't do any more than that. I wasn't going to fight him, not over this. Not when he'd swallowed so much sadness that his words slurred.

"Okay, outside," the clerk said. "Conversation outside. Bye! Have a nice night!"

"John," I said, my arm throbbing where his fist had landed. Adrenaline pumped through me: John's anxiety, Cole's tension, my own readiness feeding it. "I'm sorry. But this isn't going to help."

"Damn straight," John said, and lunged for me.

Cole was suddenly between us.

"We're all done here," he said. He was no taller than either me or John, but he towered. He was looking at my face, judging my reaction. "Let's not make things ugly in this man's store."

John, an arm's length away, on the other side of Cole, stared at me, eyes hollowed out like a statue's. "I liked you, when I first met you," he said. "Can you imagine that?"

I felt sick.

"Let's go," I told Cole. I said to the clerk, "Thanks again."

Cole turned away from John, his movements wound tight.

Just as the door swung shut, John's voice slid after us. "Everybody knows what you did, Sam Roth."

The night air smelled like gasoline and wood smoke. Somewhere, there was a fire. I felt like I could feel the wolf inside me burning in my gut.

"People just love to hit you," Cole said, still all energy. My mood fed off Cole's and vice versa, and we were wolves, both of us. I was buzzing and weightless. The Volkswagen wasn't parked far away, just at the end of the parking spaces. There was a long, pale key scratch on the driver's side. At least I knew running into John was no coincidence. A fluorescent reflection of the convenience store glowed in its paint. Neither of us got in.

"It has to be you," Cole said. He'd opened the passenger door and stood on the running board, leaning over the roof at me. "The one who leads the wolves out. I've tried; I can't hold a thought while I'm a wolf."

I looked at him. My fingers tingled. I'd forgotten the milk inside the store. I kept thinking of John swinging at me, Cole charging between us, the night living inside me. Feeling like I did, right now, I couldn't say, *No, I can't do it*, because anything felt possible.

I said, "I don't want to go back. I can't do that."

Cole laughed, just a single *ha*. "You're gonna shift eventually, Ringo. You're not totally cured yet. Might as well save the world while you're at it."

I wanted to say, *Please don't make me do this*, but what meaning would that have to Cole, who had done that and worse to himself?

"You're assuming they would listen to me," I said.

Cole lifted his hands off the roof of the Volkswagen; cloudy fingerprints evaporated seconds after he did. "We all listen to you, Sam." He jumped to the pavement. "You just don't always talk to us."

CHAPTER FORTY-NINE

· GRACE ·

Saturday, Officer Koenig came to the house to take us to the peninsula.

We all watched him pull into the driveway, peering out the living room windows. It was thrilling and ironic to be inviting a policeman over after trying for so long to avoid them. Like Mowgli asking Shere Khan in for some tea and crumpets. Koenig arrived at Beck's house at noon, dressed in a crisp maroon polo shirt and jeans that I thought he'd probably ironed. He drove a pristine gray Chevy truck that he may have ironed as well. He knocked on the door — an efficient *Knock. Knock. Knock* that somehow reminded me of Isabel's laugh — and when Sam opened it, Koenig stood there with his hands folded neatly in front of him as if he were waiting for his date.

"Come on in," Sam said.

Koenig stepped into the house, still with one hand professionally holding the other. It seemed like another lifetime that I'd seen him last, standing just like that in the front of our classroom as a bunch of high schoolers assaulted him with questions about the wolves. Olivia had leaned over to me and whispered that he was cute. Now here he was in the front entry, and Olivia was dead.

Olivia was dead.

I was beginning to understand that blank look Sam got when someone said something about his parents. I didn't feel anything at all when I thought *Olivia is dead.* I felt numb as Sam's scars.

I realized that Koenig had spotted me.

"Hi," I said.

He took a deep breath, as if he were preparing to dive. I would've given almost anything to know what he was thinking. "Well, okay, then," he said. "There you are."

"Yes," I replied. "Here I am." Cole stepped out of the kitchen behind me and Koenig's eyebrows drew down over his eyes. Cole smiled back, a hard, certain smile. I watched recognition slowly dawn on Koenig's face.

"Of course," Koenig said. He crossed his arms and turned to Sam. No matter how he moved his arms or stood, something about Koenig gave the impression that he would be difficult to knock over. "Are there any other missing persons living under your roof? Elvis? Jimmy Hoffa? Amelia Earhart? I'd just like to have full disclosure now, before we go any further."

"This is it," Sam said. "To the best of my knowledge. Grace would like to come with, if that's okay."

Koenig considered.

"Are you coming with us, too?" he asked Cole. "Because if so, I'll have to make room in my cab. Also, it's a long drive. If you have a small bladder, I'd use the facilities now." And that was that. Having established the ground rules for the day — I was a part-time wolf, Cole was a missing rock star — it was down to business.

"I'm not coming," Cole replied. "I have man's work."

Sam shot Cole a warning look. It was a look I thought probably had something to do with the kitchen finally looking like a kitchen again and Sam wanting it to stay that way.

Cole's reply was enigmatic. Well, sort of. Whenever Cole wasn't being completely flamboyant, he always seemed mysterious by comparison. "Bring your phone with you. In case I need to get ahold of you."

Sam rubbed his fingers over his mouth as if he were checking his shaving job. "Don't burn down the house."

"Okay, Mother," Cole replied.

"Oh, let's go," I said.

It was a strange trip. We didn't know Koenig at all, and he knew nothing about us except for what nobody else knew. It was made more difficult because he was being kind in a very amorphous way that we weren't certain we were glad for yet. It was hard to be both grateful and talkative.

So we sat three across on the bench seat: Koenig, Sam, me. The truck smelled vaguely like Dr Pepper. Koenig drove eight miles above the speed limit. The road took us northeast, and it wasn't long before civilization began to fall away. The sky overhead was a friendly, cloudless blue, and all the colors seemed supersaturated. If winter had ever been here, this place didn't remember it.

Koenig didn't say anything, just rubbed his hand over his close-cropped hair. He didn't look quite like the Koenig I remembered, this young guy driving us into the middle of nowhere in a civilian truck, wearing a shirt in department-store maroon. This was not who I'd expected to be putting my trust in at this stage. Beside me, Sam practiced a guitar chord on my thigh.

Appearances weren't everything, I supposed.

The truck was silent. After a bit, Sam brought up the weather. He thought it was pretty smooth sailing from here on out. Koenig said he thought that was probably true, but you never knew what Minnesota had in store for you. She could surprise you, he said. I found myself pleased by him referring to Minnesota as a "she." It seemed to render Koenig more benevolent, somehow. Koenig asked Sam what he was thinking of doing for college, and Sam mentioned that Karyn had offered him a full-time position at the bookstore, and he was considering it. No shame in that, commented Koenig. I thought about two-hundred-level classes and majors and minors and success quantified by a piece of paper and kind of wished they would change the subject.

Koenig did. "What about St. Clair?"

"Cole? Beck found him," Sam said. "It was a charity case."

Koenig glanced over. "For St. Clair or for Beck?"

"That's something I ask myself a lot these days," Sam replied. He and Koenig exchanged a look at this, and I was surprised to see that Koenig was regarding Sam as an equal, or, if not an equal, at least as an adult. I spent so much time alone with Sam that other people's reactions to him and us together always seemed to come as a shock. It was hard to imagine how one guy could elicit so many different responses from other people. It was like there were forty different versions of Sam. I'd always assumed that everyone took me at face value, but now I wondered — were there forty different versions of Grace out there, too?

We all jumped when Sam's phone rang from my bag — a bag packed with a change of clothing in case I shifted and a novel in case I needed to look busy — and Sam said, "Would you get that, Grace?"

I paused when I saw that the number on the phone wasn't one that I recognized. I showed the screen to Sam as the phone rang again. He shook his head, puzzled.

"Should I?" I asked, tipping it in my hand as if to open it.

"New York," Koenig said. He looked back to the road. "It's a New York exchange."

This information didn't enlighten Sam. He shrugged.

I opened the phone and put it to my ear. "Hello?"

The voice on the other side was light and male. "Oh — right. Hello. Is Cole around?"

Sam blinked at me, and I could tell that he could hear the voice as well.

"I think you have a wrong number," I said. Immediately, my brain processed what this meant — Cole had used Sam's phone to call somewhere. Home? Would Cole have done that?

The voice was not perturbed. His voice was lazy and slippery, like a melting pat of butter. "No, I don't. But I understand. This is Jeremy. We were in a band together."

"With this person I don't know," I replied.

"Yes," Jeremy said. "I have something I would like you to tell Cole St. Clair, if you would. I'd like you to tell him I have given him the best present in the world, and it took quite a lot of effort on my part, so I'd appreciate if he didn't just tear the wrapping off and then throw it away."

"I'm listening."

"In eighteen minutes, the present is going to air on Vilkas's radio spot. Cole's parents will be listening, too, I've made sure of that. Do you have that?"

"Vilkas? What station is that on?" I asked. "Not that I'm saying anything."

"I know what it is," Koenig said, not looking up from the road. "Rick Vilkas."

"That's the one," Jeremy said, overhearing him. "Someone has excellent taste. You sure that Cole isn't around?"

"He really isn't," I said.

"Will you tell me something? When I last saw our intrepid hero Cole St. Clair, he was not in the best of places. In fact, I might say he was in the worst of them. All I want to know is, is he happy?"

I thought about what I knew of Cole. I thought about what it meant that he had a friend who cared that much about him. Cole could not have ever been terrible through and through, if someone cared this much about him from his past life. Or maybe he was just so great before he got terrible that he had a friend that rode that through to the other side. It sort of changed the way I thought about Cole, and sort of didn't. "Getting there."

There was a pause, and then Jeremy said, "And Victor?"

I didn't say anything at all. Neither did Jeremy. Koenig turned the radio on, the volume down, and began to tune it.

Jeremy said, "They both died a long time ago. I was there to see it. You ever watched a friend die in his own skin? Ahh. Well, you can only raise so many of the dead. *Getting there.*" It took me a second to realize that he was repeating my answer from before. "I'll take that. Tell him to listen to Vilkas, if you would. He changed my life. I won't forget that."

"I never said I knew where he was," I said.

"I know it," Jeremy replied. "I won't forget that, either."

The phone went quiet in my hand. I met Sam's eyes. The almost-summer sun was bright on his face and turned his eyes shockingly, eerily yellow. For half a second, I wondered if his parents would have tried to kill a brown-eyed boy, a blue-eyed boy. Any son that didn't have wolf's eyes already.

"Call Cole," Sam said.

I dialed Beck's house. The phone rang and rang, and just as I was about to give up, the phone clicked, and a second later, "Da?"

"Cole," I said, "turn on the radio."

CHAPTER FIFTY

· COLE ·

When I started everything, and by everything, I mean *life*, suicide was a joke. *If I have to ride in that car with you, I'll slash my wrists with a butter knife.* It was as real as a unicorn. No, less real than that. It was as real as the explosion around an animated coyote. A hundred thousand people threaten to kill themselves every day and make a hundred thousand other people laugh, because like a cartoon, it's funny and meaningless. Gone even before you turn off the TV.

Then it was a disease. Something other people got, if they lived someplace dirty enough to get the infection under their nails. It was *not a pleasant dinner table conversation, Cole,* and like the flu, it only killed the weak. If you'd been exposed, you didn't talk about it. Wouldn't want to put other people off their feed.

It wasn't until high school that it became a possibility. Not an immediate one, not like *It is a possibility I will download this album because the guitar is so sick it makes me want to dance,* but possibility in the way that some people said when they grew up, they might be a fireman or an astronaut or a CPA who works late every single weekend while his wife has an affair with the guy who drives the DHL truck. It became a possibility like *Maybe when I grow up, I will be dead.*

Life was a cake that looked good on the bakery shelf but turned to sawdust and salt when I ate it.

I looked good when I sang *the end.*

It took NARKOTIKA to make suicide a goal. A reward for services rendered. By the time they knew how to say NARKOTIKA in Russia, Japan, and Iowa, everything mattered and nothing did, and I was tired of trying to find out how both of those things were true. I was an itch that I'd scratched so hard I was bleeding. I had set out to do the impossible, whatever the impossible might be, only to find out that it was living with myself. Suicide became an expiration date, the day after which I no longer had to try.

I had thought I had come to Minnesota to die.

At two fifteen in the afternoon, Rick Vilkas had just finished his first commercial break. He was a music god who'd had us play live on his show and then asked me to sign a poster for his wife, who he said would only make love to our song "Sinking Ship (Going Down)." I'd written *Rock the boat* under my picture and signed my name. Rick Vilkas's on-air persona was confidant, best friend over beer, passing along a secret in a low voice with an elbow in your side.

His voice now, coming through speakers in Beck's living room, was intimate. "Everyone who listens to this show knows — hell, everyone who listens to the radio knows — Cole St. Clair, front man of NARKOTIKA and damned fine songwriter, has been missing for what — almost a year? ten months? somewhere in there. Oh, I know, I know — my producer, he's rolling his eyes. Say what you like, Buddy, he might have been a number one screwup, but he could write a song."

There it was, my name on the radio. I was sure it had been on the radio plenty of times in the past year, but this was the first time I'd been there for it. I waited to feel something — a sting of regret, guilt, agony — but there was nothing. NARKOTIKA was an ex-girlfriend whose photo no longer had the power to evoke emotion.

Vilkas continued, "Well, it looks like we have some news, and we're the first to break it. Cole St. Clair's not dead, folks. He's not being held captive by a pack of fangirls or my wife, either. We've got a statement from his agent right now that says that St. Clair had a medical complication related to drug abuse — fancy that, did you people imagine that the lead singer of NARKOTIKA might have a substance abuse problem? — and that he went with his bandmate for some under-the-radar treatment and rehab out of the country. Says here he's back in the States but is asking to be left alone while he 'figures out what to do next.' There you have it, folks. Cole St. Clair. He's alive. No, no, don't thank me now. Thank me later. Let's hope for a reunion tour, right? Make my wife happy. Take all the time you need, Cole, if you're listening. Rock'll wait."

Vilkas played one of our songs. I turned the radio off and rubbed my hand over my mouth. My legs were cramped from crouching in front of the stereo.

Six months ago, there would have been nothing worse in this world. There had been nothing I wanted more than to be thought missing or dead, unless it was to actually *be* missing or dead.

On the couch behind me, Isabel said, "So now you're officially reborn."

I turned the radio back on so I could catch the end of the song. One of my hands lay open on my knee and it felt like the whole world lay on my palm. The day felt like a prison break.

"Yes," I said. "Looks that way."

CHAPTER FIFTY-ONE

· SAM ·

As soon as I saw the peninsula, I knew it was the solution.

It wasn't that the entrance was exceedingly propitious. There was a rough-hewn log entranceway with the words KNIFE LAKE LODGE burned into it, and on either side of that was stockade fencing. Koenig swore softly over the combination lock on the gate until it yielded, and then he showed us how the stockade fence gave way to box wire fencing U-nailed to evergreen trees every few feet. He was polite and matter-of-fact, like a realtor showing potential clients an expensive piece of land.

"What happens when it gets to the water?" I asked. Beside me, Grace slapped a mosquito. There were a lot of them, despite the chill. I was glad that we'd come so early in the day, because the air had teeth up here.

Koenig gave the wire a tug; it remained snugly pinned to the ragged bark of the pine. "It goes a couple of yards into the lake, like I said. Did I say that before? Would you like to take a look?"

I wasn't sure if I wanted to take a look. I didn't know what I was looking for. Overhead, a thrush called continuously, sounding like a rusty swing set in motion. Slightly farther away, I could hear another bird singing like someone rolling their *r*'s, and beyond that one, another bird keening, and beyond that, another still — the kind of dense, endless layers of trees and birds that you got when there was not a human footprint in hundreds and hundreds of acres. Standing in this old conifer forest, long-since abandoned by people, I smelled a herd of deer and creeping beavers and small rodents turning over rocky soil, and as nervous excitement tapped through my veins, I felt more wolf than I had in a long time.

"I do," Grace said. "If you don't mind."

"It's why we're here," Koenig said, and set off through the trees, sure-footed as always. "Don't forget to check yourself for ticks when we're all through."

I trailed after, content to let Grace look at the concrete details of life while I walked through the forest and tried to imagine the pack here. These woods were dense and difficult to walk through; the ground was covered with ferns that hid dips and rocks. The fence was enough to keep out large animals, so unlike Boundary Wood, there were no natural paths worn through the underbrush. The wolves would have no competition here. No danger. Koenig was right; if the wolves were to be moved, you couldn't ask for a better place.

Grace squeezed my elbow, making so much noise on the way to me that I realized I had been left far behind. "Sam," she said, and she was breathless, as if she might have been thinking the same thing I was. "Did you see the lodge?"

"I was looking at the ferns," I said.

She grabbed hold of my arm and laughed, a clear, happy laugh that I hadn't heard in a long time. "Ferns," she repeated, and hugged my arm. "Crazy boy. Come over here."

Holding hands felt strangely fanciful when done in the presence of Koenig, possibly because it was the first thing he looked at when we emerged in the clearing that held the lodge. He had put a baseball cap on his head to ward off deer flies in the open area — which somehow managed to make him look more formal, not less — and stood in front of a faded wooden cabin that seemed enormous to me. It was all windows and rough-hewn timber and looked like something tourists imagined Minnesota looked like.

"That's the lodge?"

Koenig led the way, kicking debris off the concrete pad in front of the building. "Yeah. It used to be a lot nicer."

I had been expecting — no, not even expecting, merely *hoping for* — a tiny cabin, some remnant of the resort's former life that members of the pack could shelter in when they became human. Somehow, when Koenig had said resort, I hadn't thought he'd really meant it. I'd thought it was a slightly aggrandized retelling of a failed family business. This must have been something to look at when it was first built.

Grace pulled her hand away from me so she could investigate better. She peered in a dusty window, cupping her hands against the glass. A vine rested on top of her head; the rest of it crawled up the side of the lodge. She stood in ankle-deep weeds that had sprung up in the crack between the concrete pad and the foundation. She looked very tidy in comparison, clean jeans, one of my windbreakers, her blond hair spread over her shoulders. "Seems pretty nice to me," Grace said, forever endearing her to me.

It seemed to endear her to Koenig, too. Once he realized she wasn't being sarcastic, he said, "I suppose so. There's no power here, though, not anymore. I guess you could get it put back on, but you'd have to have meter guys come out here then, once a month."

Grace, her face still smushed against the glass, said, "Oh, that sounds like the beginning of a horror movie. That's a big fireplace in there, though, isn't it? You could make it livable without power, if you were clever." I stood next to her and pressed my face against the window. Inside, I saw a dim great room dominated by a massive fireplace. Everything looked gray and abandoned: rugs made colorless by dust, a dead potted plant, a mounted animal head rendered unidentifiable by age. It was an abandoned hotel lobby, a snapshot of the *Titanic* under the ocean. A small cabin seemed more manageable all of a sudden.

"Can I go look at the rest of the land?" I asked, drawing back from the glass. I pulled Grace gently away from the climbing vine; it was poison ivy.

"Be my guest," Koenig said. Then, after a pause, he said, "Sam?" There was a cautious note to the way he said it that made me think I wasn't going to like what he said next.

"Yes, sir?" I asked. The *sir* slipped out before I even thought about it, and Grace didn't even glance over in my direction at it, just looked at Koenig herself. It was that sort of way that he'd said, *Sam?*

"Geoffrey Beck is your legal adoptive father, correct?"

"Yes," I said. My heart jerked in my chest at the question, not because my answer was a lie, but because I didn't understand why he was asking it. Maybe he was going to change his mind about helping us. I tried to sound nonchalant. "Why do you ask?"

"I am trying to decide if I regard what he did to you as a crime," Koenig said.

Even though we were far out of context, here in Nowhere, Minnesota, I knew what he meant. This was what he meant: me, pinned in a snowbank in front of an ordinary house, wolf breath hot on my face. Now my heart was really going. Maybe he had never intended to help us. Maybe this entire trip, every single conversation, had been to incriminate Beck. How did I know what this was about? My face felt hot; maybe it had been naive of me to think that a cop would so willingly help us.

I held Koenig's gaze though my pulse was fast. "He couldn't know that my parents would try to kill me."

"Ah, but that makes it more odious, I believe," Koenig replied, so quickly that he must've known how I would counter him. "If they hadn't tried to kill you and removed themselves from the picture, what were his intentions? Kidnapping? Would he have taken you if they hadn't made it easy?"

Grace interrupted, "You can't charge someone for something they might have done."

I glanced at her. I wondered if she was thinking the same things I was.

Koenig continued, "But he did have those two wolves attack Sam, with an intent to harm."

"Not harm," I muttered, but I looked away.

Koenig's voice was grave. "I consider what he did to you harm. Would you walk up to someone else's child, Grace, and bite them?"

Grace made a face.

"How about you, Sam? No? Just because most of the world doesn't know about the weapon that Geoffrey Beck used on you doesn't make it less of an assault."

On the one hand, I knew he was right, but on the other was the Beck that I knew, the Beck who had made me who I was. If Grace thought I was a kind person, a generous one, it was because I had learned it from Beck. If he was a monster, surely I should have become a tiny monster in his image? All of these years, I had known the facts of my coming to the pack. The slow car, the wolves, the death of Sam Roth, son of middle-class parents in Duluth, one of whom had worked in the post office, the other of whom had worked in an office doing nothing that looked like work to a seven-year-old. As an adult looking back, the wolf attack was clearly no accident. And as an adult, I knew Beck was behind it. That he'd *engineered* it — "engineer" was such a purposeful word, hard to mitigate.

"Did he do anything else to you, Sam?" Koenig asked.

For one long minute, I didn't realize what he meant. Then my head jerked up. "No!"

Koenig just looked at me, reproachful. I hated him then for taking Beck away from me, but I hated Beck more, for being so easily taken. I missed right and wrong and nothing in between.

"Stop," I said. "Just stop. Please?"

Grace said gently, "Beck's a wolf now. I think you'd find it very hard to prosecute him, and even if you did, I think he's serving his sentence right now."

"I'm sorry." Koenig held up his hands as if I were pointing a weapon at him. "Cop-brain. You're right. I just — never mind. It's very hard to get it out of your mind, once you start thinking about it. Your story. The pack's story. Do you want to go inside the lodge? I'm going inside for a moment. I want to make sure there is nothing in there that any family members might be tempted to come back for."

"I'm going to walk first," I said. I felt hollow with relief, that Koenig was really as he seemed. Everything about this plan felt fragile. "If that's okay."

Koenig nodded sharply, still looking apologetic. He tried the handle of the door. It opened without protest and he didn't look at us as he went inside.

Once he'd disappeared inside, I headed around the back of the lodge, Grace following after she'd plucked a tick from the leg of her jeans and crushed it with her fingernail. I had no fixed thought of where I wanted to go, just away, just farther into the wild, just *more*; I suppose I had an idea I wanted to see the lake. A wooden plank path led us one hundred feet away from the lodge and back into the trees before giving way to ferns and thorns. I listened to the birds and the sounds of our feet through the underbrush. The afternoon sun was painting everything shades of gold and green. I felt very quiet and small and still inside.

Grace said, "Sam, this could work."

I didn't look at her. I was thinking about the miles of road between us and home. Beck's house already felt like a wistful memory. "That lodge is scary."

"It could be cleaned up," Grace said. "It could work."

"I know," I said. "I know it could."

There was a massive outcropping before us, the slender rocks longer than the Volkswagen, flat as shingles. Grace only paused for a moment before climbing up the side. I scrambled up after her and together we stood, higher than we had been before, but still not high enough to see the tops of the tallest trees. There was only the humming feeling one gets up high, that feeling that the ground was moving slightly, to say that we were any closer to the sky than we were on the ground. I had never seen pines this tall in Mercy Falls. One pine slanted close to the top of the outcropping and Grace dragged her fingers along its trunk, her face wondering. "It's so beautiful." She had to pause, her hand rested on the bark, to tip her head all the way back to see the top. There was something lovely in the way her mouth looked, lips parted with amazement, something lovely about just the line of her back and legs altogether, at home on top of this massive pile of rock in the middle of nowhere.

I said, "You make it easy to love you."

Grace dropped her fingers from the tree and turned to me. She turned her head sideways as if I'd told a riddle and she had to work to puzzle it out. "Why do you look so sad?"

I put my hands in my pockets and looked at the ground beyond the rock. There were a dozen different shades of green down there, if you were really looking. As a wolf, there wouldn't be a single one. "This is the place. But it's going to have to be me, Grace. That's what Cole wants. We can't trap all of the wolves and we don't have enough people to drive them out. The only chance we have is to lead them out, and it has to be a wolf with some sense of human direction. I wanted Cole to do it. I thought about this: If everything were fair and logical, it would be him. He likes being a wolf; it's his science, his toys. If the world were a fair place, he would be the one to lead them out. But no. He told me he couldn't hold anything in his head when he was a wolf. He said he wanted to, but he couldn't."

I heard Grace breathing, slow and cautious, but she didn't say anything.

"You don't even shift anymore," Grace said.

I knew the answer to that. With utmost certainty. "Cole could make it happen."

Grace pulled one of my hands out of a pocket and rested my curled fingers in her palm. I felt her pulse, light and steady, against my thumb.

"I was beginning to take these for granted," I said, moving my fingers against her skin. "I was beginning to think I'd never have to do it again. I was beginning to like the person I was." I wanted to tell her how badly I didn't want to shift again, how badly I didn't even want to think about shifting. How I was starting to finally think of myself in present tense, life in motion instead of life, preserved. But I didn't trust my voice to take me there. And admitting it out loud wouldn't make what had to be done any easier. So again I was silent.

"Oh, Sam," she said. She put her arms around my neck and let me rest my face against her skin. Her fingers moved through my hair. I heard her swallow. "When we —"

But she didn't finish. She just squeezed my neck hard enough that my breath had to ease by her body to escape. I kissed her collarbone, her hair tickling my face. She sighed.

Why did everything feel like saying good-bye?

The forest was noisy around us: birds singing, water splashing, wind whispering *sh-sh-sh* through the leaves; this was the sound of its breathing before we arrived and would keep being such after we left. The cloth of this natural world was made of private, unspoken sorrows, and ours was just another stitch on the hem.

"Sam." Koenig stood at the base of the outcropping. Grace and I stepped back from each other. I had one of Grace's hairs in my mouth. I removed it. "Your phone rang and dropped the call before they could leave a message. There's not enough reception out here for anyone to get through, really. It was your home number."

Cole.

"We should get back," Grace said, already climbing down with the same aplomb that she'd made the ascent. She stood beside Koenig and together they surveyed the rock and the surrounding forest until I joined them.

Koenig made the smallest of head gestures to the forest around us. "What do you think?"

I looked at Grace, so Koenig did, too. She just nodded.

"You, too?" Koenig asked me.

I smiled ruefully.

"That's what I thought," he said. "This is a good place to be lost."

CHAPTER FIFTY-TWO

· COLE ·

In one hour, I called Sam's cell phone as many times as I'd called Isabel's cell phone in two months. To the same effect. Nothing. I could take it personally, but I liked to think that I'd learned my lesson. Patience. It was a virtue.

It had never been one of my strong points.

I called Sam. The phone rang and rang until my ears were tricked into believing that every other ring was longer.

The minutes stretched out indefinitely. I put on music, and even the songs moved in slow motion. I was irritated every time a refrain came around; it felt like I'd already listened to it one hundred times before.

I called Sam.

Nothing.

I trotted down the basement stairs, up to the kitchen. I'd cleaned my stuff up, mostly, but in the spirit of benevolence and distracting myself, I used a wet paper towel to wipe the kitchen counter and make a small pyramid of escaped coffee grounds and toaster crumbs.

I called Sam. More ringing. I jogged back down to the basement, then to my stash of things in my bedroom. I rummaged through all the supplies I'd gathered over the past several months, not really needing anything, just wanting to be busy, to move my hands. My feet ran whether or not I was standing up, so I might as well stand.

I called Sam.

Ring, ring, ring, ring. Ring, ring. Ring, ring.

I got a pair of sweatpants and a T-shirt and took them down to the basement. I laid them on the chair. Wondered if I should get a long-sleeved shirt or a sweater. No. A T-shirt was fine. No. Maybe a sweater. I got a Berkeley sweatshirt out of a drawer.

I called Sam.

Nothing. *Nothing.* Where in hell was he?

I jotted in Beck's notebook that was now mine. I went back down to the basement. I checked the thermostat. I turned it as hot as it would go. I got space heaters from the garage. I found wall sockets in the basement and plugged them in. It was a barbecue down there. Not hot enough. I needed it to be summer inside these walls.

I called Sam.

Two rings. Three.

"Cole, what is it?" It was Sam. His voice was staticky, indistinct, but it was him.

"Sam," I said. I sounded a little peevish at this point, but I felt I deserved it. I looked down at the wolf body on the floor in front of me. The sedatives were starting to wear off. "I've caught Beck."

Chapter Fifty-Three

· SAM ·

I hadn't realized until Cole caught Beck that it was Chinese Day.

For the longest time, I'd thought Chinese Day was a real holiday. Every year on the same day in May, Ulrik or Paul and whoever else was there would take me and Shelby and head out for a day of festivities — balloon in my hand, museums visited, fancy cars we didn't intend to buy taken for test drives — that concluded with an epic meal at Fortune Garden in Duluth. I didn't eat much but the spring rolls and fortune cookies, but the association with the day of revelry made it my favorite restaurant regardless. We always ended up with a dozen white takeaway boxes that populated the refrigerator for weeks. Long after dark, we'd pull into the driveway and I'd have to be dragged and prodded up the stairs to bed.

Beck never came with us. Paul gave a different excuse every year. *He has work and needs us out of the house* or *He was up late* or *He doesn't celebrate Chinese Day*. I didn't think about it, really. There were plenty of other things going on that day to hold my attention. The truth was I was young and self-involved and, in the way of youth, I didn't think about what my guardians did when I wasn't with them. It was easy for me to imagine Beck working hard in his home office on that day, if I imagined anything at all.

So for years, Chinese Day came and went. Up at the crack of dawn and out of the house. As I got older, I began to see more details that I'd missed when I was younger. As we left, Ulrik or Paul would always take the phone off the hook, and they'd lock the front door behind us, as if no one were home.

By the time I was thirteen or fourteen, I no longer fell asleep the moment we got home. Usually I would feign sleepiness so that I could retreat to my room with whatever new book or possession I'd acquired on that particular Chinese Day. I would creep out of my room only to pee before I finally turned out my light. One year, though, as I left my room, I heard — something. I still don't remember what it was about the sound that made me pause in the hall. Something about it was out of place, unfamiliar.

So for the first time, I silently padded past the bathroom toward where Beck's bedroom door was cracked open. I hesitated, listening, glancing behind me to make certain I wasn't being watched. And then I took another soundless step forward so that I could see into Beck's room.

The small lamp on his bedside table weakly illuminated his room. There was a plate in the middle of the floor with an untouched sandwich and browning slices of apple on it, and a full coffee mug beside it, an ugly ring around the edge where the milk had separated. A few feet away from that, sitting on the floor at the end of the bed, facing away from me, was Beck. There was something shocking to me about his posture, something that later I could never forget. His knees were drawn up to his chest like a boy's and his hands were laced behind his head, pulling it down toward his body as if he were protecting it from an oncoming blast.

I didn't understand. And then I heard the soft sound again, and saw his shoulders shake. No, not his shoulders, but his entire body, a tremble more than a shake, the intermittent, silent sobs of someone who has been at it for a while and is saving his strength for the long haul still to come.

I remember feeling nothing but absolute surprise that Beck should have had something like this living inside him and that I had never known, never even guessed. Later I'd learn it was not the only secret Beck had, just maybe the best-kept one.

I left Beck up there, him and his private grief, and I went downstairs to find Ulrik, flipping listlessly through television stations in the living room.

I said simply, "What's wrong with him?"

That was how I learned about Beck's wife, and how she had died on this day in May, nine years earlier. Right before I was bitten. I hadn't made the connection, or if I had, it wasn't in any important way, not in any way that mattered.

Now, it mattered.

Chapter Fifty-Four

· SAM ·

As we pulled into the driveway, my cell phone rang again. Koenig didn't even put the truck into park. He put his foot on the brake pedal. He looked at his watch and then in his rearview mirror as we climbed out.

"Are you coming in?" Grace asked him, leaning in. It hadn't occurred to me that he might want to.

"No," Koenig said. "I'm pretty sure that whatever is going on in there is — I would just prefer to have plausible deniability. I never saw you today. You are talking to your parents later, correct?"

Grace nodded. "I am. Thanks. For everything."

"Yes," I said. It wasn't really enough. The phone was still ringing. It was still Cole. I needed to say more to Koenig, but — Beck. Beck was in there.

"Call me later, when you decide," Koenig said. "And, Sam, pick up your phone."

Grace shut the door and patted the side of the truck, twice, sending Koenig off.

"I'm here," I said, into the phone.

"Took you long enough," Cole said. "Did you walk back?"

"What?" I asked. The afternoon light was coming in strong and low through the pine trees; I had to blink and look the other way. I thought I hadn't understood him right. "I'm in the driveway now."

Cole paused before saying, "Good thing, too. Hurry the hell up. And if you get bitten, remember, this was your idea."

I asked Cole, "Do I even want to know?"

"I may have misjudged doggie tranquilizer dosages. Not everything you read online is true. Apparently wolves require more than neurotic German shepherds."

"Jesus," I said. "So Beck is loose in the house? Just wandering around?"

Cole's voice sounded a little terse. "I'd like to point out that I did the impossible part for you already. I got him out of the woods. *You* can get him out of your bedroom."

We hurried to the front door. In this light, the windows of the house were mirrors full of the sun. Once upon a time, this would be dinnertime. I'd be walking into a house full of microwaved leftovers, pending algebra homework, Iron Butterfly pounding out of the speakers, and Ulrik playing air drums. Beck would say: "Someone once said European men had great taste. That someone got it really wrong." The house would feel filled to capacity; I'd retreat to my room for some peace.

I missed that sort of noise.

Beck. Beck was here.

Cole made a hissing sound. "Are you inside yet? God bless America and all her sons. What is taking you so long?"

The front door was locked. "Here, talk to Grace," I said.

"Mommy isn't going to give me a different answer than Daddy," Cole said, but I handed her the phone anyway.

"Talk to him. I have to get my keys out." I dug in my pocket and unlocked the front door.

"Hi," said Grace. "We're coming in." She hung up on him.

I pushed open the front door and blinked to get used to the dimness. The first impression I got was of red striped over the furniture, the long afternoon light coming in the window and lying over the furniture. There was no sign of Cole or a wolf. He was not upstairs, despite his sarcastic response.

My phone rang.

"Sheesh," Grace said, handing it to me.

I held it to my ear.

"Basement," Cole said. "Follow the smell of burning flesh."

I found the basement door open and heat emanating from the stairs. Even from here, I could smell wolf: nerves and damp forest floor and growing spring things. As I descended the stairs into the dim brown light of the basement, my stomach twisted with anxiety. At the bottom of the stairs, Cole stood with his arms crossed. He cracked every knuckle on his right hand with his thumb and started on his left. Behind him, I saw space heaters, the source of the choking heat.

"Finally," Cole said. "He was a lot groggier fifteen minutes ago. What took you so long? Did you go to Canada? Did you have to invent the internal combustion engine before you could leave?"

"It was a couple of hours' drive." I looked at the wolf. He lay in an unlikely, twisted position that no fully conscious animal would adopt. Half on his side, half pushed up onto his chest. Head weaving, eyes half closed, ears limp. My pulse was shallow and fast, a moth destroying itself on a light.

"Speeding was an option," Cole said. "Cops don't get tickets."

"Why the heaters?" I asked. "That won't make him change."

"Might keep a career werewolf human a little longer if this works," Cole said. "If we don't all get savaged first, which is a possibility if we dick around for much longer."

"Shh," Grace said. "Are we doing this or not, Sam?"

She looked at me, not Cole. The decision was mine.

I joined her in a crouch beside the wolf, and at my presence, his joints jerked as he became suddenly responsive. His ears were instantly more alert and his eyes flicked to meet mine. Beck's eyes. Beck. *Beck.* My heart hurt. I waited for that moment of recognition from him, but it never came. Just that gaze, and then uncoordinated paws scrabbling, trying to move his drugged body.

Suddenly the idea of sticking him with a needle full of epinephrine and God knew what else seemed ludicrous. This wolf was so firmly a wolf that Beck could never be pulled out of him. There was nothing here but Beck's eyes with no Beck behind them. My mind grabbed at lyrics, something to get me out of this moment, something to save me.

Empty houses don't need windows
'cause no one's looking in
Why would a house need windows, anyway
If no one's looking out again

The idea of seeing him again, just *seeing* him, as him, was such a powerful one. I hadn't realized until this moment how much I had wanted it. Needed it.

Cole crouched down next to us, the syringe in his hand. "Sam?" But really, he was looking at Grace, who was looking at me.

Instantly, my brain replayed that second where the wolf's eyes met mine. His gaze, without any understanding or reasoning behind it. We had no idea what we were working with here. No idea what effect the drugs would have on him. Cole had already guessed wrong on the dosage for the Benadryl. What if what he had in that syringe killed Beck? Could I live with that? I knew what choice I would make — *had* made — in the same situation. Given the choice between dying and having the chance to become human, I'd taken the risk. But I had been given the choice. I had been able to say yes or no.

"Wait," I said. The wolf was starting to stumble to his feet, his upper lip pulling back slowly from his teeth in a warning.

But then there was this: me pushed into the snow, my life traded for this one, car doors slamming, Beck making the plan to bite me, *taking* everything away from me. I had never had a choice; it was simply forced upon me on one day that could've been no different from any other day in my life. He'd made the decision for me. So this was fair. No yes or no then. No yes or no now.

I wanted this to work. I wanted it to make him human so I could demand an answer to every question I'd never asked. I wanted to force him into a human so that he could see my face one last time and tell me why he'd done this to me out of every human being on the planet, why me, why anyone, *why*. And, impossibly, I wanted to see him again so I could tell him I missed him so badly.

I wanted it.

But I didn't know if he did.

I looked at Cole. "No. No, I changed my mind. I can't do it. I'm not that person."

Cole's green eyes, brilliant, held mine for a moment. He said, "But I am."

And, fast as a snake, he stuck the needle into the wolf's thigh.

· COLE ·

"Cole," Grace snapped. "I can't believe you! I just can't —"

Then the wolf twitched, stumbling back from us, and Grace fell silent. It was convulsing with angular spasms that racked its body in time with a rapidly ascending pulse. It was impossible to tell if we were witnessing death or rebirth. A spasm rippled along the wolf's coat, and it jerked its head upward in a violent, unnatural movement. A slow, ascending whine escaped from its nostrils.

It was working.

The wolf's mouth cracked open in a gesture of silent agony.

Sam turned his head away.

It was working.

I wanted, in that moment, to have my father standing there, watching, so I could say: *Look at this. For every test of yours I couldn't do, look at this.* I was on fire with it.

In a sudden, shivering movement, the wolf backed out of its skin and lay on the worn carpet at the base of the stairs. No longer a wolf. He was stretched out on his side, fingers clawed into the carpet, muscles hard and stringy over prominent bones. Colorless scars nicked his back, like it was a shell instead of skin. I was fascinated. It was not a man, it was a sculpture of a man-shaped animal, made for endurance and hunting.

Sam's hands were limp at his sides. Grace was looking at me, her face furious.

But I was looking at Beck.

Beck.

I had pulled him out of that wolf.

I walked my fingers across the wall until I found the light switch at the base of the stairs. As yellow light pooled in the basement, illuminating the bookshelves that lined the walls, he jerked to cover his eyes with his arm. His skin was still twitching and crawling, as if it wasn't sure it wanted to remain in its current form. With all of the space heaters humming down here, the temperature was suffocating. The heat was pushing me so firmly into my human skin that I couldn't imagine being anything else. If this inferno didn't keep him human, nothing would.

Sam silently climbed the stairs to shut the basement door to eliminate any drafts.

"You are really lucky that didn't turn out badly," Grace said, her voice low, for me alone.

I raised an eyebrow at her and then looked back to Beck. "Hey," I said to him, "once you're done with all that, I have clothing for you. You can thank me later."

The man made a soft sound as he exhaled and shifted positions, the sort of sound someone makes without thinking when they're in pain. He pushed his upper body off the ground in a move that seemed more wolf than man, and finally, he looked at me.

It was months ago, and I was lying in the body I'd ruined.

There is another way out of all this, he had said. *I can get you out of this world. I can make you disappear. I can fix you.*

After all this time — it felt like years since he had injected me with the werewolf toxin — here he was again. It was a pretty damn perfect piece of circularity: The man who'd made me a werewolf was the wolf that I'd made into a man.

It was clear from his eyes, though, that his mind was still far, far away. He had pulled himself into an odd, animal position somewhere between sitting and crouching, and he regarded me warily. His hands were shaking. I didn't know if that was from the change or from me sticking him.

"Tell me when you recognize me," I said to him. I got the sweatpants and sweatshirt from the chair I'd left them on, never quite turning my back to him.

I balled the fabric and tossed it in Beck's direction. The clothing *swuff*ed gently to the ground in front of him, but he didn't pay attention to it. His eyes glanced from me to the bookshelves behind me to the ceiling. I could actually see the expression in them transition, ever so slowly, from escape to recognition as he rebooted as Beck, the man, instead of Beck, the wolf.

Finally, he jerkily pulled on the sweatpants and faced me. He left the sweatshirt lying on the floor. "How did you do this?" He looked away from me, as if he didn't expect me to have the answer, and instead looked at his hands, his fingers spread wide. He studied both sides of them, backs and then palms, his eyebrows drawn together. It was such a strange, intimate gesture that I glanced away. It reminded me of our funeral for Victor for some reason.

"Cole," he said, and his voice was thick and gravelly. He cleared his throat, and his voice was a little better the second try. "How did you do this?"

"Adrenaline." It was the simplest answer. "And some of adrenaline's friends."

"How did you know it would work?" Beck asked, and then, before I had a chance to reply, he answered himself. "You didn't. I was the experiment."

I didn't reply.

"Did you know it was me?"

No point lying. I nodded.

Beck looked up. "I'd rather that you had known. There are wolves that should stay wolves in those woods." He suddenly seemed to realize that Grace was standing opposite from me. "Grace," he said. "Sam — did it work? Is he —?"

"It worked," Grace said softly. Her arms were crossed tightly in front of her. "He's human. He hasn't shifted back since then."

Beck closed his eyes and tipped his head back, his shoulders collapsing. I watched him swallow. It was naked relief, and it was sort of hard to watch. "Is he here?"

Grace looked at me.

I heard Sam's voice from the stairs, sounding like nothing I'd ever heard from him.

"I'm here."

· SAM ·

Beck.

I couldn't keep my thoughts together. They scattered down the stairs, across the floor.

      he is a hand on my shoulder

car tires hissing on wet pavement

        his voice narrates my childhood

the smell of the forest on my suburban street

      my handwriting looks like his

wolves

        he shouts across the house, *sam, homework*

snow pressed against my skin

      hold on, he said. *don't be afraid. you're still sam*

my skin rips open

      my new desk for all my books

I

      my hands sweaty on the steering wheel of his car

never

      endless evenings, all the same, standing by the grill

wanted

        you're the best of us, Sam

this

Chapter Fifty-Five

· GRACE ·

My first thought was that Sam needed to talk to Beck, to sort out all of the conflicted emotions in him, and my second thought was that Cole needed to talk to Beck about the various scientific concepts he'd tried out on himself, but my third thought was that I seemed to be the only one remembering exactly the reason why we absolutely needed to talk to Geoffrey Beck.

"Beck," I said, feeling a little weird addressing him, but neither of the boys were, so what else was there for it, "I'm so sorry that we have to ask you questions when you feel like this."

It was clear that he was suffering; Cole had made him human, but only barely. There was a scent and energy to the room that was wolfish still; if I'd closed my eyes and used my hidden senses to focus on Beck, I doubted I would've pictured him as human.

"Do it," Beck said. His gaze jerked to Cole, to Sam, and then back to me.

"Tom Culpeper got an aerial hunt approved. In a week." I waited for that to sink in, to see if I had to explain more what that meant.

Beck said softly, "Shit."

I nodded. "We were thinking that we could move the pack. We need to know how."

"My journal . . ." Beck, inexplicably, pressed one of his hands over his shoulder for a moment, holding it. He released it. It was harder, I thought, to watch someone in pain than to be in it yourself.

"I read it," Cole replied. He stepped closer. He seemed less distressed than me by Beck's discomfort; maybe he was more used to seeing people hurting. "You said Hannah led them out. How? How did she keep the destination in her head?"

Beck glanced up to where Sam still stood silently on the stairs, then he answered, "Hannah was like Sam. She could hold some of her thoughts while she was a wolf. Better than the rest of us. Not as well as Sam, but better than me. She and Derrick were thick as thieves. Derrick was good at sending the images. She and Paul brought the wolves together, and Derrick stayed human. He kept that image of where we were going in his head and gave it to her. She led the wolves. He led her."

"Could Sam do it?" Cole asked.

I didn't want to look at Sam. I knew that Cole already believed that he could.

Beck frowned at me. "If either of you is able to send him images while you're human."

I glanced to Sam now, but his face betrayed no thoughts whatsoever. I didn't know if the brief, uncontrolled moments we had counted, when he'd showed me the golden woods when I was human, and when I'd showed him images of us together way back when we were in the clinic, injecting him with meningitis-infected blood. The latter, at least, had been close, intimate. I'd been right next to him. It wasn't like I was tossing the images from a car window while we ran from the woods. Losing Sam to his wolf form again for a plan as shaky as this . . . I hated the idea of it. We'd fought so hard for him to stay in that body. He despised losing himself so much.

"My turn," Beck said. "My turn for questions. But a demand first. When I shift back here, put me back in the woods. Whatever happens to the wolves out there, I want to happen to me. They live, I live. They die, I die. Is that clear?"

I expected Sam to lodge a protest, but he said nothing. *Nothing.* I didn't know what I should do. Go to him? There was something far-away and terrifying about his expression.

Cole said, "Done."

Beck didn't look disappointed. "First question. Tell me about the cure. You're asking about Sam leading the wolves out, but he's human. So the cure didn't work?"

"It worked," Cole said. "The meningitis is battling the wolf. If I'm right, he'll still shift, every so often. But eventually he'll stop. Equilibrium."

"Second question," Beck said. He grimaced, pain written in the creases of his forehead, and then his face cleared. "Why is Grace a wolf now?" When he saw me looking at him sharply, he pointed to his nose with a wry expression. It was somehow gratifying that despite every-thing, he remembered my name and was concerned about me. It was hard to dislike him, even on Sam's behalf; the idea that he'd ever hurt Sam seemed so impossible when he was actually in front of you. If this was how conflicted *I* was after only meeting him a few times, I could only imagine how Sam was feeling.

"You don't have time to hear that whole answer," Cole said. "Short answer: because she was bitten and chickens come home to roost eventually."

"Okay, then, third question," Beck said. "Can you cure her?"

"The cure killed Jack," Sam said, the first words he'd spoken. He hadn't been there, like I had, to watch Jack die from the meningitis, his fingers turning blue as his heart gave up on them.

Cole's voice was dismissive, "He took on meningitis as a human. That's an unwinnable battle. You did it as a wolf."

Sam's attention was on Cole and no one else. "How do we know you're right?"

Cole gestured broadly to Beck. "Because I have yet to be wrong."

But Cole *had* been wrong before. It was just that he kept being right in the end. It seemed like an important difference.

Beck said, "Fourth question. Where are you moving them?"

"A peninsula north of here," Cole said. "A cop owns it now. He found out about the wolves and wanted to help. Out of the kindness of his heart."

Beck's face was uncertain.

"I know what you're thinking," Cole said. "I've already decided; I'm going to buy it from him. Kindness is great. A deed in my name is better."

Startled, I looked at Cole, and he looked back at me, his mouth set into a little line. Later, we had to talk to him about this.

"Last question," Beck said. Something about his voice reminded me of the first time I'd ever spoken to him, on the phone, when I was being held hostage by Jack. There'd been something so sympathetic about his voice, something so kind, that it had almost broken me when nothing else had. And everything about his face now seemed to reinforce that: the honest squareness of his jaw; the lines by his mouth and eyes that seemed like they'd rather be smiling; the concerned, earnest set of his eyebrows. He rubbed a hand through his cropped auburn hair and then he looked up at Sam. He sounded absolutely miserable. "Are you ever going to speak to me?"

· SAM ·

Here was Beck in front of me, and he was already on his way back to being a wolf, and every word that I'd ever said had left me.

"I'm trying to think of what I can say," Beck said, his eyes on me. "I have maybe ten minutes to raise my son who I didn't think would live past eighteen. What do I say, Sam? What do I say?"

I held the banister in front of me, my knuckles white. I was the one who asked the questions, not Beck. He was the one with the answers. What did he expect from me? I couldn't step without putting my feet into the prints that he'd left.

Beck crouched in front of one of the space heaters, not taking his gaze from me. "Maybe, after all this, there isn't anything to say. Ah, I . . ." He shook his head a little and looked at the floor. His feet were pale and scarred. Something about them looked like a kid's feet.

The room was silent. Everyone was watching me, as if the next move was up to me. But his question was mine: What did I say, in ten minutes? There were a thousand things that *needed* to be said. That I didn't know how to help Grace, now that she was a wolf. That Olivia had died, the police were watching me, Cole holds our fates in vials, what do we do, how do we save ourselves, how do I be Sam when winter means the same things as the summer?

My voice was rough and low when I spoke. "Were you driving?"

"Yeah," Beck said softly. "Yeah, you would want to know that, wouldn't you?"

I had my hands in my pockets. Part of me wanted to take them out and cross them, but I didn't want to look anxious. Grace looked like she was moving even though she was standing still, like she wanted to move but her feet hadn't made up their mind yet. I wanted her here with me. I didn't want her to hear his answer. I was made of impossibilities.

Beck swallowed again. When he looked back up at me, his expression was a white flag. Surrendering the truth. Offering himself up for judgment. He said, "Ulrik was driving."

I heard myself make a sound — barely audible — as I turned my face away. I wanted to get one of my boxes out of my head and climb into it, but Beck was the one who had told me about the boxes in the first place. So instead, I had this. Me lying in the snow with my skin gaping at the sky and there was a wolf, and it was Beck.

I couldn't think of it.

I couldn't stop thinking of it.

I closed my eyes, and it was still there.

A touch on my elbow made my eyes open. It was Grace, looking carefully at my face, holding my elbow as if it were made of glass.

"Ulrik was driving," Beck said again, and his voice got a little louder. "Paul and I were the wolves. I — I didn't trust Ulrik to stay focused. Paul didn't want to do it. I bullied him. I know you don't have to forgive me. I haven't. No matter how much *right* I do after that, what I did to you will always have been wrong." He stopped. Took a long, shaky breath.

I didn't know this Beck.

Grace whispered in my ear, "At least look at him, Sam. You don't know when you'll see him again."

Because she asked, I looked at him.

"When I thought you didn't have another year, I —" Beck didn't finish. He shook his head, like clearing his thoughts. "I never thought that the woods would take you before me. And now I had to do it again — find someone to take care of us. But, listen to me, Sam. I tried to do it *right* this time."

He was still watching me for a reaction. I didn't have one. I was apart from this. I was somewhere else. I could find, if I tried now, a collection of words to pull into lyrics. Something that would remove me from this moment and take me somewhere else.

Beck saw it. He *knew* me, like no one else knew me, not even Grace, yet. He said, "Don't — Sam. Don't go away. Listen: I have to tell you this. I had eleven years worth of memories to reenact, Sam, eleven years of the look on your face every time you realized you were about to shift. Eleven years of you asking me if you really had to do it this year. Eleven years of —"

He stopped then, and put his hand over his mouth, shaking fingers holding his jaw. He was so much *less* than the Beck I'd last seen.

This was not the Beck of summer. This was the Beck of a dying year. There was none of the power in his body now; it was all in his eyes.

Suddenly, Cole's voice punched through the room. "Sam, you know I was trying to kill myself when he found me. I was getting really good at it, too." His eyes were on me, a challenge, unflinching. "I'd be dead now if it wasn't for him. He didn't force me. Victor, either. We both chose it. It wasn't like you."

I knew this was true. I knew that there had been and probably always would be two Coles: the Cole who silenced the crowd with a smile and the Cole who whispered songs about finding his Alps. And I knew that Beck, somehow, in pulling Cole from the stage, had unearthed that second, quieter Cole, and given him a chance to live.

And me, too. Beck had bitten me, but it had been my parents, not him, who'd destroyed me. I had come to him as a crushed piece of paper that he had slowly smoothed. It wasn't just Cole that he'd rebuilt.

There were so many different versions of him. It was countless versions of a song, and they were all the original, and they were all true, and they were all right. It should have been impossible. Was I supposed to love them all?

"Okay," Beck said, voice taking a moment to solidify. "Okay. If I only have ten minutes, Sam, this is what I want to say. You're not the best of us. You're more than that. You're better than all of us. If I only have ten minutes, I would tell you to go out there and live. I'd say . . . please take your guitar and sing your songs to as many people as you can. Please fold a thousand more of those damn birds of yours. Please kiss that girl a million times."

Beck suddenly broke off and ducked his head down to his knees; he clenched his hands on the back of his skull. I saw the muscles in his back twitching. Not lifting his head, he whispered, "And please forget all about me. I wish I had been better, but I wasn't. Please forget about me."

His hands were still white-knuckled fists on the back of his head.

So many ways to say good-bye.

I said, "I don't want to."

Beck lifted his head. His pulse was beating visibly in his neck, fast and hard.

Grace let go of me, and I knew that she meant to send me off, down the stairs. She was right. I went down the stairs, two at a time. Beck tried to stand, unsuccessfully, at the same time that I knelt swiftly down to meet him. Our foreheads were almost touching. Beck was shivering, hard.

So many days before this, it had been Beck crouching to meet me, me shivering on the floor.

I felt as unsteady as Beck, just then. It was like I'd unfolded all my paper crane memories and found something unfamiliar printed on them. Somehow along the way, hope had been folded into one of those birds. My whole life, I had thought that my story was, again and again: *Once upon a time, there was a boy, and he had to risk everything to keep what he loved.* But really, the story was: *Once upon a time, there was a boy, and his fear ate him alive.*

I was done being afraid. It had started that night, me and my guitar in the bathtub, and it would end with me disappearing into a wolf again. I wouldn't be afraid.

"Dammit," Beck whispered, soft as a sigh. The heat was losing its grip on him. We were forehead to forehead again, father and son, Beck and Sam, the way it had always been. He was every devil and every angel.

I said, "Tell me you want us to cure you."

Beck's fingertips were white and then red, pushed against the floor. "Yes," he said quietly, and I knew he was saying it for me, just me. "Do what it takes." He looked up at Cole. "Cole, you are —"

And then his skin tore, violently, and I leaped to push the heater out of his way before Beck crashed to the floor, jerking.

Cole stepped forward and pushed a second needle into the crook of Beck's arm.

And in that split second, as Beck's face turned toward the ceiling, his eyes unchanging, I saw my own face.

CHAPTER FIFTY-SIX

· COLE ·

EPINEPHRINE/PSEUDOEPHEDRINE MIX 7
METHOD: INTRAVENOUS INJECTION
RESULT: SUCCESSFUL
(SIDE EFFECTS: NONE)
(NOTE: ENVIRONMENTAL FACTORS STILL DICTATE
     SHIFT BACK TO WOLF)

Chapter Fifty-Seven

· SAM ·

I felt dirty after Beck shifted back, like I'd been complicit in a crime. I was reminded so acutely of my life before, when I'd hidden from the winter and when I'd had my family, that I could feel my thoughts slipping away to protect me. I wasn't the only one, apparently: Cole announced that he was "going for a drive" and left in Ulrik's old BMW. After he'd gone, Grace trailed after me as I made bread as if my life depended on it, and then I left her watching the oven as I went to shower. To scrub the memories off me. To remind myself that, for now, I had my hands and my human skin and my face.

I wasn't sure how long I'd been in there when I heard the bathroom door open and close.

"This is good," Grace said. The closed toilet lid creaked as she tried to find a way to make it a comfortable seat. "Good job, Sam."

I couldn't see her, but I could smell the bread. I was oddly discomfited by the knowledge that she was in the room while I was standing there under the running water. Somehow taking a shower with her in the room was more intimate than sex. I felt about one thousand times more naked, even behind the dark shower curtain.

I looked at the bar of soap in my hand. I applied it to my ribs. "Thanks."

Grace was quiet, inches away on the other side of the curtain. I couldn't see her, so she couldn't see me.

"Are you all clean in there?" Grace asked.

"Oh my God, Grace," I replied, and she laughed.

There was another pause. I washed between my fingers. One of my fingernails was battered from rubbing against a guitar string. I studied it to see if I needed to do something about it; it was hard to properly diagnose it in the orange half-light provided by the shower curtain.

"Rachel said she would go with me, tomorrow, to see my parents," Grace said. "Tomorrow night. That's when she's free."

"Are you nervous?" *I* was nervous, and I wasn't even going, by Grace's request.

"I dunno. It just has to happen. It'll get you off the hook. Plus, I need to be officially alive for Olivia's funeral. Rachel said they cremated her." She stopped. There was a long space full of nothing but the water hitting me and the tile. She said, "This bread is excellent."

I got it. Subject change. "Ulrik taught me how to make it."

"What a talented guy. Speaks with a German accent *and* makes bread." On the other side, she poked the shower curtain; when it touched my bare hip, I shied away in an undignified fashion. "You know, this could be us, in five years."

I had no body parts left to clean. I was a prisoner in the shower unless I could reach my towel from behind the curtain or persuade Grace to hand it to me. I didn't think she would hand it to me. "Making bread with a German accent?" I suggested.

"That's exactly what I meant," she said. I heard the withering tone in her voice. I was glad to hear it. I could use levity at the moment.

"Will you give me my towel?"

"You have to come and get it."

"Vixen," I muttered. There was hot water left. I stood in it and looked at the uneven grout on the tiles under the showerhead. My fingers were getting pruney and the hair on my legs had stuck together to form soaked, matted arrows toward my feet.

"Sam?" Grace said. "Do you think Cole's right about the cure? About the meningitis working if you have it while you're a wolf? Do you think I should try it?"

This was too hard of a question to answer after the evening with Beck. Yes, I wanted her cured. I wanted more proof than me, though, that it would work. I wanted something to make the fate Jack had suffered a lower percentage of the possible outcomes. I had risked everything for this, but now that it came to it for Grace, I didn't want her to do the same. But how could she have a normal life without it?

"I don't know. I want more information." It sounded formal, like something I'd say to Koenig. *I am collecting more data.*

"I mean, we don't have to worry about it until winter, anyway," she said. "I was just wondering if you felt cured."

I didn't know what to tell her. I didn't feel cured. I felt like what Cole said — *almost* cured. A war survivor with a phantom limb. I still felt that wolf that I'd been: living in my cells, sleeping uneasily, waiting to be coaxed out by weather or a rush of adrenaline or a needle in my veins. I didn't know if that was real or suggested. I didn't know if one day I would feel secure in my skin, taking my human body for granted.

"You *look* cured," Grace said.

Just her face was visible at the end of the shower curtain, looking in at me. She grinned and I yelled. Grace reached in just far enough to shut off the tap.

"I'm afraid," she said, whipping the shower curtain open all the way and presenting me with my towel, "this is the sort of thing you'll have to put up with in your old age."

I stood there, dripping, feeling utterly ridiculous, Grace standing opposite, smiling with her challenge. There was nothing for it but to get over the awkwardness. Instead of taking the towel, I took her chin with my wet fingers and kissed her. Water from my hair ran down my cheeks and onto our lips. I was getting her shirt all wet, but she didn't seem to mind. A lifetime of this seemed rather appealing. I said gallantly, "That better be a promise."

Grace stepped into the shower in her sock feet and wrapped her arms around my damp chest. "It's a guarantee."

CHAPTER FIFTY-EIGHT

· ISABEL ·

I heard a soft knock on the mudroom door. Stepping over boots and a trowel and a bag of bird seed, I opened it.

Cole St. Clair stood in the black rectangle of the doorway, his hands in his pockets.

"Ask me in," he said.

Chapter Fifty-Nine

· GRACE ·

It was properly dark by the time Rachel and I got to my parents' house on Sunday night. Rachel, due to fascinating driving habits frowned upon by the Minnesota State Police, didn't have a driver's license, so I had had to pick her up. She'd showed me a beaded purse with a smiley face on the side by means of a hello and smiled a thin white smile in the dark. It was the dark, I thought, that made it so surreal to be pulling up in my parents' driveway. Because with only the porch light to illuminate the front of the rambler and a corner of the drive, everything about the house looked precisely the same as the night that I left.

I pulled up the parking brake beside the car I'd gotten with the insurance money from my last one — I remembered, all of a sudden, yet another night, the one when a deer had smashed through my Bronco's windshield and I'd thought that I was losing Sam to the wolves for good. That seemed like a million nights ago and hours ago at the same time. Tonight felt like a beginning and an ending.

Next to me, Rachel opened her beaded smiley face purse and removed some strawberry lip gloss. She applied two coats of fruity armor with fierce determination, and ferociously zipped it back into the purse. Then we marched to the front door, sisters in battle, the sounds of our shoes on the concrete sidewalk our only war cry. I didn't have a key, so I had to knock.

Now that I was here, I really didn't want to go through with it.

Rachel looked at me. She said, "You're like my favorite older sister, which doesn't make sense, because you're the same age as me."

I was flattered, but I said, "Rachel, you say weird things."

We both laughed, and our laughs were uncertain creations with almost no sound.

Rachel dabbed her lips on her sleeve; in the yellow glow offered by the moth-filled porch light, I saw evidence of where she'd done it earlier, a small collection of kisses on her cuff.

I tried to think of what to say. I tried to think of which of them would open the door. It was almost nine. Maybe *neither* of them would open it. Maybe —

It was Dad who opened the door. Before he had a chance to react to the fact that it was me, my mother shouted from the living room, "Don't let the kitten out!"

Dad stared at Rachel and then at me, and in the meantime, a brown tabby cat the size of a rabbit crept around the doorjamb and shot into the yard beyond us. I felt ridiculously betrayed by the presence of the cat. Their only daughter had disappeared and they'd gotten a *kitten* to replace me?

And it was the first thing I said. "You got a cat?"

My father was shocked enough by my presence that he answered honestly. "Your mother was lonely."

"Cats are very low maintenance." It was not the warmest of replies, but he hadn't exactly delivered the warmest of opening lines, either. I had expected, somehow, to find evidence of my absence on his face, but he looked as he always did. My father sold expensive real estate and he looked like he sold expensive real estate. He had well-groomed hair from the '80s and a smile that encouraged sizable down payments. I didn't know what I was expecting. Bloodshot eyes or pouches beneath his eyes or ten years added to him or weight gain or weight loss — just some concrete evidence of time passing without me, and it not being easy for him. That was all I wanted. Concrete proof of their anguish. Anything to prove that I was making the wrong decision confronting them tonight. But there was nothing. I sort of wanted to just go then. They'd seen me. They knew I was alive. I'd done my job.

But then my mother came around the corner of the hall. "Who is that?" She froze. "Grace?" And her voice broke on that one syllable, so I knew I was coming in after all.

Before I had time to decide if I was ready for a hug, I was in one, my mother's arms so tightly around my neck and my face pressed into the fuzz of her sweater. I heard her say, *God thank you Grace thank you.* She was either laughing or crying, but when I pulled back I couldn't see either a smile or tears. Her lower lip trembled. I hugged my arms to keep them still.

I hadn't thought coming back would be so hard.

I ended up sitting at the breakfast table with my parents across from me. There were a lot of memories living at this table, usually me sitting by myself, but fond nonetheless. Nostalgic, anyway. The kitchen smelled weird, though, like too much take-out food, odors from eating it, storing it, throwing it away. Never quite the same as the smell you got from actually using a kitchen to cook. The unfamiliar scent made the experience seem dreamlike, foreign and familiar all at once.

I thought Rachel had abandoned me for the car, but after the first couple moments of silence, she came down the hall from the front door, holding the tabby kitten under her arm. She wordlessly put it down on the couch and came to stand behind me. She looked as if she would rather be anywhere but here. It was rather valiant, and my heart sort of swelled to see it. Everybody ought to have friends like Rachel.

"This is very shocking, Grace," my father said, across from me. "You've put us through a lot."

My mother began to cry.

I changed my mind, right then. I no longer wanted to see evidence of their anguish anymore. I didn't want to watch my mother cry. I had spent so long hoping that they had missed me, wishing that they loved me enough that it would hurt that I was gone, but now that I saw my mother's face, guilt and sympathy were making a solid lump in my throat. I just wanted to have had the conversation already and be back on the way home. This was too hard.

I started, "I wasn't trying to put you —"

"We thought you were dead," my father said. "And all this time, you were with him. Just letting us —"

"No," I said. "I was not with him all this time!"

"We're just relieved that you're all right," Mom said.

But Dad wasn't there yet. "You could have *called*, Grace," he said. "You could have just called so we knew you were alive. That was all we needed."

I believed him. He didn't really need *me*. He needed proof of me. "Last time I tried to talk to you, you told me I couldn't see Sam until I was eighteen, and completely talked over the top of m —"

"I'm calling the police to tell them you're here," Dad said. He was halfway out of his seat.

"Dad," I snapped. "First of all, they know. Second of all, you're doing it. You're not even listening to half of what I say."

"I am not doing anything," he said. He looked at Rachel. "Why did you bring Rachel?"

Rachel twitched a bit at the sound of her name. She said, "I'm the referee."

Dad put his hands up in the air like he gave up, which is what people do when they're not really giving up, and then he pressed them against the table like we were having a séance and the table was trying to move.

"We don't need a referee," Mom said. "There's not going to be anything unpleasant."

"Yes, there is," Dad said. "Our daughter ran away from home. That's a crime, Amy. An actual crime in the eyes of Minnesota law. I'm not going to pretend it didn't happen. I'm not going to pretend that she didn't run away to live with her boyfriend."

I wasn't sure what it was about that statement that made me suddenly see everything with perfect clarity. Dad was going perfectly through the motions of parenting: an autopilot setting that was completely reactionary and probably learned from television shows and weekend movies. I studied them: Mom huddled with her new kitten, which had wandered from the couch to jump on her lap, and Dad staring at me as if he didn't recognize me. Yes, they were grown-ups, but I was, too. It was like Rachel had said about me being her older sister. My parents had raised me to be an adult as fast as they could and they couldn't be offended when I turned into one.

I pressed my hands onto the table, too, an echo of Dad's posture. And then I said what I'd wanted to say for a long time. "And I'm not going to pretend that I didn't almost die in your car, Dad."

"Oh, come on, now," he said.

My stomach hurt with my indignation. "No, I won't *come on, now.* It's just a symptom. You forgot you had a kid in your car. And before that, I was dragged off the swing by wolves while Mom was upstairs painting. And yeah, I had my boyfriend sleeping in my bed here, but it took you weeks to realize it. Did you even notice *I* was sleeping here? You gave me thirty miles of free leash. Did you think I wouldn't use it?"

Rachel frantically applied lip gloss again.

"Okay," Mom said. The cat was crawling around her neck. She pulled it off and handed it to Rachel, which I thought was probably against referee rules. Rachel did look happier with the kitten, though. "Okay. So where does that leave us? I'm not going to fight anymore. God, Lewis. I don't want to fight with her. I thought she was dead."

Dad's lips made a thin line, but he sealed his mouth shut.

I took a deep breath and steeled myself. I had to get this out right. "I'm moving out."

"You are not," Dad said immediately.

"That is why I'm moving out," I replied. "You don't get to tell me what to do all of a sudden. You can't just wait until I start to choose my own family and my own life and my own happiness and say, no, Grace, that's not allowed. Go back to being lonely and miserable and a grade-A student! It's not fair. It'd be different if you were *there* like Rachel's parents or Sam's parents."

My father made a face. "The ones who tried to kill him?"

"No, Beck," I said. I thought about that afternoon, Beck and Sam, head to head, that silent bond so strong that it was visible to bystanders. I thought about Sam's gestures, putting his hands behind his head, how he had gotten them from Beck. I wondered if there was anything of my parents in me, or if who I was was entirely cobbled from books and television and teachers at school. "Sam would do whatever Beck asked him to do, because Beck's always been there for him. You know who's always been there for me? Me. Family of one."

"If you think you're going to convince me," my father said, "you're not. And the law is on my side, so I don't *need* to be convinced. You are seventeen. You don't get to make decisions."

Rachel made a noise that I thought was her refereeing but turned out to be just the kitten biting her hand.

I hadn't really thought I would persuade Dad that easily. It was principle now, I could see, and Dad wouldn't back down from that. My stomach squeezed again, nerves crawling up into my mouth. I said, my voice lower, "Here's the deal. I'm going to do summer school to finish high school, and then I'm going to go to college. If you let me move out now, I will actually talk to you guys after I hit age eighteen. Or you can call the cops and force me to stay and I will sleep in that bed and follow all your brand-new rules, and then, when midnight rolls over on my birthday, that room will be empty and I will never come back. Don't think that I'm joking. Look at my face. You know I'm dead serious. And don't talk to me about the law, Dad! You *hit* Sam. Tell me what side of the law that's on?"

My stomach was a disaster zone. I had to will myself not to say anything else, to shove words into the empty space.

There was complete silence at the table. My father turned his face away and looked out the window at the back deck, though there was nothing to see but blackness. Rachel pet the kitten furiously and it purred as if it would split its ribs, loud enough that it filled the room with the sound. My mother's fingers rested on the edge of the table, her thumb and forefinger pressed against each other as she moved her hands back and forth, like she were measuring out invisible thread.

"I'm going to suggest a compromise," she said. Dad glared at her, but she didn't look back.

Disappointment sat in my chest, heavy. I couldn't imagine a compromise that would come anywhere near to being acceptable.

"I'm listening," I said, voice flat.

Dad burst out, "Amy! A compromise? You can't be serious. We don't need that."

"Your way's not working!" Mom snapped.

Dad leveled a glare at my mother, charged with so much anger and disappointment.

"I can't believe you're going to condone this," he said.

"I'm not condoning. I talked to Sam, Lewis. You were wrong about him. So now it's my turn to talk." To me, she said, "This is what I suggest. You stay here until you turn eighteen, but we treat you like an adult. You can see Sam and you won't have a curfew as long as you" — she paused as she came up with her conditions on the spot — "keep up with your summer school and seem to be keeping up with your academic goals. Sam can't stay here overnight, but he can stay here all day long for all I care, and we'll try to get to know him better."

She looked at Dad. His mouth worked, but he just shrugged. They both looked at me.

"Oh —" Mom said. "And you still talk to us after you turn eighteen. That's part of it, too."

I pressed my fingers against my lips, my elbows leaned on the table. I didn't want to give up my nights with Sam, but it was a fair compromise, especially when I hadn't seen any way to a compromise. But what if I shifted? I couldn't move back in until I was sure that I was stable. That had to be soon. Maybe now? I didn't know. Cole's cure would come too late to be useful.

"How do I know you're not going to try to change the rules on me again?" I asked, stalling. "Sam is not negotiable, for instance. I'm keeping him. Forever and ever. I should put that out there right now. He's the one."

Dad made another face but didn't say anything. Mom, to my amazement, nodded a little. "Okay. I said we'd try. And not stop you from seeing him."

"And no more punching," Rachel put in. I shot her a look. I felt it was a bit of cheating, waiting until the conflict had mostly subsided to fulfill her referee duties.

"Right," Mom said. "Grace, what do you think?"

I glanced around the room: From here I could see the kitchen and the breakfast area, and it made me feel weird. I had thought this would be the last time I came here. That it would be a big fight and I would slam that book shut and never see it again. The idea of coming back to this house and climbing back into my old life was simultaneously relieving and exhausting. I thought of Sam's dread of shifting again after he'd thought he was done and understood it infinitely.

"I . . . I have to think about it," I said. "I want to sleep on it."

"Can't you sleep on it here?" Mom asked.

Rachel shook her head. "No, because she has to take me back home, anyway. Referee says."

I stood up, making it not an option. I didn't understand why my stomach still burned with nerves after the worst had gone by. "I'll think about it and come back to talk about it."

Mom stood up then, too, so fast that the kitten started and hissed in Rachel's arms, a tiny sound like a sneeze. Mom came around the table and hugged me again — a tight, weird-fitting hug that made me realize I couldn't remember the last time, before this night, that she had attempted it. I wasn't exactly sure where to hug her back, now that the time had come. She seemed all boobs and hair, so I just — squeezed in a general way.

"You will come back?" she said into my ear.

"Yes," I said, and really meant it.

Dad stood up and gave me a draping shoulder-hug, as if possibly he knew he'd also find me all boobs and hair if he tried for a better one.

"Here's your cat," Rachel said, and handed my mother the kitten.

"Thank you for bringing her back," Mom said. I couldn't tell if she was talking about the cat or me.

Rachel shrugged and hooked arms with me. "It's what I do." And with that, she towed me out of the house and back into the car. My parents stood at the doorway and watched the car, oddly forlorn looking, as we backed out and headed down the road. I felt giddy and ill.

The car was quiet for one minute.

Then Rachel said, "I can't believe they replaced you with a cat."

I laughed, and it made my skin crawl. "I know, right? Thank you for coming. I mean, thank you. They were reasonable because you were there."

"They were reasonable because they thought you were dead. Do you — feel okay, Grace?"

I had missed a gear and the car gasped until I shifted to the right gear. I wasn't the greatest with a stick shift, and suddenly it felt like too much effort to focus on. My stomach clenched again then, at the same time that a tremble worked its way up my arms, and I realized that what I'd put down as nerves was something worse.

"Oh, no," I said, nausea rolling inside me. "I have to pull over. I'm sorry, I —"

The night road was deserted. I jerked the car to the shoulder and opened the door. I promptly threw up behind the car. Rachel's face was white in the gloom; I hadn't realized she'd gotten out.

She flapped her hands. "What do I do? I can't drive a stick shift!"

I was starting to shiver now, hard, involuntary tremors that clicked my teeth together. "Rach, I'm so, so sorry. You need to —" I stopped to curl against the side of the car. Oh, God, I hated this part. My bones were breaking. No, no, no.

"Need to what? Grace, you're freaking me out. Oh, no. Oh, no!" It was suddenly dawning on Rachel what was going on.

"Call Sam," I managed. "Tell him I've shifted and to come get you. Cole can — ugh. Cole can drive the other car — oh — Rachel — go — wait in the car. Don't —"

My knees didn't want to hold me. They were loosening, getting ready to grow into something else. I was suddenly afraid of what she would think, watching me shift. She had to wait in the car. She couldn't watch — it would ruin everything between us. My skin felt like someone else's. I thought I must look terrible already.

But Rachel hugged me, a huge hug around my body and her cheek leaning against my tense one. I stank of wolf and I must have looked like a monster, and she was hugging me hard enough that I could feel it over the top of the pain. She was so brave that she made a tear escape.

"Does it hurt?" Rachel whispered, letting me go.

I shook my head fiercely. I balled my hands up against my body. "I just love you and it's making me . . . making me . . ."

"Turn into a wolf," said Rachel. "I know." She wiped her nose with the back of her hand. "I have that effect on people."

I tried to say something else, but I lost my footing. The stars were brilliant above me, and I remembered yet another night: me and Sam under the stars, watching the northern lights. In my head the pink lights of the aurora borealis became the lights of the dash reflected in every broken piece of my Bronco's smashed windshield, Sam and I behind it, saying good-bye, and then it was just me, broken into pieces, slivered like glass, made into something new.

CHAPTER SIXTY

· SAM ·

It was oddly distressing to lose a night of sleep with Grace like this — out of the blue, with me far away from where she'd shifted. After dropping off Rachel, I wanted to go look for her, but Cole convinced me that it was useless; she wouldn't come to me, and if she shifted back near her parents' house, at least she'd know where she was. I didn't think that I would fall asleep without her, but after Cole talked me out of driving back to where Rachel had left her, I lay in my bed and stared up at my paper birds and Christmas lights and pretended I was just waiting for Grace to come to bed. The long day stretched out behind me, and when I couldn't hold all of the things that had happened in my mind at once, sleep found me.

I dreamed I was walking around the house, going from room to room. Each room was empty, but it was a full, breathing emptiness, like I might turn and see someone behind me at any moment. The house itself felt inhabited — not recently, but *currently* — as if the residents had merely gone outside to investigate the weather and would shortly return. The bedrooms, certainly, bore signs of life: On each bed was a suitcase or a backpack filled with clothing, shoes placed carefully beside it, personal effects laid out, waiting to go. Ulrik's bed had his laptop and his electric razor. Paul's had a pile of guitar picks and some burnt DVDs I had never heard of. Even the room with the bunk beds had supplies on their beds: Derek's earbuds tangled on top of his camera, and Melissa's sketchbook beside her shoes. Beck's bed was empty.

I went from room to room, turning off lights in each room as I did. Good-bye to Beck's room, never occupied. Good-bye to Ulrik's room, where we'd watched horror movies on his laptop. I went downstairs without going to my room. Good-bye to the living room, where I had once sat with Grace on the sofa, nearly a wolf, where Isabel had helped stop Cole's seizure. I turned the light off. Good-bye to the yellow room that Cole lived in and Jack died in. Lights off in the bathroom I had avoided for a decade. Good-bye to the kitchen, with its photographs of us pinned and taped to every cabinet, one thousand smiles, every one of them genuine. I turned off the light and headed to the basement.

And here, in Beck's library, surrounded by books, were Beck's things that had been absent from his room, his suitcase and his shoes, sitting on the ottoman of his reading chair. His tie was folded neatly by them and beside them both was a CD with tangled branches on the cover. The title was scrawled in the only available white space: *Still Waking Up*.

All around me was Beck, living inside all of these books that he had read. He inhabited every page. He was every hero, every villain, every victim and every aggressor. He was the beginning and end of everything.

Die letzte aller Türen

Doch nie hat man
an alle schon geklopft

(The last of all doors

But one has never
knocked on all the others)

This was the last good-bye. I turned off the light.

There was only one place left. I slowly climbed the stairs to the ground floor and then to the second floor. Walked down the hall to my room. Inside, my paper birds trembled on their strings, caught in the premonition of an earthquake. I could see each memory that the birds contained, images playing across their wings like a television screen, all of them singing bright songs that I had sung before. They were beautiful and terrified, jerking to be free.

"Bad news, Ringo," said Cole. "We're all going to die."

I woke up to the sound of the telephone.

Adrenaline shot through my half-asleep body at the sudden noise, and the first clear thought I had, inexplicably, was *Oh, no, not here.* Half a moment later I realized the noise was just the telephone, and I couldn't think why I had thought that. I picked up the receiver.

"Sam?" said Koenig.

He sounded very, very awake.

"I should have called earlier, but I was on midnights and I — it doesn't matter." Koenig took an audible breath. "The hunt's been moved up."

"It — what?" I thought perhaps I was still asleep, but my cranes hung perfectly still.

Koenig said, a little louder, "It's tomorrow. Dawn. Five forty-seven A.M. The helicopter got freed up suddenly and they've moved it. Get up."

He didn't have to tell me. I felt like I would never sleep again.

CHAPTER SIXTY-ONE

· ISABEL ·

I wasn't quite asleep when the phone rang.

It was a little after midnight, and I was trying to sleep mostly out of self-defense. Tensions were running high in the Culpeper household as the date of the hunt and the threat of California moved closer, and my parents were enjoying one of the screamathons that I'd been missing so sorely for the past few weeks. It sounded like my mother was winning — at least she'd roared more salient points than my father had in the last twenty minutes — but it also sounded like they had several more rounds to go.

So my bedroom door was shut and I had my earbuds in, making white noise with offensive lyrics. My room was a rose-and-white cocoon made less stark by the lack of sunlight. Surrounded by my stuff, it could be any day of any year since we'd moved here. I could go downstairs, down the hall, and yell at Jack for not letting my dog out while I was gone. I could call my friends back in California who still remembered me and hatch plots to return and make plans to tour college campuses close to their houses. That the room was so unchanged and that night could play such tricks on me was endearing and horrifying at the same time.

Anyway, I almost missed it when my cell phone rang.

Caller ID: BECK'S HOUSE.

"Hi," I said.

"Guess what your asshole father has done now?" Cole sounded a little out of breath.

I didn't feel like answering. This wasn't exactly how I'd hoped my next phone call with Cole would begin.

"Screwed us," Cole said, not waiting for me to answer. "Over the hood of a foreign car. The hunt is happening at dawn. They've moved it."

As if on cue, the landline rang from its base on my bed stand. I didn't touch it, but even from here, I could see the caller ID: LANDY, MARSHALL. That meant that my dad and I were going to have the exact same conversation, basically, at the same time, with two different people.

The fighting downstairs had ceased. It was taking a long time for this to sink in.

"What are you going to do?" I asked.

"Well, first I'm going to make Sam functional," Cole said. "Grace shifted tonight and she's in the woods, so he's gone off the reservation."

Now I was awake. I pulled out the single remaining earbud I still had in and sat up. "Grace is out there? That's not acceptable."

It was more than not acceptable. Grace versus Thomas Culpeper, Esquire, was not a battle that I wanted to ever see, because I knew how it would end.

"I know, princess," Cole said tersely. "What I would like for you to do is to go to your father and tell him to get on the phone and make this stop."

But I knew how that would end, too.

"That won't work," I replied. "This is bigger than him now."

"I. Don't. Care," Cole said, slowly and patiently, like I was a child. "You find that bastard and make him stop. I know you can."

I could feel myself prickling at his tone. "Okay, first of all, you

337

don't tell me what to do. Secondly? All that will happen is I will go down there, make him completely pissed off at me for no reason, and maybe, if I'm really lucky, he'll start to wonder why it is that I'm suddenly feeling so freaking friendly toward the wolves and maybe it will just open a can of worms that I will have to deal with for the rest of the year. And you know what he will say? It's beyond him now. It's time for you to do your thing."

"*My* thing? My thing only worked if Grace was here to make it work. Without Grace, I have an emotionally unbalanced wolf and a Volkswagen."

The house was stone quiet in comparison to the shouting before. I tried to imagine going down there and confronting my father about the hunt. It was too ludicrous to even contemplate.

"I'm not doing it, Cole."

"You owe it to me to try."

"Owe?" I laughed, harsh and short. For a moment, my mind skittered over every encounter we'd ever had, trying to think if there was any truth to what he'd said. I couldn't think of anything. If anything, he owed me, big time. "Why do I owe you anything?"

Cole's voice was completely level. "Your son of a bitch father killed Victor and threw him in front of my face."

I felt my face getting hotter.

"I'm not him. I don't owe you jack shit, Cole St. Clair. I might have considered going downstairs to talk to my dad before that, but now, screw you."

"Oh, that's nice. Grown-up way to handle your problems. Find a technicality, pitch a fit, and make it someone else's problem. You really are daddy's little girl."

It stung, so I laughed at him. "You're one to talk. The only thing that surprises me about all this is you sound remarkably sober. If it goes badly, you can always kill yourself, right?"

He hung up.

My pulse was racing, my skin searing, and suddenly I felt light-headed. I sat back and put hands over my mouth. My room looked exactly the same as it had before I'd picked up his call.

I threw my phone at the wall. Halfway through its flight, I realized that my father would kill me if I destroyed it, but it smacked the wall and slid to the ground without any pieces falling off it. It looked exactly the same as before.

Nothing had changed. Nothing.

CHAPTER SIXTY-TWO

· SAM ·

Cole burst into the kitchen like a nail bomb. It was nearly one A.M., and in four and a half hours, the wolves were going to begin to die.

"No go, Ringo. Culpeper can't call it off." There was something chaotic in his eyes that wasn't in his voice.

I hadn't thought Culpeper would, but it seemed stupid to not at least try. "Is Isabel coming?" My voice sounded normal, to my surprise, a recording of me played back when the real me had lost my voice.

"No," Cole said. Just like that. Barely a word. Just part of an exhalation. He pulled open the fridge with such ferocity that the condiments in the door cracked against each other. The cold air crept out of the fridge and around my ankles. "So it's up to us. Your friend Koenig coming?"

It would've been nice: someone practical and on the positive side of the law with infinitely less emotional involvement than me sounded like a wonderful thing to have. "He found out the news because he was working. His shift ends at six A.M."

"Perfect timing." Cole grasped a handful of vials and syringes with one hand and dumped them on the island in front of me. They rolled and whirled in misshapen circles on the counter surface. "Here are our options."

My ears rang. "We have more than one?"

"Three, precisely," Cole said. He pointed to each in turn. "That one makes you a wolf. That one makes me a wolf. That one gives us both seizures."

But there weren't really three options. There was only one. There'd only ever been one. I said, "I have to go in and get her."

"And the rest?"

"Her first." It was the most horrible thing I'd ever had to say. But anything else had to be a lie. She was the one thing I'd remembered as a wolf, when there was nothing else. She was the one thing I knew I would hold on to. Had to hold on to. I would save the others if I could, but it had to be Grace first.

I didn't think I'd been very persuasive, but Cole nodded. His nod made it real, and now that it was a plan, I felt sick. Not vaguely, but in a way that made my ears hum and my vision speckle in the corners. I had to become a wolf. Not in some distant future. Now.

"Okay, then here's the plan, again. I'll go to the lake," Cole said. Now he was the general, sliding the syringe that would make him a wolf into one of the pockets of his cargo pants, pointing at some imaginary map in the air to demonstrate where we were going. "The parking area by Two Island Lake. That's where I'm going to wait for you. You. Grace. Whoever you can bring with. Then we really need to be across that sparse area on that side of the woods well before dawn. It'd be like fish in a barrel, otherwise, with no cover. Are you ready?"

He had to repeat it. I thought about sitting in the bathtub with my guitar, singing "Still Waking Up." I thought about pulling Grace's dress over her head. I thought about Cole telling me that everyone listened to me, but I didn't always say anything. I thought about everything that made me *me* and how afraid I was to lose it.

I would not lose it.

"I'm ready."

There was no more time.

Outside, I carefully stripped out of my clothing and stood there while Cole tapped the syringe until the bubbles in it rose to the top. It was surprisingly light out here; the moon was nearly a week until full, but there were low clouds and mist that took what light there was and threw it everywhere. It made the woods behind the house look eerie and infinite.

"Tell me what you're thinking," Cole said. He took my arm and turned my palm toward the sky. My scars were puckered and ugly in the moonlight.

I was thinking: Grace's hand in my hand, Beck shaking in the basement, burying Victor, becoming human. I was thinking, somewhere, maybe Grace is looking for me, too. I focused on the thoughts I wanted to bring with me. "I am Sam Roth. I am finding Grace. Finding the wolves. Bringing them to the lake."

Cole nodded. "You damn well better be. Okay, this one has to go in a vein. Hold still. Say it again. Wait, tell me where your keys are, again, before I do."

My heart thumped with nerves and fear and hope. "In my pocket."

Cole looked down.

"I'm not wearing my pants anymore," I said.

Cole looked at the step. "No, you aren't. Okay. *Now* hold still."

"Cole," I said. "If I don't —"

He heard the tone of my voice. "No. I'll see you on the other side."

Cole traced a vein from my scars to the inside of my elbow. I closed my eyes. He slid the needle in.

Chapter Sixty-Three

· SAM ·

For one second, one part of a second, one fraction of a breath, pain wiped all of my thoughts away from me. My veins were molten. My body was remapping itself, charting new courses, planning new bones while it crushed the others to dust. There was not a part of me that wasn't negotiable.

I had forgotten the agony of it. There was no mercy to this. The first time I had shifted, I'd been seven. My mother had been the first to see. I couldn't even remember her name right now.

My spine crackled.

Cole threw the syringe onto the step.

The woods were singing in the language I only knew as a wolf.

The last time I had done this, it had been Grace's face in front of me. The last time I had done this, it had been good-bye.

No more. No more good-byes.

I am Sam Roth. I am finding Grace.

Chapter Sixty-Four

· ISABEL ·

It took me five minutes after Cole hung up on me to think that what he had said wasn't as bad as I'd thought. It took me ten minutes to think that I should've called him back right away. It took me fifteen to find out he wasn't answering the phone. Twenty to think I shouldn't have said the bit about killing himself. Twenty-five to realize that it might end up being the last thing I ever said to him.

Why had I said it? Maybe Rachel was right with her bitch comment. I wished I knew how to set my weapons to *stun* instead of *eviscerate.*

It took what felt like half the night to realize that I couldn't stand myself if I didn't try to do something about the hunt.

I tried Cole's number and then Sam's one last time — nothing — and then I headed downstairs. In my head I rehearsed what I would say to my father. First the arguments, then the pleas, and finally, the justification for my concerns that wouldn't lead it back to Sam and Beck, because I knew that would go nowhere with my father. This was going to go nowhere anyway.

But at least I could tell Cole that I'd tried. Then, maybe, I wouldn't feel so sick.

I hated it. I hated this. I hated feeling so terrible because of someone else. I pressed my hand to my right eye, but the tear there stayed safely inside.

The house was dark. I had to flip light switches on as I went down staircases. There was no one in the kitchen. No one in the living room. Finally I found my mother in the library, reclining easily on the leather sofa, a glass of white wine in her hand. She was watching a hospital reality show. Normally the irony of such a thing would have amused me, but right now, all I could think about was the last thing I told Cole.

"Mom," I said. I tried to sound casual. "Where's Dad?"

"Hm?" Something about her *hm* focused me, made me feel more solid. The world was not collapsing. My mother still said *hm* when I asked her questions.

"My father. The creature that mated with you to make me. Where is he?"

"I wish you wouldn't talk like that," my mother said. "He's gone to the helicopter."

"The. Helicopter."

My mother barely looked up from the television. There was nothing new in my tone to alarm her. "Marshall got him a seat. Said because he was such a good shot, it wouldn't be wasted. God, I'll be glad when this whole thing is over."

"*Dad* is riding in the helicopter that is shooting the wolves," I said. Slowly. I felt like an idiot. Of course my father would want to ride on the front lines with an elephant gun. Of course Marshall would make that happen for him.

"It takes off at some terrible hour," Mom said. "So he headed out now to meet Marshall for coffee. So I get the TV."

I was too late. I had spent too long debating with myself and now I was too late.

There was nothing I could do.

Cole had said, *You owe it to me to try.*

I still didn't think I owed him anything. But, taking care not to signal my clawing distress to my mother, I slid out of the library and back through the house. I got my white jacket and my car keys and my cell phone and I pushed the back door open. Not that long ago, Cole had stood there as a wolf, his green eyes on mine. I'd told him that my brother was dead. That I wasn't a nice person. He'd just watched me, unflinching, trapped in that body he'd chosen for himself.

Everything had changed.

When I left, I hit the gas pedal so hard that the wheels spun in the gravel.

CHAPTER SIXTY-FIVE

· SAM ·

I am Sam Roth. I am finding Grace. Finding the wolves. Bringing them to the lake. I am Sam Roth. I am finding Grace. Finding the wolves. Bringing them to the lake.

I burst into the woods at a gallop. My paws pounded the rocks; my strides ate the ground. Every nerve inside me was on fire. I was holding my thoughts like an armful of paper cranes. Tight enough to keep them. Not tight enough to crush them.

I am Sam Roth. I am finding Grace. Finding the wolves. Bringing them to the lake. I am Sam Roth. I am finding Grace. Finding the wolves. Bringing them to the lake.

There were one thousand things to hear. Ten thousand things to scent. One hundred million clues to countless forms of life in these woods. But I didn't need countless. I needed one.

She was leaning back against me, breathing in the scent of a candy shop. Every color that I couldn't see now was painted on the walls and labels around us.

I am Sam. I am finding Grace. Finding the wolves. Bringing them to the lake.

The night was bright underneath a half-moon; the light reflected off a few low clouds and ragged strands of mist. I could see endlessly ahead of me. But it wasn't sight that would help me. Every so often I slowed, listening. Her howl. It was for me, I was certain.

The wolves howled; I stood at her window, looking out. We were strangers and we knew each other like a path we walked every day. *Don't sleep on the floor,* she said.

I am Sam. I am finding Grace. Finding the wolves. Bringing them.

There were other voices now, responding to her calls. It wasn't difficult to pick them apart. It was difficult to remember *why* I needed to pick them apart.

Her eyes, brown and complicated, with a wolf's face.

I am Sam. I am finding Grace. Finding the wolves.

I faltered as my paws slid on wet clay, sending me slithering. I heard something drop into water, close by.

A voice hissed at me in the back of my head. Something about this was dangerous. I slowed, cautious, and there it was — a massive pit, water for drowning at its base. I minced around it before listening. The woods had fallen silent. My mind tripped and stumbled, aching for — I tipped my head back and howled, a long, trembling bay that helped ease the ache inside me. A few moments later, I heard her voice, and I set off again.

I am finding Grace. Finding the wolves.

A flock of birds exploded in front of me, startled from their roost by my progress. They burst into the air, white against the black, and something about the multitude of their forms, the identical stretch of their wings, the way they suspended above me, fluttering in the wind, stars lit behind them, reminded me of something.

I struggled and struggled to grasp it, but it slid away from me. The loss seemed crushing, though I could not think of what I'd lost.

I am finding Grace.

I would not lose that. I would not lose that.

finding Grace.

There were some things you could not take from me. Some things that I just could not bear to give up.

Grace

Chapter Sixty-Six

· COLE ·

Two thirty-four A.M.

I was alone.

The lake stretched out beside the parking area, the still water reflecting a mirror-perfect image of the imperfect moon. Somewhere on the other side of the water was the Culpeper property.

I wasn't going to think about that.

Two thirty-five A.M.

I was alone.

It was possible that Sam wasn't coming.

· ISABEL ·

It was three twenty-one A.M. and there was no one at Beck's house. I found a pile of clothing and an abandoned syringe by the back door, and inside, Sam's cell phone sitting on the kitchen island — no wonder my call hadn't been picked up. They were gone. They'd done just what I said to do — gone through with Cole's plan without any of my help. I walked through the rooms downstairs, my boots clicking on the hardwood floor, though if there was anyone there, I was sure they would've answered me.

At the end of the hall was the room Jack had died in. I reached in and turned on the bedroom light. Instantly the room turned the same abusive shade of yellow I remembered from before. It was clear that this was Cole's room now. A pair of sweatpants walked across the floor unattended. Glasses and bowls and pens and papers covered every available horizontal surface. The bed was unmade, and riding on the crest of rumpled bedspread was a bound leather book, like a journal or diary.

I climbed into the bed — it smelled like Cole that day he'd come over and had been trying to smell nice — and lay on my back, thinking of Jack dying *right here*. It was a hard memory to conjure, and it wasn't strong enough to bring emotion with it. That made me feel simultaneously relieved and sad; I was losing him.

After a few moments, I reached over and picked up the journal. A pen was put in it to hold the page. The idea that Cole might have his private thoughts written down was strange to me; I didn't think he could really be honest, even on paper.

I opened it up and scanned the pages. It was at the same time nothing that I expected and everything. Honesty, but no emotions. A bland chronology of Cole's life for the past month. Words jumped out at me.

Seizure. Chills. Moderate success. Uncontrollable shaking of hands, approx. two hours. Shifted for twenty-seven minutes. Vomiting extensive; suggest fasting?

It was what was unwritten that I wanted from this journal. Not what I needed, but what I wanted. I paged through, looking to see if his entries became wordier, but they didn't. I did find what I needed, however, on the last page: *Meet at Two Island parking area, then up 169 then north on Knife Lake.*

It would take me awhile to find where they meant on Two Island Lake; it was massive. But now I knew where to start.

CHAPTER SIXTY-SEVEN

· GRACE ·

And now, finally, here he was, as I remembered him, after all this time.

I was standing in a woods made out of white-barked trees when he found me. My howls to him had gathered two other pack members by the time that we got within sight of each other. The closer we got, the more anxious I became; it was difficult to howl instead of whimper. The others tried to console me, but I kept showing them images of his eyes, trying to convey — something. I couldn't believe it was really his voice. Not until I saw his eyes.

And then, there he was, panting, uncertain. He trotted into the clearing and hesitated when he saw the other two wolves flanking me. But his scent apparently identified him to them, and a flurry of images passed between us, him playing, him hunting, him among the pack.

I bounded to him, my tail up, ears pricked, ecstatic and quivering. He threw me an image so strong that it brought me up short. It was the trees around us, the white tree trunks with the black weals up the side, the leaves falling, humans standing among them.

I threw one back, me galloping here to find him, using his voice to guide me ever closer.

But again, he threw me the image.

I didn't understand. Was this a warning — were these humans coming? Was it a memory? Had he seen them?

The image shifted, twisted: a boy and a girl, leaves in hands, the image soaked in wanting, longing. The boy had my wolf's eyes.

Something inside me hurt.

Grace.

I whined softly.

I didn't understand, and now I felt that familiar pang of loss and hollowness inside me.

Grace.

It was a sound that meant nothing and everything. My wolf stepped carefully toward me, waiting for my ears to prick before he licked my chin and nosed my ears and muzzle. I felt like I had been waiting for a lifetime for him to be here; I was trembling with it. I couldn't stop pressing against him, pushing my nose against his cheek, but it was okay, because he was just as insistent. Affection required touching and jostling.

Now, finally, he sent me an image that I could comprehend: us, our heads thrown back, singing together, calling the other wolves from all over the woods. It was toned with urgency, with danger. Those were both things that I was familiar with.

He tipped his head back and howled. It was a long, keening wail, sad and clear, and it went further toward making me understand that word *Grace* than his images had. After a moment, I opened my mouth and howled as well.

Together, our voices were louder. The other wolves pressed in against us, nosing, whimpering, and, finally, howling.

There wasn't a place in the woods you wouldn't hear us.

CHAPTER SIXTY-EIGHT

· COLE ·

It was five fifteen A.M.

I was so tired that I couldn't imagine sleeping. I was that tired that made your hands shake and your eyes see lights at the corners of your vision, movement where there was none.

Sam was not here.

What a strange world this was, that I could come here to lose everything about myself, and instead lose everything but me. It was possible that I'd thrown one too many Molotov cocktails over God's fence. It would be, after all, a divinely ironic punishment to watch me learn to care and then destroy the things I cared about.

I didn't know what I would do if this didn't work. I realized, then, that somewhere along the way, I'd started to think that Sam could really do it. There hadn't been a part of me, even a small part, that had believed otherwise, and so now this feeling I felt rumbling in my chest was disappointment and betrayal.

I couldn't go back to that empty house. It was nothing without the people in it. And I couldn't go back home to New York. It hadn't been home for a long time. I was a man without a country. Somewhere along the way, I'd become the pack.

I blinked, rubbed my eyes. There was movement at the edge of my vision again, miscellaneous floaters, consolation prizes for actual sight in this dim light. I rubbed again, rested my head against the steering wheel.

But the movement was real.

It was Sam, his yellow eyes regarding the car warily.

And behind him were the wolves..

Chapter Sixty-Nine

· SAM ·

Everything about this was wrong. We were in the open, we were bunched together, we were too near the vehicle. Instincts made my hackles rise. The light of the moon glowed inside the mist, making the world artificially bright. A few of the wolves started to retreat back into the darkness of the trees, but I broke into a run, herding them back snugly by the lake. Images flashed briefly into my mind: us, by the lake, all together. Me and her. *Grace.*

Grace. finding the wolves. the lake.

I'd done those things. What now? There was no *what now.*

Grace could smell my anxiety. She nosed my muzzle, leaned into me, but I wasn't comforted.

The pack was restless. I had to break off again to drive a few stragglers back to the lake. The white she-wolf — Shelby — snarled at me but didn't attack. The wolves kept looking up to the vehicle; there was a person in it.

What now, what now?

I was torn by the unknown.

Sam.

I jerked. Recognition rang through me.

Sam, are you listening?

Then, clearly, an image. The wolves running down the road, freedom ahead, and something — something menacing behind.

I swiveled my ears, trying to find the direction of the information. I turned back to the vehicle; my gaze was met by the young man's steady one. Again, I got the image, even more clearly this time. Danger coming. The pack pelting down the road. I took the image, honed it, threw it to the other wolves.

Grace's head instantly snapped up from where she was doing my job: keeping a wolf from wandering back into the trees. Across two dozen moving bodies, I met her gaze and held it for the briefest of moments.

In my paws, I could feel the vibration of something unfamiliar. Something approaching.

Grace tossed another image to me. A suggestion. The pack, me at the head, leading them away from whatever threat promised to arrive from behind us. Her alongside, driving them after me.

I couldn't mistrust that image being sent to me from the car, because it came with this, again and again: *Sam*. And that made it all right, even if I couldn't quite hold the entire concept of it in my head.

I sent an image to the pack. Not a request. An order: us moving. Them following me.

By all rights, the orders should have been given by Paul, the black wolf, and any others punished for their subordination.

For a moment, nothing happened.

Then, we broke into a run, nearly simultaneously. It was like we were on a hunt, only whatever we chased was too far away to see.

Every wolf listened to me.

Chapter Seventy

· COLE ·

It was working.

The moment I started to follow in the Volkswagen, though, they scattered and it took them a long moment to regroup. It was almost dawn; we didn't have the time for them to get used to the car. So I got out, tossing images as best I could — I was getting better, though I had to be close — and I ran on foot. Not stupidly close to them; I stayed on the shoulder of the road mostly, to keep my bearings, and they were dozens of yards away. I just tried to stay close enough to keep tabs on their direction. I couldn't believe I'd cursed their slowness before. If they'd been more focused, I wouldn't have been able to keep up. Instead, here I was, running with them, almost part of the pack again, as they coursed along under the waning moonlight. I wasn't sure what would happen when I got tired. Right now, fueled by adrenaline, I couldn't imagine it.

And I had to say, even as a cynic, it was something to see the wolves, leaping and jumping and ducking and surging with each other. And it was something else again to see Sam and Grace.

I was able to send images to Sam, sure, but it obviously took an effort for him to understand. Sam and Grace, on the other hand, both wolves, with their connection — Sam would barely turn his head and Grace would fall back to encourage a wolf that had stopped to investigate a fascinating smell. Or Grace would intercept one of my images and translate it for Sam with a flick of her tail, and suddenly they would have changed directions as I wanted them to. And always, as they ran, though there was an urgency to the pack, Sam and Grace were touching, nosing, bumping against each other. Everything they had as humans translated.

Here was the problem, though: North of Boundary Wood, there was a large, flat tract of land covered only with scrub trees. As long as the wolves were crossing it to the next stretch of woods, they were easy targets. I'd driven past it before, and it hadn't seemed like too wide of an area. But that was me in a car going fifty-eight miles an hour. Now we were on foot going maybe six, eight miles an hour. And the edge of the horizon was pinking as the sun contemplated coming up.

Too soon. Or maybe we were too late. The scrub stretched out for miles ahead of us. There was no way that the wolves would be across it by the time the sun came up. The only thing I could hope for was that the helicopter was slow to get started. That it started on the far side of Boundary Wood and was more concerned with why there didn't seem to be any wolves in it anymore. If we were lucky, that would be how it worked. If the world were fair.

CHAPTER SEVENTY-ONE

· ISABEL ·

By the time I found the Volkswagen, abandoned in the parking lot by the lake, it was dawn. I swore at Cole for leaving Sam's phone behind, for leaving the car behind, but then I saw that the pack had left cluttered tracks in the dew. More wolf prints than I'd ever seen before. How many was that? Ten wolves? Twenty? The brush was beaten down where they'd waited, and then the prints led back out to the road. Like the journal had said. Heading up 169.

I was so pumped to know that I was on the right track that I didn't realize, at first, what it meant that I could see the tracks so clearly. The sun was coming up, which meant we were running out of time. No, we were *already* out of time, unless the wolves were well away from the woods. There was a big, ugly stretch of alien wasteland on 169 leading out of Boundary Wood and Mercy Falls. If the wolves got caught there, they'd be totally exposed to my father and his enterprising rifle.

All I could think was that things would be fine if only I could get to the wolves. So I sent the SUV speeding down the road. I was freezing, I realized; even though it wasn't that cold, just normal early-morning chill, I couldn't seem to keep warm. I cranked up the heater and gripped the steering wheel. I didn't pass any traffic — who would be out on this hick road at dawn except for wolves and the people hunting them, anyway? I wasn't sure which category that put me in.

And there, suddenly, were the wolves. In the half-light of dawn, they were dark spots against the scrubby ground, only presenting themselves as different shades of gray and black when I got closer. Of course, they were smack-dab in the middle of the alien wasteland, strung out in a long, orderly line, two and three across, perfect targets. As I got closer, I saw the wolf that was Grace up at the front — no way could I forget the shape of her body and the length of her legs and the way she carried her head — and next to her, Sam. I saw a white wolf, and for a brief, confused moment, thought it was Olivia. But then I remembered, and realized it must be Shelby, the crazy wolf that had followed us to the clinic so long ago. The other wolves were strangers to me. Just wolves.

And there, far ahead of me, running by the side of the road, a human. The low sun stretched his shadow out one hundred times taller than him. Cole St. Clair, running alongside the wolves, side-stepping debris on the roadside every so often and sometimes jumping the ditch for a few strides and then back again. He held his arms out for balance as he leaped, unself-conscious, like a boy. There was something so fiercely *big* about the gesture of Cole running with the wolves that it made the last thing I said to him ring in my ears. Shame warmed me when nothing else could.

I had a new goal. I was going to tell him sorry, after all this.

It occurred to me then that something in my dash was rattling. I pressed my hand on the dashboard, then on my door panel, trying to locate it.

And then I realized it wasn't coming from inside the SUV at all. I rolled down the driver's side window.

From the direction of the woods, I heard the sound of the helicopter blades beating the air as it approached.

· COLE ·

The next part happened so quickly, I couldn't really keep any of the events straight or make them make sense.

360

There was the *thump thump thump* of the helicopter, every thump coming twice as often as the crashing of my heart in my ears. It was fast, compared to us, and low, and louder than an explosion. In this light, it was black against the sky; even as a human, it looked like a monster to me. It felt like death. Something in me prickled, a wary premonition. The tempo of the blades exactly matched one of my old songs, and the lyrics sprang into my head, unbidden. *I am expendable.*

The effect on the wolves was immediate. The sound hit them first, and they began to move erratically, bunching together and spreading. Then, as the helicopter itself came closer, they twisted their heads up as they ran. Now there were tails tucked between legs, ears flattened.

Terror.

There was no cover. The people in the helicopter hadn't seen me here, or if they had, I didn't interest them. Sam's head was half-turned toward me, listening for my direction. Grace was close by, trying to keep the wolves together as they panicked. I kept throwing out the image of making it to the woods on the other side of this open ground, but the trees seemed far away and out of reach.

I took in the wolves, the helicopter, the ground, trying to formulate some new plan, something that could save them in the next twenty seconds. I saw Shelby lagging near the back. She was worrying at Beck, who had been guiding the wolves from the rear. He snapped at her, but she was relentless. Like a mosquito, returning again and again. For so long, she'd been unable to challenge anyone in the pack because of him, and now, when he was distracted, she was making her move. She and Beck were falling farther behind the rest of the pack. I wished I'd fought better when I'd met her in the woods before. I wished I'd killed her.

Sam somehow sensed that Beck was falling behind, and so he lagged, too, leaving Grace to lead. His eyes were on Beck.

The sound of the helicopter was so loud, so all-consuming, that it felt like I had never heard anything else. I stopped running.

And that was when it all started to go too fast. Sam snarled at Shelby, and she abandoned Beck as if she had never cared about attacking him. For a moment, I thought that Sam's authority had won out.

Then she threw herself at Beck.

I thought I'd sent a warning. I should have sent a warning.

It would have been too late, anyway, even if they were listening to me.

Dirt kicked up around them, scattershot, and before I understood what it was, Beck fell. He scrambled back up again, biting at his spine, falling again. There was another crackle, barely audible over the helicopter, and this time, he went down and stayed down. His body was a wreck, in pieces.

I couldn't think about it. Beck. He was jerking, snapping, scrabbling without getting up. Not shifting. Dying. His body was too ruined to heal itself.

I couldn't look.

I couldn't look away.

Sam jerked to a halt, and I saw his mouth form a whimper that I couldn't hear from here. We were both transfixed; Beck could not die. He was a giant.

He was dead.

Taking advantage of Sam's distraction, Shelby hurled herself against his side, shoving him to the ground. They rolled and came up painted with mud. I tried to send Sam images, telling him to shake her off and get on the move, but he wasn't listening, either because he couldn't see anything but Beck or because Shelby was taking all his concentration.

I should have killed her.

Ahead of them, the helicopter was still flying slowly after the wolves. There was another explosion of dirt, and then another, but no wolf fell this time. I only had a moment to think *Maybe Beck will be the only one* when a wolf in the middle of the pack fell mid-stride, rolling and twitching. It took several long minutes for the two guns in the helicopter to finish the job.

This was a disaster.

I'd led the wolves out of the woods to be picked off slowly, one at a time, death in seven slow bullets.

The helicopter banked. I would have loved to think that it was abandoning the chase, but I knew it was just coming back around to get a better shot on the wolves again. The pack was badly scattered from fear; with Sam fighting with Shelby, they had virtually ceased all forward movement. The wolves were so close to the woods, though. They could almost make it to cover, if they could just move. They just needed some moments without that helicopter terrifying them.

But we didn't have moments. And with Sam and Shelby separated from the rest of the pack, I knew that they were the next to go.

I could still see Beck's death.

I couldn't let that happen to Sam.

I didn't even think. My shadow, stretched out in front of me, dug into the pocket of my cargo pants at the same time I did. I flipped out the syringe, pulled the cap off with my teeth, and jabbed it into my vein. No time to consider it. No time to feel noble. Just — a rapid, jagged surge of pain through me and then the silent push of the adrenaline helping speed the shift. I was a world of agony and then, I was a wolf, and I was running.

Shelby. Kill Shelby. Save Sam.

That was all I had to remember, and the words were already sliding away when I hit Shelby with everything I had. I was nothing but my jaws and my snarl. My teeth snagged around her eye just like I'd learned from her. She twisted and snapped, knowing that this time I was playing for keeps. There was no anger in my attack. Just relentless determination. This was what our fight should have been earlier.

Blood filled my mouth, either Shelby's or mine, from my tongue. I tossed an image to Sam: *Get out.* I wanted him up with Grace. I wanted him away from me, back with the pack, one of many instead of a solitary, nonmoving target.

Why wouldn't he leave me? *GET OUT.* I couldn't make it any more of a request. There were ways to convince him, but my mind no longer catalogued them. Then an image from Grace came back to us. The pack, directionless, scattering, the woods so close, but so far out of reach without him. The helicopter was returning. Beck was dead. They were terrified. Him. They needed him. *She* needed him.

He didn't want to leave me behind.

I let go of Shelby to snarl at him with everything in me. His ears flagged, and then he was gone.

Everything in me wished I was going with him.

Shelby lurched to follow, but I tore her down again. We rolled across the grit and the rocks. I had dirt in my mouth and eyes. She was furious. Over and over, she sent me the same images, almost overpowering me with the weight of her fear, jealousy, anger. Again and again, she sent me images. Her killing Sam. Her killing Grace. Her scrabbling her way to the top of the pack.

I grabbed on to her throat. There was no joy in this revenge. She twisted, but I hung on, because I had to.

CHAPTER SEVENTY-TWO

· GRACE ·

The pack was completely disoriented. At first, my wolf had sent me images, and strangely enough, so had the boy who ran with us. Now, we had neither, and I had to regroup them as best as I could, but I wasn't him. I had only just learned to be a wolf myself. He needed to be the one to pull them together. But his own misery was humming too loudly in my head to allow room for anything else. *Beck, Beck, Beck,* which now, somehow, I understood was the name of the first wolf to fall. My wolf wanted to go back to Beck's body, but I had already seen the images passed to me. His body destroyed, little to support that he was ever a living creature. He was gone.

The thundering vehicle, black against the sky, was approaching again, deafening. It was a leisurely predator, taking its time to cover us.

I frantically passed my wolf an image of the pack stabilizing under our guidance, escaping into the cover of the trees. All the while I darted around the wolves closest to me, goading them into moving again, pushing them toward the trees. As my wolf loped to meet me, his images were a wall of sights and sounds that I couldn't interpret. I caught one in a hundred. None of them made sense, strung together. And still, here came the monster from over the trees.

My wolf sent me an urgent, scattered thought.

Cole. Shelby.

And maybe because of the force of the thought, or maybe because the sun was warming me and I felt some shadow of someone else I used to be inside me, I knew who he meant.

I looked back over my shoulder, still half running sideways to keep from losing momentum. There, sure enough, were Cole and Shelby, locked in a fight breathtaking in its savagery. They were almost too far away for me to see clearly, way down on the flat slope we were on. But there wasn't anything to block my view when the black creature roared through the air behind them.

There was a series of pops, barely distinguishable from the rumbling above, and then Shelby released Cole.

He scrambled back from her as she lashed out, directionless. Right before she crumpled, she turned toward me. Her face was a red mess, or perhaps it was a red mess where her face used to be.

The helicopter roared low.

A second later, Cole fell, too.

Chapter Seventy-Three

· ISABEL ·

Somehow, I'd never really believed it could come to this.

Cole.

The white wolf was still kicking, just one feeble back leg, but Cole — Cole was motionless at the place where he dropped.

My heart crashed in my chest. Tiny explosions of dirt tracked my father's shots farther up in the pack. Sam and Grace were galloping in earnest now, flat out toward the trees they would never reach. The remainder of the pack strung out behind them.

My first thought was a selfish one: *Why Cole out of all the wolves? Why the one I care about?*

But then I saw that the ground was littered with bodies, that Cole was just one of half a dozen to fall. And he had thrown himself into all this, when he'd seen that Sam was in danger. He'd known what could —

I was too late.

The helicopter broke off to follow a straggler. The sun was a ferocious red disk at the edge of the horizon; it glinted off the identification letters on the side of the helicopter. The doors were open and behind the pilot, two men sat with their guns trained on the ground, one out each side. One of them was my father.

Certainty settled inside me.

I couldn't . . . I couldn't save Cole.

But I could save Sam and Grace. They were almost to the woods. So, so close. All they needed were a few more moments.

The straggler was dead. I didn't know who it was. The helicopter swung slowly back around for another approach. I glanced back at Cole; I hadn't realized how much I'd hoped that he was going to move until I saw that he hadn't. I couldn't see where in his body he'd been shot, but I saw that there was blood around him, and he lay very flat and small and very, very unfamous looking. At least he wasn't the wreck that some of the other wolves were. I couldn't have taken that.

It must have been fast. I told myself it had been fast.

My breath stuttered in my chest.

I couldn't think about that. I couldn't think about him being dead. But I did.

And suddenly I didn't care that my father would be angry with me, that it would cause a million problems, that it would make every bit of progress we had seemed to be making go away.

I could stop this.

And as the helicopter came in again, I threw my SUV off the road and onto the scrubby ground, climbing up over a bit of embankment that was by the road here. The SUV was probably never really meant to be off road, and it was bouncing and making sounds like it was falling apart and souls of hell were trying to escape from its undercarriage, and I thought I was going to probably break an axle if such a thing was possible.

But despite the rattling and bumping, I was faster than the wolves, and so I drove into their midst, right between two of the pack members, scattering them and forcing them ahead of me.

Instantly, the shooting stopped. Dirt roiled up behind me in massive clouds, hiding the helicopter overhead from my view. In front of me, I could see the wolves leaping into the woods after Sam and Grace, one after another. I felt like my heart was going to explode.

The dust sank down around me. The helicopter hovered above me. Taking a deep breath, I opened my sunroof and stared out of it toward the sky. There was still dust floating between us, but through the open sides of the copter, I knew my dad had seen me. Even that far up in the air, I knew that face. The shock and dismay and embarrassment all rolled up into one.

I didn't know what was going to happen now.

I wanted to cry, but I just keep staring up there until the very last wolf had disappeared into the woods.

My phone buzzed on the seat beside me. A text from my father's cell phone.

get out of there

I texted back.

when you do

CHAPTER SEVENTY-FOUR

· SAM ·

I shifted back to human with no ceremony. Like it wasn't a miracle. Just this: the sun on my back, the heat of the day, the werewolf running its course through my changeable veins, and then, Sam, the man.

I was at the lodge, and Koenig was waiting. Not remarking on my nakedness, he gave me a T-shirt and sweatpants from his car.

"There's a pump out back if you want to get cleaned up," he said, though I couldn't be dirty. This skin I wore right now was freshly minted.

But I went around the back of the lodge, wondering at my stride, my hands, my slow human heartbeat. When the water started to spurt from the old metal pump, I realized my palms and knees were grubby from when I'd changed back.

I scrubbed my skin and put on the clothing and took a drink from the pump. By then, my thoughts were swirling back to me, and they were wild and swelling and uncertain. I had done it — I had led the pack here, I had shifted back to me, I had been a wolf and kept myself true, or if not all of myself, at least my heart.

It was impossible, but here I was, standing at the lodge, wearing my skin.

And then I saw Beck's death, and my breath was a ship pitching at sea, uneven and perilous.

I thought of Grace in the woods, both of us wolves. The feeling of running beside her, having what I'd dreamed of all of those years before I'd known her properly as a girl. Those hours spent as wolves together were exactly what I'd imagined they'd be, no words to get in the way. I'd wanted winters of that, but I knew now that we were destined, again, to spend those cold months apart. Happiness was a shard rammed in between my ribs.

And then there was Cole.

This impossible thing had only been made possible because of him. I closed my eyes.

Koenig found me beside the pump. "Are you all right?"

I opened my eyes, slowly. "Where are the others?"

"In the woods."

I nodded. They were probably finding someplace they felt safe enough to rest.

Koenig crossed his arms. "Good job."

I looked into the woods. "Thanks."

"Sam, I know you don't want to think about this right now, but they'll come back for the bodies," he told me. "If you want to get th —"

"Grace will shift soon," I said. "I want to wait for her."

The truth was, I needed Grace. I couldn't go back there without her. And more than that, I needed to *see* her. I couldn't trust my wolf memories to know she was all right until I saw her.

Koenig didn't press me. We went into the lodge, and then he retrieved another set of clothing from his car and laid it outside of the lodge door like an offering. He returned with a styrofoam cup of convenience store coffee while drinking one of his own. It tasted awful, but I drank it, too grateful for the kindness to refuse.

Then I sat on one of the dusty chairs in our new home, my head in my hands, looking at the floor, sifting through my wolf memories. Remembering the last thing Cole had said to me: *I'll see you on the other side.*

And then there was a soft knock on the door, and it was Grace, dressed in a slightly too-large T-shirt and sweats. Everything I'd meant to say to her — *We lost Cole. Beck's dead. You're alive* — dissolved on my tongue.

"Thank you," Grace said to Koenig.

"Saving people's lives," Koenig said, "is my job."

Then she crossed to me and hugged me, hard, while I buried my face in her shoulder. Finally, she pulled away and sighed. "Let's go get them."

CHAPTER SEVENTY-FIVE

· SAM ·

In comparison to our journey that morning, it took no time at all to get back to the field where the helicopter had found us.

And there Beck was, his body a wreck. There were all kinds of internal parts lying outside of him that I'd never considered him having.

"Sam," Grace said to me.

His body was so flat and thin looking now, like it had nothing left in it. And maybe it didn't. Maybe it had all been annihilated from the blast. Those pieces, though. That he had dragged with him before he died. I remembered the bird that Shelby had killed in our driveway.

Sam.

The mouth was parted open, the tongue laying over teeth. Not like a dog would pant, but in a strange, unnatural way. The angle of the tongue made me think that the body must be stiff. Just like a dog hit by a car, really, just another dead body.

sam

say

his eyes, though

something

it had his eyes

sam

and I had so much left to say to him

you're scaring me

I would be fine. I was fine. It was like I had known all along that he would die. Be dead. That we would find his body like this, ruined and undone, that he would be gone from me and we would never fix what had been broken. I would not cry, because this was just the way it would be. He would be gone, but he had been gone before, and this wouldn't feel any different, this absolute gone, this forever gone, this gone without hope of spring and warm weather bringing him back to me.

I would feel nothing, because there was nothing to feel. I felt I'd lived this moment a thousand times, so many times that I had no energy or emotion left to bring to the scene. I tried out the idea in my head, *Beck is dead, Beck is dead, Beck is dead*, waiting for tears, for feeling, for anything.

The air smelled like spring around us, but it felt like winter.

· GRACE ·

Sam just stood there, shaking, hands beside him, silent and staring down at the body at our feet. Something terrible in his face made tear after noiseless tear slide down my cheek.

"Sam," I begged. "Please."

Sam said, "I'm fine."

And then he just crumpled gently to the ground. He was a curled form, hands up behind his head, pulling his face down to his knees, so far beyond crying that I didn't know what to do.

I crouched beside him and wrapped my arms around him. He shook and shook, but no tears came.

"Grace," he whispered, and in that one word, I heard agony. He was running a hand through his hair again and again, knotting and releasing fistfuls of it in his palm, ceaseless. "Grace, help me. Help me."

But I didn't know what to do.

CHAPTER SEVENTY-SIX

· GRACE ·

I used Koenig's phone to call Isabel.

Sam, Koenig, and I had spent an hour picking our way over the scrub, performing the morbid job of counting the wolf bodies and seeing if Sam recognized them. Seven wolves dead, including Beck. We hadn't gotten to Shelby's or Cole's bodies yet.

Sam stood a few feet away, looking out into the woods, his hands linked behind his head. As always, it was a gesture that was at once intensely Sam but also Beck. I didn't remember if I'd ever told Sam that. I didn't know if it would help or hurt to tell him now.

"Isabel," I said.

Isabel just sighed.

"I know. What is it like for you there?"

Isabel's voice was unfamiliar. I thought maybe she'd been crying. "Oh, the usual. I'm grounded for the rest of my life, which is, like, until next week, because after that, they'll kill me. I'm in my room right now because I'm tired of screaming."

That explained her voice.

"I'm sorry," I said.

"Don't be. I got there a little late, didn't I?"

"Don't beat yourself up, Isabel. I know that's what you like to do, but you didn't owe the wolves anything, and you came anyway."

She didn't say anything for a long time, and I wondered if she believed me. Finally, she said, "And they're sending me to California to live with Nanna until they can sell the house."

"*What?*"

I spoke so sharply that Sam looked over to me, frowning.

Isabel's voice had no intonation at all. "Yeah. I'm taking my finals and then I'm on a plane with my stuff. Isabel Culpeper. This is her noble end. Back to California with her tail between her legs. Do you think I'm weak for not just taking off?"

Now it was my turn to sigh. "If you can keep your parents, I think you ought to. Your parents love you, even if your dad is a jerk. It doesn't mean I don't want you to go." Isabel in California? "I can't believe it. Are you sure they won't change their minds?"

She scoffed. It was a raw sound, a new wound.

"Tell her thank you," Sam said.

"Sam says to tell you thank you."

Isabel laughed. *Ha. Ha. Ha.* "For leaving the state?"

"For saving our lives."

For a moment, we didn't say anything. From the direction of the lake, a loon cried. If I hadn't known, logically, that I had been here this morning, I wouldn't have remembered it. As a wolf, everything about this place looked different.

Isabel said, "Not everybody's lives."

I didn't know what to say to that, because it was true. It wasn't really her fault, still, but I couldn't tell her it wasn't true. Instead, I said, "We're in the field. Where was Cole's — uhh — where did he —"

She interrupted, "There was a bank by the road. There should be my tire tracks. He was a few yards before that. I have to go. I have to —"

The phone went dead.

I sighed and closed my phone, relaying the information. Together we followed the directions, which led us to Shelby's body. It was surprisingly unmolested, except for her face, which was so destroyed that I couldn't bring myself to look at it. There was a lot of blood.

I wanted to feel compassion for her, but all I could think was *She is the reason Cole is dead.*

"She's finally gone," Sam said. "She died as a wolf. I think that would please her."

All around Shelby's body, the grass was smeared and spattered and stained with red. I didn't know how far away Cole had died. Was this his blood? Sam was swallowing, looking at her, and I knew that he saw past the monster to something else. I couldn't.

Koenig muttered something about needing to make a phone call and moved off, giving us some distance.

I touched Sam's hand. He was standing in so much blood that it looked like he had been wounded himself. "Are you doing okay?"

He rubbed his own arms; it was getting cool again as the sun went down. "I didn't hate it, Grace."

He didn't have to explain. I could still remember that feeling of joy at seeing him bound toward me as a wolf, even if I had no way to remember his name. I remembered exchanging images with him at the head of the pack. They all trusted him, like I did. I said softly, "Because you were better at it."

He shook his head. "Because I knew it wasn't forever."

I touched his hair and he bent his head to kiss me, quiet as a secret. I leaned on his chest and together we stood, buffered from the cold.

After several long minutes, Sam stepped back from me and looked at the woods. For a moment I thought he was listening, but of course, no wolves would howl from Boundary Wood now.

He said, "This is one of the last poems Ulrik had me memorize.

> *"endlich entschloss sich niemand*
> *und niemand klopfte*

und niemand sprang auf
und niemand öffnete
und da stand niemand
und niemand trat ein
und niemand sprach: willkomm
und niemand antwortete: endlich"

"What does it mean?" I asked.

At first, I didn't think that Sam was going to reply. His eyes were narrowed against the sun, looking out into the woods we'd escaped into an eternity ago, and then, into the woods we used to live in, an eternity before that. He was such a different person than the one that I had first met, bleeding on my back doorstep. That Sam had been shy, naive, gentle, lost in his songs and his words, and I'd always love that version of him. But it was okay, this change. That Sam couldn't have survived this. For that matter, the Grace I'd been then couldn't have.

Sam said, looking at Boundary Wood,

"at last no one decided
and no one knocked
and no one jumped up
and no one opened
and there stood no one
and no one entered
and no one said: welcome
and no one answered: at last"

Our shadows were as tall as trees with nothing to block them. It was like we were on another planet, here in this scrubby area, shallow stretches of water suddenly glowing orange and pink, the exact same color of the sunset. I didn't know where else to look for Cole's body.

There was no sign of it for yards around, other than his blood, dotted on blades of grass and pooled in hollows.

"Maybe he dragged himself to the woods," Sam said in a flat voice. "Instinct would tell him to hide, even if he was dying."

My heart sped. "Do you think —"

"There's too much blood," Sam replied. He didn't look at me. "Look at all of it. Think of how I couldn't even heal myself from a single shot in the neck. He couldn't have healed himself. I just hope . . . I just hope he wasn't afraid when he died."

I didn't say what I was thinking: But we'd all been afraid.

Together, we combed the edge of the woods, just in case. Even as it fell dark, we kept looking, because we both knew that scent would help us more than our sight anyway.

But there was no sign of him. In the end, Cole St. Clair had done what he did best.

Disappeared.

CHAPTER SEVENTY-SEVEN

· ISABEL ·

When we first moved to this house, the piano room was the only room that I loved. I'd hated that we'd moved from California to a state equally far from both oceans my country had to offer. I hated the old, moldy smell of the house and the creepy woods around it. I'd hated how it made my angry brother even angrier. I hated the way my bedroom had slanted walls and the stairs creaked and the kitchen had ants, no matter how expensive the appliances were.

But I'd loved the piano room. It was a round room made up half of windows and half of short wall sections painted deep burgundy. There wasn't anything in the room but the piano, three chairs, and a chandelier that was amazingly non-tacky, given the rest of the house's lighting decor.

I didn't play the piano, but I liked to sit on the bench, anyway, my back to the piano, and look out the windows into the woods. They didn't seem creepy from inside, with a safe distance between me and them. There might have been monsters in them, but nothing that could contend with twenty yards of yard, an inch of glass, and a Steinway. The best way to experience nature, I'd thought.

I still had days when I thought that was the best way to deal with it.

Tonight, I ventured down from my bedroom, avoiding my parents, who were talking in hushed voices in the library, and crept into the piano room. I shut the door so that it wouldn't make any sound and sat cross-legged on the bench. It was night, so there was nothing to see outside the windows except for the circle of grass lit by the back door light. It didn't really matter that I couldn't see the trees, though. There were no monsters in them anymore.

I pulled my hoodie around me and drew my legs up to my chest, sitting sideways on the bench. It felt like I'd always been cold here in Minnesota. I kept waiting for it to get to summer, but it never seemed to make it that far.

California didn't sound like a terrible idea at the moment. I wanted to dig myself into the sand and hibernate until I didn't feel so hollow inside.

When my phone rang, I jerked and slammed my elbow into the keyboard of the piano, which let out a low, agonized thud. I hadn't realized the phone was still in my pocket.

I pulled it out and looked at the caller ID — Beck's house. I really wasn't up for sounding like the Isabel that they knew. Why couldn't they just give me one night?

I put it to my ear. "What?"

There was nothing on the other end. I checked to make sure the phone had a signal. "What? Hello? Is there anybody there?"

"Da."

I had no bones left in my body. I slid off the bench, trying to hold the phone to my ear still, trying to hold my head up because my muscles felt completely unequal to the task. My heart was clubbing so painfully in my ears that it took me a moment to realize that if he'd said something else, I wouldn't have heard it.

"You," I snarled, because I couldn't think of anything else to say. I was sure the rest of the sentence would come to me. "You scared the shit out of me!"

He laughed then, that laugh that I'd heard at the clinic, and I started to cry.

"Now Ringo and I have even more in common," Cole said. "Your father's shot both of us. How many people can say that? Are you choking on something?"

I thought about picking myself back off the floor, but my legs were still unsteady. "Yeah. Yeah, that's exactly what I'm doing, Cole."

"I forgot to say that was who was calling."

"Where *were* you?"

He made a dismissive noise. "In the woods. Regrowing my spleen or something. Also, parts of my thighs. I'm not sure my better parts work anymore. You're welcome to come over and take a look under the hood."

"Cole," I said, "I have to tell you something."

"I saw," he replied. "I know what you did."

"I'm sorry."

He paused. "I know you are."

"Do Sam and Grace know you're alive?"

Cole said, "I'll have a joyous reunion with them later. I needed to call you first."

For a moment, I let myself just bask in that last sentence. Memorized it for replaying in my head over and over later.

"My parents are sending me back to California for what I did." I didn't know any way to say it other than just throwing it out there.

Cole didn't answer for a moment.

"I've been to California," he said finally. "Sort of a magical place. Dry heat and fire ants and gray imported cars with big engines. I'm imagining you next to a decorative cactus. You look delicious."

"I told Grace I didn't want to go."

"Liar. You're a California girl anyway," he said. "You're just an astronaut here."

I surprised myself by laughing.

"What?"

"Because you have only known me for, like, fourteen seconds, and seven of those were us making out, and you still know more about me than all of my friends here in this stupid place," I said.

Cole considered this. "Well, I'm an excellent judge of character."

Just the idea of him sitting over at Beck's house, alive, made me want to smile, and then smile some more, and then start laughing and not stop. My parents could be angry at me for the rest of my life.

"Cole," I said. "Don't lose this number."

CHAPTER SEVENTY-EIGHT

· GRACE ·

I remember lying in the snow, a small spot of red going cold, surrounded by wolves.

"Are you sure this is the place?" I asked Sam. It was October, so the cold night air had pulled the green from the leaves and turned the underbrush red and brown. We stood in a small clearing. It was so small that I could stand in the middle and stretch my arms out to either side and touch a birch tree with one palm and brush the branches of a pine with the other, and I did.

Sam's voice was certain. "Yes, this is it."

"I remember it being larger."

I'd been smaller then, of course, and it had been snowy — everything seemed more vast in the snow. The wolves had dragged me from the tire swing to here, pinned me down, made me one of them. I'd been so close to dying.

I turned slowly, waiting for recognition, for a flashback, for something to indicate that this really was the place. But the woods remained ordinary woods around me, and the clearing remained an ordinary clearing. If I'd been out walking by myself, I probably would have crossed it in a stride or two and not even considered it a clearing.

Sam scuffed his feet through the leaves and ferns. "So your parents think you're going to . . . Switzerland?"

"Norway," I corrected. "Rachel really is going, and I'm supposed to be going with her."

"Do you think they believed you?"

"They don't really have a reason not to. Rachel turned out to be very good at deception."

"Troubling," Sam said, though he didn't sound troubled.

"Yes," I agreed.

What I didn't say, but we both knew, was that it wasn't crucial that they believed me, anyway. I had turned eighteen and gotten my high school degree over the summer, as I'd promised, and they'd been decent to Sam and let me spend my days and evenings with him, as they'd promised, and now I was free to go to college or move out as I pleased. My bag was packed, actually, sitting in the trunk of Sam's car in my parents' driveway. Everything I needed to leave.

The only problem was this: winter. I could feel it stirring in my limbs, turning knots in my stomach, coaxing me to shift into a wolf. There could be no college, no moving out, no Norway even, until I was sure I could stay human.

I watched Sam crouch and sort through leaves on the forest floor. Something had caught his eye as he scuffled. "Do you remember that mosaic, at Isabel's place?" I asked.

Sam found what he was looking for, a bright yellow leaf shaped like a heart. He straightened and twirled it by the long stem. "I wonder what will happen to it now that the house is empty."

For a moment we were both quiet, standing close to each other in the small clearing, the familiar sensations of Boundary Wood around us. The trees here smelled like no other, mixed with wood smoke and the breeze over the lake. The leaves whispered against each other in a way that was subtly different from the leaves up on the peninsula. These branches had memories caught in them, red and dying in the cold nights, in a way that the other trees didn't.

One day, I supposed, those woods would be home and these woods would be the stranger.

"Are you sure that you want to do this?" Sam asked softly.

He meant the syringe of meningitis-tainted blood, of course, that was waiting for me back at the lodge. The same almost-cure that had helped Sam and killed Jack. If Cole's theories were correct and I fought the meningitis as a wolf, it would slowly fight the werewolf inside me and make me human for good. If Cole was wrong and Sam's survival had been random, I faced overwhelming odds.

"I trust Cole," I said. These days, he was a powerful force, a bigger person than when I first met him. Sam had said he was glad Cole was using his powers for good instead of evil. I was glad to see him turning the lodge into his castle. "Everything else he's figured out has been right."

Part of me felt a prickle of loss, because some days, I loved being a wolf. I loved this feeling of *knowing* the woods, of being a part of them. The utter freedom of it. But more of me hated the oblivion, the confusion, the ache of wanting to know more but being unable to. For all that I loved being a wolf, I loved being Grace more.

"What will you do while I'm gone?" I asked.

Without answering, Sam reached for my left hand, and I let him have it. He twisted the stem of the leaf around my ring finger so that it made a bright yellow band. We both admired it.

"I will miss you," he said. Sam let go of the leaf and it drifted to the ground between us. He didn't say that he was afraid that Cole was wrong, though I knew he was.

I turned so that I was facing my parents' house. I couldn't see it through the trees; maybe once it was winter, it would be visible, but for now, it was hidden behind the fall leaves. I closed my eyes and let myself breathe in the scent of these trees once more. This was good-bye.

"Grace?" Sam said, and I opened my eyes.

He reached out his hand to me.

AUTHOR'S NOTE

It's a little odd to be saying good-bye to a world I've lived in for almost four years, a series that changed my life pretty completely, but here I am. Now that I've come to the end of it, I figured it's a good time to say something about the parts of my story that really exist outside the pages of the books.

First of all, the wolves.

I've tried to stay true to actual wolf behavior throughout the series (although I wouldn't recommend kissing one anytime soon). For readers who'd like to find out more about wolf behavior, I recommend the documentary *Living with Wolves* as a good starting point. The roles of Ulrik and Paul and Salem are all standard ones in a real wolf pack: the peacemaker, the alpha, and the omega. The reality of pack dynamics is fascinating stuff.

It's also real that a wolf's place in our world is highly debated. The hunt Tom Culpeper helped instigate is based on real wolf hunts staged in the western United States and Canada as ranchers and wolves struggle to find equilibrium. The facts remain — wolves are lovely but powerful predators and humans are jealous keepers of their territory and their livelihoods — so more wolves will meet their death at the end of a hunter's gun or in the shadow of a helicopter before this is all done.

Second of all, Mercy Falls, Minnesota.

I've been told by many readers that it's impossible to find on a map, and I'm sorry. *Shiver* originally took place in Ely, MN, which is a real place, then Bishop, MN, which is not, and finally Mercy Falls. In my head Mercy Falls is quite near Ely and the Boundary Waters. Outside of my head, it's quite near nothing at all, as it doesn't exist. That part of Minnesota, however, does host a very real population of gray wolves.

Other real places in the books include the candy shop (based on Wythe Candy in Williamsburg, VA), the Crooked Shelf (based on Riverby Books in Fredericksburg, VA), and Ben's Fish and Tackle (although I won't reveal where the store it was based on is located, to protect the identity of the sweaty man who owns it).

Third of all, the people.

Some of the characters are loosely based on real people. Dmitra the sound engineer is a real person, although in real life she doesn't have a big nose, nor is she female. Grace's parents are real, though they're not mine. And Ulrik is an actual person, although he's not a werewolf.

Fourth of all, the poetry.

As Sam's favorite, Rilke is most prominent, but there's also Mandelstam, Roethke, Yeats, and other assorted German poets. Even if you are a die-hard poetry un-fan like myself, I still recommend Stephen Mitchell's beautiful translations of Rilke and *German Poetry in Transition, 1945–1990*, edited by Charlotte Melin.

And finally, the love.

Many, many readers have written me asking wistfully about the nature of Sam and Grace's relationship, and I can assure you, that sort is absolutely real. Mutual, respectful, enduring love is completely attainable as long as you swear you won't settle for less.

So this is good-bye to Mercy Falls. It's time to find other uncharted worlds.

ACKNOWLEDGMENTS

It's going to be impossible to thank everyone involved in bringing this series into being, so rest assured that this is only the tip of the iceberg.

I need to thank Scholastic for being incredibly supportive of the series and very tolerant of my quirks. In particular: my editor, David Levithan, for not sending villagers with pitchforks after me after I threw it all away; the ever-smiling Rachel Coun and the rest of marketing, for their animal cunning; Tracy van Straaten, Becky Amsel, and Samantha Grefe for cookies, sanity, and bathroom breaks; Stephanie Anderson and the production team, who make me look more clever than I am; Christopher Stengel, for continued impeccable design; the incredible foreign rights team of Rachel Horowitz, Janelle DeLuise, Lisa Mattingly, and Maren Monitello — it's not easy to make me feel at home 3,000 miles away, but they pull it off absolutely every time.

And in non-Scholastic thanking, a few folks.

Laura Rennert, my agent, whose voice on the phone always sounds like sanity coming home to roost.

Brenna Yovanoff, for standing next to the wounded gazelle when all signs recommended to the contrary.

The folks at Loewe — Jeannette Hammerschmidt, Judith Schwemmlein, and Marion Perko — for saving my bacon at the absolute last moment. I owe you guys more cookies than I can carry in the overhead compartment of a passenger plane.

Carrie Ryan and Natalie Parker, for reading in short order and alternatively patting my hand and smacking my wrist when I needed it.

My parents and siblings, for knowing when "Go away, I'm working!" means "Please help babysit!" and when it means "Rescue me and take me out for chimichangas!" Kate, in particular — you know you're the reader I write for.

Tessa, you were as married to this thing as I was, and it never sent us presents on our anniversaries. I'll never forget that.

Ed, who made me tea and let me sleep after all-nighters and suffered and sweated alongside me. This is all your fault, you know, because why else would I write a love story but you?

And finally, Ian. You won't ever read this, but I have to say it anyway: Thank you for reminding me.

THE SCORPIO RACES

· SEAN ·

There's a girl on the beach.

The wind's torn the mist to shreds here by the ocean, so unlike on the rest of the island, the horses and their riders appear in sharp relief down on the sand. I can see the buckle on every bridle, the tassel on every rein, the tremor in every hand. It is the second day of training, and it's the first day that it isn't a game. This first week of training is an elaborate, bloody dance where the dance partners determine how strong the other ones are. It's when riders learn if charms will work on their mounts, how close to the sea is too close, how they can begin to convince their water horses to gallop in a straight line. How long they have between falling from their horses and being attacked. This tense courtship looks nothing like racing.

At first I see nothing out of the ordinary. There is the surviving Privett brother beating his gray *capall* with a switch and Hale selling charms that will not save you, and there is Tommy Falk flapping at the end of the lead as his black mare strains for the salt water.

And there is the girl. When I first see her and her dun mare from my vantage point on the cliff road, I am struck first not by the fact that she is a girl, but by the fact that she's in the ocean. It's the dreaded second day, the day when people start to die, and no one will get close to the surf. But there she is, trotting up to the knee in the water. Fearless.

I make my slow way down the cliff road to the sand. Any wicked thoughts Corr might have had this morning have been jolted out by his earlier trot. But the two mares are neither as tired nor as tame as Corr. Their hooves jangle every time they dance sideways; I've tied bells around their pasterns, reminding me every moment that I cannot let down my guard. The worse of the two mares wears a black netted cloth over her haunches. The cloth, passed down from my father, is made of thread and hundreds of narrow iron eyelets: part mourning cloth, part chain mail. I hope it weighs her to the ground. It's the sort of thing I'd never use on Corr — it would only make him irritable and uncertain, and in any case, we know each other better than that.

Now, closer to the surf, I see why the girl's so brave. Her horse is just an island pony, with a coat the color of the sand, legs black as soaked kelp.

I want to know why she's on my beach.